FALL FOR NOW

Bob Howard

Cover design by: Getcovers

This book is dedicated to my wife, children, and grandson.
They have been my constant source of happiness.

CONTENTS

INTRODUCTION

When I started Fall for Now, I had an idea that was suggested to me by my wife. She said I should write about Niagara Falls. I mentioned the suggestion to a friend of mine, Danny Gahan, because he's from Utica, New York. He said a few things about the area that I didn't know, and the research started. Although this is a work of fiction and the locations are altered through imagination and necessity, the area was a natural fit for this story. Thank you to both of them for the great ideas.

NEWLYWEDS

Niagara Falls - 2016

Mrs. Tori Cassidy, formerly Ms. Tori Mathers, couldn't believe her wedding had only been a day ago. It had been a whirlwind of choreographed plans beginning before sunrise and culminating in a limousine that carried the newlyweds away from the reception. The party probably continued for hours after they left. Her father had promised the guests the party wasn't over until the food and booze were gone. He said if he was going to pay for everything, it wasn't going home in doggy bags or with the staff of the reception hall.

Tori rolled over on her side to watch the majesty of the water that rushed over Niagara Falls, and she wasn't sure which was more spectacular, the size of the diamond on her finger or the view. Randy had given her a list of choices for the honeymoon, and she had demurely asked if she could pick more than one. Randolph Cassidy could afford whatever his new bride wanted, so he had given her three.

Niagara Falls was where they would languish in the care of a five-star hotel for a week. Room service, spa treatments, and fine dining were the plans. The next destination was a beach on a Pacific island that featured privacy for guests in search of romantic getaways. The cabins were suspended over a calm lagoon where they could soak up the sun and feel like they were alone in the world. The final stop would be in Las Vegas, where they would do their best to prove that the casinos didn't always win. Tori planned to spend money shopping during the day and gambling as much as she could at night. The next three weeks would be the best ever, and she had a feeling nothing could go wrong.

Randy, Tori's handsome new husband, was still sleeping off the effects of the reception. He was experienced in the art of recovery because frat parties at college taught him everything he needed to know about overindulging. Actually, he had developed a tolerance to alcohol that would prove to be a useless survival skill for anyone in a few days. When Tori nudged him, her husband showed no outward signs that he even noticed. At thirty years of age, he had developed the ability to sleep anywhere and through any disturbance. Tori was only two years younger, but it seemed to her he had more experience than most people his age. Maybe it was because his parents had pushed him to travel so much when he was a teenager. She decided to let him sleep as long as he wanted while she ordered room service and enjoyed the morning.

As promised, an efficient young man arrived with an elegantly presented breakfast of scrambled eggs that would have made her favorite TV chef proud. The waiter suggested that she would enjoy her meal more if she ate inside because the ever-present roar of the falls would wear upon her senses, but she had always dreamt of the moment when she would lose herself in that sound while enjoying a savory meal. She thanked him but asked him to serve her on the private balcony anyway.

It was everything Tori had imagined, and she closed her eyes between bites of fluffy scrambled eggs served over toast. She smiled as she finished each bite and thought this was how she was supposed to live. She was so deep into the pleasure of the tastes and sounds that she couldn't process what she saw when she opened her eyes for the fourth time. Her focus was on the plate of food, but she always took in a glimpse of the falls before sliding her fork under the next piece of toast. Something had passed through her field of vision that wasn't supposed to be there. A speck of darkness against the bright colors of the water came and went just as quickly.

Tori thought about how her father had complained when he had gotten a *floater* in his eye. At first, he thought it was a fleck of dirt that could be removed, and he was furious when a doctor informed him it was permanent. It was inside his eye, and it would drift aimlessly around, appearing out of nowhere like a piece of junk. It would distract him and then disappear to wherever it was *floaters* went when they didn't want to be seen.

The pepper flake stain in the water was that fast, and Tori wondered how old she would have to be to get a floater. She attempted to see if she could make it reappear, and she closed her left eye to focus through her right. Nothing...until she shut her right eye as she opened the left. In that split second, she saw the dark spot go from the top of her field of vision and then drift downward. It took her several seconds to understand that it wasn't a black spot inside her eye. Instead, it was something that had gone over the falls and disappeared into the mist below. Her exquisite breakfast was forgotten when three more spots appeared at the top of the falls then began their long descent together. This time, she saw arms and legs as they flailed helplessly.

With both eyes open and firmly fixed on the top of the falls, Tori watched as a dozen bodies jostled for position before following the last trio. She dropped her fork. It clattered and bounced through the railing to begin a descent of its own, but Tori couldn't have cared less. Unless someone was playing a cruel joke on her, she had just witnessed more deaths in a few seconds than most people saw in a lifetime.

"Randy," she shouted while her body remained paralyzed in

her chair. "Call 911."

She yelled it three more times before realizing the sliding glass door was closed. The door was designed to muffle the roar of the falls and, in this case, Tori Cassidy's screams. When she broke free of her paralysis, she rushed for the door and violently slid it open as she screamed again.

Randy Cassidy, like most people, wouldn't remember the dream he was having for more than a few seconds after he woke up. Especially since the dream was replaced by some very vivid images of his new wife in the advanced stages of hysteria. Tori was screaming to call 911, but she had also begun to blubber and cry as she screamed. Randy had no idea why he should call 911 or why Tori wasn't calling 911 herself. All he knew was that he had been deeply asleep until Tori screamed.

"What? Why do we need to call 911? Are you hurt? Is someone else here?"

Randy suddenly bolted from under the sheets and charged out of the bedroom. When he changed directions and returned, Tori was still standing at the open door with her arms spread and tears running down her cheeks.

"What are you doing?" she asked. "Did you call 911?"

"I was looking for my golf clubs, but then I remembered that I didn't bring them with us."

Tori wanted to ask him why he needed his golf clubs, but Randy, still disoriented, had gone into the bathroom before she could stop him. Something crashed in the bathroom, and Randy emerged with an expensive but heavy porcelain towel bar. He wielded it like a baseball bat and was prepared to do battle.

"Where are they?" he asked.

"What are you going on about? Who are you looking for?"

Randolph Cassidy was almost a genius when it came

to financial decisions. He was a firm believer that people preferred to do business with someone who stayed in shape, so he worked out at the gym, played golf at least once a week, and watched what he ate. He also knew good food when he saw it.

"You ordered room service? Why didn't you wake me?"

Tori was surprised when her husband brushed past her onto the balcony. He seemed to have forgotten that he was in his underwear and carrying a porcelain towel rod. He grabbed a plate and served himself scrambled eggs and assorted slices of fruit. He lowered himself into a chair and was about to take his first bite when he saw a logjam of people in the water only a few yards from the top of the falls. The current was pulling them forward so fast that he didn't have the chance to say anything before their bodies rained over the edge and disappeared under tons of water.

"Tori, call 911."

******

The front desk wasn't answering the phone, so Randy tried making the call to 911 on his cell phone. The call didn't go through, and he was surprised to see there was no service. Tori's phone was the same.

"We should call my father," she said. "He'll tell us what to do."

Randy said with a touch more sarcasm than he intended, "I don't think he can hear you from here."

"What?"

He held up his cell phone and shook it like they could hear broken parts inside it.

They both stood on the balcony and watched as a steady stream of bodies reached the crest of the falls and slipped over the edge. Randy reached across the table to the serving tray and heaped cold eggs onto a slice of toast. He folded it messily and ate it like a sandwich. Tori watched him chew as he stared at the falls. At first, she was appalled, but then she felt the same urge to eat while she could. She had never eaten a scrambled egg sandwich, but at the moment, it seemed like the right thing to do. They sat down and ate their breakfast in silence.

The bodies kept arriving and falling. Eventually, the honeymooners were full, but there was no sign that the mass suicide, or whatever it was, had subsided. If anything, it was increasing.

"I should've ordered more food while I could," said Tori.

"I'm glad you ordered it when you did, and there's plenty left. We'd be starving by now if you hadn't. Did the server say when someone would come back for the cart?"

Tori shook her head.

"This is stupid," said Randy. "We can't just sit here and watch people die."

"Maybe it's some kind of stunt. You don't think they're making a movie or something, do you?"

It was Randy's turn to shake his head.

"We have to do something," he said.

He pushed his chair away from the table and stood up as if he had decided what to do. He still had his eyes on the bodies and was vaguely aware of the way they pinwheeled and collided with each other, changing directions as they fell. In a split second, his field of vision was blocked by the body of a man who was much closer than the raging waterfalls because he had fallen from a balcony directly above theirs. The man's body was spinning just like the others sliding over the falls, and one flailing arm hit the top rail of the balcony where Randy and Tori had eaten breakfast. He disappeared in the same direction as Tori's fork.

Tori let out a yelp of surprise, and Randy would never admit it, but his yelp was pitched slightly higher than hers. Tori ran to the railing and was in time to see the man hit another balcony, but this time, he didn't bounce away. His trajectory had apparently been altered toward the balconies when he had hit their railing, and his body was draped over a similar railing a few floors below. She felt sick when she saw the man lift his head and move his arms. She turned back to tell Randy what she had seen just as another body fell from above. It missed her, but she felt the rush of air as it went by. Randy and Tori both backed away from the railing and pressed their bodies against the sliding glass door.

It didn't take long for the newlyweds to pack. Whatever was happening, they didn't want any part of it, and they decided to leave for the Pacific island part of their honeymoon ahead of schedule. As they packed, Randy tried every number in the hotel that provided service. The front desk, the concierge, room service, and the parking valet could all be contacted individually, but the phones rang as if the staff had all gone home.

"How am I going to get our car if I don't even know where it is?" asked Randy. "They even have my keys."

"I have the spare set you gave me," said Tori.

She didn't know why, but Randy oddly brushed her answer aside like it wouldn't matter.

"I hope they don't expect me to carry all of my luggage to the lobby by myself," said Tori.

The couple was so determined to leave the hotel that they didn't even consider turning on the television in their room. If they had, it probably wouldn't have made them change their minds about blaming the hotel for everything, but it would have at least given them an idea of how much safer they were in their room than they would be outside.

"Let's leave the luggage here," suggested Randy. "We can send a porter to the room after I give the front desk a piece of my mind."

As soon as Randy opened the door to their suite, the gravity of the situation became obvious. They weren't the only customers who were leaving, and judging by the mass of people near the elevator doors, they were late arrivals in the chaos. The hallway outside their room was crowded in both directions, and Randy made an instinctive judgment call. The crush of people moving in both directions had kept him from going further than the open door, so Tori was still behind him. He backed toward her and pushed the door forward, locking it as it clicked shut.

"Let's stay in the room a bit longer."

"Why? I want to get out of here and get to the airport."

A loud thud against the other side of the door made them both jump. They could hear cursing as people raised their voices, and the first thud was followed by several more.

"That's why," said Randy. "I'm not sure we could even make it to the stairs through that crowd."

"Why would we take the stairs? Aren't the elevators working?"

"The elevators are probably stopping on every floor because everyone's trying to leave at the same time, and when the door opens, there isn't even room for anyone else to get in."

******

Randy was just making a guess, but he didn't know how right he was. When one of the elevators arrived on their floor, it was already full, and no one was planning to let more people squeeze in with them. The occupants yelled at the people in the hallway to quit blocking the automatic door, and the people trying to get inside insisted that there was room for at least a few more. What the people in the hall didn't realize was that the same scenario had been played out on the floor above and on every floor since the elevator had started its journey from the top floor. With twelve floors to go, it would be repeated over and over like a well-rehearsed stage performance.

Something had to give as the doors repeatedly bounced against people and luggage, retreating to the fully open position and starting the timer over again. A large man who was pressed against the rear wall of the elevator picked up a wheeled suitcase and used it to knock back the entire front row of would-be passengers. They fell against each other in the hallway as threats and curses were shouted. Before the door closed completely, someone threw a wall-mounted fire extinguisher over the heads of the crowd into the elevator cabin.

"Let's get him when the door opens on the next floor," yelled one of the people who had been knocked to the floor. His nose was bleeding profusely from the impact of the suitcase.

As the elevator descended to the next floor, the occupants inside were shouting in outrage. The fire extinguisher had hit a woman in the face and knocked her into unconsciousness. Her husband was screaming to let them out. He needed to get her some help, and he didn't want to ride in an elevator that was going to stop on every floor. What he didn't consider was the separate exodus that was already in progress on the stairs, and it was about to become worse when it was joined by the vigilante squad from the previous floor.

By the time the elevator door opened into the next crowded hallway, the occupants inside were veterans. The people outside eased forward, expecting to ride the elevator to the lobby, but the angry veterans inside surged outward, aided by the man who wanted to get his unconscious wife to safety and the large man who wielded the suitcase like a club. The sudden, outward burst of people created a temporary void between those who wanted to stay inside the elevator and the people who were blocked out of the entrance. The door closed after disgorging passengers, and the elevator descended only half full.

While the elevator had ejected half of its occupants, the vigilantes from the previous floor had forced their way into a stairwell that was already at its capacity. As gravity tends to do, it assisted their efforts to reach the next floor before the elevator could depart because they blindly forced their way downward. The pile-up on the landing at the halfway point caused several of them to collide with the mass of people who were ignorant of the dispute at the elevator. The man with the bloody nose was the first one to go over the railing, and bystanders on the stairs watched helplessly as his body careened against metal and concrete until reaching the bottom floor. Then, the rest of the people on the stairs panicked and moved faster.

A second wave of panic happened when the distraught husband of the unconscious woman forced his way into the stairwell. With no room on the overcrowded stairs, people pushed back, and he was ironically the second person to go head-first over the railing, leaving his still-unconscious wife on the landing, where people apologized as they stepped over her.

*****

Unaware of what they were missing, Randy and Tori paced restlessly around their suite, spouting suggestions and snapping at each other. They had a shared epiphany when they both realized at the same time that there could be something on the news about the bizarre events of the morning. They frantically searched for the remote. When Tori found it, she fumbled for the ON button and pressed it. The television screen grew bright, displaying an apocalyptic scene in a city somewhere, but just as quickly went black. Silence seemed to flood the room as the lights went out, and the gentle breeze from the air conditioning stopped. The silence was only interrupted when the screaming in the hallway changed from concern to panic, then terror.

Tori pressed the ON button again, but nothing changed. She threw the useless remote across the room and sat down heavily on the bed. She buried her face in her hands and had a fleeting thought about how happy she had been only a couple of hours earlier. The only sound was from the hallway outside, where people continued to force their way to one end of the hall or the other. Some tried to reach the stairs, while others pushed the dead buttons next to the elevator doors, but almost all of them were yelling.

When she lifted her head, Tori saw that Randy was on the balcony with his back to her.

"What are you doing?" she asked.

Randy didn't answer or even act like he had heard her, so she left her spot on the bed and walked up behind him. Randy flinched when she touched his arm, and she saw why he hadn't answered. He had a mouthful of food and was chewing as if he were starving. The eggs were cold, and the toast was hard, but there was plenty of it.

Tori was angry at first, but something inside her said she could be mad later. In the meantime, they should eat what little food they had before it spoiled, even if they weren't hungry. She grabbed a plate and helped herself to her share. Neither of them had noticed a covered tray that hid the bacon. When they did, they divided the slices between their two plates.

"There won't be any more food from room service," said Randy. "I wasn't going to eat all of it."

Tori gave him an icy glare, but she didn't waste time answering him. She kept chewing her food and occasionally lifted her head to watch the water flow over the falls. The bodies still bobbed and bumped into each other before being swept over the top and disappearing in the mist and spray. Her vantage point didn't give her a clear view of the area downstream, but she didn't really want to see what that was like.

Randy stayed silent while he ate, knowing he should have asked her to eat with him. He couldn't explain it, but it occurred to him it was like Tori's attempts to turn on the TV. He had begun eating because of a survival instinct. He knew she would figure it out on her own if he waited for her to calm down. Besides, for the first time in his very successful life, he didn't know what to say. He was at a total loss for any ideas that would keep them from becoming like the people in the hall, the people in the water, or the man who had fallen from somewhere above them.

Tori finally broke the ice.

"Do we have anything we can wrap the leftovers in so we can save some for later?"

It was such a good suggestion that it made Randy think about what else they should do. Up until that moment, he had just been caught up in the events and was mentally paralyzed.

"We should fill the bathtub with water," he said. "We'll need water more than food."

He didn't wait for her to answer, but he heard her ask as he dashed from the balcony to the bathroom, "Are we staying?"

By the time Randy got back from the bathroom, Tori had figured out a few things on her own. Some of their clothing was still packed in plastic from the dry cleaners, and Tori had used it to wrap the leftovers from breakfast. Their suite had a sizable minibar, and she unceremoniously swept the little bottles of liquor onto the floor to make room for the food.

"I did it as fast as I could so the refrigerator would still be a bit cold," she said. "I'm sorry for the stupid question."

"What?"

"I asked if we're staying," she said. "Of course, we're staying. Where else are we going to go? We don't need a TV to tell us what we already know. There's nothing so special about us that would make whatever it is that's happening just happen to us."

Randy knew that giving his wife the wrong answer was a slippery slope.

"It wasn't a stupid question. Up until you mentioned wrapping the food, I wasn't exactly having flashes of brilliance. That was a good idea to use the minibar. Is it too early to have one of those?"

Tori saw that he gestured toward the miniature bottles on the floor next to her. She handed him a bottle of bourbon and took one for herself.

"I think we could both use something to settle our nerves right now," she said.

They sat on the floor next to each other and leaned their backs against the bed. They sipped their bourbon straight from the little bottles while watching the door to the hallway. The shouting hadn't stopped, but it was definitely not the chaos it had been before.

"I'm trying hard not to fill in the blanks," said Tori.

Randy knew exactly what she meant. He had been replaying everything they knew like a video loop, and he kept feeling like parts of the movie were missing.

"You're trying to explain what's happening, but we're short on facts. All we know is what we've seen."

She nodded, "But things were fine when I ordered breakfast from room service."

"The waiter didn't say anything when he brought the food?"

"No, he wasn't in a rush or nervous or anything. Whatever this is, it happened fast."

Randy reached for another bottle of bourbon, but he offered it to Tori first. She shook her head, but then she changed her mind.

"One more," she said, "then we should only drink them when it's safe."

Tori wasn't even sure what she meant when she said that, but she had a feeling that something permanent had happened. Things were never going to be the same again.

Randy surprised her by letting out a short laugh.

"What's so funny?"

Randy held up the little bottle of bourbon and said, "I was just thinking we should fill these with water as we drink the alcohol."

Maybe the bourbon had calmed their nerves the way they had hoped it would, but they both laughed…longer this time. They were still laughing hysterically when two loud sounds in the hallway interrupted them. They froze, and they listened for a clue as to what made the sounds, but both of them suspected they were gunshots.

"You locked the door?" asked Tori.

"Yeah, I'm sure I did."

The shouting in the hallway earlier had been the sound of anger and frustration. What they heard following the gunshots was different. The screaming out there was the sound of pain and fear.

"Give me a hand," said Randy.

Together, they managed to drag the heavy sofa from the living room of their suite until it was wedged into the short hallway inside their door. Randy positioned the other end of it against the entrance of the kitchenette. They retreated to the bedroom without speaking and waited. They sat on the floor with their backs against the bed and watched the door.

******

When the sun went down, the only things that had changed were the sounds coming from the hallway. There had been sporadic outbursts from angry people, more screams, and then periods of silence. Around midnight, they heard someone shouting orders, and a man yelled that he was a police officer. They thought they were about to be rescued, but the verbal commands were followed by more gunshots.

Someone with a deep voice yelled, "Move, move, move."

More muffled gunshots came from farther away, and the next time they heard the deep voice, they could tell the man, probably a police officer, had kept going. Tori and Randy didn't need to talk about whether or not they should follow the voice. They held hands and stayed where they were.

Eventually, they both gave in to the fatigue that mental stress could cause, and they fell asleep leaning against each other. That was okay for a short nap, but the slightest movement jolted them both awake. The room was totally dark, and they sat frozen, unable to force themselves to assault the monsters or demons that stood in the dark corners of the room. To their bleary eyes, there even appeared to be someone sitting in a lounge chair by the window.

"Did you hear something?" whispered Tori.

"No, did you?"

"No. I think I fell asleep. Can we get on the bed?"

"You can," said Randy. "I think I need to find out what's happening outside."

"Are you sure that's a good idea?"

She hated how scared she sounded, but she sounded exactly how she felt.

"I'm just going to take a look."

Tori gripped Randy's hand tighter, but he pulled away when he stood up. Despite what he said about her getting on the bed, she let her body slide to the floor and then eased sideways until she was under it. She tugged at the bedspread and drew it across her hiding place like a curtain.

Randy went to the door of the suite and sat on the armrest of the sofa they had used as a barricade. He listened with his ear pressed against the door. If there was anyone in the hallway, he couldn't hear them. He tried the peephole and couldn't detect even a faint light. The only way he was going to find out what was happening was to go out there, and he wasn't sure that was the smartest thing to do.

He alternated between listening, peering through the peephole, and sitting on the couch, thinking about what to do. The short nap had done nothing for his tingling nerves because a small bump in adrenaline had awakened him too far, and he felt like he had to do something…anything to get them out of this mess.

Randy didn't even realize that he had deviated from his loop of peering, listening, and sitting until he had moved the sofa far enough from the door to make room for it to open. It was so quiet that the sound of the door unlocking might as well have been a gunshot, but it didn't stop him from opening the door. He pulled it toward him and put his face in the gap.

There was total silence in the darkness, and he couldn't see around the corner of the small alcove outside the door. Something told him he would know if someone was there, and he held his breath so he could focus on the sound of someone else breathing. Nothing…no movement and no breathing.

When Randy let out his breath, he pressed his lips together. His next breath was inhaled through his nose, and he was forced to give up all hope of remaining quiet. The stench in the hallway made him gag and cough. He grabbed at his mouth and nose first to try to block out the smell, but then he grabbed his stomach as spasms forced undigested food up his throat. As he choked back food and bile, Randy pushed himself back into the room and slammed the door shut. Out of reflex, one hand dropped to the lock and loudly turned it to the right. He fell more than sat on the sofa and gasped for clean air.

On the other side of the door, something bumped against the wall where Randy had been standing, and he was sure the groan came from the same deep voice he had heard earlier. In the bedroom, Tori heard the choking sounds, but she was so paralyzed with fear that she couldn't move. All she could do was hold her own breath as silent tears rolled down her cheeks.

ABANDONED
PROJECT

1969

After the government accepted the idea that shelters were a necessity for the survival of elected officials, Titus Rush felt like he had to be everywhere at once, and as if he didn't have enough to do, he was constantly being dragged to closed-door meetings to defend the projects. There were a few shelters that were being built without a hitch despite their challenges, but a few were proving to be nothing but a pain in the neck. The Finger Lakes shelter in New York was a prime example of the second group. Titus wondered at times whether or not he could have done the same thing with private funding instead of fighting through all of the red tape with the government, but he had to admit, they had quite often given him a sharp pair of scissors to cut through a lot of that red tape.

"Red tape is nothing but accountability for taxpayers' dollars," he said more than once, and he always added, "We're giving the taxpayers something for their money...they just don't know it yet."

Privately, Titus Rush held the belief that there was no way to guarantee the safety of people who weren't already inside a shelter when an apocalypse began. That was why he felt *exposed* when he had to leave his own shelter. He told himself that he was going to stop building shelters and just follow the philosophy he had adopted for himself. He was going to go inside the Mud Island shelter, shut the door, and not go outside for any reason. He also wouldn't open the door for anyone. He believed that would be how a shelter would become contaminated by the apocalypse outside, no matter what it was. Still, as much as he wanted to adhere to the rules that would ensure his own survival, he felt sorry for the masses who would flock to the shelters once word got out that they existed.

His own personal shelter was discreetly hidden on an island off the coast of South Carolina, and it was doubtful that the *masses* would flock to the door of his shelter because it was such a remote area. There were contractors who knew about it, but they were busy with their own lives, and to them, it was just another eccentric customer with money who wanted a home near the beach that would last longer than most.

He wasn't sure it was possible, but sometimes he hoped that a few of his shelters would be built to accommodate as many people as necessary instead of just a handful of politicians. If a million people showed up at the doors during an emergency, there would be a problem, but that wasn't likely to be the case. Of course, if he was right, the shelters should be occupied before the apocalypse began, not after.

Titus had a theory that it wasn't a question of when the emergency would happen. In his mind, it was already happening. Even as he spoke with the members of his survivor's club or with the government, he felt like he was supposed to be inside his shelter. It would always be too late to leave for the shelter if an apocalyptic event occurred. That's why a million people trying to get inside the shelters at the same time would be a problem. They needed to be inside the shelters now, and if they couldn't be in them now, the shelters needed to be big, and there had to be a way to get everyone inside fast while screening them, or the apocalypse would come in with them. It just wasn't feasible.

Knowledge of the shelters had been compartmentalized at the beginning, and a large number of shelters were built before too many people in Congress knew where the money had gone. Once that changed, Titus was forced to defend the shelters and even had to broaden his views about who was allowed to use them. He couldn't count the number of times he sat across from congressmen and thought, "I shouldn't be here. I should be inside my shelter."

"Imagine the line at the door," he told a group of politicians at one of the many unscheduled Senate committee hearings that questioned the need for the shelters. "Now imagine your family in that line."

One of the senators replied, "So, you're saying we should run for cover now?"

That drew a laugh from the other senators but not from Titus.

"You're missing my point, Senator. I'm not saying I believe the country could even continue to function if we all ran for cover now. I'm saying it will be too late for most people to run for cover once it starts, so we should make sure there's room for everyone who makes it to a shelter in time. We won't be overcrowded if we plan for more people than the ones who show up, and we need to have contingencies for deciding who can come inside."

The senator wasn't persuaded.

"Mr. Rush, some of these shelters are going to be nothing more than underground hotels without a lot of people checking in. I'm not going to use money that could be put to better use above ground, so I'm not going to divert funds from the Niagara Falls Refurbishment Plan for your pet project. We also need to give more funds to the New York State Canal System. Your shelters are taking away from both of those projects."

Titus could feel his temper rising and knew he wasn't going to be able to control it. He did his best to make his point without sounding like he was insulting the senator.

"So, you think the country would benefit more from fixing a tourist attraction than developing a network of safe havens during an apocalypse?"

The senator became red-faced and answered, "When was the last apocalypse, Mr. Rush? Wasn't it when the dinosaurs got wiped out? If you gave a million people the choice between spending a few days at Niagara Falls and moving into one of your shelters, there'd be a lot of tourist dollars spent at Niagara Falls. I'm stopping the diversion of funds to the New York shelter project. We need to get Niagara Falls up and running again. The voters want to see where their money is being spent, not read about it in the paper."

Losing the funding for one of the shelters wasn't such a significant loss to Titus. He just wanted the senator to think it was. Then again, the senator didn't know how much money Titus had already gotten, not to mention his use of the Army Corps of Engineers to build the shelters. He would just have to hope the New York shelter wasn't overrun by an evacuation when the need arose.

As for the voters getting to know where their money was being spent, he had serious doubts about how many Americans even knew that Niagara Falls was undergoing a facelift. The government had actually stopped the water from flowing over the Falls so they could fix places where nature was doing what nature does best. There were tons of debris at the bottom of the Falls that they wanted to get rid of, and to Titus Rush, none of that would matter if there weren't any people left alive to see it.

Titus left the meeting with a vague plan to arrange private funding for the shelter, but he also wanted a guarantee that the senator wouldn't be allowed inside any of the shelters if there was ever a need to survive a disaster. He hoped the senator could get a room at a hotel overlooking Niagara Falls and ride out the apocalypse there.

******

When Titus began making a pitch to politicians about surviving an apocalypse, he appealed to their egos. All he had to do was ask, "How would civilization survive without you?" Private investors were a different breed because they weren't all motivated by the same things. Some were interested in the survival of their families, some were driven by greed, and some were in agreement with his philosophies. There was a wide range of motivations. He just needed to figure out what made each of them tick.

The patriarch of the Warren family in Ithaca, New York, was a mixture of motivations, but it didn't take long for Titus to understand what Mansfield Warren wanted to protect the most. He was fiercely protective of his family, his money, his property, and his privacy, so Titus knew from the start that the scale of the shelter would be smaller than he had hoped, but at least it would be built. Warren didn't want a million people to show up at the door, so security measures had to be included in the design. He only wanted his family to have a place to go, but he made a few compromises that were important to Titus, and the construction of the shelter was back on track without the help of the senators.

The salt mines were an ideal location for a shelter because the family business was already in operation. Mining could continue without interruption, and no one would question why the excavation was being done. It was the perfect cover for the construction of a secret shelter because thousands of tons of salt were extracted every day. Excavation of the mine could be done on all sides of the shelter, and no one would know there was an oasis in the middle except the Warren family and the people who built it.

As soon as the Army Corps of Engineers received its new orders, they pulled out their people and equipment and moved everything to Niagara Falls. The bulk of the work had already been done, and all Mansfield Warren had to do was use his own money to finish and modernize the shelter. He wanted to be as secretive as possible, so he only used contractors from the West Coast or foreign countries. He also compartmentalized the purpose of the work and only had the contractors work on small sections of the shelter, so no single company knew the full scope of the project.

Mansfield Warren had considered running for the Senate in New York, but he felt like it would expose the extent of his wealth to public scrutiny. It was a source of great amazement to him that people took it for granted that there would always be salt on the roads during the winter. They never considered where the salt came from. It never occurred to people how much of a monopoly he had built. The wealth it gave his family made it possible for him to provide everything in his shelter that Titus Rush suggested, and he immensely enjoyed the long hours they spent discussing the perfect shelter.

As the years passed, the Warren family routinely summoned Titus to their home to discuss advances in technology and improvements to the shelter. Although Titus preferred the privacy of his own shelter on Mud Island, he considered the Ithaca shelter to be one of the best in his network. He knew that the family would continue to make upgrades even if he was no longer around to advise them, and he was grateful that they included him in the discussions.

One of the features that set the Ithaca shelter apart from the others was something that Titus never fully embraced. The shelters were protected from being discovered by hiding them in plain sight. Decoy shelters were built near them to keep people from suspecting there were superior shelters nearby. Mud Island had a simple houseboat tied to a dock, and the Guntersville shelter had an entire village built above it. Stealth was a defining defensive feature of the shelters built by Titus Rush. The Ithaca shelter, however, had a more lethal security system that Titus discouraged. Mansfield Warren actively sought technology that would keep people out of the shelter, and he said he wanted them to rival the pyramids. If curses were real, he would find one that kept intruders from opening the shelter doors.

Titus was invited to supper with Mansfield Warren to discuss the security system, and it was the last time they spoke with each other. Titus warned his host that the security measures installed to keep people out were dangerous to the occupants of the shelter. Titus suggested that the best security was already in place because the tunnels within the mine were endless. There were hundreds of miles of tunnels that snaked away from the center where the shelter was located, and without provisions, people weren't likely to wander so far from the entrance of the mine. Titus attempted to explain his own belief that a decoy shelter would keep anyone from venturing too far into the mine, but a security system would spark curiosity.

Warren would accept none of it, and despite a stern warning from Titus, he ended their relationship in the same manner the senators had. He paid Titus a generous consulting fee and informed him that they had concluded their business.

Titus returned to Mud Island with the belief that he had done his best to persuade Warren to do the right thing, but all he could see in the future was the disaster that would unfold in the right circumstances. Something was tugging at the back of his mind, and he wasn't sure why he hadn't thought of it before.

He rummaged through his collection of architectural plans and found the designs for the Ithaca shelter. He unrolled them across a large table and sorted through the stack of drawings until he found one that showed the surface area surrounding the mine. He checked the scale at the bottom of the drawing and calculated the distance from the main entrance of the salt mine to the nearest of the Finger Lakes. The banks of Lake Cayuga were only one hundred yards from the mine.

Titus flipped through the sheets of paper and found the map of the tunnels below the surface. He stared in disbelief at the complexity and depths of the tunnels.

"Why didn't I see this before?" he asked himself.

According to the charts, the tunnels descended more than five hundred feet below the surface, but Titus was alarmed to see they also extended below Lake Cayuga. The lake itself had a depth of four hundred and fifty feet, and Titus could only wonder about the pressure exerted on the tunnels by that much water.

Titus asked himself out loud, "What would happen if the Canal System fails and more water is released into Lake Cayuga? Have the mining engineers ever considered that?"

TENNESSEE

Blue Ridge Foothills - 2025

We were walking through tall grass next to an old cemetery when I saw one tombstone that stood out. It was more obvious because someone had placed flowers on top of the weather-worn and curved slab. It leaned slightly to the left, so the flowers were off-center. The chiseled sentence cut into it was still legible even though the date said the occupant had died in 1840.

It said, "Here lies Nicholas Dollar...stole a horse and wore the collar."

Jean saw that I had stopped at the wrought iron fence that still formed the boundary of the small cemetery and came back to stand next to me.

I felt that familiar flash of warmth I always got in her presence, even after eight years. I never took that feeling for granted. From the first moment when I met her until now, I still felt a sense of awe at how attractive she was to me. She was still the little pixie who teased me the first time I had met her on the boat, and it wasn't a surprise that she found something appropriate to say about the headstone.

"Friend of yours, Eddie? Oh, wait...great-grandfather?"

I should've known better, but not to be outdone, I answered, "No, my great-grandfather died from a head injury. There was speculation that it was inflicted by my great-grandmother after he gave her a cast iron skillet for her birthday."

"A skillet? Isn't that what you got me last year?"

I had to think about it for a moment, but it was enough time for me to realize I would never win the ongoing battle of quick, witty remarks, so I conceded by changing the subject. It wasn't the first time, and it wouldn't be the last.

"Those flowers are fresh, and why are they on that headstone? There can't be a living relative who still misses Nicholas."

Both of us realized our mistake at the same moment, and in that flash of a split second, we reacted as we had so many times before. Jean dropped to the ground to the right and disappeared into the tall grass. I did the same thing to the left. The bullet that was intended for one of us, probably me, exploded the grave marker into fragments.

Years ago, when I moved into the Mud Island shelter, I was only good at video games and cooking instant noodles. I hadn't even mastered Hot Pockets. That was a long time ago, and since then, I acquired survival talents that came just as naturally to me as knowing where the buttons were on a video game controller.

Without even thinking about it, I stopped moving for the crucial few seconds that would tell me where the shooter was, and I was sure Jean was doing the same thing. If either of us made a sound, it would help the unknown assailant. I heard the sound of a bolt being pulled back and then pushed forward, and I knew the shooter was taking aim. I could also tell where he was.

The Chief had told me that if I ever found myself in this moment, there were two possibilities. If the hunter couldn't see his prey, he would have reloaded and aimed at the last place he saw the rabbit hide, or he would have waved the rifle over the general area, waiting for the rabbit to run. Either way, he wouldn't pull the trigger until he was sure.

Jean and I had faced worse situations, and we had learned to trust our instincts. My instincts were screaming that the shooter had intended the first bullet for me because I stood over a foot taller than Jean. I was more of a threat. I hoped I was right when I decided to trust the Chief's advice. I had to stay frozen where I was until Jean found the shooter. It could take a while.

In the tall grass to the right of where they had stood, Jean also heard the bolt moving backward and forward, and she had a moment of panic as she worried that her husband might be bleeding to death. In her mind, she replayed the sounds and decided the bullet had hit the gravestone with too much force to have gone through Ed first. She hoped she was right about what her husband was doing. Ed was waiting for her to make a move on the shooter, and she was thinking she had to be the one to try. Whether it was logical or anger, she wanted the threat to be gone, and the shooter had most likely been too focused on Ed to see where she had gone. Without disturbing the tall grass around her, she eased out of her backpack and crawled toward the sound of the rifle bolt.

Over the years since the arrival of the infected dead, there had been no end to the differences between philosophies about survival. Some people believed there was strength in numbers, and some survivors trusted only themselves. For those people who banded together, their success depended upon their collective rules. Sadly, rule number one was often that no one was allowed to keep a bite wound a secret. Groups that didn't put that rule at the top of the list didn't survive very long. Rule number two was to be faithful and protective of the group against outsiders.

Some groups had one leader who made all of the decisions, while others established loose governing councils. Regardless of which one they chose, they didn't always accept that other groups they encountered were trustworthy. Shortages of supplies caused larger groups to destroy smaller groups, and while people honored rule number two and called themselves families, they became something they never thought they would become...tribes. Territorial and paranoid, tribes established boundaries around the land they considered to be their own, and trespassers were eliminated as fast as the infected dead.

The question on Jean's mind as she quietly crawled toward the shooter was whether or not it was someone with the group mentality or if it was someone who had the philosophy that a living person always had something he needed to have. Worse...they had something he was entitled to take. The fact that he shot first meant he didn't plan to negotiate a trade.

******

A second bullet sliced through the grass to my left, and I had to force myself not to run. The only thing that helped me stay calm was knowing a random shot in my direction was one more chance for Jean to stay undetected. Part of me wanted her to just get away, but the years of surviving together made me sure that the second shot had only improved my chances of coming out of this alive.

******

When the rifle fired for a second time, Jean was surprised by how close she was to the shooter. The blast was so loud that it almost drowned out the bolt action as the shooter pushed another round into the chamber. She gently parted the grass and saw she was only a few feet below the barrel of a hunting rifle that protruded from the end of a hollowed-out log. The back end of the log was on the ground, but the part that was above her head rested across another log at a thirty-degree angle. The shooter had probably placed it there and then slid feet-first into the log.

"How has this guy stayed alive so long?" she muttered to herself.

Jean knew he was blind to any movement on his sides, so she could move freely without the shooter knowing she was there. She didn't want the next shot to be the one that found Ed, but there were only two obvious ways to end this. She could shoot the side of the log from point-blank range, knowing she wouldn't miss the man inside, or she could flush him out.

From the start of the zombie apocalypse to now, the Mud Island survivors had done what they could to draw people into their group, so Jean chose the second option. She pulled a cigarette lighter from her pocket and held it against the dry bark on the underside of the log. The fire caught quickly and spread upward toward the open end, where smoke curled over the lip of the opening. She heard a cough first. Then there was the panicked scrambling inside the log that meant someone would be coming out in a hurry.

The man extended one arm from the opening with a firm grip on the rifle. Jean held her 9mm Smith & Wesson pistol against his head with one hand while she grabbed the rifle with the other.

"I'll take that. You won't be needing it anymore."

Jean was surprised that the man tried to keep his grip on the rifle at first. She saw through the shaggy hair and beard covering most of his face that he was one of the crazy survivors. He was angry at her for flushing him out, but he was probably angrier that she was a petite woman with a gun at his head. He let go of the rifle but took a swing at the Smith & Wesson with his other hand as he pushed himself out of the burning log. He missed the pistol because Jean only needed to step backward.

I arrived at that moment. An easy swing with the stock of my own rifle was all it took to knock the man out.

"You made that look easy," I said as I gave Jean a quick hug.

We both grabbed the man by his arms and pulled him out of the log the rest of the way. We dumped him unceremoniously, face down on the ground. It went without saying that we wouldn't have made him suffer a painful death, but judging by his appearance, we weren't going to become traveling companions either. We had run into plenty of solitary people like him, but they were like some of the homeless people before the apocalypse. Most of the solitary survivors were alone by choice, and plenty of them were mentally ill. This one was likely to be in that category.

"It was too easy," said Jean, "but I take that as a good sign."

"How so?"

"That was a dumb hiding spot. He didn't have a backdoor, he was blind on the sides, and he didn't have an escape plan. That means he hasn't been getting tested out here. We might be in one of those areas where there just haven't been that many infected dead."

We had seen places like that before. There were places with natural features that seemed to defy the existence of the infected dead. Places surrounded by cliffs, rivers, and natural predators caused the infected to be exterminated with very little assistance from the living. Unfortunately, those places were like the parts of cities where the homeless people used to go. Somehow, the homeless found those safe zones, but the biggest difference was the formerly defenseless homeless were carrying guns and determined to hang onto their zones.

Both of us had the same thought. If it was a safe zone, it was either going to have a settlement nearby, or there would be more crazies. The man I had knocked out was still unconscious, so we took a minute to check our surroundings. The trees were tall in all directions, but we could see clearings that we had avoided. There was also a chance that he was one of the crazies who didn't belong to a settlement, but there were others just like him nearby that he tolerated. They weren't in alliances, but they avoided conflicts with each other.

"Where are we?" asked Jean.

"Hang on a second."

I pulled a zip-tie and a map out of my backpack. After I finished securing our hairy friend, I spread the map out on the ground and ran a finger along the trail I had marked as we hiked northeast into the Appalachian Mountains. We were still in the foothills, but we could see that the valley we were following would take us into the mountains in about two more days.

"Here's one of the natural barriers."

I put a finger on Chickamauga Lake to the north.

"I still don't understand why they called that thing a lake when they named it. It's so long that it should be a river."

Jean nodded her head and said, "I agree, but it's too far to the north to make this a safe zone. There must be something else about this area that made this guy survive for a long time.

Aren't we still close to the Georgia border above Atlanta?"

I answered by showing her that we were close to Big Frog Mountain. Our plan was to stick with the state roads as much as possible to avoid the heavily populated areas and give us a chance to cross or navigate around rivers.

Jean lifted her head as if she had heard something nearby, but it was just the way the log was burning. The angle of the log made it act like a smokestack, sending a plume of smoke and ash high into the air. It seemed like there was only one thing the infected dead liked better than living people, and that was a good bonfire. The Chief had said more than once that the infected would've been a lot of fun at pep rallies.

"We can't stay here long," I said. "That smoke will draw people, and the fire will draw the infected."

"What about him? We can't just leave him here."

Despite the fact he had shot at us, neither of us had become so cynical that we would leave someone to die. I pulled my canteen from my belt and unscrewed the cap. When I splashed water on the man's face, he jolted awake but froze when he saw a semiautomatic gun a few inches from his head. The scowl he had worn on his face when he first laid eyes on Jean returned but faded quickly. He opened his mouth to say something, but Jean put a finger across her own lips to indicate she didn't want him to speak.

"My husband and I don't care. We don't care who you are, and we don't care why you shot at us. All we care about is that you shot. Now you're going to pay for it. We're leaving, but we're keeping the rifle and any ammo you have for it."

"Wait, you can't do that," he blurted. "I'll die out here without a gun."

"You're not doing a very good job staying alive with it," I answered. "You would still own a gun if you hadn't used it in our direction."

With his hands still tied at his back, I searched his pockets and satchel for the rest of his ammo. Besides the bullets, there was an odd assortment of wedding rings and personally engraved items like watches, money clips, and cigarette lighters. It was fair to conclude that we weren't the first people the man had laid traps for. It made me angry to think about the survivors who had died because of this man's petty greed. I gave the cigarette lighters to Jean, but I threw the personal items in every direction.

I was so angry at the man that I grabbed him by his beard, pulled his face close to mine, and said, "Maybe I should just tie you to that cemetery fence and leave you for dead."

When he protested, Jean put one hand on my arm and waited. She knew that words weren't necessary. I slipped a knife under the tie straps around the man's wrists and cut him loose. He didn't have to be told what to do, and once he was on his feet, it only took a minute for him to run far enough to disappear into the woods.

We gathered up our gear without talking about it and left the area quickly. Several times, we ducked for cover and waited for the infected dead to go by in the opposite direction. Judging by their agitated behavior, we knew they were being drawn to the burning log. The gunshots had started them moving, but the crackling flames and smoke kept them interested. After crossing a stream and climbing some rock-strewn hills, we were far enough from the old cemetery to slow our pace.

Jean broke the silence when we reached the crest of a hill and saw the valley stretched out ahead of us.

"We have a long way to go."

"You aren't regretting the decision again, are you?"

"A little," she answered. "We could've waited. The Chief and the others will be back in a couple of weeks. It would've been safer to wait for them and then fly to New York. It's going to take us longer than that now that we're on foot."

I had to admit Jean was right. Despite all of our planning, we had run into enough bad luck to last a lifetime. Still, waiting a couple of weeks might mean the difference between life and death for a lot of people, so we felt like we had to try.

"If it makes you feel any better," I said, "when the others get back to Guntersville, Doc Bus will tell them where we went, and they'll come looking for us. We'll pop a flare when we see the plane, they'll figure out where to land, and we'll meet them there."

Jean said, "You left off the part about what the Chief will do to us when he finds out we went out on a mission without him and the rest of the gang. He'll work me over a bit, but he'll go easier on me because I'm a woman. I'll bet he's going to wear you out."

"Thanks for reminding me. Instead of popping a flare, maybe we should just hide. Better yet, would you like to go back?"

Jean appeared to be giving it some thought, but she shook her head. Even though her dark hair was cut short, it moved enough for him to know she meant it.

"If we don't run into more bad luck, we can still do this," she said. "You don't think the Chief will think we had a good enough reason to make this trip?"

"I think he'll be okay with the reason, but I think he's going to disagree with the plan. You know how he is with plans. Every plan A has a plan B. I think he's going to say our plan A was so bad that no plan B would save us. At the very least, he's going to think we should've taken along a squad of soldiers, and don't expect him not to bring up the fact that we left our own child behind to go off on a rescue mission."

Jean said, "There wasn't time to get a squad together, and they were all assigned to other duties, and I already feel guilty for leaving Josh, so don't remind me about him. We'll be fine, and so will he."

"Speaking of time," I said, "we would've had plenty of time to make it to the designated spot if we hadn't lost our transportation so soon. We should have taken that much into consideration at the start. Practically every mission we've ever done has had a transportation failure of some kind. If I remember correctly, the very first time we left Mud Island, our plane took a bullet that kept us from getting back to the shelter."

"We made it back," said Jean.

"But we were less than a hundred miles from home, and we had help from Hampton in Georgetown. We're going to need some major good luck to make it to New York on time. Maybe we'll meet another person like Hampton."

We walked in silence for the next hour, but I was sure Jean was thinking the same thing that I was. We had a long trip ahead of us, and we would most likely be better off if we turned around and went home. Her optimism was probably the only thing that kept us moving north.

As if Jean could use willpower to bring good luck into existence, we spotted a cabin on the side of the mountain only a couple of miles away. Smoke curled upward from a chimney. In our experience, survivors who advertised their locations were generally best avoided, but there were a few who were helpful if they were approached carefully. Carefully was usually defined as respectfully. If they didn't feel threatened, then they wouldn't overreact, and at least in our minds, we didn't appear to be threatening.

I had gained a few pounds over the years, and the exercise I got from having a more active lifestyle as an apocalypse survivor had turned some of those pounds into muscles, but I still had the good fortune to have a perpetually young look. If it were still a normal world, I would get carded buying beer at the grocery store. As for Jean, no one was ever afraid of a cute little brunette who stood just under five feet tall and had a pretty smile. If she were given the chance, she would charm someone into helping us, but if that didn't work, she would at least keep us from getting shot. We decided we had to at least try to get some help from the people in the cabin.

It took close to three hours for us to cross the heavily wooded valley. We talked in whispers about how we would approach the people, but we both knew that we wouldn't have a clue how to do it until we were closer. We had to scout the area around the cabin to be sure we weren't sneaking up on a tribe. If we made that mistake, nothing else we did would matter.

We also planned to spend some time finding the traps that were likely to be hidden in the woods as we got closer. We had seen snares, nets, pits, and landmines near settlements. The more sophisticated the traps were, the more likely we would be spotted before we got close to the cabin, but the most important thing the traps told us was whether or not the people were too dangerous to approach. If the traps were set to kill, we would circle the cabin and leave. If they were set to capture, we would spring one and hide.

Of course, what we planned to do and what we did were often two different things, and that proved to be true this time when we heard a woman's voice behind us.

"This looks like as good a place as any for us to talk. How about you two lowering your weapons to the ground before you turn around?"

She didn't need to say she had a gun aimed at us. That much, we could assume.

Jean said, "How long have you been following us?"

"Why's that matter?" asked the woman.

"I'll get a better idea about whether or not you're going to kill us," said Jean. "If you've been following us a long time, then you would've killed us by now."

The woman laughed, and I was grateful for Jean's ability to be an ambassador. The laugh sounded genuine.

She said, "Long enough to see Henry Shackley running through the forest without his rifle. Would that be his rifle you're carrying, mister?"

I eased the strap of the rifle from my shoulder and lowered it to the ground with my arm extended as far as I could reach.

"If Henry Shackley is that crazy, long-haired guy who shoots at innocent people, then it's probably his rifle," I answered.

"I suppose you're going to tell me you're innocent, but you somehow got Henry's gun after he shot at you. Sound about right?" she asked.

Jean took over again, and I preferred it that way.

"You said you saw him running through the woods. That means we didn't shoot him after we took his gun. I'd say that makes us decent people if not innocent."

"Taking a man's gun out here is about as bad as shooting him these days," said the woman.

Jean countered quickly, "That was his only gun?"

This time, the woman laughed longer, and it was more than genuine. It sounded like she had been saving up for something big to laugh about.

"Honey, you have Henry figured out. He was running fast so he could get another gun and come back after you. He's not very bright, but it's been good to have him out there as my early warning system."

"Can we turn around now?" asked Jean.

"Won't hurt," answered the woman.

The woman was around seventy years old and thin, but she wasn't likely to be starving. She had been living off the grid for a long time and cradled a high-powered hunting rifle like she knew how to use it. She had gray hair pulled back in a ponytail and was wearing a Braves baseball cap. She was still smiling about what Jean had said, so she didn't come across as threatening, but I knew we had to do more than make her laugh if we wanted to earn her trust.

"I'm Jean, and this guy is my husband, Eddie."

"You two are actually married? Who has time to get married these days?"

She didn't wait for us to answer before going on, "I'm Ruth, and that guy over there is my brother. Wally, come out where they can have a look at you."

Jean and I were both surprised to find the woman wasn't alone. Wally was about my height, but like Ruth, he was thin and wiry. He emerged from behind a tree, and I could have sworn he blended into the background so well that he really didn't need to hide.

"Let's get inside before sunset," said Ruth as she gestured in the direction of the cabin with her rifle.

******

We walked to the cabin behind Ruth, but Wally was behind

us. It didn't matter because I could tell Jean was relaxed. They could have killed us already if that was what they planned to do. Besides, it was getting dark, and it was a good idea to have shelter for the night.

The door didn't have a lock, but as soon as we were inside, Wally laid a heavy steel bar through mounts on both sides of the door. We used the same drop-bar door brackets on the front gates of the village in Guntersville, and I knew they worked well against most attacks. Wally's appeared strong enough to withstand an attack by a horde and maybe even getting rammed by a vehicle. Jean and I surveyed the cabin and saw that it was as neat as a pin...almost too neat. There was a fire burning in the fireplace with a big cast iron pot suspended above it, but there was something that stood out about the furniture and the normal accessories. Ruth saw the way I was taking everything in.

"You figure something out, Eddie?"

"As a matter of fact, yes," I said. "I feel like I'm in a showroom. Why?"

Ruth said to Jean, "He's smarter than he looks. No wonder you married him."

When Ruth nodded at Wally, he opened a small closet and reached for a spot inside and above the door. He pulled on a latch, and the back wall of the closet moved out of the way to reveal a set of stairs. A bright light came from the bottom of the stairs, and Ruth gestured for us to go in.

Jean went first with me behind her. Ruth followed and talked as we went down the stairs. Wally closed the hidden door before coming down behind his sister.

"My late husband, Reggie Stone, was a survivalist. I thought he was nuts when he built this place, but I guess we know by now that he wasn't."

I reached the bottom of the stairs and stood next to Jean. We were in a spacious room that reminded me of the Mud Island shelter. There wasn't a huge vault door that could withstand a nuclear blast, but the room was well-furnished and decorated. A hallway in the far corner went back toward other rooms that I assumed were bedrooms and bathrooms. Of course, there had to be plenty of storage, and the power had to be sophisticated because I didn't hear a generator chugging away.

Ruth took us on a tour, and we were impressed. The shelter had a storeroom that was stocked well enough for the two of them to survive for years. She explained that her husband had sunk their entire savings into the shelter because he expected a war. He died about a year before the infection began, and she had come to the shelter for peace and quiet. Wally showed up and told her what was happening to the world.

"You didn't have a TV or the internet?" I asked.

"I did, but I wasn't watching TV or checking the news. I would have sooner or later, I suppose, but I just wanted to be alone."

I was dying to know how she managed the power requirements, and I wasn't disappointed. She said her husband always believed in having a backup plan.

"Sounds like someone we know," said Jean.

Ruth added, "He was always that way, and it paid off for me. One floor below the storeroom is the power plant, and it has a big battery storage capacity. The electric generators are quiet and don't need a vent system. There are solar panels outside that are hard to find if you don't know where to look for them."

"What's the backup plan?" I asked.

"The first backup is a supply of solar panels in storage. If we can't use them, there's a tunnel that goes into the caves under the mountain, and we have generators in a large cavern. These mountains have caves everywhere, and they're so big you don't need to bother with vents or the noise. If anyone hears them and does manage to find them, they aren't likely to find their way back out."

I hated to ask, but she needed to know for her own sake.

"Is the fuel still good?"

"My husband had it stored in tanks that stir the fuel from time to time. I expect it won't last forever, but no one has found the solar panels yet, so we haven't worried about it. We've also been making biodiesel for years, but I'll tell you about that later."

After the tour, Ruth and Wally took us back to the main room, where we settled in for dinner. We talked well into the night because there was a lot to tell her, and sooner or later, the discussion had to get around to why we were going to New York and how we wound up without transportation. It was a pleasant surprise when Ruth said she might be able to help us out.

THE WARREN FAMILY

Virginia Beach, Virginia - 2016

It seemed like it was never easy to find a stretch of beach that wasn't heavily populated, but the Warren family was enjoying more space than usual. There was an all-day concert in Norfolk that was drawing a large crowd of the tourist population away from the coast, and the Warrens were making the most of it. There were still a few people scattered here and there in the distance, but they were so far away that Brad and Denise were comfortable giving the children more room to run than usual. They positioned themselves comfortably on folding chaise lounge chairs while Jacob and Jalen worked with their plastic shovels to create the ultimate sand castle.

A stiff breeze rushed across the wet sand just as a cloud covered the sun, and the temperature drop signaled the unwelcome arrival of rain. The sudden change caused both parents to lift their heads away from their books. The cloud shifted and allowed the bright light of the sun to burst through just as they focused their eyes on their children, and their dark sunglasses and changing scenery made them unsure of what they saw.

"Who's that?" asked Brad.

It was a natural question, but so was the irritated response from Denise.

"How am I supposed to know? It's not like I know everyone on the beach."

The arrival of the stranger came as such a surprise that there was a frozen moment when neither of the parents reacted, and they watched as he approached the boys. Jacob was leaning so far into the hole he had dug in the sand that he was totally unaware that they weren't alone. Jalen was packing wet sand into a bucket between his knees to shape it before adding it to a castle wall. He was watching the man in that curious way a kid would stare at something he thought might be dangerous. He was sitting on both of his legs, but he was already bunching his muscles for a fast retreat.

"Jacob?"

Jalen's voice squeaked out his older brother's name as a question. Jacob felt like he was making more progress digging the hole than any ten-year-old in history, so he kept digging without answering.

"Jacob? There's someone coming."

"Tell Mom and Dad."

Jalen took his eyes off the man who was making steady but slow progress in their direction, but his stranger-danger alarm had already detected that the man wasn't dressed for a day at the beach. He was wearing a long-sleeved shirt and denim pants that were soaked to the knees. Jalen turned toward his parents and saw his father wasn't in attack mode yet, but he was in the process of standing next to his chair. His mother had removed her sunglasses and was sitting up straight on her chair.

Brad Warren wasn't what people would call a hothead. He didn't get upset in traffic, he didn't get impatient if the lines were long at the store, and he never sent a meal back to the kitchen in a restaurant. He was easygoing until his family was threatened, and the indecision he had felt when he noticed the man bothered him more than his wife's snappy answer. He slid his feet into his sandals and moved to close the distance between himself and his boys. His six feet four-inch frame and long legs enabled him to get there quickly.

"Can I help you?" he said after positioning himself between the boys and the man.

Even though the stranger was at least ten yards away, Brad knew he had heard the question. It caused the man to adjust his course slightly toward Brad, which was what Brad wanted. If the man wanted to cause trouble, Brad wouldn't want the boys in the middle of it.

Jacob finally lifted his head out of the hole when his father's shadow passed over him. He dropped his shovel when he saw why his brother had tried to get his attention. Whoever the man was, there was something wrong with him. He walked like he was hurt. Jacob came to the conclusion that the best place for him to be was by his mother, and Jalen fell in behind him as he ran toward her.

Brad Warren wasn't happy with the man's lack of response, but he wasn't ready to escalate the confrontation yet.

"I asked if I could help you, buddy. The polite thing to do would be to answer me."

He felt like the man heard him well enough because it sounded like he let out a grunt. It wasn't much more than an exhalation of air, but Brad heard it and waited for more. The next sound that came from the man's mouth was louder and more drawn out into a groan that made the fine hairs on the back of Brad's neck stand up. It was his signal that it was time to escalate. He held out his right hand with the palm facing the man.

"That's close enough, friend. I've given you a chance to say whatever it is that you want, but now it's time for you to leave."

The distance between the two men closed more quickly, and from the place where Denise was huddled with the boys, it seemed like the man was attracted to her husband's outstretched hand. The stranger lifted both of his hands toward Brad's as he drew closer. Brad saw the way the man seemed to reach for his hand as if he was offering him something, but he kept his arm extended for a few heartbeats to be sure. At the last second, Brad moved his hand to the right but kept it level with the stranger's eyes. There was no mistaking the intentions of the man as he lunged after the moving hand with both hands, and as he grasped at the empty air where the hand had been, his mouth opened in a grotesque attempt to bite the exposed flesh.

Brad used his hand as bait in order to line up a perfect left hook. The man was slightly off balance already, and the right side of his head was fully exposed, but the man turned his head toward Brad at the last moment. Brad's fist solidly collided with the man's mouth, and the punch, combined with the man's momentum, caused the stranger to land face down in the sand.

Because Brad had always taken the high road when faced with confrontational individuals, he had seldom been forced to follow through with a punch. Judging by the way his hand felt, he was instantly worried that he had committed the crime of murder. Even Denise had heard the impact, and Brad turned toward her with guilt written on every line of his face. He wanted to say to her that he felt like he had been given no other choice, and at first, he was sure she agreed. Then he saw her expression change to confusion. She pointed to the spot beyond her husband.

Brad turned to see that the man was on his hands and knees, facing away from him, and he was arching his back to pull his right foot forward. Brad's mouth hung open as the man fell over on his face for a second time, but he renewed his efforts to stand almost immediately. He eventually got both feet under him and stood upright, facing away from Brad, and if not for the fact that Brad had just hit him with a killer left hook, he would have assumed the man was admiring the view of the ocean. That impression changed as the stranger stumbled in the sand, but he gradually turned around to face him. Gone was any semblance of life in the stranger's eyes. Milky gray cataracts with red streaks stared at Brad, and the guttural grunts combined into one long, phlegm-filled groan.

"What happened to you?" said Brad.

One backward step by Brad was enough to make Denise scream. Brad's left leg disappeared into the hole Jacob had been digging, and he landed flat on his back. It was a good thing that Jacob had vacated the hole to stand by his mother and younger brother while Brad confronted the man. The fall wasn't painful, but Brad could tell by the odd angle of his leg that he would suffer later when it started to swell. His more immediate problem was walking toward him with both hands extended downward.

To Denise, everything seemed to speed up and then slow down. Brad was falling quickly into the hole, and the strange man was reaching for him as he stumbled slowly forward. The man didn't seem to know how to walk on loose sand, and his feet dug deep trenches as he walked. He would have eventually reached Brad, but Jacob rushed back to help his father. He picked up his sand shovel and stuck it between the man's knees. The man fell face-first into the sand for a second time and just short of where Brad had landed. Brad crab-walked away from the prone man and then got his feet under him. Jacob circled around behind Brad, and they made their way back to Denise and Jalen.

Denise looked to her husband for an explanation of what had happened, but other than what both of them had already seen, he had nothing to offer her. When he suggested that he felt like they had spent enough time in Virginia Beach, she didn't object. When they left the beach, the stranger had gotten to his feet but then fell again without the help of anyone else when he stepped in the same hole that tripped Brad.

******

It only took the Warren family about two hours to get back to their hotel, pack, and drive to the private airstrip near the airport. Brad Warren had paid in advance to have his Cessna C172S refueled, so he called ahead and asked the maintenance crew to file a flight plan and do the preflight checks. Brad preferred to do his own preflight checks, but Denise was pushing hard for them to be on their way home, and this was one time when he didn't disagree.

They didn't talk about what had happened on the beach until they were airborne and headed northwest. The shaking in their voices was a surprise to both of them because there had been a couple of hours between the beach and the airplane. They both felt violated, and it must have been because they had to protect their children. If it had happened without the children there, they would have dealt with it, and it would have been just a topic of conversation. Now, it was like PTSD, and talking about it meant admitting their children had been exposed to real danger.

"What was that?" asked Denise.

They were wearing headsets, and the boys couldn't hear them in the passenger compartment. Just asking the question made her feel a lump rise in her throat, and she almost sobbed. Over the sound of the plane, Brad heard the effort she made to hold it in.

"I have no idea," he answered. "There was something really wrong with that guy."

"You mean he was sick?"

"Let's put it this way," said Brad. "If he had been lying down, I would've thought he was dead."

"From where I was, he just looked sick."

"From close up, he looked dead."

They didn't talk again for a few minutes. Brad concentrated on flying the plane, and Denise seemed to be lost in thought.

"You hit him hard. I thought you killed him. I know it sounds stupid, but all I could think of was that you were going to be arrested in front of your children."

"I thought I killed him, too," said Brad. "My hand hurt like hell, so I can imagine what his face felt like."

He held up his left hand, and Denise saw he had one of those tan ACE bandages wrapped around it. There was a rust-colored stain on the part of the bandage that covered his knuckles.

"Did you hurt yourself when you hit him?"

Brad held his hand out to get a better look at it. He flexed his fingers and winced. It felt like a thousand needles went through the knuckles all the way to his fingertips and wrist.

"I think I cut my hand on his teeth."

"We should stop at the doctor's office after we land at home," said Denise. "You may need a shot or some antibiotics to keep it from becoming infected."

Brad wanted to say he was fine and didn't need to see a doctor, but even he wasn't stubborn enough to ignore the red streaks that ran in jagged lines from his knuckles down the back of his hand. Denise couldn't see them because they were hidden by the bandage, and he wanted to keep it that way for a while.

"There's an Urgent Care by the airport. It'll be faster to go there. Doctor Foster is always booked up and will want me to make an appointment. Besides, I don't know if I broke a bone or something, but it really hurts."

"You want me to take a look at it?"

The last thing Brad wanted was for Denise to see what he saw before he wrapped it, so he shook his head in a matter-of-fact way.

"Naw, I'll be fine."

Denise didn't push the issue, so Brad was careful not to let it show that it was bothering him. Time passed slowly for Brad, and he was relieved to see that their flight was almost over. He contacted the air traffic control tower and asked for clearance to land just as the sun was setting. There was a longer pause before the air traffic controller responded, and Brad was just about to repeat his request when the answer came.

"Cessna N52737, you have no clearance to land at this time. Divert at present altitude to Niagara International."

Brad had never been denied permission to land, so the response left him speechless.

"Cessna N52737, confirm receipt of instructions."

"Uh, this is Cessna N52737…say again. I need clearance to land at Ithaca Tompkins Private Terminal. Your instructions to proceed to Niagara International are not possible."

Brad knew from his flight training that there was really only one thing that could get you clearance to land if you were told to divert to another airport, so he quickly added it to his request before the controller could respond.

"Cessna N52737 requests clearance to land at Ithaca

Tompkins due to a medical emergency."

The air traffic controller's tone of voice sounded almost cold when he answered.

"Cessna N52737, what is the nature of your emergency?"

Brad knew that his answer had to be more than a cut on his hand to be allowed to land, but if he made more of it than it was, he would be in big trouble when they found out he had lied.

"Uh, the pilot of Cessna N52737 is having difficulty due to a cut on his hand, which is causing a deterioration of performance. Niagara International may be too far to fly."

Another period of silence went on longer than he expected, and Brad saw that Denise was watching him closely. He told her in a low voice with a hand over his mic that he was okay and just trying to get permission to land, but he saw her concern. If he were more honest with himself, he would admit that he wanted to have a doctor take a look at his hand sooner rather than later.

"Cessna N52737, proceed to Niagara International. They have been notified of your arrival and will have medical personnel on standby."

Brad was stunned by the answer and more than a little angry. He was glad that they showed him the courtesy of arranging medical treatment, but he was more interested in landing closer to home. Landing at Niagara International meant he would have to rent a car and then drive all the way back to Ithaca.

"Ithaca Control," he began to make his request again, but the controller cut him off.

"Cessna N52737, proceed to Niagara International...over and out."

There was no mistaking the emphasis on the last word.

Denise asked Brad, "Can you make it to Niagara? I can take over if you can't."

"I'm fine," he snapped a bit more harshly than he intended. "You haven't gotten your license yet. Besides, it isn't that bad. I just don't understand why they wouldn't clear me to land, especially after I said it was a medical emergency."

"It seemed to me like they were more adamant about not giving you clearance after you told them you cut your hand," said Denise.

Brad had wondered about that, too, almost like his cut was contagious or something. All he could do was continue northwest to Niagara. It was a short trip by plane, but he figured it would be well after midnight before they landed, got treatment for his hand, rented a car, and made the drive back home.

By the time they were within hailing range of Niagara International, Brad's left hand felt like someone had doused it in gasoline and held a match to it. He radioed the control tower and was immediately given clearance to land at the private terminal.

Paramedics and a police officer met the plane, and Brad and Denise were surprised by the lack of professional courtesy. Brad was virtually pulled away to the back of an ambulance while Denise and the boys were ordered to stay on the plane. When Denise opened her door, the police officer pushed it shut and, through the window, asked her if she or anyone else on the plane was injured. It all happened so fast that they felt like they had done something wrong.

"We're not criminals," shouted Brad. "I don't know why we're being treated like this."

"Just calm down," said the female paramedic. "How did you hurt your hand?"

The other paramedic, a large man with hands that gripped Brad's arms like vises, held him in place from behind while the woman unwrapped Brad's hand.

Brad was feeling a bruise forming on his ego because he had so little control at the moment. He practically spat out his answer.

"I punched a guy in the face."

The two paramedics seemed to become frozen in place.

"You weren't bitten?" asked the woman.

"No, I already told you. There was a guy bothering us at the beach, so I punched his lights out."

Brad wanted to sound a lot tougher than he was, and to him, it seemed to work because the big paramedic loosened his grip on Brad's arms, and the woman began packing up their gear.

"We don't have time for this," she said. "Here's a bottle of acetaminophen that should help with the pain. When you get wherever it is you're going, you should check with a doctor about your hand. You might have broken a bone, Mr. Macho Man."

Just as quickly as they had arrived and manhandled him away from the plane, the paramedics and police officer were gone. They didn't apologize for their rude behavior or even wish them luck. Brad stood where the ambulance had been and was dumbfounded. Denise got out of the plane and walked over to his side. Together, they watched the taillights fade away in the distance.

"What was that all about? What's happening?" she asked.

Brad was actually smiling when he answered, "I don't have a clue. I feel like someone's going to pop out from behind a camera and yell surprise. Let's get that rental car and get on the road. I don't want to hang around here any longer than we have to."

As it turned out, the Warrens were going to be forced to hang around in Niagara much longer than they expected. After unloading their luggage, Brad went to the main terminal to get a rental car. He was surprised by the heavy police presence and the number of people who were yelling at the agents behind the ticket counters. He got in line behind six people who also needed a car, and it didn't take long for his anxiety to get kicked up another notch. He heard the people ahead of him escalate when they were told there were no more cars available.

"What do you mean you don't have any cars?" yelled the man at the front of the line. "You have a whole parking lot full of them."

"Sir, please lower your voice. As I already explained, those cars were reserved in advance. When people arrive on their flights, they're going to expect to find their rental cars waiting for them."

Brad knew the agent behind the counter had a valid point. Every time he had flown and reserved a car, it had been waiting for him to arrive. As a matter of fact, they had just turned in a rental in Virginia Beach, and he would have been offended if they had been told there were no cars available when they had arrived for their vacation.

After the verbal abuse the young lady had endured from the six people ahead of him in line, she expected no less from the man with the bandaged hand. She was relieved when he smiled.

"People can be jerks, Miss. Can you tell me when you expect to have something available?"

He was so kind that she would have gladly given him her own car if she didn't need it, but the best she could do was let him know when cars were due to be returned. She already knew that the next expected arrival was not until the next morning.

"Sir, I wish I could be more helpful, but if you can wait until the morning, I can book a hotel room for you in a nice place with a view of Niagara Falls. We have a partnership with them that will allow me to give you a great discount."

She hoped he would be happy with her offer, and Brad knew it was the best deal they could get. There probably wasn't even a bus to Ithaca, so he thanked her and took care of the reservation. She arranged for a shuttle to meet them at the plane and carry them to the hotel.

Brad didn't want to burst the young lady's bubble, but he had seen Niagara Falls plenty of times, and even though he thought they were a spectacular sight, he didn't really care about the view from the room. All he really cared about was getting control of the endless stream of setbacks he and his family seemed to be enduring. If he could soak his hand in a hot bath and go to bed, he would be satisfied.

Denise also seemed to be at her limit, and she didn't object to spending the night in one of the best hotels the area had to offer. Once they got settled in, she treated it like a vacation and ordered a late supper from room service. The boys enjoyed their expensive cheeseburgers while she cut into a really expensive fillet.

Brad didn't say no when she asked if she could order for him, but he was more interested in the minibar and a hot bath. He took several of the small bottles and a bucket of ice with him. Alone in the bathroom, he was disturbed by the sight of his hand. The bandage had stubbornly pulled at the cut as he unwrapped it, and when he dipped his hand in the hot water that filled the bathtub, he immediately shot down the contents of a mini bottle. The bourbon felt good going down, and Brad began to feel better about how the day was ending, even if it hadn't gone well earlier.

Before collapsing onto the bed, Brad found that his impressive wife had asked the concierge to send a first aid kit to the room. They both thought it was odd when he told her she wasn't the first hotel customer to ask for one, but he was able to deliver everything she needed. With a little help, they did a decent job of replacing the old bandage with a fresh one. Denise hid her dismay when she saw the swollen tissue on her husband's hand. Brad felt more tired than usual and passed on supper, so Denise did her best to get his food into the minibar. The young man from room service earned an extra tip by providing her with aluminum foil from the kitchen.

Denise got the boys tucked into their beds in a separate room and went to check on Brad. He was so sound asleep that she just turned off the lights and shut the door.

******

Jacob Warren was in the fourth grade and liked to sleep later in the morning as if he were already in high school. Jalen was in the second grade, and he had his mind set on pancakes and the cartoon channel. He woke Denise up early to get his wishes. Denise figured she could go back to sleep after she got him situated. The sun was just below the horizon, and its glow was spreading, but not enough to bother her if she shut her eyes again.

The room service man told Denise it was a good thing she got the order in early because the word was they were closing the kitchen soon. When she asked how a five-star hotel could stop room service in the morning, he said she should just turn on the TV. He left before she could ask him why. He seemed to be in a hurry and didn't hang around waiting for a tip.

When she checked on Jalen, he wasn't watching cartoons. He was happily eating his pancakes, but he was flipping through the channels on TV with the remote in his free hand.

"I can't find the cartoon channel, Mom."

He held the remote out to her, and she aimed it at the TV. Before hitting the button that would show her the guide, she had a chance to see what was already on the channel where Jalen had stopped. She was surprised that some parents would let their children watch horror movies, but so far, she had managed to steer her boys away from them. This particular movie looked too realistic. As a matter of fact, she wasn't so sure it was a movie.

It was a local news broadcast from a cameraman who was obviously on one of the tour boats that carried people out to the bottom of the waterfalls. She didn't think they started the tours before sunrise, and judging by the number of police officers behind the wet reporter, she didn't think it was a scheduled tour. The boat moved closer to the falls, and the spray made the camera lens wet, so the cameraman was constantly wiping it with a piece of cloth. Denise saw the police officers pointing upward and then toward the water. She saw a shadow through the spray that appeared at the top of the TV screen and disappeared at the bottom. She felt like her imagination was playing games with her eyes because the shadow was shaped like a human body. It had four limbs that were extended outward from the right places.

The boat moved even further into the water that rained down from above, and the reporter turned around to watch as the police officers leaned over the port bow railing with long poles that had hooked tips. She had seen crews on boats use those poles for line handling, but sometimes, they used them to retrieve things or even people from the water. Several policemen concentrated their efforts on one pole, and it was obvious they weren't handling lines. They pulled on the pole together, and Denise saw she had been right about the shadow that had fallen from above. The officers lifted a woman over the railing, first pulling on the pole but then shifting to get their arms around her.

It wasn't clear to Denise if the woman was conscious, but they laid her on the deck and immediately began doing chest compressions on her. An officer pulled her chin down, inspected the inside of her mouth, and gave her a rescue breath. He went back to doing chest compressions while his fellow officers resumed their rescue attempts with the poles. Denise was shocked when they pulled a second woman over the railing.

"What's happening?" she asked herself out loud. "Multiple suicide attempts?"

The second woman was placed on the rocking deck of the boat only a few feet from the first one, and a man dressed as a paramedic took over to do the life-saving compressions. He and the officer were almost working in unison when the unthinkable happened. There were no warnings. No one saw it coming.

In a split second, the body of a man entered the top of the field of view on the TV and landed awkwardly across the bodies of the two women, the police officer, and the paramedic. The officer and paramedic were knocked unconscious and sprawled across the deck. Denise felt numb when she saw the two women appear to move. She could have sworn their arms and legs moved a few inches, and the head of the woman closer to the cameraman turned to face him. Smokey, white eyes stared at the camera.

The reporter, a young woman who had thought she was in the middle of the story of the century, screamed when the body landed. She disappeared somewhere to the left of the cameraman, but her mic was still open, and she was sobbing uncontrollably. When the woman on the deck turned her head toward the cameraman, the reporter screamed again, but this time, her screams faded away as she ran for safety somewhere out of view.

"Mom, can I watch cartoons now?"

Denise had forgotten all about Jalen, and she was torn between getting her son out of the room and the spectacle on the bow of the ship. Everything seemed to be happening faster. The women were attempting to get up from under the man, who had to weigh at least two hundred pounds and had fallen from somewhere above the boat. The officers using the poles abandoned them and rushed to help the injured officer and paramedic. The cameraman was determined to get everything recorded.

Denise made her decision and hit the off button on the TV.

"Cartoons aren't on TV today, Jalen. Eat your breakfast without TV. I need to talk with your father."

TRANSPORTATION

Blue Ridge Foothills - 2025

Ruth and Wally had never seen a big horde. They had ventured a few miles from their shelter to see what was happening in the world but never went too far. They saw a small group of the infected dead and thought that a dozen was about as many as they had ever seen at one time. When I told them we had seen hordes numbered in the thousands, they didn't believe me at first, but when I told them about the massive horde that descended onto Charleston, South Carolina, I could see them trying to imagine what it had been like. No one could tell the story better than the Chief, and I wished he was here to describe it.

I told them about the infected dead that Hampton and Colleen had fought near Charlotte and how they were caught between two hordes. Then, there was the horde that filled the moat behind Mud Island and the one that trapped the crew of Executive One at the airport in Columbus, Ohio. They got the picture, and they understood just how lucky they were.

Ruth was the first one to admit she understood that she would be lucky if she got to live out the rest of her life in the shelter without being bitten by one of the infected dead. She even said it with a serene smile.

"Wally, just make sure when my time comes that I'm in my bed."

Jean said gently, "Ruth, there are some ugly things you should know about before that time comes."

We took turns filling in the details of what would happen after someone died of old age, and Ruth accepted it as gracefully as she could, but the serene smile faded, and we saw that Wally wasn't making eye contact with her.

"What's wrong?" I asked. "I mean, aside from the zombie apocalypse."

I tried to add a lighter tone to the conversation, but Wally was checking out his fingernails, and Ruth found a spot on the wooden table to stare at.

"Wally wants to leave," said Ruth. "When he came out here to the mountains to tell me what was happening, he left his family in Lynchburg, Virginia. He was planning to just come out and get me to go back to help him find them. I told him he should've brought his family with him, but he said they were evacuated by soldiers before he could get home from work. He figured I would know what to do."

Wally, Walter Merrill, didn't talk as much as Ruth. He added a few words here and there, but I could tell by the way he seemed to always have his eyes lowered that he had a badly damaged conscience. Now, I knew why. He felt guilty for coming after his sister and not finding his family first. He was about fifteen to twenty years younger than her, and he had always turned to his big sister for help.

He said in a low voice, "I know my wife and son probably aren't alive anymore, but I want to know for sure what happened to Sally and Glenn. Now, you're telling us that I need to put my own sister down after she dies a peaceful death, just so she won't come back to life. Even if I stay here and do that, where does that leave me? Who's gonna put me down when my time comes?"

"You could come with us," said Jean. "I mean, you have it good here. You have it a lot better than most people who survived, but as good as this place is, it's not a permanent solution."

"Come with you where?" asked Wally.

It had already crossed my mind that this small, hidden shelter was, in many ways, what my crazy uncle, Titus Rush, had envisioned when he talked about survival. It couldn't survive a nuclear attack, and it could be discovered and ransacked by people who only considered their own survival to be more important, but it had served its purposes. I could already see how it could be used as a way station between the big shelters. It could be fortified, resupplied, and populated with a few more permanent residents.

"You could live in one of our big shelters," said Jean. "There's no need to live out the rest of your lives by yourselves, and it's obvious you both have skills we could use. I think you would like the shelter in Guntersville, Alabama, the most because you can spend more time outside there. It's a lot like this part of the country, but the village is at the top of a small mountain."

"Give it some thought," I added. "If you decide to go with us after we come back from New York, we would be more than happy to give you a permanent home."

"That's what I've been waiting to hear you explain," said Ruth. "Why are you going to New York, and do you know how long it takes to walk there? You won't get there before winter, and then you'll freeze to death."

I took a deep breath and told them how we got to their neck of the woods. Flat tires and a blown engine were the reason why we were walking, but the reason why we were going to New York was more complicated.

"Our friends in Guntersville were against us making the trip," said Jean.

Ruth was quick to answer, "You should have listened to them."

"Imagine this, Ruth. You turn on a shortwave radio, and you hear a broadcast from a kid who says he's Wally's son. Would you be able to stop him from going to the place the broadcast came from?"

"Well, no, I wouldn't. He'd probably go right through me if I got in his way. Did you get a broadcast from your family?"

Jean shook her head.

"They weren't our family, but they said enough for us to learn they were on their own. They need help from someone, and the way we see it, there are so few people left alive compared to the infected dead that we should all consider ourselves as members of a family."

Ruth said jokingly, "I'll bet you don't think about Henry Shackley as family."

"Henry shot at us," said Jean. "We would still save his sorry neck if he was cornered by a bunch of the infected dead, but we wouldn't talk to him at family cookouts."

That got a laugh out of Ruth and me, but it seemed to have the opposite effect on Wally. It wasn't because he liked Henry Shackley but because it made him realize he wouldn't have saved Henry's neck. It made him wonder if anyone really tried to help his family.

His eyes were red-rimmed when he said, "What are the odds that my family made it?"

Getting his hopes up by lying wasn't going to do anything but get him killed, but Jean did her best to answer in a way that would make him understand that the odds couldn't be the reason to give up hope.

"People survived, Wally. We're proof of that. You, Ruth, and even Eddie most likely survived because you were in a safe place when it began. I wasn't that lucky. I was out there in the middle of it, but I survived because a few people around me were determined to survive. What are the odds? I don't really know because it all depends on whether or not your family was around someone like my friends. As long as there are good people left alive who help each other, more people will have better odds."

Something in what Jean said made Wally grin.

"So, we should make sure Henry Shackley stays alive so he can help people."

"There are exceptions," I answered. "We've run into our share of really bad people who survived because they were bad, and we've even been forced to eliminate a few of them. We also saw plenty of stupidity at the beginning that caused more people to die. I think we've seen the best and worst that people can be."

"And people who were in between," added Jean.

Ruth said, "Most people are in between until they're faced with a choice, and right now, I'm getting the feeling that would apply to us."

"What do you mean?" I asked.

Ruth took a moment to answer, and she studied our faces as if she wanted to be sure of something.

"I know Wally is a good person, but we just met you. You both seem like good people, and if what you're saying is true, then we should be making the choice to help you."

"You already have," said Jean. "You took us in and gave us a safe place to spend the night."

"That's not what I meant. We should be helping you to do more. Instead of staying here or going to one of your shelters, we should be coming with you."

"We can't ask you to do that," said Jean.

Wally said, "Why not? Wouldn't it be safer with four of us, and isn't Lynchburg between here and there?"

Wally didn't have to say the rest. If there was even a remote possibility that his family survived, he had a right to try to find out. It was more likely that there wouldn't be conclusive evidence either way, but if it was one of us in his situation, we would at least want to check the area. As for them helping us get to New York, it did make sense. Four people would be better than two.

Ruth said, "This may sound crazy, but I never felt like hiding in this shelter while the rest of the world died was the same thing as living. Especially if there's someone out there who we could save."

What Ruth said was like an echo of everything we had said since the infection began. Titus Rush had the philosophy that I should go to the shelter, shut the door, and not open it again for any reason. He wasn't a bad person, but I had come to believe you had to open the door whenever it meant someone else would survive. That was living, and if I had listened to him, I wouldn't have Jean sitting next to me in Ruth's shelter, and we wouldn't have a little boy named Josh waiting for us at home.

"The pickup backfired before it stopped?" asked Wally. "How old was your gasoline?"

I nodded as I said, "It was old. Do you figure that's what it was? We tested the fuel before leaving Guntersville, but we knew it was going to be useless soon. I guess it was stupid to think we could use it for a trip that far."

"Wally was a pretty good mechanic back before the infection," said Ruth. "He still is, as a matter of fact. He's also got a real knack for making his own biodiesel fuel. When the fuel goes bad in our generators, he's going to modify them to run on the new stuff."

Jean said, "You mentioned that earlier. Are you just storing the biodiesel until you need it?"

"Wally's been planning to make a trip to Lynchburg sooner or later. He's already modified the engine of a king-cab pickup. I suppose now that he knows the truth about what happens after we die, he might as well go. If I die and turn into one of those things, I suppose I won't be a danger to anyone else if I'm locked inside my shelter, but if we go with you, maybe I can be of a little use before my time is up."

Jean and I could both see that the topic was a sore spot for both of them, but it was also something they couldn't ignore. There was always a slim chance that Wally's family was safe somewhere, but it was more likely they had been evacuated to an overcrowded military shelter, and we had seen what happened to those.

"A king-cab pickup truck?" I said. "Sounds just right to carry four people instead of two, and like you said, Lynchburg is on the way."

"It's settled," said Ruth. "You can walk to New York, or you can ride with us."

******

Breakfast was like a going-away celebration. Ruth had a large supply of fresh eggs, and they wouldn't keep long in the truck, so she kept making them until everyone was full. She used what was left to make enough cornbread for a small army.

"Nothing wrong with loading up on protein before we go," said Ruth.

We helped her secure the shelter and pack the things she needed to bring. She was upbeat and optimistic that we would return and decided she only needed to bring a picture of her late husband. The rest of her mementos would be waiting for her when we got back.

Ruth had managed to raise a few chickens and goats, but it made more sense to let them run loose before we left. Despite the big breakfast, we had the truck loaded and the chores around the shelter done before noon.

"I'll drive for a bit," said Wally. "I think I'm too nervous to be a passenger right now."

Jean and I both knew what he was going through. It wasn't going to be an easy trip for him, whether he was driving or riding along, but we didn't mind if he thought it would be easier for him to drive. That didn't mean we wouldn't be offering him some tips. Driving since the apocalypse began meant you could never assume the road was clear around the next curve.

The drive wasn't going to break any speed records, but we made decent time. About an hour after we began our journey, we stopped to clear away a tree that blocked the road. Judging by the way the branches pulled easily away from the trunk, it had fallen years ago, and the wood had become dry on the hot asphalt. We were lucky it was so brittle because there was no way around it, and using a chainsaw on a quiet mountain road was an invitation for the infected dead to join the party.

One side of the road sat below a slope that was too steep to climb, and the right shoulder had a low guardrail that was flattened by the fallen tree. We naturally threw the branches over the guardrail and watched them drop to the bottom of a ravine at least eighty feet below us. When the branches landed, we saw that they stirred up movement in a large pile of the infected dead.

I said, "My guess is at least fifty infected."

Jean watched them for a moment and said, "They probably didn't arrive all at the same time. If this tree is as old as it appears to be, they most likely accumulated over the years."

"What makes you say that?"

She pointed to the left and right of the pile and said, "The ones toward the outside edges of the pile crawled away before the ones in the middle fell. They made it pretty far without getting smashed."

"Good point," said Ruth before she tossed a big branch over the guardrail. "Notice anything else?"

It only took us a moment to guess what she was quizzing us about. The infected that were around the periphery of the pile were all missing arms and legs.

"Predators?" I asked. "What kind?"

That was when I realized there should have been carrion-eating birds circling above us. There weren't any, and that could be a bad sign.

Ruth said, "Imagine what it was like when it started. Vultures used to feed off of animals that were either hit by cars or remains left by a kill made by a larger predator. When the infected dead showed up, they didn't have to wait for cars to collide with deer that got pinned in their headlights, and they didn't have to wait anymore for a bear or wolf to get done eating their fill. They learned that the infected dead are food that's still moving."

Wally had joined us out of curiosity, and he added, "I remember one time when I saw a bunch of vultures sitting in a circle around one of the dead that was still moving. It was like they couldn't decide if they could eat it or not. It smelled right, but when one would get close enough, the dead would try to grab it, and it was making a snarling sound."

"What happened?" I asked.

"Something I've never seen before. The smell probably got to the vultures, and they went for its feet. The strangest part, though, was that one of the vultures stayed up by the head and pecked at it."

"You mean it was distracting the dead so the other vultures could feed?" said Jean.

Wally nodded, "Yep. Never seen carrion birds work together before, but then again, I guess they didn't have to. If they ever came across a dying animal, they would wait for it to die because they knew from past history that it would die sooner or later. They could tell by the smell. The infected dead must've made them impatient as hell. That also explains why I saw a flock of vultures take down one that was still walking," he added.

Wally leaned far enough out over the guardrail to make me uncomfortable. I was about to grip him by his shirt when he backed away from the rail.

"We need to get out of here, and don't throw the branches over the guardrail. Maybe they won't come after us if they don't smell us over the stink down there."

I didn't have to ask what he saw because Jean saw them too and pulled me back to a spot on the road.

"Wolves," she said. "We couldn't have seen it from here, but there might be a cave entrance at the base of the cliff right where the infected dead have been landing. There's a litter of pups that just came out to feed on the bodies. Their mom and dad must be around here somewhere."

We worked more quickly to clear a path just big enough

to drive through, and we piled into the truck as soon as we finished. As we drove through the opening and increased speed, Wally told everyone to look out the back window. We learned that we needed to be more careful about whatever dangers there were in the mountains besides the infected dead. Four large wolves were sniffing at the branches we had piled to the sides of the road, obviously recognizing the scent of warm blood, preferable over the pile of carrion at the bottom of the cliff. Wally pushed his foot down a bit farther and increased our speed.

The weather cooperated nicely as we worked our way east. Aside from a few clouds, we didn't have to slow down for most of the day to navigate problems caused by rain. Toward evening, we came to our first challenge after the tree, and it took some skillful driving from Wally for us to get the truck past it.

Years of unchecked rain and rockfalls had caused the road to collapse. Large rocks falling around the same few feet of road had punched holes in the asphalt. Heavy rains and more falling rocks beat on the cracks until pieces washed away, leaving ruts and deep holes. Left unrepaired, the dirt under the asphalt eventually broke apart and left a gap that was wide enough to make Wally slam on the brakes. It didn't take an expert to know we would have damaged the truck beyond repair if we had driven straight into it.

We all got out and studied the gap in the road. It wasn't like we could fill it in, and our first thoughts were how far we would need to backtrack to make a detour. Wally surprised us by suggesting that we should all get into the bed of the pickup truck and hold onto the left side for ballast.

I didn't know if he was planning to do something that came under the category of, "It seemed like a good idea at the time," or if he really was sure it would work, but I hesitantly got into the back with Jean and Ruth. Wally had me help him move all of our spare fuel cans over to the left and secure them in place. Their combined weight was probably close to what the three of us weighed, so the truck had plenty of ballast on the left side.

All Wally said before he got behind the wheel was, "Hang on tight, and if you feel like you have to jump, jump to the left. I wouldn't want to roll over top of anyone."

He backed the truck away from the washed-out gap until we were about thirty yards down the road. We could tell he was planning to go around the gap on the left side of the road by driving at an angle onto the side of the steep slope and then letting gravity pull the truck down the slope on the other side. If he waited too long to cut the wheel to the right, gravity would get us there by rolling the truck down the hill. We would probably go off the other side of the road and drop to the bottom just like the infected dead back by the tree. It was far too late for any of us to protest.

I felt weightless for a couple of seconds after the truck's initial bounce tossed us all into the air, but I somehow managed to keep my grip on the safety rail that ran along the edge of the truck bed. Jean and Ruth both screamed, and I probably did. For a moment, I wished I had tied my hand to the railing. Then we were on the other side going down the slope, and all I wished for was that Wally could stop before driving over the guardrail on the other side of the road. When he did, we were thrown forward to the window on the back of the cab. This time, we let go of the railing, and the three of us slammed into a pile in the truck bed. We were on the other side of the collapsed section of the road and safe, but Ruth was cursing at Wally.

"I don't know how I was able to hold on," said Jean.

She was rubbing at the side of her head, and I checked the spot for her.

"You must have hit your head. You have a lump coming up."

"Do you think?" she said.

Despite the harrowing rollercoaster ride, I had to laugh at the way she said it. We were on the other side and safe, but I wasn't sure I would agree if Wally wanted to do that again. He had gotten out of the cab and crawled under the truck. He emerged from his inspection of the underside of the pickup with a big smile.

"No damage," he announced.

The three of us who had been in the back of the truck were happy to be alive, but the experience had left us feeling a bit drained. We decided to take a break to eat and to determine our location on a map. If we were correct, we wouldn't reach Lynchburg by nightfall, and none of us wanted to drive at night. When we started driving again, Wally was in the cab by himself while the rest of us stood in the back and surveyed the treetops for cabins. It took two bumpy hours, but we finally spotted a hunting lodge on the side of a hill. We felt like we were in luck when we found the overgrown driveway that had a metal gate across it. A NO TRESPASSING sign hung at an angle, only secured by a wire through one hole in the right corner.

We cut away the bushes and vines that had wrapped themselves around the gate, and I broke the rusty lock without much trouble. We pulled the gate shut after Wally drove through in the hope that it provided at least a little security if anything wandered by it, and then we piled inside the truck. Wally navigated down a narrow driveway with tree limbs scratching at both sides of the truck, and there were times when I wasn't convinced he was still driving on anything that was meant for the truck, but the large cabin emerged from the gloom that was gathering on the mountainside just in time.

I patted Wally on the shoulder as we came to a stop and said, "Good job. I thought we might be sleeping in the truck tonight after all, but you found it."

Jean was already standing outside the truck, taking in the size of the cabin. It was much bigger than we had thought when we spotted the roof. We had probably missed countless smaller cabins that weren't tall enough to be seen from the road, but this one had a second floor, which meant there could also be something useful to salvage.

"I'm glad we have enough light left to clear this place. I wouldn't want to do it after dark," she said.

"We're still going to be using flashlights," I said. "With a place this big, I'd be surprised if it's empty."

"Thanks," said Jean. "I really needed to hear that."

"Just keeping it real," I answered. "Our luck has been better than what most people have. This place is big enough to have a basement, and have you noticed anything about the front porch?"

I pointed at the front of the house, where a set of steps went up to a long front porch. A bench swing hung from the overhang on one end, and a pair of rocking chairs sat near the other end.

Ruth came up beside us and answered my question for Jean.

"The porch is clean. There's no debris, no bodies, and it even appears to have been repaired in a couple of spots."

"Recently repaired," added Wally. "Even a well-built wooden house should have some warped boards after eight years of sitting in the woods. Not to mention the leaves and other junk that should have collected against the walls during storms."

"Well, I guess we should announce ourselves if we don't want to get shot," I said.

We found out soon enough that it wasn't necessary to announce ourselves. The people who had been living in the cabin had most likely met their end recently. The cabin door was unlocked, and when I pushed it open, the air inside wafted across us. While the outside air smelled crisp and clean, the smell of blood mixed with antiseptic cleansers made the cabin smell like the inside of a hospital emergency room on a busy day.

Haunted houses were popular at county fairs back before the arrival of the infected dead. I can't count the number of times I've wondered how they would do now. Everyone I knew had been in a close call with an infected dead or a crazy living person. Having them pop out into the open, or even worse, having one grab you from behind, wasn't my idea of fun.

The good news was that Ruth's husband had the good sense to store batteries in one of the caves near their shelter. Some batteries lasted as long as ten years if stored properly, but there was no guarantee. Batteries from the same package performed differently from others. Now that we had taken them out of the cave, some were already failing.

"Let's go in pairs with one flashlight per pair," I said. "Turn the other one on if you have to, but we don't want both flashlights going dark at the same time. Call out if that happens, and wait for the other pair to reach you before you move."

We got a break on the main floor of the cabin because we could see most of it from the door. It was big, but whoever built it wanted an open-floor concept. Judging by the number of chairs around a dining room table and the sofas arranged near a fireplace, it had been a hunting lodge. The source of the smell was the dining room table itself. There was a body stretched out on its surface with one arm crudely amputated. Judging by the black stain on the floor, the patient had bled to death. Flies circled and crawled on the body, and we were forced to put rags over our faces.

We hadn't split up into pairs yet, so we were all drawn to the table and what must have happened. The severed arm was lying on the floor, and in the beam of my flashlight, we could see the bite marks. I aimed the light at the man's head and saw where someone had shot him after the failed attempt to save his life.

"Does that actually work?" asked Ruth.

Jean said, "I was a nurse before the infection, and I wouldn't want to try it without sterile equipment, but the facts speak for themselves. The reason for cutting off a limb if you get bitten is to prevent the infection from spreading. It takes less than one minute for the heart to pump blood to every cell in the body. That means you don't have time to sterilize the equipment. I've seen people go into shock over less severe wounds, and an amputation is likely to kill you before you bleed out. It can be done, but most people won't survive."

"Sorry I asked," said Ruth.

Wally asked Jean, "How long ago did this happen?"

"Within the last day," she answered.

I panned my flashlight around the room and saw more black stains that were probably blood. The sun was setting outside and was barely above the trees, and what little light came through the cracks of the windows was useless. I had to admit the obvious.

"I think we're sleeping in the truck, after all. The smell in here would be too much for me. We can search the house at sunrise for anything useful."

No one needed to be convinced. We retreated from the house and worked quickly to set up a perimeter using string and tin cans, but Wally had another idea. The overhang of the front porch was broad and flat, and it wasn't difficult to reach by climbing the rough logs of the cabin. Wally climbed up to take the first watch, and the rest of us settled in for the night inside the truck.

Randy & Tori

RANDY & TORI

Niagara Falls - 2016

"The toilet won't flush."

Tori stood in front of the toilet and stared down at it in disbelief.

In the middle of the night, Randy had already discovered the malfunction. Now, he was faced with the reality that Tori, in her entire pampered life, had never been exposed to this particular problem. He had a splitting headache that had been brought on by sleeping on the sofa by the door of their suite. He had slept fitfully, and each time he woke up, he had listened to the sounds that came from the hallway.

Around three AM, someone had apparently tried to leave their room down the hall. Randy had strained to see what was happening through the peephole, but it was too dark to make sense of the shapes moving past their door. He could tell there were people, but that was all. He heard someone talking in cautious whispers that suddenly escalated into screams.

A woman's voice pleaded, "Stop…no, please stop."

He wanted to open the door and help her, but he didn't know what to do without light. The voices receded further from the door as the pleading turned into screaming. It eventually became silent again, and Randy drifted off to sleep.

He stood behind Tori and knew that anything he felt like saying about the toilet not flushing was going to come out wrong, so he didn't say anything.

"Did you hear me?" she said louder. "The toilet won't flush."

"Keep your voice down," said Randy.

Tori couldn't believe Randy had a tone when she needed his help, but she stopped talking when a loud thump on their door interrupted her. It was just one dull thump, but it was all she needed to be reminded of what they had seen and heard on the previous day.

They had the balcony door open to let fresh air into the suite, and the noise from the waterfalls helped to drown out the sounds in the hallway, but it seemed like whatever it was that was patrolling outside their door had exceptional hearing. Randy wandered out onto the balcony and stood with his weight resting on the railing. He leaned outward to see the terrace behind the hotel and got an instant reminder that people had fallen from the floors above his. He yanked himself backward, expecting to see a body falling toward him.

Nothing was falling from above, but there was something different. About four floors above him, someone was lowering himself from the balcony. Randy couldn't tell what the daring individual was using for rope, but he also didn't think the man just happened to have enough rope to successfully reach the first floor. He watched the man use his feet to catch the railing of the next balcony. The man managed to swing himself over the railing and disappear for a moment.

Randy was captivated by the man's daring and wondered if he could do the same thing. He turned his attention to the terrace again and counted the number of balconies below him. There were eleven, and while he didn't doubt he could risk the climb, he couldn't ask Tori to try. When he lifted his head again, he saw that the man above him was leaning over the railing. Randy knew it was too late to hide, but that's what he did. He ran for the balcony door, shut it behind him, and drew the curtains. He tugged at the handle to make sure he had securely locked it.

The man yelled when he saw Randy.

"Hey! Mister...wait!"

If he yelled anything else before Randy shut the door, he didn't catch it.

It took about thirty minutes for the climber to reach the balcony outside their room, and Tori had to cover her mouth to stifle a scream when he pounded on the glass door. He hit it so hard that they both were sure it would break. At first, the man pleaded with them, but eventually, his pleas turned to anger. He insisted that he wasn't going to hurt them, but when he became desperate, he told them what he was going to do to them when he got inside. It was a colorful description beyond any threats either of them had ever heard.

It was quiet for a few minutes, and they thought he had possibly decided to continue on his downward journey. Randy risked a peek around the corner of the thick curtains, and he was shocked to see the man lifting the heavy serving cart that had been left on the balcony since breakfast was delivered the day before. The man was burly but not tall, and he lifted the cart as if it were as light as a feather. All Randy had time to do was yell at Tori to move out of the way.

The man rushed toward the glass door and propelled the serving cart forward as hard as he could. The door shattered with an eardrum-splitting crash, taking out the door but not landing completely inside the room. The curtains hung down across the cart as it lay in the place where the door had been, and as the man leaned into the gap and parted the curtains, he was surprised to see an aerosol can of hairspray in front of his face. There was a click, a flicker of flame from a lighter, and the hiss of the hairspray before a fireball erupted in his face.

The man fell backward and stumbled as he hit the balcony railing. His makeshift rope dangled in space, and for a moment, it seemed like he would catch it, but he missed. He went over the railing headfirst and screamed until he reached the terrace below.

Randy was shocked at the quick and brutal reactions of his new wife. A few minutes earlier, she had been staring helplessly at a toilet that didn't flush, but in the face of real danger, she had most likely saved their lives.

"Where did you learn to do that?" he stuttered. "Better yet, where'd you get a cigarette lighter from? I thought you quit smoking."

Tori shrugged her shoulders at him and said, "Okay, so maybe I still have one from time to time. Would you have preferred that I didn't have the lighter?"

They stepped over the cart and went to the railing. The man had landed on his back, and his hair was still smoldering.

"There must be something wrong with me," said Tori. "I just killed that man, and I don't feel as bad about it as I'm supposed to. Do you think I'll go to jail? Can I claim self-defense?"

"Something tells me you won't have to worry about that. We need to figure out what we're going to do next. You thought of that trick with the hairspray fast enough. Why can't you think of anything that helps us get out of here?"

"Because I don't have a clue what's going on. Why don't you explain that to me so I can think of something?"

Randy had to admit, they were both clueless. They hadn't gotten enough from the news to know anything, and they didn't know what was happening in the hallway. If they hadn't felt so threatened by the man Tori had just killed, they might have learned something from him.

"The bodies are still going over the falls," said Tori.

Randy said, "I wonder why."

They were so deep in thought that the tone that blasted from their cell phones made them grab the railing of the balcony and duck. They had forgotten all about their phones because there hadn't been any cell service. They both ran to get them, and they saw at the same time that it was an alert tone. The screens were illuminated in red with a warning.

This is an emergency broadcast. If you receive this message, seek shelter immediately. Do not attempt to render first aid to anyone. If you are sheltered, remain as quiet as possible. The infected are drawn by sound. End message.

The tones stopped, and they stared at each other in disbelief, but Randy had a moment of clarity as he pieced together the things they knew for sure.

"Tori, it all adds up."

"What does?"

"We don't know what's happening, but we know some details. If it was safe to go out in the hallway, that man wouldn't have been playing Spiderman and climbing down the outside of the building. Why isn't it safe to go out there? This message says there's an infection, and infected people are probably why it isn't safe to go out there."

Tori wasn't connecting the dots about why that would be useful to them.

She said, "We already know it isn't safe to go out there. How does that help us?"

Randy had felt like he was on the verge of an epiphany about their dilemma, but Tori's question stopped him short. He realized they had more information, but there wasn't much they could do with it.

"I don't know," he answered. "Maybe it doesn't help us get out of here, but there has to be something we can do."

They sat down on the bed, and the silence was only broken when something bumped against their door. At least, that was all they heard until their cell phones scared them again. This time, they pounced on their phones quickly to stop the alert tone, but they could still hear it in the distance. It took a minute for them to understand they were hearing other cell phones in the hallway outside their door. The tones gradually stopped, but before they did, it had become obvious that whatever was outside had left their door and gone toward the last cell phone that was still sounding the alert.

"We can use that," said Randy. "That's how we're getting out of here."

"How? Cell phones?"

"We can put your cell phone on the balcony and then open the door to the room. We can find a good place to hide and then call your phone. Those people in the hallway will go out onto the balcony after your phone."

Tori frowned.

"I might be missing something," she said, "but what are we going to do with a balcony full of infected people? We don't even have a door on the balcony anymore."

Even though Randy had accepted the problem with the toilet with more understanding than Tori, he realized he had never been faced with questions of survival, either. His wife had just saved them from a brutal attack, but he could only come up with a half-baked plan to get them out of the room.

Tori continued, "And how do we know if we got all of them to go from the hallway to the balcony? What if there are more?"

"Okay, let's take each problem one at a time," said Randy. "What can we do to them when they get to the balcony? Can we push them over the railing? Maybe you could do your hairspray thing again?"

Tori just stared at him and waited.

Randy finally said, "Yeah, I forgot about problem number two. More of them could come into the room while you're setting them on fire."

"Not just that," said Tori. "Pushing burning people over a balcony railing can't be that easy."

They both came up with a possible plan at the same moment. Randy snapped his fingers, and Tori pointed at him.

They both said, "I've got it."

"We have to knock the railing off the balcony," said Randy. "They'll walk into the room, rush out onto the balcony, and go right over the edge."

Tori added, "We can hide in the bathroom until we're sure they're all gone."

"How will we know?" asked Randy.

"We won't know for sure. We just need to hide in there as long as we can. We'll just keep calling your phone until we think there aren't any of them still out there in the hallway."

Randy and Tori worked harder over the next hour than they had in their whole lives. The railing around the balcony was meant to keep people from having a good reason to sue the hotel. They tried kicking at the top rail until their feet and backs hurt, but neither of them could swear they had loosened it at all. What finally did the trick was repeatedly ramming it with the serving cart. It was one more reason to be grateful that Tori had gotten up early and ordered breakfast on that first morning.

The railing snapped on their last hard push, and the cart flew over the edge. It landed with a loud crash twelve floors below, but neither of them approached the edge to watch. The thought of looking over the edge of the balcony without the protection of the railing made them both queasy. All that was left of the balcony were a couple of broken mounts where the railing had been fastened to the concrete.

Satisfied with their ability to complete the first part of their plan, they moved on to the second part. They emptied the contents of the small refrigerator and carried everything to the bathroom. They didn't know how long it would take to lure all of them to the dangerous balcony, but on the off chance it took a long time, they would at least have a little food and something to drink.

Randy took Tori's cell phone out to the balcony and used a couple of her hair ties to secure it to one of the broken mounts. If the plan worked, he didn't want the cell phone to go over the edge with the people. He chose a mount close to the wall on one side so the people wouldn't kick it when they walked onto the balcony. He made sure the volume was turned up as high as it could go.

When they were as ready as they thought they could be, Tori went into the bathroom and waited while Randy made sure the path was clear from the balcony to the door. He peered through the peephole and waited for his eye to adjust to the darkness on the other side. He couldn't be one hundred percent sure, but he didn't think there was anything outside the door. He quietly turned the handle and pulled the door open about six inches, and then he ran to the bathroom as fast as he could. He pulled the bathroom door shut behind him.

"Now," he said.

Tori dialed the number to her phone.

Every plan has a hole in it somewhere, and the hole in their plan was the assumption that they had cell service just because the alert tones had sounded. They discovered their mistake when Tori dialed the number and nothing happened. They had that sinking feeling you get when you realize that you messed up and you can't fix it. There wasn't even the familiar message that said, *Your call could not be completed as dialed.* They didn't think to test it before executing the rest of their plan. If they had, they would have at least been able to set an alarm on the phone, and they could have selected to have the alarm go off once every fifteen minutes or so.

Outside the bathroom, there was a now-familiar thump that announced the arrival of someone who found the open door of their suite. They heard clumsy footsteps as they went past the bathroom door. They had no way to be sure where the person went after that. What they didn't know was that the first infected dead to walk into their suite walked straight toward the demolished balcony door. It was drawn by the sound of the waterfalls outside. The infected had been a man who was staying in the suite next to theirs, but now he stumbled over the bottom frame of the balcony door and dove headfirst off the building. He was followed by three more infected dead in rapid succession.

In the darkness of the hallway, the sound of the waterfalls was equal to the roar of a freight train to the infected. They streamed toward the open door as if they were being summoned, and they followed each other like lemmings. One by one, they tripped over the door frame and fell forward. If any managed to keep from falling on their own, they were pushed by the arrivals behind them. They tumbled over the edge and fell to the terrace in surprising numbers. If the torrent of falling bodies was an indication of how many there were on each floor, then the hotel was populated by hundreds of the infected.

"What are we going to do?" whispered Tori.

"I don't know. I guess we have to stay in here until we think there aren't any out there."

"Then what?"

"I said I don't know."

It came out just a bit more harshly than Randy had wanted, but he was frustrated by the whole ordeal. It would have been different if he had known what was happening outside the bathroom door. Knowing that the infected dead were streaming through their suite like it was a freeway would have made him feel a little better, but even if they had known what was happening, they would still have been faced with not knowing when it would be safe to leave the bathroom.

"Let's get some rest, Tori. I didn't mean to snap at you. I'm just mad at myself for not checking the phone first."

"It's not your fault. We dreamt up the plan together. Do you think if we stay in here long enough, we can at least go out and shut the door again?"

"That's all we can plan to do for now. Like I said, let's get some rest. I can try to go out there in a couple of hours."

They got as comfortable as they could, but neither of them felt like sleeping. They sipped mini bottles of liquor and snacked on chips and mixed nuts. There was an occasional thump near the door. They kept track of the time and the thumps, and they eventually came to the conclusion that it had been over two hours since the last one. It had apparently slowed down, but they were at a loss for how to be sure there was no one out there.

Another hour went by, and there were still no more sounds from their suite. Randy got up and put his ear to the door. In the dim light from his cell phone, he found the bathrobes on their hooks and pulled the belt from one of them. He handed the other robe to Tori, and she put it on. It wasn't cold in the bathroom, but the comfort of the plush material was welcome.

Randy tied one end of the belt to the door handle as tight as he could, and then he fastened the other end to a towel bar that was securely mounted on the ceramic tile to the left of the door. He tested it to be sure it had about two inches of slack and was satisfied, but he hoped the towel bar held better than the one he had yanked out of the wall by the shower.

"What're you doing?" asked Tori.

"I'm going to open the door just a couple of inches. If someone out there tries to push the door open the rest of the way, this belt should help me get it shut again. If I can open it far enough, I'll be able to see the balcony door from here. I have to check before it gets dark outside, or I won't be able to see what's happening out there."

Randy still had a hand on the doorknob, but he leaned over and gave Tori a kiss.

"That's for luck," he said.

"This is our honeymoon," said Tori. "Get back here safe, and I'll do better than a kiss for luck."

Randy smiled, then turned the knob as gently as he could. The door opened a couple of inches, and he listened closely for anything that would tell him it was safe. Nothing pushed against the door, but it was too soon to relax. All he could hear was the rushing water as it went over the falls. He pictured it in his mind, and he still saw the bodies being carried over the falls, but he didn't picture anything hanging around in their suite.

He nodded at Tori and untied the belt from the door.

"Close it behind me," he said.

Randy stepped through the gap in the door and felt it close.

He kept his back against the wall and peered toward the open door to the hallway. Nothing was there, so he slid across the bathroom door and along the wall toward the entrance of their suite. The light was dim, but he saw the dark footprints on the carpet. The trail led from the door of the suite all the way to the open balcony door, and for the first time since the failed phone call, Randy felt like they had a chance of getting out of there alive.

The door to their suite closed quietly, and he turned the lock. He heard it make the tiniest sound as the lock clicked into place, but it was faint. Randy let out a breath he didn't notice he had been holding until that moment. Stepping around the patches of blood on the carpet as best as he could, he tiptoed from the door to the balcony. He didn't know why he hadn't seen the woman before, but she was standing with her back to him outside. She was wearing one of the complimentary bathrobes and standing at the very edge of the balcony. It was too easy.

Randy stepped carefully over the frame of the sliding door and reached across the balcony at the same time. A slight push between the woman's shoulder blades was all it took. She didn't scream or try to catch her balance as she went over. He waited a few seconds and heard the distant sound of her reaching the bottom.

The light was beginning to dim outside, so Randy turned his attention to the cell phone still attached to the broken mount. He pulled it free, and he wasn't surprised to see that it didn't say there had been a missed call. He stepped back over the door frame while he still had his eyes on the bright screen of the phone and collided with someone at least four inches taller than him. The collision knocked him backward, and he pinwheeled his arms in an attempt to stop, but the big man followed closely. They collided a second time, and Randy felt weightless as he went over the balcony in the embrace of the stranger. There was an odd, searing pain on his face, but it was gone in seconds when he hit the pile of bodies on the terrace. Ironically, he landed on top of the woman in the bathrobe. She was trying to get up when he and the big man crushed her. She resumed her efforts moments later.

******

Tori waited for Randy to come back, but she was too afraid to check on him. She kept telling herself that he would be back any moment, but as time passed, her worst fears began to win over her internal argument about why he had been gone so long. She told herself that he would have yelled for help, but then she answered stubbornly that he wouldn't have put her in danger. Then she told herself maybe he had left the room to see if there were more of those sick people on the same floor as them. That would be more like Randy. He would go check the rest of the floor while she was safe.

Her worst moment, after she convinced herself he was just off somewhere being her hero, came when it occurred to her that he may have locked himself out of their room. There she was, waiting helplessly for her hero to come back, and he was outside praying that she would unlock the door. She decided that she had to find him.

At the moment when Tori reached for the bathroom door knob, another alert came through her phone. The tone seemed a hundred times louder in the bathroom, and she screamed. She dropped the phone and watched as it bounced hard over the tile floor. The screen cracked, and the tone stopped. Then the screen went black. That was the moment when she had a clear image of the phone Randy had fastened to the mount on the balcony. She knew why the tone got cut off in the bathroom, but she should be able to hear the tone coming from the other one...unless the tone was done. She mentally focused on the previous alert tones and knew they had been longer in duration.

Tori retrieved the broken phone and held it up like a weapon. With her other hand, she pulled the door open and braced herself for an attack. She stared out at the dark room and saw that it was after sunset. The door to the suite was closed, and she couldn't see much in the bedroom, so she didn't know if she was alone or not. She forced herself to leave the bathroom to check the door. It was locked, but she could only see blackness through the peephole. She wanted to open the door to see if Randy was out there, but she couldn't shake the feeling that she was being watched from the bedroom.

For a moment, Tori realized just how ridiculous she must look to be walking around with a dead cell phone in her raised hand, but she kept it up there as she eased around the corner into the bedroom. Without thinking, she ran her free hand along the wall, hunting for the light switch. When she found it, she flipped it upward and got ready to throw her weapon. When the lights didn't come on, all of her willpower drained out of her body. She was vulnerable. She had given away her position and announced her presence. If there were anything in the room with her, it would be on her in seconds.

Tori felt her legs go numb, and she collapsed into a pile against the wall. Resigned to her fate, she waited for her turn to die. When it didn't come, she cried in deep, heaving sobs. She didn't know where Randy was, but he certainly wasn't in their suite, or he would have rushed to her side and comforted her. He wasn't there, but through the tears that swam across her eyes, she could see every dark corner in the room, and they were all hiding something terrible. She shut her eyelids and gave in completely to her worst fears. Randy was gone.

It wasn't really sleep that overcame her. It was more like she shut down. Her body slumped over the rest of the way to the floor, and she curled into a fetal position. She stayed like that until sunlight washed over the room and illuminated those dark corners.

Tori had to force her eyes to open. They were crusty the way they had sometimes gotten in her childhood, and she wondered absently if she was sick. Her throat was dry, and it was hard to swallow. As she pushed herself into a sitting position against the wall, she let out a loud groan from the joints that weren't used to the hard floor and the position she had stayed in for too long. One hand was numb, and she shook it to get feeling back in the fingers that seemed to have needles in them.

"What happened?" she croaked.

Even the sound of her voice was foreign to her. Her surroundings were vaguely familiar as she fought to bring back memories that would remind her that everything that had happened wasn't just a bad dream. Even though she knew deep down that it was real, her mind tried to escape to a more pleasant reality. She imagined she would be able to get up from the floor to find Randy in the bathroom shaving, or on the balcony making her a plate of food from room service. Then she remembered him leaving and saying he would be right back.

"Where are you?" she asked the empty room.

Tori listened for any answer, but all she could hear was the water rushing over the falls. She was beginning to tune out that sound the way people tune out tinnitus, that constant buzz or whine that never goes away. She pushed it into the background and focused on other sounds. Somewhere far away, she could hear what she thought might be the sound of someone in pain. It took a moment for her to understand it was the sound of a lot of people, but it was real.

Her joints cracked in protest when she pushed herself up to a standing position, and she had to use the wall for support. She crossed the room by the balcony and didn't even glance at it, but she was aware that under the sound of the waterfalls was the sound of those faraway people. She didn't know why she wasn't drawn to see what the people were doing or where she was even going until she got there. She went straight to the bathroom sink and turned on the cold water spigot. All she wanted to do was drink water to take the dry ache from her throat. She stared at the faucet as if it would take time for the water to come out. Then she remembered.

Six bottles of water were left in the cache of supplies they had carried into the bathroom, and she drank two of them. The cool liquid restored her body in more ways than just quenching her thirst. She also became aware of the different smells she hadn't noticed before. She drew in a breath through her nose and attempted to sort them out.

As she breathed in, Tori stepped out of the bathroom. She saw the trail of dark stains on the carpet and remembered the first time she had smelled blood. She had gone to a meat market with her mom when she was nine years old, and the coppery smell had stayed with her since. The smell that came from the carpet was worse. She recalled that the meat market and the man behind the counter who weighed their purchase were at least clean despite the smell. There was something dirty about the big stains that led to the balcony.

Tori didn't think about what she did next. She just did it. She followed the trail of stains toward the open door. When she reached the balcony, she got down on her knees and then onto her stomach. She crawled forward to the edge of the balcony and looked down to the brick terrace twelve floors below.

A crowd of people was gathered below her...hundreds of people. Some were lying in a large pile directly below her, and she guessed they had fallen from her balcony and the ones above. The people who were walking were milling around as if they didn't know where they were going, and the sound she heard in the background of the waterfalls was coming from them.

She instinctively turned her head upward to the balconies above her. There were faces at the railings of a few. Some waved at her as if they were excited to see her, and they yelled with their hands cupped around their mouths. She couldn't understand what they were yelling, but she waved back. There were also balconies where the people were different. She thought they were waving at her at first, but she gradually caught on that they were reaching for her. Some hung perilously far over the railings, and on one balcony, the railing was beginning to lose the battle to keep the people from falling.

Somewhere high above the reaching and waving people, Tori saw something else, and she knew it was more bad news for her. Black smoke was pouring out of the building. She imagined it would be worse if it came from a floor below hers, but that was a small consolation. She crawled backward away from the edge as if some unknown force was going to pull her over, and she heard the snap of breaking metal just as she reached the door behind her. At least twelve people rained past her balcony on their way to the crowd below, and she could have sworn none of them screamed as they fell.

NO CARTOON CHANNEL

Niagara Falls - 2016

"Brad?"

Denise sat on her side of the bed and reached over to touch her husband's shoulder. There wasn't even the faintest response. She moved her hand to his forehead and was shocked by the heat he radiated.

"Oh, my God, Brad. You're burning up. I'll get you a cold washcloth."

As she ran by Jalen, he whined about the TV again, but she ignored him. She didn't have time to explain why the Cartoon Channel wasn't on TV, and she felt a level of irritation she seldom reached. Her usual calm demeanor was gone.

Denise grabbed a washcloth and wet it with cold water, then she checked the refrigerator and found a small supply of ice. It wasn't much, but she wrapped it up in the washcloth.

Jacob came out of the bedroom, rubbing his eyes, and asked her, "What's wrong, Mom?" He could tell by the way she moved that she was frantic. The only time he had seen her like that was when he was bleeding after being hit in the nose with a baseball.

"Daddy's sick, Jacob. I need to cool him down. Can you be a big boy for me and take the ice bucket down the hall and fill it up?"

Jacob did his fair share of complaining about why he had to do chores while Jalen watched TV, but this time was different. He could see it in his mother's face, and the TV was turned off.

"Yes, Ma'am."

He grabbed the ice bucket from the table next to the refrigerator and left their two-bedroom suite in search of the ice machine. He had stayed in hotels with his family before and knew they were usually in a room near the elevators or vending machines. Through the crowd streaming toward the elevator, he saw an alcove down the hall to his right and headed for it.

Jacob couldn't recall ever seeing so many people in a hotel hallway at the same time. Since they were only on the second floor, he was also surprised by how many were trying to squeeze into the elevator when the stairs would have been just as fast. When he waded through the crowd by the stairway door, he saw why they rushed toward the open elevator. The stairs reminded him of a highway traffic jam, and the traffic wasn't moving. Angry voices of frustrated customers stuck in the middle of the crowd on the stairs expressed their displeasure in very colorful language. He had heard a drunk parent talk like that at a Little League game, and other grown-ups had made the man leave. No one was telling anyone to behave in the crowd on the stairs. Instead, they used the same bad words back at each other.

The ice machine was full, probably because so many people were already leaving, Jacob thought. He used the scoop to fill the bucket and began navigating back to the room. On his way to the ice machine, Jacob had moved against the current in the river of human bodies, and they had generally moved out of his way when he wanted to get by. Now, he was going downstream, and the forward progress was slower. All he wanted was to get by them at the elevator and the stairs, but everyone blocked him as he tried to get through.

"Hey, kid. Wait your turn."

The demand came from an older guy. In his mind, everyone over eighteen was an older guy, but this man was like his father. The man moved into Jacob's path, and when Jacob automatically stepped to the other side to get by, the man rudely grabbed him by his collar and pulled him backward.

"I'm just trying to go to our room, mister. My dad is sick. He needs this ice."

Jacob had hoped his appeal would gain him clear passage, but he couldn't have expected the reaction of everyone who heard what he said.

The crowd around him spread out like Moses parting the Red Sea. He heard someone scream something about his dad being sick, and someone else echoed it but added, "He might be sick, too."

Jacob saw his opening as men and women flattened themselves against the walls, and he sprinted between them. Word reached the logjam on the stairs that someone was sick, and as he ran past them, he saw the crowd collapse downward to the first floor. The traffic was moving to fill every square inch of space between the people in the frantic mob. There were more screams, some angry and some from pain.

Despite the chaos, Jacob managed to reach the door to their room. The doors to the suites weren't flush with the hallway. Instead, they were recessed inside small alcoves that gave the occupants a small sense of privacy. Jacob leaned against one wall in the alcove by their door to catch his breath. He held the bucket of ice tightly to his chest and cried. Everyone was being so mean, and he didn't understand why.

They didn't usually act that way toward a kid. He had been raised to be polite to everyone, and even though he wouldn't have totally understood what it meant if someone told him he was sensitive, he would have felt like it was a good thing. The problem with being sensitive was that he had learned to expect the same behavior back from adults that he showed to them. When he had tried to get by the people in the hallway, he had politely said, *Excuse me, Sir*, and *Excuse me, Ma'am*. Instead of respecting his good manners, they treated him like he had done something wrong. That was new to Jacob.

As he cried, Jacob tugged at the handle on the door, but he had forgotten to take his key with him. The hallway continued to fill with new arrivals wanting to reach the elevators and the stairwell, and he felt claustrophobic in the alcove. He slapped his palm against the door, and between sobs, he called out to his mother.

"Mommy! Let me in...please let me in!"

It seemed to take forever, and Jacob was in full panic mode by the time the door opened. His brother was confused by the sight of his big brother crying. Jalen held the door open as Jacob seemed to fall into the room as if he were running for his life. Even though he was only seven years old, he knew there were too many people in the hallway. Most of them paid him no attention, but a few seemed almost ready to come inside with Jacob. He was frozen where he stood by the open hostility on their faces.

Jalen had no way of knowing that the flood of hotel customers had already surged into a suite at the far end of the hallway. A few people who weren't able to reach the stairs or the elevators had gone through the suite when the occupants opened their door, and despite protests from the guests inside, they had gone straight to the balcony and climbed over the railing. They were willing to jump from the second floor of the hotel rather than wait in the crush of the crowded hallway.

Jalen slammed the door just as a man got the same idea and stepped into the alcove. He heard the man curse and hit the door with his fist. Denise came around the corner behind him and pulled her son away from the door. It sounded like the man outside was ramming it with his shoulder. In a cheaper hotel, the frame would have split, and the door would have crashed open, but Denise was grateful for the way it withstood the attack. The man pounded, yelled, and kicked, but finally gave up.

Denise hugged Jacob and told him she was sorry she had sent him out there. She wanted to wrap the ice and place it on Brad's feverish head, but she had to take a few minutes to make Jacob feel safe again. Jalen kept asking his brother what happened, but Jacob didn't know how to explain it. He had felt as though he would never reach their room and see his family again. Separation anxiety is something every child experiences, but Jacob had never felt anything come that close to the real thing.

By the time Denise returned to Brad, her husband had pushed himself to an upright position on the bed. He was trying to stand, but his whole body was shaking from the effort. He was so weak that Denise was able to easily coax him back to bed, and he shivered in long spasms. She didn't have a thermometer, but his forehead was hotter than anything she had ever experienced. As the mother of two children, she had felt their foreheads and easily knew when they needed to see a doctor. This was different. She thought her husband might be sick beyond what a doctor could fix. She decided to call 911 and ask for an ambulance to take Brad to the Emergency Room.

Denise tried her cell phone first, but when she pressed the numbers on the screen, the call didn't go through. She couldn't remember a time when there wasn't even a recorded message that said to try again later, so she thought there was something wrong with the phone. Her worst fears were realized when she tried the hotel phone. She tried to dial out directly, but this time, she got a message that said all lines were busy. Denise angrily stabbed at the number to the front desk. It rang immediately, but it just kept ringing. Eventually, it stopped ringing and began beeping rapidly.

Brad moaned loudly and rolled over the side of the bed. He hit the floor hard, and to make matters worse, his head struck the corner of the nightstand. He was lying face down on the floor on the right side of the bed, but she could see the trail of blood from the nightstand to the carpet below his head. She dropped the phone and grabbed the washcloth she had been using as an ice bag. She got on her knees next to him and reached around to the cut. She pressed the cloth against it with one hand while using the other to roll him onto his back.

Denise recoiled as her husband's face came into full view. He didn't look like Brad anymore. He had a strong resemblance to that man on the beach, and the smell that came off his body was the smell of decay. The bandage on his hand was brown and yellow where body fluids had leaked through. She sat back on her heels and replayed the last twenty-four hours in her mind. Brad had punched that man in the face. It was not something she had ever seen him do before, but it hadn't really surprised her. He would do anything to protect his family. He had cut his hand on the man's front teeth.

"Two plus two equals four," she said out loud.

Her voice sounded like it came from someone else. It was mechanical and matter-of-fact. It was her way of saying she had known from the start that the cut wasn't normal. The man on the beach wasn't normal. The trip home wasn't normal. Now, as she sat staring at her husband, she saw he wasn't breathing, and the fact that he might be dead from a cut on his hand wasn't normal.

"What's happening, Brad? What am I going to do? How do I

tell the boys?"

For a fraction of a second, she thought she had been wrong. One of his legs jerked so slightly she almost missed it, and an eyelid fluttered. She was about to jump back into the role of family nurse when both of his eyes opened. The formerly green eyes that belonged to her husband were the same off-white as chicken eggs. They were wet and shiny, but there was no spark of life in them. His lips parted, and even though Denise didn't think he was going to speak, she never expected the fetid odor that came out with the deep groan.

Denise thought about the news broadcast from Niagara Falls and knew she had seen the same faces on the women pulled from the water. She had made the connection between them and the man in Virginia Beach, but she hadn't allowed herself to make the connection between them and the terrible infection on her husband's hand. Now, she had to force herself to accept it for the sake of her children. Denise pulled the blanket from the bed and draped it over the thing her husband had become. She watched as he struggled to push it aside, and in a detached sort of way, she understood that he had no idea of how to actually do it.

To buy herself more time, Denise ran around to the left side of the bed and pushed the mattress until it slid off onto her husband. It wasn't extremely heavy, but she knew it would be harder to push aside than the blanket. She kept one eye on the mattress as she gathered her belongings. She hadn't unpacked her suitcase because they weren't going to be in the hotel for more than a night, so it didn't take her long. Something told her that Brad only had one thing with him that was worth taking along besides the money in his wallet. His pants were draped over a chair, and she quickly dug through the pockets and found his keyring. She didn't have a car, but she did have an airplane parked at the local airport's private terminal.

The boys were just finishing breakfast when she pulled the

bedroom door shut behind her. She had engaged the lock on the handle on the other side and was essentially just locking them out of the bedroom, but she figured if the new Brad couldn't navigate himself out from under a blanket and a mattress, he might not be able to figure out how to unlock the door.

Both of them looked up at her from plates covered in maple syrup, and they wore the same expectant expression. Their eyes were wide, and they could tell something was wrong because their mother had her suitcase and an armful of assorted necessities. Their father wasn't with her, and the closed door was blocking them from seeing him.

"Where's Dad?" asked Jacob. Jalen was nodding as if he had the same question.

"Daddy's going to stay here while we go home."

She knew it was a lie...a big lie, and she would have to tell them the truth sooner or later, but Jacob had just recovered from something that had traumatized him in the hallway. She didn't know what it was, but she didn't want to send him back into shock by telling him his father was most likely dead.

Before they could ask her questions about why their father wasn't going with them, she said, "Let's get your things together. Let's go...now."

Judging by the tone of her voice, the boys knew she meant business. They both threw glances at the closed bedroom door as they packed the backpacks they had brought with them from the plane, but they were ready to leave in a few short minutes. Jacob was holding himself together, but he kept wiping at his eyes. If Denise could have spared the time to grieve, she would have sat down with them and pulled them into a hug where they could let it all out. She had to keep telling herself there would be time for that later.

******

Staying in the hotel wasn't a choice Denise wanted to make, but leaving also didn't appear to be an option. To say it would be impossible was an understatement. She learned that as soon as she opened the door of their suite. She shut it quickly and stood staring at its blank surface, trying to process what she had seen. It was *standing-room-only* in the hallway, and the people in front of their door had turned toward her with utter hatred written on their faces. She didn't know why they looked at her that way, but it frightened her. They weren't like her husband, but they were clearly hostile to her. Denise understood better what Jacob had gone through.

Denise locked the door and leaned toward the peephole as if she expected to be attacked by someone on the other side. Her right hand was still resting on the handle, and she saw a man reaching for it on the other side. She felt the vibration in the metal, even though it was a solid door. She pulled away her hand and backed up at the same time, shielding the boys behind her. The loud *thump* from the door could only mean he had rammed his shoulder against it.

"Come with me, boys," said Denise as she turned and ushered them away from the door to the balcony.

Denise stopped them just short of the sliding door and thought about what she was considering. They were only one floor up from the courtyard outside, but she had to ask herself if she was really considering having her boys drop over the side of a hotel balcony.

"Wait here," said Denise.

Denise redirected the boys to the sofa in front of the

TV before going to the balcony alone. Before leaving them, she picked up the TV remote and aimed it while pressing the ON button. Any distraction for the boys would be good at the moment. Nothing happened, and she stabbed at the button again. That was when she noticed the power was off. There was no distant hum of electricity or draft from the air conditioning vents, and a lamp she had left on was now off. Jalen's lower lip was quivering, and she knew he was scared but didn't think she had the time to waste reassuring him. She also thought it might already be too late for them to leave. That thought was confirmed when she stepped outside.

The brick courtyard was supposed to be an outdoor dining area where guests could enjoy a leisurely meal with a view of Niagara Falls. Each table had a large umbrella over it, and it wasn't uncommon for the courtyard to be crowded, even on rainy days. Denise saw that the crowd was much larger than usual. Every table was occupied, but so was every square inch of standing room between the tables. Over the background roar of the waterfalls, she could hear the shouts and curses of angry patrons. There were threats and shoving as people attempted to squeeze through the courtyard into the entrance of the hotel. While all of this was happening, the overflow crowd seemed totally oblivious to the view of Niagara Falls, where bodies washed over the edge and fell into the mist below. It wasn't news anymore...it was a reason to go somewhere else.

It was confusing at first, but Denise finally understood that everyone was doing exactly what she had intended to do. They just wanted to leave, and even though many of them had most likely decided not to bother going to the front desk to check out, there were still the ones who didn't want to be billed for an extra day if they didn't turn in their room keys on time. There were also at least a hundred more in line at the car rental desk. When they had arrived the night before, the lady said there would be no more cars until the next morning when some were returned, but it was obvious that wasn't going to happen. Even if she could walk straight to the front of the line, there wouldn't be a car for them.

Someone tried to open the door to their suite again, and it dawned on Denise that people who were stuck in the traffic jam in the hallway wanted to use her room as a shortcut. If she opened the door, they would stream through and climb over her balcony. She didn't know it was already happening further down the hallway, but she saw evidence of her theory when she looked that way.

To her left and right, crowds were gathering on balconies and climbing over the railings. There were no tables directly under the balconies, but luggage of all sizes was being thrown over the railings, and it crashed heavily into the umbrellas and people below. The jumpers followed, and the screams were testimony to the number of sprained and broken ankles. As newcomers pushed harder for their turn to jump, there were more in front who fell before they were ready, and they landed awkwardly on top of the injured who were attempting to crawl away from human waterfalls. Then, the human rainstorm began.

Denise became a witness to the true horror that followed as bodies rained past her balcony from the floors above. When she looked upward at an angle, she saw some dropping from well above the tenth floor. What she thought was odd was the way they fell. They didn't even attempt to point their feet toward the ground or wave their arms. They fell like sacks of meat.

When they landed on top of the jumpers who landed before them, the sounds of impact were unlike anything Denise had ever heard. It was a lot like dropping a watermelon from the top of a building, but it was difficult for her mind to accept that the sound was coming from human bodies.

One male jumper clearly intended to catch the railing of

her balcony before he reached the ground, but when his hands wrapped around the metal bar along the top, she heard the snapping sounds in his forearms a split second before sharp, white bones tore through the skin. He screamed and fell into the tangle of people below, and Denise retreated to the safety of the room.

******

Denise and her sons huddled on the floor between the TV and the sofa, listening to the muffled sounds from three places. There were still occasional thumps on the door and the mashup of voices, but they decreased throughout the night. The noise outside the balcony door rose and fell until it sounded like a large crowd of people talking in low voices. There was no shouting or screaming...just an amplified murmur of the single voice that was coming from the master bedroom. Sometimes it was by the door, and sometimes it was more distant. She knew her husband was moving around the room, and she did her best to distract Jalen and Jacob.

Nothing changed throughout the night. The boys slept fitfully, and Denise didn't sleep at all. She thought the door to the suite would hold, but she wondered what she would do if the bedroom door suddenly opened. She stared at the pale rectangle across the room, and sometimes, her tired mind made it move. Eventually, she noticed she could see the door better, and sunlight was filtering through the curtains that hung over the sliding glass door to the balcony.

The boys were still asleep against the sofa cushions she had pulled onto the floor. Jalen had slept against her most of the night, and she had tried hard not to move. He rolled over about an hour earlier and was wrapped around his big brother now. Jacob would normally have protested, but he was already sensing that he needed to protect his little brother now. Her joints were stiff as she eased her body away from the boys and crawled to the curtains. She pulled open a corner near the floor and squinted against the bright light. She could see Niagara Falls in the distance, and there were still bodies dotting the surface at the edge before plunging out of sight.

The view of the courtyard was partially blocked by her balcony, but she could see enough of it. There wasn't a line at the car rental counter anymore. As a matter of fact, everyone she could see was just milling around. At first, she wondered if they had been out there all night and why they hadn't left. Then she saw the way they moved and how much they reminded her of her husband. She blinked her eyes again to clear them of their sleep-deprived dryness and focused on individuals. One man was missing his right arm, but the long bone of his upper arm, the humerus, was still attached to the shoulder but stripped of flesh. She searched the crowd and saw that they all had injuries…even the children.

Denise covered her face and cried softly. She didn't want her sons to end up like that, but she felt totally lost and out of ideas. She left the curtains and crawled back to her pocketbook to find her cell phone. There was still no service, but this time there was a big message on her screen that said in bold letters, *National Emergency Broadcast System*. She had turned the volume and ringer off to keep from drawing attention to them, and she was glad she did. If it had blasted one of those awful alerts they used on TV, it would've scared them to death.

About an hour later, the boys opened their eyes and were confused about why they were on the floor in the living room. The realization came to them as they remembered the day before, and they both cried when they asked about their father. The vague answers she gave them only upset them more, and when they cried louder, it drew the attention of the thing in the bedroom.

"Come with me," said Denise. "You two need to brush your teeth and wash your faces."

She grabbed a bottle of water and helped them get to their feet.

"Listen to me," she said. "Church rules...that means no talking or playing around. Let's just take care of business."

Denise had hoped the distraction would take longer, but they returned from the bathroom much faster than it always took at home when she was trying to get them ready for school in the morning. She retrieved leftovers from breakfast the day before and did an inventory of the refrigerator. There wasn't much, but she figured she could ration it for a day or two until the police showed up. There was bound to be some kind of rescue in progress.

"Maybe it will be the National Guard," she thought.

Either way, she had to entertain two small boys until help arrived. She could only hope it was soon.

******

Denise Warren couldn't remember a longer day in her life. Busy days always went by in a flash. She could barely remember the details of her wedding day because it was all a blur. There was so much to do, and it all had to be done on a clock. She regretted that they hadn't made it less formal. Maybe it would've been more fun. She also thought about the home she and Brad had built outside Ithaca. They had drawn up the plans themselves and then bothered the contractors the entire time. They wanted it to be their *forever* home where the boys would always have a place they could come back to.

Those were the best memories, along with watching Brad grow his own business. He had been happy from the start. It seemed like most of their friends, especially acquaintances from down south, took what Brad did for granted. He was always happier when he could get into the heavy equipment and drive down into the Ithaca salt mines for a hard day of digging and hauling, but he knew why he was doing it. Brad knew that a rough winter in New York would require hard work from him in the summer months. The salt that was mined, refined, and bagged ahead of time would all be gone by the end of the snowy season, so they mined an astounding amount of salt in advance. He had told her they averaged ten thousand tons per day, but she couldn't wrap her mind around that number. He always laughed when she would suggest they should slow down so they wouldn't run out of places to mine.

Denise remembered when Brad would come home from work. She could always tell when he had done his job as the owner of the business and stayed in the office or when he had pulled on his work gloves and his helmet and worked alongside his crew.

Her mind came back to the present, and she once again picked up the ongoing assessment of their situation. The boys were playing games they made up, which meant Jacob usually made rules that ensured he would win, but Jalen went along with them because he loved the attention he got from his big brother.

In the afternoon, she made sure they each ate enough of their meager supplies to get enough calories, but it was painfully obvious that they didn't have enough to last a few days, even if they stretched it. There was no sign of change outside, and she was beginning to doubt the existence of the saviors who were supposed to come to their rescue. Denise began to make her own plan. It was a bad plan, but she didn't know what else to do.

Nightfall came again, and it was quiet in the bedroom and the hallway. Denise made several trips to the front door and stared through the peephole. It was always the same thing. Dark shadows passed by the door, and even though there was very little light, she could tell by the way they moved that they were just like the people in the courtyard...and her husband in the bedroom.

Time went by at different speeds, sometimes fast and sometimes slow, and Denise lost track. She filled her time reading useless pamphlets about Niagara Falls, and the boys entertained each other better than she had hoped they would. She stretched their water and food until she knew they would die if they stayed in the room. Maybe it was her own lack of food that was making her move without thinking, but somehow, she found herself on the balcony. She stayed on her stomach and studied the random movements of the crowd. She came to a startling conclusion. They were not totally random. She checked her watch and waited.

A fun fact in one of the pamphlets said tourists could get some great pictures of the boats near the base of the waterfalls if they listened for the bell that would ring on the other side of the courtyard. On normal days, the bell would ring, and tourists would rush away from their tables with their cameras. On this *not-so-normal* day, the bell could be heard faintly over the guttural sounds of the crowd in the courtyard, and there was a shift in the way they moved. Just as if they were tourists getting ready to take pictures, the mass of damaged bodies crowded at the railing in the distance, and Denise could see the railing bend under the strain.

"That bell must be operating under some kind of battery power," she thought, "and when that railing breaks, it might be enough of a distraction for us to go."

Denise hurried back inside and told the boys they were

leaving. She helped each one with a backpack and told them not to speak unless they had to. She led them onto the balcony and crouched in the left corner by the wall. When she took a quick look over the edge, she saw she had been right. It was clear along the side of the building. The throng in the courtyard was packed on the side farthest from her, and they were getting louder.

When the railing broke, it was chaos as the ones in front were pushed over the steep cliff behind the hotel. Denise went over the balcony railing first. She lowered herself until she dangled a few feet from the ground before she let go. Then she motioned for Jalen to come next.

"Do it just like Mommy did, Sweety. Don't worry if you fall. I'll catch you."

Jacob helped Jalen over the railing, and Denise was proud of both boys. They seemed to sense that they were being asked to do something important, and they were being very serious about it.

Jalen dropped harder than Denise expected, but she managed to catch him. She felt a twinge in her back, but she would take it any day over having to coax him to jump. Jacob did it better, but she still had to help him break his fall when he landed.

So far, so good. The crowd was still surging in the opposite direction, but Denise saw stragglers coming around the corner of the hotel about a hundred yards away. They couldn't hear the bell from where they were and were being drawn by the chaos of the crowd as the railing broke. The narrow path along the first floor of the building was clear, with the exception of the newcomers and piles of people who had jumped from balconies, and Denise knew they had to get by them. Some of the people in the piles moved, but Denise kept her eyes on the ones that were walking.

Taking her sons by the hands, Denise led them in that direction, hoping that the stragglers would stay focused on anything but them. She kept her sons close to the wall, and she whispered to them to get ready to run when she said to. She wasn't entirely sure what was around the end of the hotel, but a quick glance backward told her there was no turning back. The party at the railing was breaking up, and the crowd of injured people in the back rows had already begun to wander away.

Denise felt the blood rush from her head to her feet. That numb feeling of helplessness washed over her when she saw every straggler, at least twenty, turn in their direction. Behind them, another two dozen were making a deliberate attempt to cross the courtyard to where they were. She pushed her small boys against the wall and shielded them with her body.

The nearest of the strange, damaged people was only a few yards away, and they were reaching for her and her children. She turned in all directions to find a way to escape, but there was nothing besides the wall, a smooth door with a deadbolt lock and no handle, and a balcony above her.

"No," was all she could say.

She screamed when the door opened, and a hand shot out to grab her by the arm.

TORI

Niagara Falls - 2016

It was quiet in the hallway when Tori opened the door far enough to be able to see outside. The walls of the alcove at the entrance of their suite prevented her from seeing very far, but if she tried hard enough to block out the sound of the waterfalls behind her, she felt like there was only silence in the hallway. She kept one foot inside the door to keep it from locking her out of the suite, and she leaned out as far as she could. There was only faint light filtering in from somewhere on the left and right, and she waited while her eyes adjusted to the darkness.

There was no way to describe the stench that came from all directions, but judging by the smell of the carpet inside her own suite, she didn't need to be able to see the carpet in the hallway to know it was worse. She could also make out some of the shapes that were scattered on the floor as far as she could see. Some of the shapes were abandoned luggage, and some were bodies. She wondered if one of them was Randy.

After nearly two days, Tori Cassidy knew very little about what was happening, but she had a feeling she was about to get answers to some of her questions. Her most recent question was whether or not Randy was dead. She had wondered why she had phrased the question that way instead of, "Is Randy still alive?" It was a "glass half full" question, but Tori wasn't feeling too optimistic at the moment. Part of her brain said Randy could still be alive, but a bigger part of her brain said Randy would still be with her if he were alive.

Randy kept showing up in her thoughts even as she ventured from the hotel suite into the hallway, and when he did, her emotional side railed against the "unfair" situation. This was supposed to be their honeymoon, and it was always the first thing that she thought of when his face popped into her mind. She pushed her thoughts about Randy aside and focused on what she knew for sure. There was a fire somewhere in the building above her. That meant she had to get out fast.

Tori leaned down and dropped a towel in the doorway to keep the door from closing. She didn't plan to return to the suite unless there was no other choice, but she still felt better knowing she could retreat if she was forced to. She grabbed the handles of the bag she had packed with a few necessities. She felt like she had done a good job of sorting out the things she didn't really need. Even though she had been gripped by disbelief when the toilet wouldn't flush, she recognized that the reality was that she was very likely going to die. There were suddenly far worse things in the world than toilets that didn't flush. She also took the time to put on a pair of jeans and a T-shirt. Randy had teased her about bringing sneakers with her on the honeymoon, but she had told him he would regret not bringing his. She wished he were there for her to say, "I told you so."

One of those "worse" things than a nonfunctional toilet was lying on the floor about ten feet from her door, and as Tori got closer, she could see that it was a young woman about her own age. She was dressed in a uniform that had the emblem of the hotel on her chest. On the other side was a name tag that said, "Rose." Tori didn't know what had happened to Rose, but a lot of her was gone. The fact that so much of her body was missing only gave Tori more questions that needed to be answered.

Tori felt that she should do something. She should tell someone in authority that Rose was dead and that something really bad had happened to her. It was what she would have done under normal circumstances, but she had left "normal" behind a long time ago.

"Or did normal leave me behind?" she asked herself out loud.

The sound of her voice caught the attention of something farther down the hallway. It was another dark lump on the floor, but this one was crawling. As it crawled in her direction, it made the same sounds she had heard out on the balcony, and she could tell it was reaching for her.

In the dim light, she could make out some of the details of the crawling lump, and in many ways, it resembled Rose. It was also a woman who had been severely injured. One of her legs stayed where it had been when she crawled away, and other places on her body were serious wounds that should have prevented her from crawling at all.

Tori found herself comparing the two mortally damaged women and saw one difference. Rose had a butter knife stuck in her head. That difference registered in Tori's mind, but it was partly because it meant Rose had been murdered.

"Or had she? What if Rose had been like you?" Tori said to the woman crawling toward her.

Anger flared inside Tori as she saw the possibility that someone or something had done this to Randy. That he was lying on a floor somewhere, or worse yet, crawling along a hallway.

Tori gripped the butter knife on the side of Rose's head

and pulled. She was surprised by how hard it was to pull it free. Rose's head kept coming with it until Tori put her foot on Rose's cheek to hold her head down while she pulled. The knife pulled free with a scraping sound that made Tori think of a movie she had seen where an insane doctor was sawing through bones. She was still in control of her thoughts and knew this wasn't a movie. There was something she had to do with the knife before she changed her mind. She rushed down the hallway and dove at the other woman.

It wasn't really a question that was answered for Tori when she stabbed the woman. It was more like a learning experience. Her first stab was to the top of the head, and the knife cut into tissue but stopped against hard bone. The shock to Tori's wrist hurt badly, and she knew she would feel it more later.

The woman on the floor reached for her and grabbed Tori's arm. Tori was appalled when she saw the woman extend her head forward as far as she could with her teeth bared.

"Oh, no, you don't," said Tori as she stabbed the woman again.

This time, she buried the knife to the hilt in the woman's temple, and the woman dropped to the floor, as dead as Rose.

"I have to remember that," said Tori.

She got up from the floor and went back to retrieve her bag near Rose when a small sign on a door caught her eye. Unlike the stylish number that would indicate it was a suite, there was an engraved plaque that said, *Guest Services Staff Only.* She didn't know why that might be the best place for her to go, but she had already figured out a couple of things for herself without bothering to verify them. She tested the knob on the door and wasn't surprised that it was locked.

One of those things she had figured out was that people wouldn't be jumping from balconies or playing Spiderman if they had another way out of the building. Tori decided she didn't need to check the stairwells or the elevators to find out what had happened to them. The elevators had probably lost power, and she had no doubt they had done so while they were in use. She didn't know how many elevators were in the hotel. Her guess, if she had to make one, was that there were at least ten, and if they were full when they lost power, there were over a hundred people stuck in elevators.

Stairwells were the preference for the throngs of guests who either didn't want to wait for an elevator or were standing at the doors of an elevator when the power failed. They felt like they were the lucky ones because they hadn't been inside the elevators at that moment, but they had plenty of regrets when they saw the traffic on the stairs. Hundreds of people carrying suitcases down through the confinement of a concrete and metal obstacle course was a difficult task on a good day. When there was electrical power, they could at least see where they were going.

Tori had no way of knowing that the stairs had been a bigger nightmare than jumping from the balconies. Emergency lighting failed after the electrical power was lost, and panic caused people to move more quickly. They tripped, fell, and generally threw their weight onto the backs of the people below them. The logjam of bodies pressed down on the lowest floors, and no amount of screaming from the people on the bottom was going to stop them from coming. It was like pouring sand into a hole. Eventually, the hole would be full.

Tori knelt over Rose and searched her uniform pockets. Her hand closed on a metal ring with several keys on it, and she pulled it free. She hoped one of the keys would unlock the Guest Services door. Tori couldn't see the lock too well in the dim light, so she forced herself to take her time. It wasn't easy because she thought there was a faint smell of smoke drifting down the hallway. The third key slid into the lock easily, and she unlocked the door.

She had hoped the door would give her a way off the floor where she and Randy had been staying, but it was beyond expectations. There was a set of elevator doors that were shut, and the small lights for up and down weren't illuminated, so she didn't bother to try to open the doors. Besides, she had a momentary fear that the doors would open and release the people who were trapped inside.

Next to the elevator was a door that opened onto a stairwell. Tori opened the door and listened. It was dark, but it was as silent as a tomb. Going down twelve floors in the dark wasn't what she hoped for, but if it was the only way out, she had to take it. She pulled her cigarette lighter out of her pocket and thought about Randy again. She had promised to quit smoking, but she was glad she hadn't. The thought made her take in a deep breath, the way smokers do when they want a cigarette. She considered lighting one, but she reminded herself she wasn't going out to see the sights. She was trying to save her own life.

"Here goes nothing," she whispered as she stepped into the darkness.

The door sounded way too loud as it clicked shut behind her, and she stood still to listen for a response. There was only silence, and Tori realized she couldn't hear the sound of Niagara Falls anymore. As she stood with her back against the door, Tori thought about the employees who had used these stairs and the hundreds of times they used them to get some peace and quiet, or maybe to sneak a cigarette break, or the inevitable romantic hookup. She hoped none of them were still lurking in the depths of the stairs.

Tori found it to be incredibly easy to walk down the stairs without making a sound. The steps were concrete, and as long as she didn't bump against the railing with her bag, she would remain undetected. She put one foot in front of the next and reached the first landing before the darkness became too much for her. It was so pitch black that she couldn't see the railing or even her own feet. She decided she would stop at each landing and use the cigarette lighter to calm her own fear of the dark. She clicked the wheel with her thumb, and the little flame jumped out.

The light was too weak to penetrate the darkness more than a few feet, so she held it downward toward the next landing. She wasn't one hundred percent sure, but it appeared to be safe. When she reached the next landing, she saw a door identical to the one on her floor, and she knew there would be a Guest Services room beyond it. She held her lighter up in front of the door and saw a smear of something dark on the small window. She hoped the smear was on the other side of the glass.

"One floor down and eleven to go," she whispered. Her voice was shaky, but in her mind, she told herself it had a right to be shaky.

******

Tori's hopes of reaching the first floor without running into problems were dashed when she made the turn onto the seventh-floor landing and saw the stairs disappear under a virtual junkyard of furniture. The faint glow from her cigarette lighter made long shadows on the wall behind the upended tables, chairs, and beds. She didn't see a way to get through it, and her biggest worry was getting past it before the fire reached the floor she was on. She wasn't going to be able to reach the sixth floor unless she had enough time to move the furniture, but she doubted she would be able to untangle everything even if she had all the time in the world. Her only choice was to leave the stairs and enter the seventh floor from the Guest Services room.

She held the lighter up to the small window on the door, but all she saw was her own reflection in the glass. She tapped on the window with the lighter. It sounded loud in the stairwell, but her only other option was to go back up, and she already knew that was the same thing as giving up. There was no response from the dark room on the other side, so she took the only choice left to her and opened the door.

The room wasn't large, but it seemed bigger than the one she had entered on her own floor. She imagined that some of them might be used as storage places so Guest Services staff wouldn't need to go far for supplies. She wondered if there would be anything useful, but she also knew she didn't have the time to do a thorough search.

Morbid humor has a way of helping people get through life-threatening situations, and Tori had to push back a laugh. When she thought about the supplies that might be in the room, the first thing she thought of was toilet paper. Tori put one hand over her mouth to keep from saying it out loud, but she thought, "It might be useful as currency in a week or so." Other than the toilet paper, it occurred to her that there might be candles and matches, and she decided she at least had to take a minute to investigate.

Tori felt like she was in a tomb because the air was different. It had a musty smell to it, and there was a large draft. Without windows or air conditioning, she wondered where the draft was coming from. The room made her feel exposed, and the slightest movement of her feet seemed to echo. It was so dark that she couldn't see the door that would go out onto the seventh-floor hallway, and she was afraid to use her lighter too much. She noticed how much smaller the flame was than when she began her trip down the stairs.

If the room was laid out the same as the one upstairs, the elevator would be on her right, and beyond it was the entry to the hallway. She decided she could make it that far without the lighter, and that was when she discovered the source of the draft.

Tori placed her hand on the wall to her right and slowly walked toward the place where the door to the hallway should be. She felt the smooth sheetrock under her fingertips, the useless light switch, and then the smooth metal frame around the elevator. When she passed her hand over the frame, she automatically let her hand search for the elevator door by reaching a bit deeper into the wall. Her arm straightened too far as her fingers went further than they should have gone. Her body leaned as her arm stretched for the nonexistent door, and she felt almost weightless as she teetered on the edge of the open elevator shaft.

Without light to fill in the details, all Tori could do was try to fall away from the door. It seemed impossible because her weight was moving in the wrong direction, but her left hand somehow found the recessed slot in the door on the left side. Her fingers hooked inside the metal frame, and her body swung outward. Totally blind, she hung onto the metal and felt it cutting into her fingers as her momentum caused her feet to finally lose their traction and fly up into the air. There was nothing else she could do but fall.

In the moment when she knew she was going to die by falling down an elevator shaft, she felt terror, frustration, futility, and sadness all wrapped up in one emotion...denial. Time slowed down at that moment, and even though she wanted to scream, she held it in with a single thought that if she screamed, it would give away her presence in the room. She denied that she would let herself die despite the fact that she was falling, and if she survived...*when* she survived, she didn't want anyone like the woman she had stabbed in the head to know she was there.

The fall ended more abruptly than it started. She landed on

her back on the top of the elevator, and it forced the air from her lungs in a loud grunt. Her heels were still sitting on the lip of the doorway, and judging by the bulge that pressed against her back between her shoulder blades, she had been lucky. If she had hit that spot with her head, it probably would have done more than just knock the wind out of her.

Tori gingerly pulled her feet down from above and managed to get them under her. She thought about what her chiropractor would do for the sore spot to the left of her spine where she landed on the bump, but she told herself it was better to have a few bruises than to need surgery. She pulled out her lighter and clicked the flame into life. She saw that she was even luckier than she had originally thought.

The elevator was only about a foot below the door, and she had magically fallen in between a variety of mechanical devices. She didn't know what the machinery was for, but it all had sharp or hard edges. If she had wanted to fall on her back on top of an elevator, she couldn't have picked a better place to land because the hard lump under her back was still the flattest spot on the elevator roof.

Turning in a circle, Tori took stock of her situation and decided it hadn't been the worst thing that could have happened to her. Someone else had obviously been there before her. Judging by the amount of luggage on the roof with her, more than one person had paid a visit to the elevator shaft.

"Where did everyone go?" she asked herself out loud. Then she added, "When did I start talking to myself?"

She knew the answer to the second question. She had begun talking to herself when she saw bodies washing over Niagara Falls. It became a full-time thing when Randy didn't come back.

She decided the first question probably had something to do with the trapdoor on the far corner of the roof. It appeared to be open, but it was so dark inside the shaft that she couldn't tell in the dim glow of her lighter. She moved closer to the trapdoor and knelt down with her hand extended toward it. That was when the noise inside the elevator increased.

Until that moment, Tori had only been slightly aware that there was any sound inside the shaft. It was only a rustling sound, and her mind attributed it to her unfamiliar surroundings. Since she had never been inside an elevator shaft other than within the confines of the actual elevator car, she thought it was just normal noise. Her cigarette lighter appearing over the open door caused a chaotic chorus of groans and a sound she would have described as snarling. At least a dozen hands reached upward toward her, and she caught a glimpse of the faces.

A glimpse was all Tori needed to make her pull her hand away. They weren't even close to reaching her, but she didn't feel like staying on top of the elevator was a good idea. At the very least, she couldn't think of a reason to stay.

She had half of her body out of the elevator shaft when she remembered the luggage that was piled on the top of the elevator. More questions arose in her mind, and she sorted through them in an attempt to make sense of what had happened on the elevator.

"Why is there luggage on the roof of the elevator? Did it belong to the people inside the elevator? If so, why is it still up here, and why did they get in the elevator?"

The first question was the one she answered.

"Does it matter why the luggage is here?"

"No. It only matters that it's here and there's something in it I can use."

Tori let her feet drop back to the elevator roof, and she began her search through the variety of bags. In the back of her mind, she was holding out the hope that someone had been traveling with a gun...but she wouldn't mind a pack of cigarettes, some food, or a flashlight. She tried to be quiet, but any sound she made seemed to increase the chaos inside the elevator, so she searched quickly.

Right from the start, Tori saw that among the useless junk people carried with them, there were some prizes. When those prizes were combined with each other, they made a pretty good survival kit. She emptied a backpack and examined the contents. The previous owner was obviously going camping because she found a flashlight as well as a supply of protein bars. She found tubes that had labels on the packages that said they were *Drinking Straws* for use when water is contaminated. She had never seen one before, but all of the bodies going over Niagara Falls made her an instant believer that water supplies might be contaminated. She threw away personal items and made room for anything else she might find. She had never used a multi-tool before, but the one she found had a knife on it, and she had already learned the value of a simple butter knife.

She learned the value of the pliers on the multi-tool when she discovered the rectangular case that didn't seem like a normal suitcase. It had a dial-type combination lock in the middle, and it took time, but between the pliers and the flathead screwdriver on the tool, she managed to pry the case open.

"Someone was into some serious stuff," she said as she studied the contents. "I can use this."

Tori had stayed in plenty of nice hotels where conventions were in progress, and as she examined the contents of the case, she thought about the signs she had seen on the banquet hall concourse. One of them had been World War II memorabilia.

Inside the case, there was a long blade that resembled a World War II bayonet. It was wrapped in a sheath and nestled in a slot made for its shape, and she lifted it out with both hands. It was heavy, and when she slid it from the sheath, she saw that the blade was very sharp.

Next to the blade was just what she was hoping to find.

"Well," she thought, "It's not exactly what I was looking for, but I'll bet it works fine."

A German Luger was in a holster and fit into a recessed section of the case. Next to it was a box of 9mm ammunition that held one hundred rounds. Tori had been to a gun range a few times with a boyfriend she used to date, and she had fired a variety of weapons. She had hoped to find one she was familiar with, such as a Glock, Sig Sauer, or Smith & Wesson, but the Luger seemed straightforward. Using the flashlight, she figured out how to eject the magazine and loaded it, then she happily pulled her belt loose and hung the holster on her hip.

Tori stood up and studied the way it felt to be wearing a gun on her hip. It seemed like such a long time ago that she had bemoaned the loss of luxury when she tried to flush the toilet. She remembered something her father had said to her more than once. He told her that he saw more potential in her than she saw in herself, and she should let that potential out. It had been hard for her to be anything other than what her mother had wanted. They had money, and no daughter of hers was going to excel at anything except the social graces. Her mother was old school, and that meant Tori was supposed to act like a lady. Now, as she felt the weight of the gun pulling slightly downward, she understood that her father was telling her to explore other opportunities, but to do it in a way that didn't get her mother mad. She understood that she was supposed to be upset about the toilet not flushing for Randy's sake, but now she was supposed to use her potential to survive.

She went back to her search for supplies and wondered how she could do better than finding weapons. There was plenty of room for more prizes to fit inside the backpack, and it seemed like plenty of people staying at the hotel were using antibiotics. She sorted through a variety of pill bottles and packed everything she recognized into the backpack, along with assorted bandaids and a tube of antibiotic cream. She almost passed on a sewing kit, and sewing herself up wasn't something she wanted to think about, but she kept it in case someone else would need it.

From the remainder of the luggage, Tori found a pair of hiking boots that fit well, and she swapped them for the sneakers she had been wearing. She added spare socks, underwear, and a t-shirt to the pack. Almost every suitcase had travel-sized shampoo, toothpaste, and bars of soap. She found a toothbrush that was still in its package and counted it as a valuable prize.

The one item that surprised her the most was something she had never considered buying for self-defense. Apparently, a lot of travelers felt like they might need pepper spray. Since it didn't take up much space, she kept six of the small aerosol cans.

A scraping sound from somewhere outside the elevator shaft reminded Tori that she had forgotten something very important. She had neglected to climb out of the shaft to see if the hallway door was shut.

Tori thought to herself, "You're stupid, and someone else is going to find your backpack and appreciate it."

She turned off the flashlight and sat as still as she could. As her eyes adjusted to the dark, she realized that there was no ambient light. That was how she wound up inside the elevator shaft in the first place. If the door was open, and if someone came into the room, they were just as likely to fall into the elevator shaft as she had done. If it was one of those people like the ones below her inside the elevator, she was about to have company she didn't want. She could shoot the intruder, but the gunshot would make her ears ring so bad that she might as well be deaf, and if it turned out to be a normal human being, she didn't want to murder them. She slid the bayonet out of her belt and waited.

Tori wondered if she hadn't let her imagination get the best of her because it was quiet for so long. Her legs ached from staying still, and she finally gave in to the temptation to stand up. Her knees betrayed her by making loud pops, and she heard something in the room react. She didn't know why she thought it sounded like something reacted eagerly. Maybe it was because she pictured it as reaching for her the way the people inside the elevator and on the balconies had reached for her.

She felt and heard the weight of someone or something as it fell onto the elevator with her, and she held the long bayonet out in front of her.

"What am I doing? My only advantage is my flashlight because I can't even see what's in here with me."

She clicked the light on again and aimed it toward the entrance to the elevator shaft. The beam of light landed on a man who resembled a turtle on its back. He flailed his arms without coordination as he attempted to free himself from the same place where Tori had landed, and Tori wondered if she could do the same thing to him that she had done to the hotel employee with the butter knife. The bayonet was a big improvement.

Before she could decide to make her move, the man somehow managed to roll over. He was on his hands and knees, and his face lifted toward the source of light. The menacing expression on his face didn't change, but he uttered a growl that made her feel sick to her stomach. With clumsy, jerking movements, he stood up and took the first step toward her.

Tori backed away from the man and stepped dangerously close to the open trap door. It had been one thing to stab the employee on the hallway floor, but this guy was walking and reaching, and so were the people below her.

She thought of all the movies she had ever seen that had an action scene on top of an elevator and remembered there was always a ladder on the wall of the shaft. She panned the light around the walls and saw it...right behind the shuffling man who was coming toward her. Unable to think of anything else to do, Tori lifted the backpack and threw it at him as hard as she could. She missed. It didn't even land in his path and trip him.

Her only choice was to shoot him, but he was already so close that she was forced to back away even further. This time, she was careful to shine the flashlight downward so she could see the open trapdoor. She stepped over it and stood on the narrow edge of the elevator roof between the opening and the wall. The heels of her hiking boots hung over the side, and there was a six-inch gap between the elevator and the wall. She leaned backward as far as she could until she felt the cold concrete wall against her body and pointed the tip of the bayonet at the man's face. With the other hand, she held the flashlight aimed at his eyes. She didn't think the light blinded him, but she didn't know what else to do.

Tori saw the excitement appear to grow on the man's face as he got closer, and as his fingertips came within range, she swung at them like she was holding a fly swatter instead of a blade. She felt helpless and stupid, and the man didn't seem fazed by the sharp edges slicing his skin, but it did make him lose his balance. With his right foot, he stepped into the middle of the open trapdoor, and his body followed.

He didn't fall completely through the hole. Instead, he went through to the waist and had the upper part of his body wedged in the opening. What stopped him was his left leg.

It was pointed practically straight up in the air with his foot facing Tori. He was still reaching for her as if it didn't matter that half of his body was inside the elevator. He was also snapping his teeth together in loud clacks.

Tori kept her back against the wall of the elevator shaft, but she slid sideways until she was far enough to stand up straight again. She stepped away from the wall and walked around behind the man. He did his best to turn around, but his left leg was keeping him wedged inside the opening.

"That's gotta hurt," she said. "Let me give you a hand."

She grabbed the foot that was pointed at the ceiling and pushed downward. She was sure the loud pop she heard was the sound of his left hip coming out of its joint, and he fell the rest of the way through the hole. Feeling satisfied but just about sweating adrenaline, she climbed from the elevator shaft and closed the door to the hallway.

"This might be a good place to get some rest," she said.

LYNCHBURG

The Blue Ridge Mountains - 2025

The night was far more eventful than we expected. Before Wally climbed up to the overhang above the front porch of the cabin, he told us there were going to be predators drawn by the smell inside the house. They would come to investigate, and if they couldn't get in, they would most likely move on. The problem was that we wouldn't know when most of them were nearby.

He said, "The big ones, like the bears and the wolf packs, will move fast and make more noise than the cats. Since things changed, there have been plenty of mountain lions. They were pretty much gone from this area before the infection, but they haven't had to deal with humans hunting them. They're so quiet that you don't know they're behind you until you feel their warm breath on the back of your neck."

"That's going to help me sleep," said Jean. "I guess we need to keep the windows up."

Ruth added, "They're going to smell us anyway, so we can have the windows down an inch or two, but if a bear decides it wants to get inside, it'll open the truck like a can opener. The good news is that a bear will run if you make enough noise."

Jean answered, "That's reassuring because I'll be making

plenty of noise. They call it screaming."

Despite the warnings from Wally, it didn't take long for us to go to sleep, but it also didn't take long before the activities began. The infected dead showed up first.

Tin cans rattled as the infected stumbled through the strings, and they came straight toward the truck windows. Ruth raised the windows before they got their fingers into the gaps. There were only four of them, but they were making enough noise to attract a pack of wolves. We stayed still inside the truck while the wolves tore them apart, but I watched from a corner of a window and saw something I knew was important.

There were six wolves, and I wanted to see how they would react to the differences between an infected dead and a living person. For one thing, the wolves could inflict massive bodily injuries, but head trauma wasn't in their skill set. The infected dead were easily taken down, but they were going to keep moving regardless of the number of times they were bitten. The second thing that made them different from living people was their blood...it wasn't warm. It was one thing for the wolves to feed on the pile of infected that had landed in front of their lair, but these infected dead were walking around and making noise.

Four of the wolves took down the infected in a matter of seconds, while two stayed back and watched. The infected were all on the ground, but as I expected, if there was anything left on them that could move, it was moving. The tangle of bodies writhed as the four wolves tore at them. Eventually, the wolves sat back on their haunches and waited while the two that had been watching moved forward to inspect the kill. They sniffed at the twitching bodies and occasionally pulled their heads back quickly to avoid being bitten by the infected. It made me wonder if the wolves would die if they were bitten. So far, I hadn't seen it happen, and I told myself to ask Wally if he had ever seen a predator become infected.

The two wolves inspecting the kill finished their assessment, and the other four seemed to be waiting for their verdict. The inspectors weren't satisfied, and they raised their noses into the air in search of the scent that attracted them more. I didn't know if they could see me in the corner of the window, but I knew they would see me move if I ducked down. So, I tried not to blink as they stared at the windows of the truck. Their bared teeth seemed to reflect light back at me.

Wally must have moved slightly because all six heads turned to face him, and the pack charged toward the cabin. They were just gray shadows when they were that far away, but I could still see them well enough when they picked up our scent by the front steps. I could almost sense their fury as they circled the spot where we had all stood until they knew for sure where we had gone. They raced together back in our direction, but for the first time, I was glad to have the infected dead next to the truck. They had covered our scent enough for the wolves to be confused.

The hunt lasted almost two hours. I imagined Wally ached from head to toe from just trying to stay completely still on the roof. It was hard to sleep inside the truck, knowing that six hungry predators were circling us, but I finally dozed off. When I woke up, I saw the gray shadows disappearing into the trees, but there was a new shadow. This one was at the bottom of the steps in front of the cabin, but it seemed like it was melting into the ground.

I understood what I was seeing when the mountain lion uncoiled its bunched muscles and launched itself as high as it could against one of the main supports of the porch overhang. It came very close to getting its claws into the shingles. I didn't know if it would be able to pull itself up if it got a grip, but if it did, Wally would have to shoot as soon as its head appeared. If it got up there with him, it would be too late.

"Ruth," I said just loud enough to wake her from a light sleep. "Turn on the headlights."

Ruth didn't waste time asking me why, and the entire clearing and the cabin were bathed in the blinding lights just as the mountain lion jumped again. The sudden burst of light made it misjudge the leap, and it landed heavily on the porch. It disappeared around the corner of the cabin with incredible speed.

"Was that what I think it was?" asked Jean.

Ruth said, "I think I'm going to move the truck closer to the porch in case Wally needs to get off that roof."

The rest of the night didn't feature any new arrivals that we were aware of, but none of us could sleep. We didn't talk, but we could tell without being able to see each other that all three of us were awake. When the sun finally made its appearance, we were all relieved.

******

We didn't waste much time exploring the cabin because the smell was too hard to tolerate. There were plenty of dead batteries, camping stoves, and lanterns that used propane, but only empty propane cans. Judging by the number of equally empty matchboxes, the people who had sought refuge in the cabin were probably lighting fires with flint, but we couldn't find any.

When we returned to the front porch and breathed in the fresh air, Wally said, "I remember when it started, and I was making my way to Ruth. There were people along the roads putting their thumbs out like hitchhikers. Some had backpacks loaded with camping gear, but I'll bet none of them had enough gear to last more than a week, let alone the first winter. I don't know why I gave in and picked one up. Maybe I just wanted to find out what he knew about the infection, or maybe I felt sorry for him."

Jean asked, "Why'd you feel sorry for him?"

"He had a load of stuff on him that would be great for a weekend of camping. There were still price tags on some of the stuff. I just felt like he was a little too excited about the infection."

"Excited?" I said.

Ruth answered for Wally, "I remember when you told me about that guy. You said he was glad to see the population get thinned out a bit so the planet could recover."

Wally nodded, "Yeah, the guy kept saying we could go back to the cities in a year or two and start over. He thought people would learn from their mistakes and stop polluting everything."

I said, "Well, I can't disagree with him about the pollution, but I think he was a bit optimistic about everything getting better in a year or two."

Wally was amused by my comment and let out a short laugh.

"He was too optimistic about his own future. I asked him how he planned to survive in the mountains for two years. He said he would build a log cabin, hunt wild game for food, and make his own clothes from animal hides. He had a hatchet in his backpack. That's how he planned to build his cabin. I would bet someone took his hatchet away from him within a week, and maybe they used it on him."

Wally's amused expression faded as he thought about what had become of the young man. It always reminded him of the number of times he found the remains of other survivalists who thought all they needed was plenty of supplies.

"They weren't all naive," I said. "When it started, I had enough supplies to last the rest of my life. The difference was that I also had a location. Your hitchhiker was starting from scratch."

"The people in this cabin thought they had a location," said Ruth. "Maybe they started out with supplies, too."

Standing on the porch together, I pictured the people arriving. They must have thought they could weather the infection because they were so far off the beaten path, but the image I got reminded me of something we had missed.

"It just occurred to me that they didn't have any vehicles," I said.

"Eight years is a long time," said Jean. "If they even arrived here in vehicles, they would've run out of gas, broken down, had flat tires, been stolen, or been abandoned somewhere else. They could have gone on supply runs and not made it back. The people in this cabin now aren't likely to be the original occupants."

I knew Jean was right, and as we loaded the few useful things we had found into the truck, we felt like we were leaving a mausoleum. I also had to wonder how many more cabins there were in the mountains where we would find the same scenario.

We drove away down the overgrown path through the woods back to the paved road, and once we were out from under the shadows of the trees, we felt a sense of relief. Even though we had always been watching for survivors to bring into our shelters, more often than not, we had found the ones who almost survived. They were like the man on the table who either died from a bite or from the amputation attempt. The rest were infected and wandering around outside somewhere.

There was always the feeling that things would have been different if we had arrived a few days or weeks earlier. That was what had driven Jean and me to strike out for upstate New York on our own.

We passed the time with random stories as Wally drove at a snail's pace along the debris-littered country roads. I remembered a book I had read years ago, and for some reason, I felt like sharing it.

"I read a book about a family that was faced with the aftermath of a nuclear war," I began. "The father knew a lot about radiation because he was some kind of teacher. I think he may have been a professor. They only had a little time to get everything done before the fallout would reach them, but one thing I remember was that they were in a cellar, and they had used rolls of toilet paper as an air filter in a pipe. He said it let in enough air and would filter out the carbon dioxide from the inside and the radioactive particles from the outside."

Jean asked, "How'd it work out for them?"

"I don't remember how the book ended, but I remember thinking they would eventually run out of toilet paper."

"That's a bleak story," said Ruth. "I assume you're saying when faced with the choice between dying from radiation poisoning and running out of toilet paper, some people will die from radiation poisoning."

"Something like that," I said, "but more to the point, I'm saying that the average person won't have the ability to prepare for something like this. I mean, just think about the cost of preparing for every possibility."

Jean added, "Who knew there would be a zombie apocalypse? When Titus Rush began building his shelters, he had in mind that there would be a nuclear war, civil war, foreign invasion, natural disaster, or pandemic, right? He had zombie apocalypse on the list, but only because he knew preparing for one would make people think of more things in order to get ready."

I said, "I think he actually had an alien invasion ahead of a zombie apocalypse."

"And more things meant more money," said Ruth. "My husband was always coming up with some new thing he had forgotten. I didn't even know what water filter drinking straws were until Reggie bought a big box of them, and don't get me started about prescriptions. I ran out of blood pressure medicine years ago."

Wally let out an audible groan.

"That's why she started adding garlic to everything she cooks. Some survival book said it would lower blood pressure if you eat more garlic."

"I like garlic," said Jean.

"In pancakes?" asked Wally.

We rode in silence after that exchange until Wally slowed down at the crest of a hill. In the distance, we had a clear view of Lynchburg, and it had to be a shock to Wally's system.

He said in a low voice, "I don't really know what I expected it to look like, but it wasn't this."

******

Jean and I had seen plenty of cities that had suffered the ravages of the infection. Changes began on the first day, and we had to remind ourselves that there had always been changes even before the infected dead began roaming the streets in search of victims. One day, you would see a building on a corner, and the next day, it would be a vacant lot. A week later, the lot would have a new fast-food place on it or maybe a bank. The difference was that those changes were man-made and called progress. It was expected, and it was hard to imagine the opposite.

When the infection began, the biggest changes happened in the first few days. People fled from the inner cities into the suburbs, where they tried to hide in their homes. Some emptied their pantries and loaded their cars with luggage they wouldn't need three days later. They drove onto the already congested highways and joined the exodus of vehicles that would become brightly colored cemeteries. Most of them were on the roads that led to the mountains because word spread quickly that it was safer there.

Many people stayed inside their homes. They found every scrap of wood and every spare nail and boarded the windows and doors. They didn't want to give up the possessions they had collected as they progressed through the American dream. The big TV set, the favorite recliner, and the washer and dryer...they were all symbols of the hard work and long hours they invested to achieve promotions and larger paychecks.

Among the other prized possessions were the guns and ammunition. The photo albums were packed and ready to go if the people had to leave, but the guns were loaded and readied for battle. In the first three days, neighbors shot at each other over food shortages and made it clear that the backyard cookouts were in the past. It was ironic that one box of ammunition cost as much as seven cans of meat because people ran out of food before they ran out of ammunition.

Eventually, the boarded doors and windows became the prison bars that held the occupants inside. Too many had carried the infection into their homes on the first day as they held makeshift bandages wrapped around bite wounds. Others died from heart attacks, bullet wounds, and a variety of ailments, and the surviving relatives didn't know what their loved ones would become after they died. Empty prescription bottles littered countertops in kitchens and bathrooms, and people died from the lack of medications that sustained them.

Those who tried to fight back, the police officers, the military, the firemen, and the medical people, weren't prepared to face an enemy that didn't die. The same thing happened everywhere, and it didn't really matter how fast they learned that a headshot was the only way to stop the infected dead. There were just too many of them.

From what we could see of Lynchburg, Mother Nature had finished what the infected dead had started. The suburbs were covered with vegetation, and the rooftops of the houses that lined the streets were barely visible. We couldn't see any garbage-strewn streets or abandoned vehicles because eight years of unchecked plant growth had consumed the city. Beyond the suburbs were the tall buildings of the downtown area, and in between were strip malls that were only visible because of their asphalt parking lots. We knew from experience that there wouldn't be anything worth seeing in the strip malls or downtown because those stores were picked clean by people escaping from downtown on the first day.

Almost eighty thousand people lived in Lynchburg when the infection began. Add a few thousand transients who were in the city on business, and even though the entire population could only fill two or three major league baseball stadiums, there were enough people to cause chaos. Since that day, it was likely that the remaining population was mostly the infected dead, but we owed it to Wally to at least find out where his family had gone.

Wally was dejected by the sight of the city. Tall buildings had long, black scars on them where they had burned. Smaller buildings were consumed by vines and hidden under trees, and many of the rooftops had collapsed under the weight of falling trees. He put a pair of binoculars to his eyes, and the sound of his breathing gave away the emotion he was feeling. He held his breath and then let it out in a heavy sigh.

******

Wally said, "There are chain-link fences around so many of the strip malls, but I see holes in all of them.".

I dug out my own binoculars and scanned the city for the fences. I saw them almost immediately, and he was right. The sections that were intact had barbed wire running along the top. Inside the fences were the remnants of military equipment and trailers that had FEMA painted on their sides.

"It's hard to tell from here," I said, "but FEMA and the National Guard must've tried to set up camps in the city."

Ruth asked, "Why didn't they evacuate to the countryside? Why'd they try to set up camps in the city?"

"They didn't know better," said Jean. "I was on a cruise ship when it started, and we tried to quarantine and treat the infected. We learned pretty quickly that families weren't going to tell us if someone was infected. They hid the bites from us. When the infection spread throughout this city, they could have set up the FEMA camps anywhere, and the same thing would have happened."

Jean was instantly embarrassed for stating the obvious in front of Wally, and I was surprised I hadn't slipped up before she did.

"I'm so sorry, Wally."

He held up a hand to stop her.

"Don't apologize," he said. "You and Eddie have seen so much more than us. After seeing this, I'm glad that Ruth stopped me from coming back here before now. If I had, I would be dead just like everyone else."

Wally didn't have to add that *everyone else* included his family. Seeing Lynchburg in such a state of devastation was enough to make it painfully obvious that he had been hoping for the impossible. Even if they had been evacuated from the city, finding them would be a miracle.

Jean wanted to add that it was still possible that Wally's wife and son were alive and had been taken to a safe place, but they hadn't seen any indications that FEMA had set up camps in the mountains. FEMA's idea of a safe place had consistently been refugee camps inside chain-link fences and armed guards to shoot anything that tried to get inside. It was like no one had learned anything from Custer's last stand at the Little Bighorn.

"What are we going to do?" asked Ruth.

Jean and I knew that Wally was doing his best to let go of the hope that his family survived, but we owed him the opportunity to take a closer look at the city. I gave him a nod of approval, and he returned the gesture with a weak smile. He took his foot off the brake pedal and let the truck roll forward to the city.

We didn't get far before the roads became too congested for us to get through. The truck came to a stop on a narrow street that was tangled with rusting vehicles and crawling vines. Wally cut off the engine, and silence descended around us. It was a warm afternoon, and the fetid smell of rot hung in the air. All four of us felt the same dread as we sat in the truck and listened for any sound that would indicate there were infected dead nearby.

"Where are we?" asked Jean.

The question was aimed at Wally because he was staring at

one house in particular.

"Warwick Lane...I lived in that house," he said.

"I didn't recognize it," said Ruth. "I didn't even recognize the street."

If we had left at that moment, Wally would have accepted what he already knew, but we all saw the curtains move in the living room window, and that was something he couldn't walk away from.

"Everyone stay here," said Wally.

We knew why he said it, but we also knew there was no way we were going to let him go into the house by himself. We all got out of the truck at the same time, but Wally was halfway up the sidewalk to the door before we could stop him. He crossed the narrow porch and threw his shoulder into the door with as much force as he could. The wooden frame tore free like cardboard, and he fell into the room. He had so much momentum that he wasn't able to stay on his feet, and Wally landed heavily on top of the broken door.

Ruth had given us the impression that she was able to take care of herself, and we hadn't doubted her, but she showed us how capable she was in a matter of seconds. Even as Wally fell to the floor, Ruth brought her rifle to her shoulder and aimed at the empty space above him. She pulled the trigger and fired, and in that split second, the shape of a man appeared above Wally and then fell across his back.

We all feared the worst as we ran toward the house. Jean and I had been carrying weapons for so many years that our hands had moved reflexively to the hilts of our machetes. My legs were longer than hers, so I reached the door a few steps ahead of her, but I knew we were thinking the same thing. First, we had to eliminate the infected dead, and then we had to see where Wally was bitten. If it were an arm, we would be forced to test the question of whether or not the amputation theory worked. The image of the failed attempt in the cabin flashed through my mind, and I knew Wally would suffer either way.

I raised my machete with my right hand as I grabbed the collar at the back of the neck of the infected dead. It was so emaciated that it seemed to weigh no more than a pillow, and pulling it away took no effort. I was only vaguely aware that Jean had ducked past my upraised arm into the home to be sure the rest of the room was clear. We had cleared rooms together so many times that I knew she would be covering my flank while I took care of the infected dead in front of me. I heard her say it was clear before I let go of the collar, above which remained only part of a head. Ruth's bullet had removed the rest.

Wally rolled away from the corpse as I pulled it from his back, and things hadn't happened too fast for me to know by his expression that he was trying to make a connection between his wife and the thing I held above him. It would have been a terrible tragedy if it were her, whether she was an infected dead or not. I was relieved to hear Ruth say it wasn't her.

Ruth said in a sharp voice, "You can't do that again, Wally. What if there had been more of those things in here?"

Wally tried to protest, but she added in an even sharper voice for him to be quiet. The way she tilted her head to one side told me she was listening for something. Jean and I took her not-so-subtle hint and focused our attention on the rest of the house. There was a faint rustling sound like old newspapers being crumpled together. The moldy smell inside was certainly the same as wet paper, and it was likely that the rot in the walls and furnishings would make walking through the old house unsafe.

I pointed at the stained carpet and said, "This place has a basement. We shouldn't walk around like the floors are safe."

If I hadn't pointed at the floor when I had, we might have missed the movement under the carpet. Something traveled across the room like a mole burrowing through the ground. The bulge moved steadily toward the body of the infected dead and disappeared under it.

"Do I even want to know what that was?" asked Jean.

She was closer to the middle of the room, and the body was between us. My instincts were telling me that whatever was under the carpet wasn't something we would like if it was interested in the dead body. Wally shifted his position on the floor and pulled his left hand away as if something had touched it. There was another bulge under the carpet where his hand had been.

Jean jumped over the body of the infected dead and was out of the house in one leap. Wally was on the floor one moment and was squeezing past me only about two seconds later. All four of us stopped outside as a group and watched the carpet as new bulges appeared where we had been standing. They all converged near the body and disappeared under it, but a moment later, there was movement under the stained clothing on the back of the corpse.

The bulge that had bumped into Wally's hand moved from side to side as if it were unsure why the hand was gone. A small tear appeared in the fabric of the carpet, and as the tear grew in size, a head appeared. Long legs twitched through the opening, and mandibles chewed at the torn carpet until the creature could squeeze through. A spider bigger than a rat turned toward the body of the infected dead and ran to join others of its kind.

There was no question about whether or not we needed to search the rest of the house. Wally understood that his family wouldn't be there even if they were still alive. No one spoke until we were back in the truck and driving away.

"I don't understand something," said Ruth.

I made a guess at what she was going to say and asked the question for her.

"How did the spiders get that big?" I said.

"No, if I can believe the dead come back to life and eat people, I can believe spiders will get bigger," she said. "What I don't understand is why they didn't go after that dead guy until after I shot him in the head. I mean, it seemed like they were really interested in him after I shot him."

"Movement," said Jean. "Isn't that how spiders know when something is trapped in their webs? They feel the vibrations in the strands and follow them to the victim."

"That means the infected had been sitting still for a long time," I said, "and the whole house was like a giant web? I don't think we should go into any more houses."

We only made it to the end of the street when we saw the large FEMA sign at the entrance to a campus of some kind. Wally pointed at it and said, "I forgot about the college. It makes sense that FEMA would've set up a camp there. My wife and son could have walked to it."

The sight of the FEMA camp seemed to bolster Wally's spirits for a moment, but as he eased the truck past the broken barricade at the entrance, the hope faded from his face again. The large common area of the college campus was more like a battleground than a place of refuge. Most of the vehicles were scarred by bullet holes or fires that burned out of control. The weather-worn tents that had housed refugees were nothing more than large sheets of material draped across the cots and tables inside. They had collapsed years ago as if they were sheets placed over furniture inside a vacant home.

Wally said what we were all thinking.

"Spiders live in grass, too. I don't think I want to look under those tents."

He navigated around the abandoned vehicles and drove off the campus.

HOTEL

Niagara Falls - 2016

Tori woke up thirsty and downed a bottle of water from her supplies. She wondered why she woke up with a clear head and didn't question the reality of her situation. She wasn't even confused about where she was. She could have woken up believing it was all a nightmare.

"You would be proud, Dad. Mom…not so much," she said. "I don't think clicking my heels together twice and saying there's no place like home is going to work."

She felt around in the supplies for one of the protein bars and greedily unwrapped it. She didn't need a light to see what she was doing, and she wanted to conserve the battery, so she waited until she was done eating before clicking the button on the flashlight.

"What time is it? How long have I been here? Why am I still talking to myself?"

In her mind, she answered, "Defense mechanism."

In the bright flashlight beam, she saw she had been right about the room being a larger version of the one she had entered on her own floor, but there wasn't anything remarkable about it. She could tell the storage cabinets had already been ransacked, but she couldn't imagine what anyone found that was useful. Hotel toiletries weren't going to save anyone's life today.

For the first time since it all started, Tori was able to go beyond the events she had witnessed and consider the facts. It started in her mind as the thought about hotel toiletries saving lives, and it grew into the question of why lives needed to be saved. Bodies really were being carried over the top of Niagara Falls. Randy really was gone and probably dead. She really was sitting in a dark room with a Luger on her hip. When she played out the events in her mind, she remembered the upper floors of the hotel had been on fire.

"I need to get moving," she said. She wasn't sure if her mind was playing tricks on her, but she could have sworn the acrid smell of smoke was in the room already.

Tori gathered her supplies and put her hand against the door to the hallway. It wasn't warm to her touch, so she knew the fire hadn't reached the floor she was on. She eased the door open and peered around the edge. Every door was open as far as she could see, so the sunlight lit up the hallway well enough for her to see a group of men dragging injured people along the floor. There were three of them, and they each dragged their victims into one room. She didn't know what they were doing to the injured people, but she heard screams abruptly start and stop inside the room. Tori forced herself to leave her hiding place to see for herself. She arrived in time to see the men throw two of the victims from the balcony, and they turned around toward her before she could react.

"Get her!"

The man's sharp command made Tori jump, but she felt like she was in a dream and couldn't run. All she could think of in that split second was how she had never known those dreams were true. You really can't run just because you want to.

She didn't really know what happened next. She only knew the Luger was in her shaking hands, and she had pulled the trigger three times. The men were in a heap just outside the door of the room, but none of them were dead. They were all holding their bodies where they had been shot, and they were screaming. It was a mixture of anger and pain that made them yell at her, and suddenly, her legs were able to run.

Tori went back to the storage room and locked the door behind her. Her mind was busy sorting out what she had seen, and she made a logical assumption that the men were pulling people out of the logjam at the stairs so they could get through. She also assumed they hadn't finished their work before she arrived, so she couldn't get out of the building that way. That left her one option.

The ladder inside the elevator shaft was something she had considered for a moment before she opened the door, but she didn't like the idea of climbing down several stories in the dark. She was a little afraid that someone below would see the beam from her flashlight, and she would be stuck on a ladder while they waited for her to climb down. She couldn't wait around to find out if there were more people like the three men, and she knew she had made the right decision as soon as she jumped onto the elevator and reached for the first rung of the ladder. The loud thud of a body ramming the locked door echoed down the elevator shaft, and the profanities shouted at her from the other side left her with no doubt that she would be tossed over a balcony railing if she was caught.

Putting aside her fears about what might be at the bottom of the elevator shaft, Tori clipped the flashlight to a belt loop and forced herself to climb downward. She glanced at the darkness below her feet, but she was still too many floors from the bottom for her to see anything but blackness. The flashlight swung back and forth on her hip, and the beam didn't settle on anything except her legs and feet, but it was better than being in the dark and totally blind.

She wished she had at least shown the presence of mind to count the rungs as she climbed, but all she wanted to do was get down the ladder as fast as possible. By the time she thought of it, she guessed she had climbed down about twenty rungs, and if there were ten per floor, she had fifty to go. Her heart had been hammering in her chest when she shot the three men, but even though she was exerting herself on the ladder, it had slowed to a steady beat. Counting the rungs made her feel more calm and more aware of sounds in the darkness.

Way above Tori's head, the crowd inside the elevator had become agitated by the gunshots, and they had gone into a frenzy when her hiking boots echoed across the top of the elevator. Now, she realized she could judge the distance by how faint their clamor had become. As she got closer to the bottom, they were only a rustling noise as their feet shuffled across the floor.

Tori saw the concrete bottom of the elevator shaft a few feet below her, so she stopped long enough to use the flashlight to locate the service exit. She knew it would be locked to prevent access by hotel guests, but it would only make sense that someone inside the shaft could unlock the door. She just hoped she was right. She found it on the wall to her right.

She lowered herself from the last rung and went straight to the door, but she forced herself to slow down. She didn't want to find herself in another room full of crazy men, or even worse, more people who were like the ones crawling along the floor or groaning inside the elevator. She put her hand on the lever-style door handle and gently pushed downward. It was unlocked, and it barely made a sound as she eased the door open.

The other side of the door was as dark as the elevator shaft, and Tori was forced to give away her presence by using the flashlight. She wasn't surprised that the elevator access was located inside the hotel's power plant. She saw electrical breaker boxes and pipes that snaked away into dark corridors. Even though the electricity had been off for over a day, there was still the occasional sound of machinery cooling down. The ticking sounds made her feel like she would be lucky if she were alone.

Tori closed the door behind her as quietly as she had opened it, but she kept her hand on the lock in case she had to get back inside in a hurry. Her flashlight didn't reach every corner of the power plant, but she noticed there were no windows. It struck her as odd at first because it didn't occur to her that she had climbed past the ground floor into the basement, but as she panned the light from her flashlight around the room, she saw more steel ladders on the walls. There was movement at the top of one.

Pointing her light at the movement was more of a reflex than a decision, but when the beam stopped on a man on the other side of a metal railing, the man became animated. It didn't matter to him that she was down a level from him and that he needed to use the ladder to climb down. She kept the light on him and watched with morbid fascination as he worked his way along the railing toward the opening over the ladder. He leaned toward her and reached with expectant hands as he slid closer and closer to something she knew was inevitable.

The man found the opening above the ladder, but instead of using the handrail to help him get his foot down to the first rung of the ladder, he stepped into midair and did the ugliest head-first dive Tori had ever seen. It was far enough from the top of the ladder to the floor for him to be almost prone when he reached the bottom. He landed somewhere near the ladder out of her view, but there was no doubt in her mind that the impact would have killed a living person.

Tori had gone from being a newlywed to a murderer in a

short time, and the evolution had taken a toll on her. Her sense of humor was also a victim of circumstances.

"Whoa, that's gonna bruise," she said. "The American judge deducted points for not sticking the landing, but the Canadian judge added points for difficulty. Wait a minute...the Romanian judge docked him on style points, but they always do that."

Tori circled the room slowly, and she decided she would use a different ladder than the one where she had seen the man do the diving act. She picked the closest one and climbed the wall to a landing that gave her a better view of the whole power plant. When she saw the man again, she was shocked to see that he was limping between the rows of machinery. He was moving in the direction of the ladder she had just climbed, so Tori pulled the Luger out of its holster and got ready.

After a few wrong turns, the man found the path that would take him to Tori's ladder. She watched in amazement because she couldn't believe he could walk. One leg was badly broken just below the knee, and the skin had been flayed away from the leg from the fracture to the hip. The white bones stood out in the beam of her flashlight, and she noticed the kneecap was gone.

"How can you walk on that leg?" she asked.

The man seemed to hear her question. He groaned loudly and reached upward at her with one hand as he got closer. Tori aimed the Luger at his head, but she didn't want to waste bullets. She waited for a better shot and figured she had until he reached the top of the ladder. When he was directly below her, he kept reaching upward, but even though his hand was only inches from the metal rung, he ignored it and kept reaching for her.

"You don't know how to climb a ladder, do you? You don't even know what that metal rung is for."

Tori watched the man bump against the wall repeatedly and said, "I'll bet you'll keep doing that as long as I'm up here, but I'm not hanging around to find out. See ya later."

The level Tori had climbed to had covered windows and a door, and as far as she could see, this was where hotel maintenance people entered the power plant. A couple of desks and chairs were arranged below a wall covered with key fobs. She guessed there were at least two hundred. Tori shined her flashlight on the keys and closely examined the tags that were attached to the metal loops. The tags were numbered, but under the numbers were names. Tori realized she had found the secure area where guest services tracked the concierge parking, and she excitedly began searching for the tag that would have her last name on it.

It didn't take long before she spotted the tag with *Cassidy* scrawled on it. She snatched it from its place on the board and put it in her pocket where she could get to it in a hurry. She had a nagging feeling that everything was about to move at a faster pace once she was outside the hotel.

Tori was only a few steps away from the keys when she stopped. Her thoughts had been jumping from one thing to another as if she couldn't focus on more than one thing at a time. That was because this was all new to her. She had gone from caviar to killing and from newlywed to fugitive in a matter of hours.

"Hours?" she thought. "How long has it been?"

Tori had lost track of time. She didn't know how long she had been in the elevator shaft or the storage room. She didn't even know how long it had been since she had seen Randy the last time. Somehow, Tori realized she needed to slow down. If she opened the door and ran outside without making a plan, her luck might end. So far, she had been very lucky. Even the butter knife sticking out of the head of the woman in the hallway was good luck. If she hadn't found it, she might not have gotten past the thing that tried to bite her. She had been lucky to find the gun. If she hadn't used it when she did, the three men would have caught her.

Now, she was ready to take the biggest step of the day, and that meant she should have a plan. Something nagged at her subconscious, and she turned back to the key fobs. There was something about them that made her study the variety of keys. Of all the makes and models they represented, she knew some were better than others.

"What makes them better?" she asked herself out loud.

An answer came from the lower level, where the injured man still bumped against the wall. It was just a groan, but it reminded her it might be time to stop talking to herself.

Randy had driven them to the hotel in a rental even though he had a favorite car at home, and when he turned the keys over to the concierge, he had reserved another car. She didn't know what model it was, but his love for luxury cars didn't let him stray too far from a BMW or Mercedes. Knowing him, it was likely to be the same as the one he owned. They were certainly nice cars, but from what Tori had seen from the hotel balcony, they might not be what she needed.

"What do I need?" she asked herself in a whisper.

She pulled the fob from her pocket that Randy had given her after they checked in and read the abbreviations. The fob had an embossed BMW logo, but there was nothing to tell her more than the color and the license tag number. Something told her she wouldn't have the luxury of time that would allow her to stroll around the parking lot searching for a specific tag number.

A tool bag next to one of the desks was just what she needed. She lifted it onto the desk and then noisily dumped the contents onto the desk calendar. Her first inclination was to leave the tools, but the idea of making a plan kept nagging at her. She had to think beyond getting to a car and leaving, and tools might come in handy. When she studied the pile of metal and sharp objects and visualized what she might have to use them for, she realized she wouldn't know how to fix a broken-down car, but the claw hammer would be better than a butter knife. So could use the pipe wrench and the sharp-tipped screwdrivers.

Tori thought of a movie she saw in which a cop in a hotel said, *Now I have a machine gun.* She revised the line to say, *Ho, ho, ho…now I have a bag of weapons.*

In the end, she decided to eliminate the heaviest weapons because she had the gun and the long bayonet. The pipe wrench was way too heavy, so she left it on the pile of discarded items. Besides, she needed space in the bag for the key fobs. She couldn't take them all, and she hoped the ones she chose worked with vehicles that were more suited to whatever was happening outside. She wasn't sure what that meant, but she figured if one of the keys matched an armored car, that was what she would take.

Tori went through the desk drawers and found another flashlight to add to her collection. A candy bar in one drawer was unwrapped immediately and eaten while she searched through the things people brought with them to work. She passed on the uneaten sandwiches and a thermos of coffee, but she couldn't resist taking the unopened pack of cigarettes.

A supply locker contained a variety of items that could be found in any garage, but Tori only took the duct tape and a long-handled piece of metal that was flat and had a notch on one end. She had seen a tow truck driver use something just like it to unlock a car without a key. If nothing else, she could use it as another weapon.

"Okay…so what's the plan?" she said.

Tori had stayed away from the covered windows for fear

that someone could see her inside if she got too close to them. They were covered by wide mini-blinds that were fastened in place. If she moved one slat, they would all move. She leaned toward the end of the blinds, being careful not to touch the slats as she tried to see around them. The windows filtered the light, and she was relieved that they were tinted. That meant she could see outside, but people couldn't see in through the windows except at night if a light was on inside. She used one finger to tug at the corner of the blinds for a better look, but she jumped backward when she saw a face only inches away. She didn't stay at the window for more than a second, but it was long enough for her to see that it was bloated and marred by a normally fatal injury.

It took several minutes for Tori to work up the nerve to approach the window again. She had backed away far enough to sit down in one of the office chairs, and she had to think about her next move. The door was to the right of the window, and another set of windows was on the other side of the door. If she went out the door, she would be only a few feet from the face she had seen in the window. The only blessing was that the door opened to the left, and it would temporarily block the owner of the swollen face.

Tori thought about going back down the ladder to find another exit. She went back to the railing at the edge of her level and panned the beam from the flashlight along the opposite side. There were more doors, and one of them was labeled *GARAGE LEVEL ONE*. Below her, the man with the mangled leg groaned and waved his arms excitedly. She would have to deal with him to reach the other side, but she knew there was no guarantee that things were better on the other side of the garage door.

She went back to the desk and grabbed the handle of the tool bag, but as she lifted it from the desk, she considered how she would deal with the guy at the bottom of the ladder. She didn't want to use the gun even though she couldn't miss from where she would be standing. Tori hefted the pipe wrench from the pile of discarded items and went back to the railing. It weighed a few pounds, so she took careful aim and let it drop on the man's head.

What would have been a crippling blow to most people was only a distraction to the man. The wrench glanced off the side of his head and bounced away, but it only caused him to fall over. He recovered quickly and resumed his attempts to breach the wall by bumping into it.

Tori turned her own attention back to the other set of mini-blinds on the right side of the door, opposite from the one she had looked through before. A shadow moved across the blinds because someone was directly outside the window. She couldn't resist trying to see what was there, even though she suspected it would be more bloated faces. Tori peeked around the edge of the blinds and saw a woman reaching upward. At first, she thought reaching was something the injured people all did, but then she realized the woman wasn't just reaching... she was coaxing. A boy dropped into her arms, and as soon as she set him on the ground, she resumed coaxing. A second child fell a little more awkwardly into her arms, and then the woman backed up against the window. Her head snapped frantically to the left and right, and Tori could imagine why.

Tori still didn't have a plan, but she could see clearly that the woman wasn't like any of the bloated faces she had encountered so far. She also wasn't like the men who were throwing people over the balcony railings. She was more like the victims the men were dragging. Tori was having a hard enough time keeping herself alive, but she knew she couldn't live with herself if she didn't help the woman and the two boys.

Without another thought about what she was doing, Tori threw open the door. She felt it slam into someone, probably the guy with the fatal injury, but she pushed harder against his weight and felt it give. She had no way of knowing she had knocked three of them to the ground. She shot her free hand toward the frightened woman who had her back against the wall and her arms wrapped protectively around the boys. Tori grabbed her by the forearm and pulled as hard as she could.

The woman was caught off balance, so she fell more than she followed Tori through the door. Tori avoided being pinned under the weight of the woman and somehow held onto the doorknob. She pulled the solid door shut with her left hand and flipped the lock into place with the other. On the floor behind her, the woman shielded the boys with her own body and begged for mercy.

******

"Are you hurt? Are you okay?"

Tori kept her distance, but she prodded at the woman as carefully as she could. The woman was obviously frightened, and she had no way of knowing that she had been pulled to safety. Judging by the clamor on the other side of the door, she and the children had been only moments away from a horrible death. Tori braved another peek from the window, and she saw that a large crowd had gathered outside. Every face she saw was damaged, and above the sound of their bodies bumping against the door was an eerie moaning chorus of voices. There were no words to describe the sound.

"Are you hurt?" she asked again. "You're safe now. I'm not going to hurt you."

The woman hesitantly lifted her head and eyed her rescuer. It took a moment, but that was what finally sank in. This stranger had rescued her and her boys from certain death.

It was almost dark in the room, and the frightening sounds outside the door felt too close, but no one was attacking them, and no one was trying to bite them. Neither of them knew nor would have cared about the irony that Tori had less information about what was happening than the woman she had rescued.

Denise fussed over her sons and frantically checked each of them over. Jalen's face was tear-streaked, and his lower lip was quivering, but Jacob gave her a brave smile and told her he was fine. Tori had a moment to take in what had just happened, and she realized what her split-second decision had accomplished. If she did nothing else right in her life, it was a good feeling to know she had just saved someone's life. She stood back and waited for the woman to recover from the shock of being yanked inside.

When she was finally able to piece together what had happened, Denise said in a shaky voice, "I can't begin to thank you enough."

Tori felt an elation she had never experienced and felt like saying something dumb like, "Aw, shucks." What came out was, "Don't mention it," and that sounded just as dumb.

"My name is Denise Warren, and these are my boys, Jacob and Jalen."

"Tori Cassidy."

It was a strange feeling to shake hands, but it was still reassuring because neither of them had seen anything even close to a normal person since losing their husbands.

Tori said, "Do you have a clue what's happening? I mean, besides the obvious?"

"Only what was on the news," said Denise, "but nothing since the power went out."

"You saw some news?"

Denise nodded. "There was a news broadcast from a boat over at the bottom of the Falls. They were rescuing the people who were going over the Falls, but then the people who were pulled out of the water were attacking the police and EMTs who were rescuing them."

"Attacking how?"

Denise appeared to be reluctant to say it in front of her boys, so she mouthed the word *biting* at Tori. Tori remembered the way the hotel employee had bared her teeth at her before she stabbed her with the butter knife. She had thought the woman was going to bite her.

Tori pointed at the door and asked, "Those people out there...are they all like that?"

Denise nodded again and said, "There are hundreds out there."

"We have plenty to talk about," said Tori, "but right now, we need to find a way out of here. We can talk when we're safe. The upper floors of the hotel are on fire, and I was working on an idea when I saw you outside."

The man at the bottom of the ladder chose that moment to groan loudly, and Denise jumped between the railing and her children.

"Oh, don't worry about him. He can't reach us. My plan to get out of here includes getting him out of the way so we can reach the garage over there." Tori pointed toward the door.

Denise got closer to the edge on her knees and peered over at the man below.

"Maybe we could drop a desk on him," she said.

Tori thought she would have reached that conclusion sooner or later, but she didn't mind giving her new friend credit for the idea. While the boys waited at a safe distance, the two women combined their efforts and slid one of the heavy desks away from the wall.

"I'm glad this place didn't try to save money on the furniture," said Tori. "These things weigh more than some of the junk people call desks."

They got two legs of the desk over the edge at the top of the ladder, but the strange man wouldn't stay directly under it. He kept going to one side or the other to reach for the women.

"I have an idea," said Tori.

One of the discarded items from the toolkit was a ball of twine. She tied the loose end around a pair of pliers and carried it back to the railing. It was easy to get the man to reach for it when it was dangled in front of him, and they guided him to where the desk would land. When he excitedly grabbed the pliers, Tori and Denise pushed the desk at the same time.

The results were a spectacular success. The man not only disappeared under the heavy desk, but he was crushed in a way that silenced him for good. Tori used her flashlight to see if he was still alive, but she couldn't see him from above. She climbed down first, and since the desk was directly under the ladder, she stepped onto it before jumping to the floor. Once she was able to see under the desk, she could tell that the man wouldn't be a problem anymore. She climbed back up to retrieve the tool kit and the backpack and was pleased to find that Denise and the boys were stuffing their pockets with more key fobs.

Denise said, "One of these keys is bound to go to a car that can get out of the garage."

"I didn't think of that," said Tori. "I was thinking about needing to choose one that's going to be safe to drive. If everything's as bad as I think it is, we should hope for a Jeep or Hummer. I guess we won't know what we're going to get until we go through that door."

Tori climbed down and then helped the boys get by the desk after Denise got them started on the ladder from above. Tori led the way through the maze of machinery inside the power plant, and they helped each other again to go up the ladder to the garage door. When they shared a nod that they were ready, Tori unlocked the door to *GARAGE LEVEL ONE*. She thought she was prepared for what was out there, but she was wrong.

The garage level was dimly lit because the sky had become overcast. Hundreds of vehicles of all types were wedged against each other as if someone had pushed them inward from the outside. Tori couldn't see a clear path more than a few feet from the door, but that wasn't really good news because the only people she could see were the ones who were trapped in the small gaps between the cars. None of them appeared to be alive. Some of them could move, but most of them were pinned into place from the waist down by the cars. Getting out of the garage was going to be like walking through a minefield.

AMHERST COUNTY

Virginia - 2025

When the order came to stay indoors, don't go to hospitals, avoid strangers, and go to FEMA camps if possible, the citizens of Lynchburg did the same thing as the citizens of every other city that received the same orders. They loaded their cars with supplies and escaped from the infection by attempting to go somewhere safer. At least they thought they were going somewhere safer. For most of them, their final destination was the nearest interstate highway. We found evidence to support what we already knew to be true. The sides of the roads to the north of Lynchburg that led to interstate highways were choked with rusted vehicles of all kinds.

Wally had been focused on driving ever since giving up the search for his family. None of us could blame him for not wanting to talk. It was a burden that had been weighing on him for years, and now he was literally putting it behind him. With Lynchburg in the rearview mirror, he was trying to give the road ahead his full attention.

For Wally's sake, the rest of us were quiet, but it was just a matter of time before someone had to speak. We were on a different quest, and if Wally had wanted to stay in Lynchburg to continue his search, he had been free to do so, but no one had broached the question. We simply accepted that he was driving and we were going north.

Ruth was riding up front with her brother and broke the silence by asking a question.

"Has anyone else noticed that there are more cars on the sides of the road than in the middle?"

"It's something we've seen before," I said. "People were told to stay home, but they packed up and hit the roads anyway. When the logjams of traffic blocked roads, emergency vehicles couldn't get through, so local authorities took it upon themselves to make a path. Firetrucks, SWAT vehicles, and bulldozers were ordered to push cars out of the way. It didn't matter if they were occupied or abandoned."

"Don't forget FEMA and the National Guard," said Jean. "They had plenty of heavy equipment that was needed to carry supplies to refugee centers. At first, they had them go into the cities. Then, they had them evacuate and take everything to the smaller towns that surrounded the big cities. Their convoys were actually bigger when they left the cities because they carried refugees with them."

The last comment caught Wally's attention.

"Carried them to where?" he asked.

Jean was one of the biggest optimists in the world, especially since the living population of the world had decreased significantly, but I knew her well enough to know that she hadn't meant to get Wally's hopes up again. We exchanged a knowing glance, and she mouthed the word *sorry* at me.

There wasn't any sense in lying to him, and I could see he was watching her in the rearview mirror, waiting for an answer.

I wanted to come to Jean's rescue, but as was often the case, I made matters worse.

"A lot of the FEMA and National Guard camps were set up in places like football stadiums. They were usually surrounded by fences already to keep people from messing up the fields, and the stadium seats were a great barrier to give the authorities control from higher ground."

Wally visibly perked up, and I didn't know what I said that made a difference to him, but it was clear that I renewed his sense of purpose.

He said with a big smile, "There's a football stadium at one of the Amherst County high schools, not too far from here. If it's true that they moved cars to the shoulders so they could get through, then it sure looks like they went this way."

There was no way to take back what we had said or deter Wally from his hope that this was the evacuation he had always pictured for his wife and son. He had been told on the first day of the outbreak that they had been evacuated by soldiers, and we had inadvertently added fuel to his desire to find them. Maybe a small part of us wanted it to be true.

"It's on the way," I conceded. "It won't hurt to take a look."

Whether it was true or not that Wally's family was evacuated to the high school, something had cleared the path well enough for us to make good time. What bothered Jean and me was the possibility that it hadn't been the National Guard. We were approaching the stretch of highway that ran parallel to the high school and would be exposed as we got closer.

Jean voiced what we had silently considered by making a suggestion.

"Wally, pull over to the side of the road and park as close as you can to the other cars. We need to blend in."

"Why?" asked Wally. "We're almost there."

Ruth said in a tone that made it more than a suggestion, "Just do it, Wally."

Wally frowned but did as Ruth said. He let the truck coast along the shoulder until he saw a gap on the right side that he could slide into. The rear of the truck faced the highway, giving us a good view of the road while also providing a hiding place where we could get in and out of the truck without being seen. He shut off the engine and turned toward us in the backseat. He wasn't happy about stopping, but Ruth was quick to remind him that we had more experience on the road.

Ruth added, "Hear them out. Jean wouldn't have said to stop without a good reason."

"Something's bothering me," said Jean. "The road isn't just clear, it's too clear. I think someone's been using it to go back and forth to the city on supply runs, and why aren't there any infected dead on this stretch of highway?"

I answered for her, "Because someone has a choke point up ahead."

"What does that mean?" asked Wally. "Wouldn't that be a good thing? What if it's the National Guard?"

"That's what we have to find out," I said.

"We have to find out without taking any chances," added Jean, "and it bothers me that some of the wrecked cars aren't as old as the others. I also noticed some have bullet holes in them."

Wally wasn't completely convinced, and he wouldn't be easily deterred from his quest to find his wife and son.

He argued, "Anyone who survived this long and has the resources to keep this road clear must be a strong group. To me, that's a good thing."

"Until they take what you have, kill you, or use you for slave labor," said Jean.

Over the years, we stayed behind while our friends had gone in search of survivors and other shelters, but we learned from their stories. We knew there were good and bad people on the road, and we didn't know which they were until they showed their intentions. There were even times when good people turned against them and tried to take what they had.

Jean didn't want to sound like she was patronizing Wally, and she knew she could easily shock him with some of the things she knew people did on the road, but she decided it was best to use an example he would understand.

"Whoever they are, they could be like you and Ruth, or they could be like Henry Shackley. Imagine a whole army of people like him. We need to find out what they're like before we let them know we're in the neighborhood. You had to make a decision about us, remember?"

"And if they're dangerous people?" asked Ruth.

"Then we have to find a way around them," I answered.

We had already told Ruth and Wally everything about the Chief and our other friends, so it came as no surprise to them that we wanted to make a plan before leaving the truck. We also needed a plan B in case things didn't go well. We decided to wait until dark and then use the wreckage on the other side of the road as our cover to approach the choke point. The stadium at the high school was on that side, and we couldn't cross the road without being seen if we were too close to the school.

Our goal was simple. We wanted to avoid contact until we had a chance to learn whether or not it was safe to announce our presence. We wouldn't split up unless we had to. In the event we got separated from each other, we would do our best to get back to the truck, but only if we could do it without leading pursuers to the rest of our group. With a plan in place, we settled in to get some rest before it got dark enough to leave the truck.

******

We were lucky there was no moon, or our shadows might have been enough to give away our position. We also discovered that Jean had told Wally to pull to the side of the road at the right time because there were no more gaps after the place where we had parked. There was still an opening between us and the next car that was big enough to walk through, but nothing after that. Someone had taken great care to use the abandoned vehicles to create a barrier, and they touched each other bumper to bumper.

I took the lead, followed by Wally and Ruth. Jean deliberately followed us at a slower pace to watch for patrols that might be behind us. The Chief had told us about combat patrols using a similar tactic. He said you never knew when the enemy was already patrolling the area, and it was easy to slip into a path ahead of them. Of course, we had another reason for putting someone at the back of the group. The infected dead were noisy and easy to find in the dark because they weren't stealthy, but we didn't want to get caught between them and the choke point any more than the living.

We followed the line of derelict cars and trucks along the north side of the road, always keeping in mind that the choke point could be obvious or hidden. We estimated that we had stopped at least two miles from the school, so it wasn't likely that anyone had heard us coming, but we got our first clue about the people at the high school when we saw where they had chosen to welcome new arrivals to the area.

I held up a hand and signaled for everyone to get down, and then put a finger over my lips. When Jean caught up with us, I gestured to her by pointing at my own eyes and then at a spot on the other side of the barricade of cars. She raised her head just far enough to see what I had spotted, and then she ducked low to the ground and crawled to where we waited.

She said in a very low whisper, "I saw three infected."

"What else?" I asked.

Jean answered with her own question, "Are we at the beginning of an overpass? The road slopes upward, and I couldn't see any cars after about twenty yards from here."

"It's too dark to be sure, but we'll know in a few minutes when those infected dead reach the last cars," I said. "Wally, do you remember this stretch of highway enough to know what's up ahead?"

Wally half-stood to see what Jean and I had seen, and he nodded at me.

"This is a clover leaf, but we should be able to see more of it. I think it's collapsed at its highest point where it crosses over the highway below."

Jean said, "So if we had kept driving, we might have driven right over the edge, but even if we had stopped in time, we would've been seriously caught out in the open. What are the infected dead doing now?"

The darkness made it hard for me to spot them again, but I eventually saw they were approaching the end of the pavement. In a few more steps, they would confirm for us that the overpass was gone. I told the others in a low voice what was about to happen, and everyone stood up for a better look.

The infected dead closest to the precipice only needed one more step before he lost his balance and disappeared. It always seemed so strange when one fell from a high place. There was no depth perception or even the slightest hint that they understood what was about to happen. The other two had a few yards to go and were moving at a slower pace, and they changed directions when the first one disappeared. One of them walked toward the opposite side of the road. The other one, a woman who had long ago been ravaged by a fatal injury and then subjected to years of hot and cold weather, turned directly toward us. Everyone ducked except Wally.

"Justine?"

Ruth grabbed Wally by the back of his shirt and pulled, but she was too small and frail to move him. Wally wasn't a big man, but his wiry frame was rigid, and he wasn't in his right mind. He had kept it to himself, but ever since they had abandoned the search for his wife and son, he had been expecting to see them walking on the side of the road.

"That's not Justine," said Ruth. "Get down."

"It's her, I tell you. It's my wife."

Wally pushed Ruth away and jumped over the hood of a wrecked car before I could grab him. He ran straight toward the infected dead, and the dead woman raised her hands toward him.

"Justine, it's me, Baby. Let me help you. I'll help you, and then we can go find Andy together."

Wally rushed toward the welcoming hands, and it wasn't clear if he grabbed her or if she grabbed him. He somehow seemed to understand that she immediately tried to bite him, and even though she came dangerously close, he kept her from reaching his exposed skin by turning her from side to side. The whole time, he brought his face closer to hers, and he talked to her in a reassuring voice. It wasn't going to end well, even if I got there in time, because Wally wasn't going to be overly excited to see me drive a blade through the woman's head, even if it wasn't his wife.

Ruth was still yelling that it wasn't Justine, and Jean was pulling her away so I could get by her to go after Wally. Jean succeeded in tripping Ruth's legs from under her, and the two fell in a heap behind the wreckage of a camper. It was good that they did, and it was good that I had gotten delayed by Ruth. If not for that little bit of luck, I would have been on the hood of the car when the lights came on.

The bright spotlights were aimed toward the center of the road, where Wally was locked in an embrace with the infected dead that he thought was his wife. He had pulled her into his body so hard that her chin was on his right shoulder. As hard as she tried, she couldn't turn her head far enough to bite the invitingly close flesh of his neck, but she kept snapping at it only an inch away.

The other infected dead had turned around when Wally had called out his wife's name, and his previously slow progress became the closest thing to running that he had done in years. He stumbled forward and greedily reached for Wally.

All three were in the middle of the searing white lights, and even though the sudden burst of light had blinded me and left me fumbling to clear the spots from my eyes, I was still in the shadows and invisible to the people on the other side of the spotlights. I instinctively let myself fall onto the ground and then crawled to where Jean and Ruth were hiding behind the camper.

"What in the world do we have here?" said a rough voice.

The voice asking the question was deep, and there was no mistaking that the speaker found the situation humorous. There was something like a short chuckle at the end of the question.

A higher, more nasal man's voice asked, "Are they dancin' with each other? I ain't never seen that before."

"Naw, at least I don't think so," said the deep voice. "That guy might be dancin', but the other one has definitely got something else on her mind."

The second voice added, "That other one comin' across the road is gonna cut in. Get it? He's gonna cut in."

He laughed at his own joke, but I heard a sound that I recognized as someone racking a round into the chamber of a gun. Jean knew what the sound was, too, and she put her hand over Ruth's mouth to keep her from reacting to what was about to happen.

There was a single shot, and I risked turning my head far enough to see under the camper. I saw two people standing close together and one on the ground, so I knew someone had shot the other infected dead. The two close together were Wally and the infected dead he had thought was his wife. I wondered how Wally was keeping himself from being bitten, but he was probably in just as much danger from the two men. The problem was that I didn't have a clue how I was going to help him, and I didn't know yet if the men were good people who were just guilty of having a sick sense of humor. I got my answer less than a minute later.

I could see better than Jean or Ruth, so Jean was waiting for me to indicate one way or the other what we should do. I watched as two more sets of legs walked up to Wally and the infected dead he still held tightly. One of them stood behind Wally, while the other one circled around behind the infected dead to be face to face with him over the dead woman's shoulder.

The deep-voiced man was apparently looking Wally straight in the eyes, and he asked, "Is this a private party, mister? I mean, you do know how this is gonna end, right?"

The nasal man behind Wally said, "We know you're her type, mister, but this relationship ain't gonna work out."

Both men laughed at their own jokes, and they weren't laughing because they were the kind of people who would help someone they didn't know. If they had been good people, they would have already pulled the infected dead woman away and kept her from biting Wally in the process.

I heard Wally say something in a low voice, and even though I couldn't understand what it was, I got the impression that his momentary case of insanity had passed, and he was begging for his life. Now, he found himself embracing an infected dead, surrounded by two unsympathetic people, and most likely unsure of how it had happened. He was pleading for their help, but they were trying to decide how to have more fun with the situation.

I knew Ruth wasn't going to like it, but there was only one way for the rest of us to live through the encounter. We had to leave while they were occupied. I crawled close enough to whisper in Jean's ear and told her we had to go. She whispered the message in Ruth's ear, and at first, it seemed like she was going to fight her way loose from Jean. I had to help hold her down without making noise. Then Ruth stopped fighting, and resignation passed across her face. She nodded at me and then at Jean. We waited a few heartbeats to see if she was just faking, but we had no choice. We had to trust that she understood.

Jean relaxed her grip on Ruth, and I crawled off of them. I had to see if we had been detected when we scuffled in the dirt with Ruth, so I eased myself into a half-standing position and peered around the back of the camper. Everyone was still right where we had left them, and the two men were laughing too hard to have heard us. The nasal man was imitating Wally's pleas for mercy, and the man with the deep voice said something about needing some music.

I was surprised to see the man walk away toward the bright lights, and I couldn't see where he had gone. We couldn't move from where we were because we couldn't tell if he could see us. I jumped when the quiet night was filled with loud country music.

It was a song that was clearly meant for dancing, and one of the men shouted something about it not being a party if they couldn't all join in. My curiosity got the best of me, and I moved closer to the men. I was shocked when I saw that someone had forced a gag into the mouth of the infected dead. One of the men had pulled her away from Wally and was dancing in a wide circle with her. Her wasted body was weightless to him, and her feet swung in the air as they swirled around in the beams of light. She tried to bite him through the gag, but he just laughed even harder. I assumed it was the man with the deep voice because he was so much bigger than the other man. The nasal-sounding man was standing behind Wally with a gun to his head while he stomped his right foot to the music. Wally stood with his shoulders slumped in fear.

The nasal man yelled at Wally, "What's wrong with you? You wanted a party so you could at least clap your hands."

Wally halfheartedly raised his hands and clapped in time to the music while the big man swirled around in the road with the infected dead, swinging her like a rag doll. I turned to Jean and Ruth and was surprised to see both of them taking aim with their rifles. My fear had been that shooting the nasal man would result in one last pull of his trigger finger, but I had forgotten that Ruth was a true marksman.

Jean pulled the trigger a split second before Ruth, and the big man fell sideways onto the road. His body twitched, but Jean hadn't messed around with an attempt to wound him. Her shot had been to the side of his head. The infected dead woman fell on top of him and continued her vain attempts to bite him through the strip of cloth tied across her mouth.

When Ruth fired her rifle, the nasal man screamed as his gun hand exploded in a spray of mist and bones. He fell to the pavement, clutching his wound and sobbing. Wally was left standing in the middle of the brightly lit road, surrounded by blaring music. He still had his hands raised as if he was going to clap one more time.

I was slower than I should have been, but I had the presence of mind to make a mad dash toward the bright lights. I found a set of big halogen spotlights mounted on the hood of a pickup truck. I hit the power switch and turned it off, and then got into the truck and ejected a CD from the dashboard. It was instantly dark and quiet on the road at the top of the overpass. The only sound was the whimpering of the nasal man and a muffled growl from the infected dead woman.

About a mile away, the sky suddenly became brilliant as the high school stadium lights turned on, and we heard several engines roar to life. Whoever it was at the school, they weren't afraid of being discovered. We didn't have the luxury of waiting to find out for sure if the two men were on their own or part of the group that occupied the stadium. If the behavior of the two men was any indication of what we could expect from their friends, then we would be dead soon. If not, we would be wishing we were dead.

"We have to go now," I called out to Ruth and Jean.

Ruth answered, "There's one last thing I need to do before we go."

She may have been old and small, but Ruth was mad enough to muster up the adrenaline she needed to take care of the wounded man. Even in the darkness, we were impressed by the way she grasped the whimpering man by the back of his neck and yanked him to his feet. Before the infection, I had seen a bouncer at a club handle an unruly patron the same way. Ruth bum-rushed the man straight to the end of the road and pushed him over the edge. The sound of his scream faded as he fell and abruptly stopped. Ruth grabbed Wally above the elbow and set him in motion toward me.

Jean and I didn't have to ask her why she had to kill the man, but she told us anyway.

"When the people at the stadium get here, the first place they'll look is at the meat pile that's probably below the end of the overpass. If they see him, and if he was lucky enough to survive the fall, maybe they'll waste some time trying to figure out what happened."

We couldn't disagree with her logic.

It was a long run back to where we had left the truck, and along the way, I had a frightening thought. We had all wondered why there was one gap between the cars pushed to the side of the road. Through winded gasps for air, I told the others I suspected we may have parked in the only place the people from the stadium used as their entrance to the chokepoint at the top of the overpass. That meant we had to get there first.

We doubled our pace and sprinted as best as we could the rest of the way. When we arrived at our truck, we could hear vehicles running their engines at high speeds, and the glow of their headlights danced across the trees as they got closer. Ruth shoved Wally into the back seat ahead of her. He was moving fast enough, but he had a confused expression that made us sure we didn't want him to drive.

Jean was closer to the driver's seat, so she jumped in behind the wheel and started the engine before I could get into the passenger seat.

I managed to gasp out the words, "Keep the headlights off and don't try to run from them. Just back out of the gap and get close to the rest of the wrecked cars. Kill the engine, and everybody get down."

Jean understood. There was no way it was going to work out in our favor if we tried to win a high-speed chase, especially if they knew the area better than us. She backed the truck out of the gap and carefully maneuvered it into position against an SUV a few yards behind us. When she cut off the engine, our truck looked like it had been pushed to the side of the road along with the other vehicles. For good measure, I reached up with the butt of a rifle and rapped it against the windshield. A spider web of cracks spread across it from side to side.

We only waited below the dashboard about five minutes before the first of the headlight beams cut through our windshield and lit the interior of the truck's cab. The beam sliced across us from left to right as the approaching vehicle burst through the gap and then turned hard to the right. As soon as it straightened out to speed toward the chokepoint, a second vehicle entered the gap and followed the first one. Before the third one arrived, I lifted my head far enough to see what we were dealing with. The second vehicle's headlights were aimed directly at a pickup truck, and I was able to make out a heavy machine gun mounted high enough to shoot over the cab. Whoever the people were, they were ready for a fight.

I told the others what I had seen, and we all kept our heads down as we counted six trucks passing through the gap. When the last one roared away toward the chokepoint, Jean reached for the ignition key. I put one hand on hers and shook my head.

"These people haven't lasted this long by accident."

Jean's eyes met mine in the dark cab, and she remembered why we had her covering us from behind earlier.

"A stringer," she said. "Remind me to tell the Chief how well you filled in for him."

Almost ten minutes after the last pickup truck went by, we heard voices coming from the direction of the trees on the other side of the opening between the wrecked cars. It sounded like at least four men were arguing with each other, and they were way too loud to be formally trained for night patrols.

"How come I always have to walk? Just once, I'd like to be in one of the trucks."

"Shut up, Cole. I've had enough of your whining."

"Make me shut up, Jeff. You're not my boss."

"Both of you knock it off. What's the point in having the rear if you make so much noise? Someone could hear you two arguing a mile away."

"Did you guys see what someone did to Stevie's hand? There wasn't much left of it," said a fourth voice.

The voice that told the others to be quiet said, "Stevie probably did something to deserve it. Now shut up and keep your eyes open."

The voices faded as the men walked up the center of the road to where the trucks had reached the top of the overpass. They had undoubtedly found the big guy with a bullet in his head and the infected dead with a gag in its mouth sprawled out on top of him. By now, they were trying to find a clue as to what had transpired.

Almost an hour later, the trucks coasted at a low speed down the middle of the road and made slow turns into the gap as they drove back to their base. We waited another hour just in case their stringer patrol followed them, but our best guess was that they had been sent into the trees near the bottom of the overpass to search for whoever had shot their friends, because the men on foot never came back.

Wally seemed to snap out of his mental fog and made a suggestion we couldn't ignore. We agreed with him, and he quietly got out of the truck as Jean released the hood. He came back with a handful of relay switches that controlled the lights.

"Here," he said, "we can put these back in later when we need to, but at least no one will see our tail lights as we drive away."

Jean turned us around in the direction of Lynchburg, but we

had no idea how we were going to get around the high school football stadium to go north. At best, we would be adding another day to our trip.

STAY ALIVE

Niagara Falls - 2016

The sound of the infected dead inside the garage was so loud that it covered any noise made by the door as it opened, but some of them were facing the four frightened people from only a short distance away. They escalated their groans to a level that seemed to draw the attention of the others. It was almost as if they were communicating to the rest that there were living people nearby. To Tori and Denise, that was exactly what was happening. They had no way of knowing that the dead people were simply drawn to the increased noise being made by the others, and it wouldn't have made a difference if they had known. There was no way they were going to be able to hide their presence from the dead people as they made their way across the garage.

Tori said, "We have to get up on top of the cars and cross from one to the other until we get to the other side."

"There must be a hundred cars between us and the outside," answered Denise.

"Unless you have a better idea, it's our only chance. We can't stay here."

Tori motioned with one hand for Jalen to move closer to her, and she scooped him up in her arms.

"You're heavier than you look, buddy."

To Denise, she added, "I don't have much experience with kids, and we can take turns when I get tired, but we can do this. You can help Jacob from one car to the other."

Denise didn't have a chance to object. It wasn't easy watching a total stranger carry her younger son away toward the cars, but if they were going to live another day, they couldn't sit in the doorway of the power plant. She took Jacob by the hand and moved as fast as she could to catch up with Tori. She had already guessed she was only a few years older than Tori, but the younger woman had a more athletic body. Denise had stayed fit just by keeping up with her two boys, but it was obvious that Tori could carry Jalen easier than her.

In the dim light of the parking garage, the cars were a solid wall that blocked them from leaving. They were wedged together so haphazardly that Tori couldn't see a clear path to the outside, even going over the rooftops. She suddenly realized she had never climbed onto the roof of a car in her whole life, and she didn't know where to start. The lowest spot was the dark blue hood of a small SUV. Its smashed front end was embedded into the passenger side door of a sports car, and it would have been a good place to start if not for the dead woman who was trying to climb out the smashed window of the sports car onto the hood of the SUV. Tori thought about lifting Jalen onto the hood closer to the windshield and pushing him onto the roof of the SUV, but for her to follow him, she would be within reach of the dead woman.

Tori passed the rear of the sports car and saw that the next vehicle was a white pickup truck with oversized tires, and the bed was empty. Both sides of the truck were flush against two other cars. The sports car on the right sat so far below the truck that they couldn't see into the car. That meant the dead lady and her companion, the driver, couldn't see them.

"It's a starting point," she said to Denise. "One down with

about a hundred to go."

Tori lowered the tailgate and put Jalen into the bed of the truck. After she climbed up with him, she helped Denise and Jacob. When she stood to her full height and surveyed the garage, the scene before her was good news and bad news. The good news was that the higher vantage point helped her see multiple paths to the other side of the garage. The bad news was that she could also see that the fire from the upper floors was causing burning debris to fall onto the garage. Clouds of smoke were going to fill the bottom level before they got out if they didn't move faster.

Denise saw the same things, and as Tori searched for the best escape route, Denise remembered the key fobs. The only escape route that mattered was the one that got them closest to the cars that matched the fobs. She caught Tori by her shirt sleeve and held out a fob to her.

"We can use these. Once we know which cars they go to, we can get closer to them."

Tori took the fob from her and aimed it toward the other side of the garage. She pressed the button with a little picture of a horn on it. The horn was loud and sounded oddly metallic inside the garage. She had only pressed it once, and they weren't exactly sure which horn had sounded, but once was enough for them to know the car would be useless. It was too close to them and was in the middle of the tightly packed vehicles.

Tori raised her arm in frustration and was ready to throw the fob at the nearest infected dead, but Denise stopped her.

"Wait...we can use the horn as a distraction. We have to move fast."

Denise pointed at the smoke that was rising toward the ceiling as it entered the garage.

"Right," said Tori. "The honking horn will at least keep the attention of the dead people, and I have another idea. The smoke's coming in from the right side, so let's try to find a path around the left."

Moving against time as the smoke rolled closer, they crossed over the cab of the pickup truck and hopped onto the hood of the next car that was out of the reach of the dead people. It was hard not to trip on the places where hoods weren't buckled by collisions, and they had to backtrack twice before they were even halfway to the other side of the garage.

Tori stopped on the hood of a car and put Jalen down. She held up a palm toward Denise.

"There's no way around this spot. The gap is full of dead people," she said.

It only took two seconds for her to turn around and tell Denise they had to find another way, but when she faced the crowded gap between the cars again, Jalen was gone. As he disappeared, there was only a glimpse of the green and red shirt he was wearing. The dead people between the cars converged on the spot, and Tori could only watch.

Behind her, Denise was screaming, and Tori had to move quickly to block her as she tried to go after her son. Tori wrapped her arms around Denise and pulled her backward. Their feet were sliding out from under them, but Tori knew that letting Denise go into the middle of those dead people would be suicide. They fell onto the hood of the car behind them and then rolled together over the side. It seemed like it came from miles away, but they could hear Jalen's screams mixed in with the chaos of the infected dead.

Tori and Denise landed hard on the concrete floor of the garage. The impact knocked the wind out of both women, but Tori kept her arms firmly wrapped around Denise to keep her from getting away. Denise was still screaming and sobbing.

"My boy...my little boy! I've got to help him!"

Her words ended with a gut-wrenching sob, and she buried her face into Tori's neck in resignation. Tori held her close, not knowing what else she could do for her. Her left shoulder burned from the fall to the concrete, and despite being worried it might be serious, she bit her teeth together against the pain and squeezed Denise harder.

The pain had also made Tori wince so hard that her eyelids were pressed shut, but she felt like she would hear the awful screams for the rest of her life. When she finally opened her eyes, she saw something she didn't understand. Through Denise's thick brown hair that fell across her own face, she saw the soles of a pair of sneakers, and they were moving away from where she and Denise were wrapped around each other on the floor. They were plain sneakers worn by millions of kids, and the cuffs of the denim jeans were rolled up because they overlapped onto the shoes. Tori had noticed the cuffs of Jacob's pants when she had pulled Denise and her boys inside.

The sneakers were moving in the direction where Jalen had disappeared, and Tori saw the toes pushing against the concrete floor as if the owner of the feet was swimming away. Just as suddenly, the feet were reaching toward her a few inches at a time as the toes dug hard into the floor. There was a longer pause been each stroke, but gradually, the distance between the feet and Tori decreased, and she could see Jacob's outstretched arms dragging Jalen closer with every new purchase of his toes.

Tori crawled over Denise and reached for Jacob's ankle. He tried to kick free from her grip at first, thinking he had been caught by one of the dead people, but when he realized it was Tori, he stretched his leg toward her. Denise rolled over on her back under Tori and saw Jacob's face. Beyond him was Jalen's dirt-smudged face, streaked with tears, but crawling under the car toward her.

Denise held both of her sons against her with enough force to make Jacob complain that he couldn't breathe. When he broke free, Denise frantically checked Jalen from head to toe to see if he was hurt. He had scrapes on his elbows from crawling across the concrete, and there was a bruise on his forehead, but she was relieved to see there were no open wounds. By the time she was done with Jalen, Tori had finished her inspection of Jacob.

"He's fine...not a scratch," she said just to make them all feel better.

Denise hugged him and then ruffled his hair.

"That was very brave of you to save your little brother."

Jacob gave her a weak smile but said, "Dad would've done it if he was here."

Tori picked up Jalen and said, "We need to move, and this time, we have to do it like it's an obstacle course, and we have to beat a time limit. We can't afford to stop to measure each jump. Once we start going forward, we can't stop. Got it?"

From her knees on the floor, Denise could see the smoke above and behind Tori, and she understood. If they didn't get out before the smoke reached them, they wouldn't be able to breathe. Denise stood up and pointed toward the place where the smoke was entering the parking structure. There were dozens of dead people already enshrouded by the thickest cloud of smoke, and they weren't choking for air.

"The smoke isn't killing them," said Denise.

Tori said, "A butter knife will, but the smoke won't."

"What?"

"There's no time to explain. I'll tell you after we get out of here."

Tori told Jalen to hang on tight and climbed up onto the car again. She held out a hand and helped Jacob and Denise up. She gave final instructions to Denise before assaulting the obstacle course.

"Keep Jacob in front of you the whole time. If he can't make a jump, pick him up and throw him as hard as you can. I'll be ready to grab him."

Tori turned to face the first jump and found that the dead people were still in a pile, searching for Jalen. It made it easier for her to reach the next car, and the one after that had a clear path over several vehicles. She was allowed to develop some momentum that helped her jump a little further each time, but her legs burned as if she really was on an obstacle course in an Army basic training center. She was grateful for the fact that tennis had been her passion, and she jumped, weaved, changed course, and rushed ahead with every bit of energy she had. She pushed out of her mind the possibility that she would come to a jump she couldn't make, and she couldn't worry about whether or not Denise and Jacob were able to keep up.

The smoke closed in around Tori and burned at her throat and eyes. She held Jalen's face against her neck to protect him as she jumped, but it was becoming harder to see by the second. She thought she had misjudged the distance between two cars because she didn't feel a solid surface under her foot. She was falling, and there was nothing she could do about it.

As she hit the ground, she fell into the sunlight that barely filtered through rain clouds. She welcomed the drizzle of water that rinsed the smoke from her eyes, and she greedily gulped at the fresh air. Smoke was billowing from the parking garage, but it was running up the side of the building as if it had been trapped inside, too. Jalen coughed against her neck and rubbed at his eyes. She would normally have tried to stop him, but she had something more important to worry about. She got her feet under her again and pushed herself up from the ground. Tori felt the burning sensation in her left ankle, which confirmed in her mind that she most likely sprained it on the final jump, but she backed away and waited anxiously for Denise to appear.

If it had taken one more minute for her new friend and her son to emerge from the smoke, Tori might have gone back in to find them. Denise and Jacob both landed hard, but neither of them was bleeding. Tori let Jalen go to his mother while she helped Jacob up from the ground. She used her own shirt to wipe his eyes and reassured him that everything was going to be okay now. He coughed and gasped for air, but through each fit, he did his best to tell her he was okay. Tori hadn't known the boy before the craziness had started, but she imagined he had been someone his parents could be proud of. He had been forced to accept some unimaginable, unexplainable horrors in a short time.

One glance around the parking lot outside was all Tori needed in order for her to know they had a short window of opportunity. The chaos that existed inside the garage had not happened outside. She guessed the only explanation was that guests of the hotel hadn't made it past the garage. A sign a few yards away told her they were at the edge of the rental car lot. Another sign pointed toward the valet parking area, and Tori had an idea.

"Why didn't I think of this sooner?" she said. "Give me all of the key fobs...quick. We have to get out of here."

Denise dumped the pile of car remotes on the ground. In the middle of the colorful tags, she saw a fob with the initials RC printed on it. She felt a momentary surge of emotion that caused her to get a lump in her throat.

"Where did you get that key fob?" she asked Denise.

"I don't know," she answered. "It was just hanging on the board with all of the others."

Tori understood that Randy must have had his favorite

car delivered to the lot and given her the key as a way to make her think they would be driving the rental. It made her think of his sense of humor and wonder what had happened to him after he left the bathroom. The idea that Randy was somewhere in the hotel or outside in the courtyard with those other dead people was overwhelming. She picked up the fob that had belonged to her new husband and aimed it in the general direction of the valet parking area. She pressed the horn button once just to see if she was within range of the car. At least she knew which car to look for.

Randy could have afforded any model car he wanted, but he was really in love with his Series 4, all-wheel-drive, six-cylinder convertible. He had bought it a year earlier, and Tori had teased him about how she thought he loved the car more than her. When she would ask him to pick her or the car, he would always get a distant expression on his face as if he was considering the question. Then he would smile and tell her he would make a concession and name the car after her.

The single burst from the horn of Randy's BMW was surprisingly close, and she was glad she wouldn't need to do it again and draw the attention of the dead that were spread out in the parking area. Denise was gasping for air as much as her sons, but she also understood that they were too exposed outside of the garage. They had made it through the worst part. Now, all they had to do was drive out of the area. She knew that it was likely to be bad, but they would at least have the protection of the car.

Tori felt a sudden gut punch from the memory of Randy behind the wheel of his favorite car. Randy's handsome face would be slightly tilted to one side, and the corners of his mouth would have the faintest upward curve. She didn't realize that she hadn't even been given the opportunity to grieve, and it froze her in her tracks. She stood in the parking lot and just stared into the distance. She couldn't see the falls, but she only had one thought.

She said out loud, "This was supposed to be my honeymoon."

Denise said in her most urgent voice, "Hey, we need to go now."

She held Jalen and Jacob pulled against her protectively, and she was waiting for Tori to lead the way. She saw the way Tori's shoulders slumped, and she knew instinctively that Tori was feeling the same loss she was. They hadn't been afforded the time to talk about how they had gotten to the same place in the power plant, but Denise didn't think Tori had been at the hotel by herself. Hearing her say it was her honeymoon just confirmed what she had been thinking about her new companion. There wasn't time to talk about it before, but there certainly wasn't enough time to talk about it standing in the parking lot next to the burning hotel that was surrounded by dead people who were cannibals.

"Tori! Which car?"

Tori snapped out of it when Denise yelled, and she grabbed her backpack as she scooped up Jalen. Denise followed closely with Jacob, and they ran toward the blue BMW that Tori knew so well. They stashed the boys and their gear in the back seat and just as quickly got in the front seats. Denise was grateful, but it crossed her mind that she would rather have a solid roof over her head.

As soon as Tori backed out of the parking spot, she knew what it was going to be like navigating through the chaos, so she punched the accelerator hard. Denise felt her body sink into her seat as she groped for her seatbelt, and it crossed her mind for a second time that she would have preferred to be in something like an armored car or a tank.

The dead people seemed to be going somewhere. A few turned toward them when Tori started the car, but the vast majority were flocking in the direction of the burning hotel. The sound of the fire consuming new fuel was growing as more floors became involved. Glass exploded from windows as heat and gases built up inside the rooms, and with each burst of noise, the dead were distracted away from the parking lot.

Tori made a sharp right turn out of the aisle where the car had been parked and found herself on the main access road that would lead them to the entrance of the valet parking lot. Denise had a clear view of the hotel and stared in amazement at the number of dead people who were walking toward the conflagration. She was also stunned by how many living people were still trapped inside. She had imagined that she, her boys, and Tori were the only survivors. She didn't know what had given her that idea, but she was able to see firsthand just how wrong she had been.

The guests on the other side of the hotel had paid a premium for a view of Niagara Falls, and those rooms had most likely been full of tourists, but Denise saw people daring to jump from far more balconies than she expected. People hung from open windows that belched black smoke, and when the orange and yellow flames licked at the window sills, the people were forced to let go. She couldn't hear them, but she knew their anguished cries were summoning the dead who waited at the bottom of the building.

Tori swerved to avoid a group of dead people who walked across the road in front of them, and she yelped as the car clipped one with the right fender. It sent the man spinning like a bowling pin into the rest of them. Denise wasn't pleased with herself for getting that random thought, but the whole situation was enough to lower a normal person to that level. She didn't realize that she had voiced her random thought until Tori laughed.

Denise gripped the curved handle on the passenger door as if it were her only hold on reality and stared at Tori in disbelief.

They were in a convertible, speeding away from a burning hotel without her husband, in a parking lot full of dead people who were walking despite being dead, and her new companion was laughing. The world had turned upside down.

Tori swerved again and had to keep her eyes on the road in front of them, but she kept laughing and glancing at Denise. Denise thought Tori had lost her mind, but Tori thought Denise had indulged in some pretty good gallows humor.

"A spare?" said Tori. "Did you really just give me a spare for taking down those last three by only hitting one?"

Denise suddenly realized that she must have said it out loud, and despite her embarrassment, her gallows humor was contagious. She laughed along with Tori, and in the back seat, the frightened boys felt better. They didn't know what was so funny, but they were reassured by the laughter.

Denise caught her breath and said, "Don't try for a strike."

That caused a new round of laughter, and they let go of some of the fear and tension that had built up inside them the same way the smoke and gases had caused the hotel windows to explode outward. Tori pushed down on the accelerator to speed through an opening in the road, and just as they were leaving the chaos behind them, they were leaving behind some of their old selves. They were escaping, and that meant they had a chance to live.

The BMW leaned into the curve outside the parking lot and shot down a stretch of open road going east. Tori only slowed down to avoid abandoned vehicles in the middle of the road.

******

The congestion on the roads caused them to drive slower when they were close to populated areas, but the country roads were remarkably clear. Without much advance warning of what was happening to the world, people didn't have time to get far enough away from the infection before it overwhelmed the cities.

As it grew dark outside, the steady drone of the engine lulled the boys to sleep, but Denise kept turning the radio dial to find any news that was different from what they already knew. There were prerecorded loops from FEMA on most of the channels, but sometimes, they got bits and pieces from people who were in isolated places, and they were relaying what they were told by people who were running ahead of the infection. Denise settled on one broadcast that came through clearly, and they listened to the young man as he spoke softly about how bad it had gotten. He sounded like he had reached his limit of bad news already.

Um, this is WNPY 93.4 on your dial, and if you haven't heard yet, this would be a great time to get inside your shelter if you have one. If you don't have one, lock your doors and stay home. Repeating the news we have from FEMA and a short broadcast from the White House, there's some kind of outbreak, and it's not just local. It's a worldwide outbreak that's...um.

The man paused, but they could hear him choke back his emotions. He cleared his throat and exhaled a heavy sigh before he went on. His next piece of news may have been responsible for his need to stop.

"The outbreak has spread around the world. If you have a loved one...if you have a loved one or a friend who has been bitten by someone, the police advise you to keep them at home, isolated from everyone else. Do not take them to a hospital. There's no treatment that will help someone once they're infected."

The boys were asleep, but Denise kept her voice low anyway.

"My husband was sick."

"Was he bitten?" asked Tori.

"No, but he punched a guy in the mouth in Virginia Beach. I think he cut his hand on the man's teeth."

Tori waited for Denise to go on. She had more questions, but the young man on the radio was only saying things she already knew.

"When did he get sick?"

Denise had slipped back into her memories of the past few days, and Tori's question startled her.

"I'm sorry," said Tori, misunderstanding Denise's reaction.

"Oh, no...that's okay. I was just remembering how healthy Brad was before it happened. We were having so much fun on the beach until this strange man showed up. I mean, he wasn't dressed for the beach, you know. He was wearing clothes like he should be in an office or something. He got too close to the boys, and Brad punched him. We left, but then Brad started to get really sick."

Tori listened to what Denise was saying, but her mind went back and forth. She didn't even know what had happened to Randy. He had left her in the bathroom and hadn't come back.

"Where's your husband now?"

"I locked him in the bedroom in the hotel. Actually, I didn't know that much about what was going on outside, and if I hadn't seen that one news broadcast, I would've been clueless."

"Wait a minute," said Tori. "You were at the beach? When was that? How'd you get here?"

It was becoming obvious to both of them that they each

knew a little about what was going on, but neither of them had anything near the full story. They needed to piece their facts together if they wanted to figure out what they needed to do next.

"I guess I should start at the beginning," said Denise.

Denise started over again and explained that they had flown to Virginia Beach and that they had left in a hurry after the incident with the strange man. She told Tori what happened when they tried to land at Ithaca Tompkins Airport and about how they were diverted to Niagara International.

Denise said, "I didn't understand what was happening at the time. EMTs met our plane and treated Brad's hand, but they were only interested in how he got hurt. They wanted to know if he had been bitten, and once he told them he had cut his hand when he punched a guy, they hurried off like they had better things to do. I guess if they had made the connection and realized Brad had cut his hand on the man's teeth, they would have done something else."

"Like what?" asked Tori.

"I don't know. Maybe they would've rushed him to the hospital. Maybe they would've been able to help him."

Tori got a mental image of Rose, the hotel employee with the butter knife sticking out of her head. Something told her that Denise's husband would have faced a similar fate if the paramedics had realized he had cut his hand on someone's teeth. It wasn't exactly the same as being bitten, but the results were obviously the same.

"Anyway," said Denise, "that's how we got stuck in the hotel. We were planning to rent a car and drive back to Ithaca."

They were quiet for a few moments and listened to the voice on the radio. The man droned on about inane things like rationing canned goods, filling the bathtub with water, and cooking frozen foods while people still had power. It was all useful stuff, but he kept talking as if there was going to be help coming soon.

"What about you?" asked Denise. "How much do you know?"

For the sake of Denise and the sleeping boys in the back seat, Tori chose her words carefully.

"Randy and I were on our honeymoon. I don't even know for sure where he is."

Denise reacted anyway. Even though she had just left her husband and the father of her children locked in the bedroom of a burning hotel, she was devastated by the news that Tori had lost her husband so soon.

"You didn't see any news? I mean, before you saved me and my boys, what happened?"

Tori told Denise that she had seen what was happening at the top of Niagara Falls, but she didn't have a clue what it meant. She left out details in case one of the boys woke up, but she told her about Rose and the butter knife.

"You mean that's the only way they can be stopped?" asked Denise.

Tori nodded, but then she told her about how she had gotten to the power plant of the hotel and how she had stumbled across the Luger and bayonet in her backpack. It took a few minutes of silence for it to sink in, but it occurred to Denise that it was going to be hard to survive if they had to stab people in the head with a bayonet.

Denise said, "You know, we crushed a guy under a desk, right?"

"I don't think it made a difference to him how it happened," said Tori.

They kept talking in low whispers for the next hour until Tori yawned uncontrollably. By that time, they both knew what each of them had learned so far. Denise suggested that they could find a safe place to pull over for the night. The stress of everything that had piled up on them, and they were exhausted.

As Tori pulled off the pavement into a heavily wooded dirt road, she said, "We still don't know where we can go. I can't reach my parents to get help."

"I'm not sure what anyone can do for us, or what's happening to the world," said Denise, "but at least we do have somewhere to go that's safe."

"We do?"

"Yes, but get some sleep first. I'll tell you more about it in the morning, and it's really not that far from here."

THE CHASE

Amherst County - 2025

Stevie landed flat on his back on the *meat pile* at the bottom of the overpass. If he had been lucky, the fall would have broken his neck, and he would have died quickly. He was alive after he landed, and since his shattered hand still hurt, he knew it wasn't his lucky day. The mound of infected dead that had accumulated to create the *meat pile* cushioned his landing, but they also greeted his arrival with hungry mouths.

His screaming was what drew the attention of the first group to arrive, but the men in the truck were surprised to see it was one of their own people. They had expected it to be someone caught in the chokepoint by Stevie and his partner, Baldwin. Baldwin was one of their best men, and Stevie was never sent out on patrol by himself because he was likely to get himself killed. That was why it wasn't completely unexpected to find him on the *meat pile*, but it meant something had happened to Baldwin.

"Someone drag him down from there and shut him up before he wakes up every deadhead that can still walk. Make sure he tells you what happened before he dies."

The order came from the bald man behind the wheel of the pickup truck. Ted Branch's muscular body was big enough to make the full-sized pickup truck appear small, and he had a perpetual scowl that made the rest of the men afraid to make eye contact with him. When he gave an order to do something, he didn't want anyone to waste time by acknowledging the order. He just wanted it done fast.

The second truck came to a stop with its headlights aimed at the pile of bodies, and two men from the back of each truck climbed down and cautiously approached the reaching hands of the infected dead. They dodged hands and shook a few loose when they managed to catch the legs of their pants, but they paid closer attention to the ones that reached for them with their teeth.

One of the men managed to get a grip on Stevie's right ankle and pulled until Stevie slid down the slope of the pile toward him. Stevie screamed even more on his way down because one of the dead had sunk its teeth into Stevie's left cheek. Something had to give, and his left cheek stayed where it was as Stevie slid free. He also slid over more of the dead on his way down. There was no telling how many times he was bitten, but each new bite elicited more screams.

Despite the fact that Stevie had been a member of their group, he was dragged without sympathy away from the pile, and as soon as the back of his head touched the open ground, one of the men put a big hand over his mouth to stifle his screaming.

"Ow!"

The man yanked his hand away, and Stevie didn't wait one second to start again. It was obvious to the others, judging by the amount of blood on the man's hand, that Stevie had bitten him hard. They all backed away from him as Branch got out of the pickup truck.

"Branch," said one of the men, "he's not going to tell us anything. He's too broke up."

Even before the man finished talking, Branch delivered a solid kick to the side of Stevie's head. The screaming stopped immediately, and Branch turned his attention to the man who tried to cover Stevie's mouth with a bare hand.

The man pleaded, "No, Boss...it's not that bad, and he wasn't even infected yet. There wasn't enough time for him to be infected."

"Come on now, Tony. You don't know that," said Branch. "No one knows that."

Branch took a step toward the man and said in a softer voice, "It's alright, Tony. You know how it is. We don't know, do we?"

Tony opened his mouth to answer, but before he could speak, a burlap sack was yanked over his head from behind. It wasn't the first time they had needed to subdue a member of the group using the burlap sack. He had just kept Tony's attention long enough for a couple of the men to get behind him. The two men dumped Tony on the ground and pulled his arms behind his back.

Inside the sack, Tony flailed his head from side to side and did his best to plead his case, but the group had kept its membership largely intact by setting a few simple rules in place. The first rule was the basis for most of the other rules. Getting bitten by a deadhead was a death sentence. It was a fact that all bites were fatal, and even though there had been attempts to save lives by amputating limbs, there had never been a success. They would never know if death was a result of the bite or the brutal, improvised surgical procedure.

The second rule was a spinoff of the first rule. If there was any doubt about the nature of the bite, the victim would be bagged and tied to a bed. If they didn't develop the infection, they would get to live. Since no one knew if Stevie's bite was infectious, the bag was the only choice for Tony.

"Take him back. The rest of us are gonna find Baldwin."

The men picked Tony up and pushed him toward one of the trucks while Branch led the rest of the convoy toward the entrance of the chokepoint. The stringers were dropped off about a quarter of a mile later by the last truck in the column.

It was easy for Branch to put together some pieces of the puzzle. The deadhead lying across Baldwin's body was probably an interesting story, but Branch was only interested in how Baldwin got a bullet in his head. He didn't think Stevie shot him and then jumped from the top of the overpass. Whoever threw Stevie off must have shot Baldwin. He eyed the scrawny deadhead with a gag in her mouth. It wasn't attracted to Baldwin anymore because Branch was a living, breathing person, but it was having a hard time getting to its feet.

Branch pulled a pistol from his hip and almost pulled the trigger, but even he tried to follow the rules, and one of them was to never shoot a deadhead unless there was no other way to dispose of them. He grabbed the wasted woman by the back of the neck and walked her to the edge of the overpass, tossing her to the pile of bodies below as easily as if she weighed nothing more than an empty soda can.

When Branch turned to the rest of the vehicles, he gave rapid-fire orders. Whoever had killed Baldwin and Stevie couldn't have gotten a big head start, and he wanted them found before they could get away.

"They must be around here somewhere. I want people on the ground in all directions. Get word back to the base that I want everyone searching. No one sleeps until we catch whoever did this."

******

We didn't know if we were being followed yet, and there was barely enough moonlight to see the pavement of the highway ahead of us, so we could hardly manage to go more than ten to fifteen miles per hour. To the east of us, we could still see the way the stadium lights reflected from the clouds.

"That's not a good sign," said Jean. "Whoever they are, they must have an endless supply of power, but that many lights must be eating into their reserves."

"What's that mean?" asked Ruth.

I said, "That means we kicked a hornet's nest. They're mad enough to be mobilizing to find us no matter what it costs."

"Can we outrun them?" asked Wally.

He had been quiet up until that question because he felt like he was responsible for the mess they were in, but we didn't see it the same way. Jean was still driving, so she said what she knew I was going to say without even looking back at Wally. She probably wouldn't have been able to see him anyway.

"Listen to me, Wally. You did the same thing that most people would have done under the circumstances, but in a weird sort of way, you may have saved our lives. By giving up your position to those two morons, you kept the rest of us from getting caught. As for outrunning them, that's something I can't answer yet. It all depends on whether or not they've locked down the area."

"What's that mean?" asked Ruth for a second time.

Jean said, "It's something we've done near all of our shelters in one way or another, but you don't think that overpass collapsed on its own, do you?"

I added, "They probably blew that up a long time ago, then they created that vehicle wall on both sides of the road as a funnel for the infected dead. The dead walk up to the top and fall off. We've done the same thing with bridges. It's pretty effective."

"But we already know about the overpass," said Wally.

Even in the dark pickup truck, we could tell by the sound of his voice that he figured it out as he said it. His voice trailed off, and then he said, "But we don't know if there are others."

"Right," said Jean. "If they got the idea by watching the infected fall over the sides of the overpass or a bridge somewhere near here, they probably created more chokepoints surrounding their main camp. From the looks of it, their main camp is that high school football stadium, and we were only about a mile from it. That means they would do the same thing for about a mile in all directions."

Jean's suspicions were confirmed only a few minutes later, and it was a good thing we weren't driving at a high speed.

Ruth said, "There are cars lined up bumper to bumper on both sides of the road again."

"What's that up ahead?" I asked.

The brightest part of the sky was still the distant stadium lights, but up until that moment, we had been driving along a dark road with trees on both sides. There was an opening in the trees up ahead and the faint outline of something against the sky. We didn't have a clue what it was until we were almost to it, but Jean's comment about bridges made us recognize the shape of the outline. She braked the truck to a stop well short of the bridge and cut off the engine. The dark road and trees around us were totally silent.

"Why did we stop?" asked Wally.

"Be very quiet," said Jean. "No one talks after we get out of the truck. Don't close your doors. Even the sound of the hinges might carry too far out here."

"We may have to abandon our transportation," I whispered. "If there's debris in the road, be careful to step around it. One last thing. We have to walk single-file to reduce our profile if there's someone up ahead. Jean will lead, I'll follow her, and you two decide who should be next, but watch us for signals."

All four of us got out of the pickup truck and walked silently toward the bridge. Ruth had been right about vehicles making a solid wall on both sides of the road. Any living person could easily go over them, but the infected would just keep walking forward until they came to whatever it was the people had waiting for them up ahead. Of course, chokepoints were effective traps for living people who didn't know what they were.

I could tell that this particular trap must have been very effective when hordes traveled the roads in large numbers. Sometimes, a group of them would walk along a road and make such a racket that strays would join them out of attraction to the noise. The horde would grow until hundreds or thousands of them would be walking together, and if they came to this particular bridge chokepoint, I wondered what would happen.

I didn't have to wonder very long. Jean lightly snapped two fingers together to get my attention, and then she held her hand out to stop the rest of us from walking forward. She hardly moved her head at all when she whispered instructions for me to pass along.

"The bridge is blocked at the midpoint. Directly above the blockade is some kind of lookout shack."

I focused my eyes on the spot where I thought she meant was the midpoint. It took a moment, but I gradually made out the rectangular shape of the lookout shack.

"You have good eyes," I said just loud enough for her to know I heard her.

"Tell Ruth and Wally we're going to move to the left side of the road and crawl under a car into the trees."

I passed the instructions back to the others and then waited for Jean to move. When she stepped to the left, we all moved as a group until we were against the same vehicle. Then we lowered ourselves to the ground and slid under it.

"Why can't we just go back and find another way around?" asked Wally as we all emerged in the tall grass close to the trees.

"We can't even start the pickup truck again," said Jean. "If someone is in that lookout shack, they're probably asleep because they're bored, but the sound of the truck's engine would be like someone dropped a bomb out here."

To me, she asked, "Can you see the trap?"

"I think so. It's hard to tell without light, but I think the guardrail is gone on the right side of the bridge before the barricade. Any infected dead that walk out there would probably drop right off the side. Is there a river below the bridge?"

"I don't know," said Jean. "Wally, did you ever come this way before?"

Wally was glad to have a chance to contribute again, and he nodded as he said, "Not a deep one, but the bridge is high enough to kill you if you fall off."

Jean was the smallest member of our group. At just under five feet tall, she would be the hardest one to see, even if someone was watching from the guard shack. We both felt like we could scout the bridge, but we had been surviving together long enough to know what was best. There would be no argument about which of us would be better at it.

"I'll stay close to the left side," said Jean, "so don't expect to see me cross the road unless something goes wrong. I'll be back in less than thirty minutes."

She crawled under the last car before the bridge, and when she emerged from below the front bumper, she hugged her body against the concrete base that supported the railing along the left side. I crawled behind her but stayed under the car when she crawled away. I wanted to be able to see her for as long as I could, and I also felt like I could give her cover if she had to get off the bridge fast.

It was hard to move around under the car, but I managed to get my M4 in front of me and propped it over my backpack so it could be aimed upward at the guard shack. I dug out my binoculars and studied the dark rectangle. I could see that it was bigger than we had expected. What we had thought was a long shadow was actually the full size of it. At first glance, we could tell it was rectangular, but we didn't realize it was a cargo container turned lengthwise to the bridge, and we were just facing one end of it. There was a crude window facing our way, and I didn't doubt there were others. I lowered my binoculars a bit and strained to see if there was a rope ladder, but I couldn't find anything to indicate how guards would come or go from the top of the bridge.

I felt a tap on my foot and, for a moment, thought I had an infected dead under the car with me.

"It's us," whispered Ruth. "We have company in the trees."

Wally and Ruth both squeezed under the car with me. We were shoulder to shoulder between the rear wheels.

"How many?" I whispered.

Wally said, "No tellin' because it's so dark, but from the sound of it, there's more than one."

We couldn't crawl out from under the car into the road, so our best bet was to stay where we were and keep still. I told Ruth and Wally not to move even if they felt spiders crawling up their pant legs. I regretted it as soon as I said it because I was more afraid of spiders than both of them combined.

The infected dead showed up on our left ten minutes later. Jean said she would be gone for about thirty minutes, and I hoped she didn't come back early. Over Wally's back, I counted four sets of legs as the infected encountered the row of cars with no gaps between them. They stumbled up the slight incline on the side of the road and walked into the sides of the cars as if they could walk right through them, and then they fanned out to the left and right.

I knew Wally was petrified, and I put a hand on his arm in the hope that it would keep him from panicking. I was horrified by how badly he was shaking. If he couldn't stay still, the infected dead wouldn't hesitate to come under the car after us.

The legs I could see were spread out from the front to the back of the car, and I knew more infected dead had arrived when I heard them make contact with the car behind us. The commotion was just loud enough to get the attention of the group gathered only inches away from Wally's left arm, and it was enough to make them go in that direction. I watched them walk away on unsteady legs until they were past the rear tires of the car where we were hiding.

I let out a sigh of relief as I turned my attention back to the bridge, but I froze when I saw there was something different about the guard shack suspended above the barricade. At first, I thought it was one of the sentries who was supposed to be watching the road, but then I realized someone was climbing from the top of the cargo container and crawling inside through the crude window.

All I could think at that moment was how mad Jean would be if she saw me pulling that stunt. It was bad enough that she found a way to climb up to the guard shack, but climbing inside was crazy. I didn't know what she could see through the window, but there was no way to stop her now.

"How long has Jean been gone?" whispered Ruth.

I didn't answer because I was straining my eyes for any sign of Jean in the dark square of the window, and Ruth must have figured it out because she didn't ask again.

******

Jean crawled until she reached the barricade across the bridge. The bridge was only two lanes across, so it was easy to block it with a few cars, but someone had added large sheets of metal to the sides of the cars for good measure. She wondered why the guard shack suspended from the framework of the bridge was even necessary when the barricade was so solid, but she guessed someone wanted the extra advantage it would give them on both sides of the barricade.

She found the ladder on the outside edge of the support beam on the left end of the barricade, and she was reasonably sure that her profile was small enough that she wouldn't be seen from above if she climbed it. Directly across from her, she saw that there was a large gap in the railing on the right side of the bridge.

"So, that's how it works," she said to herself. "The infected dead walk out onto the bridge until they reach the barricade, then they walk through the opening in the railing and fall off the bridge. If survivors approach the barrier, they get a choice. They can jump from the bridge or get shot from above as they try to escape."

Jean didn't remember who called her *Pixie* the first time. It was either the Chief or Eddie. Her short height and cute haircut made people underestimate her, but after they got to know her, they knew she was fearless. She knew she couldn't assume there weren't any guards in the cargo container above, and she knew at any moment that she might see the headlights from the pickup trucks that had come from the stadium. That meant there wasn't enough time to go back and talk it over with Eddie. Besides, he would try to talk her out of it. She put her M4 across her back and pulled herself onto the outside edge of the support beam before she could change her mind.

After Jean was on the ladder and completely hidden behind the support beam, she only paused long enough to peek around it to see if there was any indication she had been spotted from above, and she glanced down once. The river that ran by under her was black and slick, and it seemed like it was right below her, but she guessed it was at least forty feet from the bridge to the water. It wasn't far enough to kill her, but there was no telling if it was shallow or deep. If she fell, she might only be landing on the muddy bottom.

There was no movement in the dark window, so she climbed the ladder as fast as she could. She was surprised by how quickly she found herself above the cargo container, and she stepped carefully down onto its roof. There was a hatch in the center, but opening it would be the same thing as knocking on it.

She thought she felt it sway a bit, but the worst part was her hiking boots. If she took another step, she was sure someone inside would hear her. Jean lowered her body carefully and untied her boot strings. Once she was free from the heavy boots, she moved softly to the edge of the roof above the window.

It was a good thing that Jean wasn't really afraid of heights, or she could never have attempted to drop down from the roof through the window, but she imagined that if Eddie could see her, he wouldn't be too choked up about it. She knew that she could do it, but she was glad it was dark enough to keep her from thinking about how high she was above the pavement. She gripped the edge of the roof and lowered her feet to the rim of the window.

Fortunately, there were plenty of places she could fit her fingers into for handholds, and she curled her toes around the metal frame of the window for balance. The interior of the cargo container was darker than the surface of the river. No light penetrated the metal walls, and it smelled bad due to a lack of ventilation. She hung in the window and waited for her eyes to adjust to the pitch black and hoped she would at least be able to make out shapes inside.

Jean thought to herself, "Why not at least open the hatch on top of the container and let air circulate through this thing? It smells like a gas station restroom."

Something stirred along the left wall near the floor, and she realized her night vision was adjusting to the lack of light. Someone was on the floor and had just rolled over to face the wall. Directly across from that person was a dark shape that appeared to be a large man asleep on his stomach. The tossing and turning of the person on the left caused the container to sway a bit, and the big man rolled over on his back, causing it to sway more.

"That's why they didn't react to the swaying I caused," she thought. "Now, what am I going to do with these guys?"

Up until that moment, Jean didn't really have a plan other than to find out if there was anyone inside the guard shack. She thought about the Chief and what he would say about the risky business she had gotten herself into, and she had to smile at the well-worn saying she knew would be part of the conversation. One of them would eventually say that you couldn't always have a solid plan, and you would have to cross the bridge when you came to it.

In front of her were two sleeping people who were most likely part of that group from the high school, and if the chokepoints and the behavior of the men on the overpass were an indication of the way these people treated other survivors, then it wasn't likely there would be a possibility of mutual cooperation. Over the years, she and her friends had rescued other survivors, and they had formed alliances with anyone who wanted to be friends. They had also been forced to take the offensive. Jean knew that their survival meant the guards had to die unless there was a way to overpower them, and that didn't appear to be an option.

Now, faced with the decision about what to do next, Jean reached into one of her deep pockets and pulled out a road flare. She had an idea of what she needed to do, but lighting the flare was going to be a problem for her, too. She couldn't afford to be blinded by it the way she wanted the guards to be. She put the flare between her teeth and let herself slide through the window until her feet reached the floor. Then she moved along the wall until she was in the corner. She sat down slowly and felt the outsides of her pockets until she found the shape she was looking for.

Jean pulled out a pair of dark sunglasses and put them on. For good measure, she pulled a knitted watch cap from her backpack and pulled it over her head. She rolled it down in front so it would cover the sunglasses and the gaps around the frames. Road flares were extremely bright for a good reason, and she had no doubt she would be able to see it even with protection, but she would only need the glasses and cap for a few seconds. The sleeping guards would only be able to see white light.

Without a sound, Jean moved closer to the sleeping men and held the flare in her left hand roughly between them. She checked the safety of the 9mm on her hip with her left hand to be sure it was off, took a deep breath to steady her nerves, and ignited the flare.

Jean only held the flare long enough to be sure the men made the mistake of looking at it. Then she made a quick flick of her wrist and let it fly to the opposite end of the container. She hadn't seen the weapons on the floor next to each of the sleeping men, but it wouldn't have mattered. Both men groped for rifles that would do them no good in such close quarters, but they also wasted time and tried to shield their eyes against the light.

Jean pulled back the watch cap but kept the sunglasses on. It only took two shots from point-blank range, and despite their few seconds of panic, Jean felt like she had been merciful. She would have preferred another way, but she already felt like she was taking too long, and for all she knew, their pursuers were already getting close. The sound was deafening, and she knew she would have ringing ears for a long time, but she couldn't have risked using her machete even with the advantage she had given herself. If she had only wounded one or both of them, she may have been one of the casualties.

******

Jean had told me she would be back in thirty minutes, but I knew that wasn't going to happen when I saw her go from the roof of the guard shack to the window. I held my breath because I was certain that anything I did to help her would just cost her whatever advantage she thought she had. All I could do was watch the window and hope Jean came out through it first.

The white light inside the cargo container was like an explosion, and to add to that illusion, the gunshots were amplified because the light and sound could only exit through the small window. I didn't know what had happened, but I knew one thing for certain. That much light and that much sound could be seen and heard for miles, and since the window faced straight down the road, the chase would be on if it wasn't already. We wouldn't have long before someone would be driving at a high speed toward the bridge.

I crawled out from under the car and helped pull Wally and Ruth to their feet. The infected dead were already gathered at the side of the car and searched for a way to get by it. They would eventually try to go under it.

"What happened?" said Ruth in a worried voice.

"I hope Jean can answer that question for us all in a few minutes," I answered.

I had lost sight of Jean when she reached the barricade, but I knew she had found a way up to the top of the bridge somehow. I kept glancing toward the light that came from the window, but I was more intent on finding the ladder. When I found it along the left side of the bridge on the outside of a beam, I was surprised to see a dark figure climbing down it. Judging by the size of the person, I hoped I was right that it was Jean.

Jean dropped from the ladder onto the pavement and pulled her boots from around her neck, where she had been wearing them with the laces tied together.

"There wasn't time to put them back on," she said.

I tied one of them for her while she pulled the other boot on.

"What happened? How'd you get out? I didn't see you come out through the window."

"There's a hatch in the roof of that thing, but I'll explain later. That thing looks like a beacon from here," she panted. "We need to get out of here."

Wally said, "That thing's really starting to burn."

We all looked upward and saw he was right. Flames were shooting out of the window, and if that wasn't a big enough problem, exploding ammunition began to add to the noise.

"Follow me," said Jean. "We can use this side of the ladder to climb around the barricade. Now that we're on foot, we need to be as far from here as possible before more company arrives."

I followed Jean when she led the way over the railing and around the barricade, but the expression on her face had me worried. I didn't know the details of what happened in the guard shack, but the fire and gunshots didn't worry me half as much as the haunted look in Jean's eyes. We had seen our share of horror since the beginning of the infection, but we had been spectators for a long time. Something told me Jean had done what she needed to do for us to survive, but it had left a scar.

THE FINGER LAKES

South of Rochester, New York - 2016

"We aren't going to make it, are we?" said Denise.

The sun was just coming up, and the clear morning sky didn't match her mood.

The question jolted Tori awake. Not that she had been completely asleep anyway, but she was slumped back in the driver's seat with her head resting against the window. She didn't realize she was so exhausted until they had pulled off the main road, but as the adrenaline was absorbed from her bloodstream, it left her feeling weak and drained of energy. If she really slept, it was probably only for a few minutes at a time.

"What makes you think that?"

Denise didn't have to answer with words. She just made a limp gesture with one hand in the direction of the highway.

Tori turned her head and felt the stiffness in her neck and the sore shoulder from her fall in the garage, but it was quickly forgotten when she saw what was happening beyond the trees where she had carefully parked the car out of sight. The road was crowded with people, but even though she didn't have a clear view, she could tell they weren't refugees like them.

"There must be hundreds of them," she whispered.

Denise answered so quietly that Tori could tell she was on the verge of a breakdown.

"They'll hear us as soon as we start the car, and we won't even make it back to the road."

Tori already knew that without Denise telling her, but it bothered her more to hear the resignation in the woman's voice. She leaned toward Denise and didn't speak until Denise made eye contact with her.

"If you really feel that way, you can get out of the car and go join them right now. Leave your boys with me. I'll make sure they get somewhere safe."

The second part of Tori's comment meant more to Denise than her suggestion that she should give up. She had almost forgotten about her sons in the back seat, and she couldn't give up on them. She was the one who knew where they had to go. She knew where they would be safe. Tori was helping to get them there.

"I'm sorry…wow, I'm so embarrassed."

"That's better," said Tori.

She sat up straight again behind the steering wheel and turned her attention back to the road. She was surprised to see that her movement inside the car drew the attention of the dead people. Even though they were almost completely shielded by the trees, the morning sun was reflecting off the windshield, and the light changed just enough to be noticed. Heads turned, and the dead people flowed from the road into the trees.

Tori could hear the shaking in her own voice when she said, "Why are there so many?"

She didn't expect an answer, but Denise said, "Rochester… they're all people who tried to get out of Rochester."

Tori had no choice but to start the car. If she waited, they would be swarming over the car in only a few minutes, and a convertible wasn't the best kind of car to be in at the moment.

As if Denise was reading her mind, she asked, "Why couldn't we be in a Hummer right now?"

The crowd of dead people was already excited by the sight of living people inside the car, but when the engine started and the car rolled backward onto the dirt road, the flow became a flood. Driving to the highway wasn't an option, so Tori pointed the car down the dirt road and drove further into the trees.

"I don't know where this road goes, but we don't have any other choices right now," said Tori. "Any ideas?"

The sudden sound of the engine and the motion of the car woke both boys in the back seat. Jalen and Jacob turned to look out the back window at the horde that was pouring through the gap in the trees where the dirt road met the highway.

"Mommy?" said Jacob. The question was left hanging in the air because he didn't know what he even wanted to ask her. He just wanted to hear her say they were going to be okay.

Denise turned toward the boys and put on her best fake smile. She told them not to look back until she told them it was safe to. The logic would only work on a child for a few minutes, but if they didn't figure something out fast, it wouldn't matter. It was like telling a child the monster under the bed would go away if they didn't look at it. All they had to do was wish really hard to make it disappear. As children often do when they're told to think really hard, both of them shut their eyes tight and held their breath.

"I have an idea," said Denise as she turned her attention back to Tori.

"Does it involve us getting rescued?"

"It's not that good of an idea," said Denise. "You won't like it, but it's all we have."

"I'm all ears," said Tori.

Denise said, "Stop the car."

"You're right...I don't like your idea."

"I'm serious," said Denise. "Let them get closer but not too close. Stay ahead of them, and just keep following this dirt road."

"You want them to follow us?" asked Tori. "Why?"

"We already passed two mailboxes on the right side of the road. There were private driveways."

Tori said, "I know. I almost drove down one of them. The houses would be safer than a convertible."

Denise shook her head. "The houses are probably full of dead people, but if I'm right, this dirt road will intersect with the highway again. We have to draw enough of them away from the highway onto the dirt road so there aren't any at the intersection."

Tori stopped the car. She didn't like the feeling of sitting still while the horde approached, but as she watched them in her rearview mirror, she imagined what would have happened if she had impulsively followed one of the private driveways. They would have most likely reached a secluded home. It would have been someone's sanctuary away from the city, but there would have been either dead people inside the home or living people waiting with a gun aimed at the door.

"Now," said Denise. She was also watching the horde get closer. "Not too fast, though."

Tori touched the gas pedal just enough to make the car roll forward. She couldn't see all the way back to the highway, but judging by the size of the crowd behind them, they were getting the attention Denise suggested they would.

"You know," said Tori, "if this doesn't work, we're going to have a big crowd close behind us when we either come to a dead end or an intersection with another road that's just as crowded."

"I already thought of that," said Denise. "Got a better idea?"

"I have to drive, or I would just shut my eyes and wish really hard," said Tori.

If wishing really hard was what made the road ahead begin to curve in the direction of the main highway, Tori would be willing to add it to her survival skills. They passed three more mailboxes, all on the right side, and Tori never drove too far ahead of the horde before waiting for it to catch up. It felt like they drove a few feet at a time for hours, and they didn't know how far they had gone, but they hoped it would be far enough. The curve began just past another mailbox.

Tori couldn't slow down and wait too long for the horde to catch up because a large group of the dead people broke away from the main procession and cut diagonally across the grass on her left. Instead of watching the horde in their rearview mirrors, they only had to look out the windows on the driver's side, and they were shocked to see how many had followed them down the dirt road. Even the boys were staring with wide eyes and their mouths hanging open.

"Punch it," said Denise.

Tori didn't need to be told twice.

The dirt road ahead of them sloped slightly upward, and they could see the intersection as Tori gained speed. She knew how well the BMW could hold the road, and even though it was a ninety-degree turn, Tori was still accelerating when she reached the pavement. A huge cloud of dust obscured their view of the horde that had followed them, but as the front end of the car swerved to the east, they saw a clear road ahead. Denise turned around to see the highway going west toward Rochester and saw that her idea had worked. The paved highway behind them was still clogged with dead people, but like a slow-moving drain, the flow was moving in the direction of the dirt road where they had begun their escape.

Tori kept her foot on the gas pedal so long that Denise had to convince her it was safe to slow down.

"If we're going too fast to stop, we'll run right into some. We don't have to crawl anymore, but we can't go a hundred miles an hour."

"Mommy, I'm hungry," said Jalen.

Denise took that as a good sign. If they were hungry, it meant they had their minds on something besides the dead people. While she dug out some power bars, Tori focused on driving but also turned on the radio. She punched at the tuner and watched the digital display scan for stations. There were public service announcements playing on most of the stations, but she finally picked up a real voice. She had punched too quickly and moved on, but she immediately found the reverse button and picked up the station.

"If you're hearing my voice," said the man on the radio, "I repeat…this is everywhere. There's no safe place to go. The infected dead can get to you wherever you are."

Denise reached for the off button, but Tori stopped her.

"We need to hear this. You at least got to see some news. I don't know anything."

"But the boys," said Denise.

Tori shook her head and said, "If this is everywhere, you won't be able to hide it from them. The more you know about it, the more you might be able to protect them from it."

Despite knowing that the voice on the radio scared the boys, Denise knew Tori was right. She turned up the volume and told Jacob and Jalen to pay close attention because the man might say something important.

The man was reading a list of the cities that he knew had fallen. He claimed to have personally verified the information by making contact with stations in those cities, and it was a long list. When he got to Ithaca on his list, Tori eased her foot off the gas pedal. She let the BMW coast, but they needed to make a plan instead of just driving straight into another dead city.

The man continued, "National Guard units have been mobilized in every state, but there are reports of FEMA camps under National Guard protection that have already been overrun. If you missed the first part of this broadcast, let me repeat...hospitals and police stations should be avoided. If you go to a hospital, you will most likely become infected. If you go to a police station, you will most likely be shot because they can't tell who is infected and who isn't. Above all, I need you to listen to this...all bites are fatal. If you are bitten, you will die. After you die, you will come back as one of the infected dead. That's as clear as I can make it."

The man stopped talking, and they thought they had lost the radio station. It wasn't until he took a deep breath and let it out forcefully that they realized he had stopped to compose himself.

"Folks, I've been on the air for almost twenty-four hours nonstop. If it were up to me, I would keep going. It's not that I would have anything new to say, but there may be someone out there who's hearing me for the first time. I'm going to get a few minutes of shut-eye and maybe something to eat. I'll be back when I wake up, but in the meantime, try to find a safe place where the infected dead can't get to you. If you do, I pray that you only open the door for someone if you know they aren't infected already. Check for bite wounds."

The car was still coasting, but it eventually came to a stop. They listened to static from the speakers until Tori finally switched the radio off.

"Where are we?" asked Denise.

Tori gestured toward the road and said, "If we got back on the same state road, then we should be close to Geneva at the top of Seneca Lake."

Denise became frantic and practically yelled at Tori to start driving again.

As they picked up speed, Denise said, "I don't know why I didn't recognize this place sooner. Fifteen minutes from here are businesses and neighborhoods. We have to go south and go around the bottom of the lake. Take the first country road you come to on the right."

"Wait a minute," said Tori. "I've been here before, too. It was a long time ago, but where are we going? Do you know about a safe place?"

"Yes, if we can get there, we'll be better than safe. It's only about forty miles from the top of Seneca Lake to the bottom, as the crow flies, but we have to stay off the straight road. It might take a couple of hours, but we're going to stick to back roads. I'll tell you when to turn."

For the first time in days, Tori allowed herself the luxury of a smile and a touch of humor.

"Okay, navigator. I'll be the pilot. Just tell me when to turn."

******

It took three hours, but there were times when they thought they wouldn't make it at all. One thing they were sure of was that they were glad they didn't have to make the drive at night. It was bad enough when they could see where they were going and if something was coming their way. Tori didn't bother to come to a complete stop at intersections, but she didn't blow through stop signs on the assumption that nothing would be crossing their path. It was a good thing because they weren't the only survivors who were trying to reach safety, and none of them were being as careful. Cars came up from behind them and flew past the BMW as if it were sitting still, and other vehicles sped by in the opposite direction. Several times, they came across wrecks and recognized the cars that had passed them. Tori didn't slow down, and Denise distracted the boys so they wouldn't have to see the unfortunate people.

The man on the radio had said to find a safe place to go, but he also said nowhere was safe. Tori was just taking Denise's word that she had a safe place for them, but she didn't know any of the details. Denise also didn't want to talk about it. When Tori prodded her a bit, Denise just said she would see it soon enough. Tori had nowhere else to go, so she quit asking.

The worst part of the trip was when they arrived at an intersection, and as Tori made another right turn, they found themselves on the same road as a horde of infected dead. It was a small group compared to the horde by Rochester, but they didn't want to test the ability of a convertible BMW to plow them out of the way. They were at least a hundred yards down the road and were walking slowly in the same direction. The good news was that they didn't act as if they had heard the BMW.

Tori put the transmission in reverse and backed up to the intersection. She smoothly turned the steering wheel and backed onto the road where they had been. She kept going until the trees blocked their view of the horde.

"Can we go to the left and still get to the bottom of Seneca Lake?" she asked Denise.

"Yes, but that road will take us straight into Watkins Glen, and I'd rather go around it if we can."

They sat in the car with the engine idling, but their choices were narrowed down to the only two options they already knew about.

"We can't just sit here," said Tori.

Denise was about to give in and say they had to make a left and take their chances going through the small town at the southern tip of Seneca Lake, but the decision was made for them by a pickup truck that approached so fast from behind that Tori almost didn't move fast enough. She saw it in the rearview mirror and threw the transmission into drive as she hit the gas and turned the wheel. The BMW was barely out of the way onto the shoulder when the pickup truck slid sideways past them into the intersection. The driver got control of the slide, and the truck accelerated in the direction of the horde. A man in the passenger seat of the truck leaned out the window toward them and extended one finger toward the sky.

Both of them were too surprised to speak for a moment, but Tori broke the silence first.

"What was that saying a football announcer was famous for?"

"I don't know what you mean," said Denise.

Tori gestured in the direction where the truck had disappeared and said, "Now, there's a fan who still thinks his team is number one."

They would have laughed longer, but they needed to see if the pickup truck had given them the opportunity they needed to get around the horde. Tori drove forward again and extended the car into the intersection just far enough for them to know.

Smoke rose from the engine of the truck. It was on its

right side in the shallow ditch beside the road. Judging by the number of bodies that were scattered around on the shoulder near the truck, they had eliminated over a dozen of the infected dead. Most of them were making an effort to get up again, but some that got missed were already gathering around the truck. The wheels on the left side were still turning.

"I think we can get by them if we go now," said Tori.

Denise nodded.

Tori had to dodge a few of the infected dead, but they were past the wreck quickly. As they drove by, one of the men in the truck was climbing out of the cab. He waved his arms at them in the hope that they would stop.

Tori said, "The man on the radio said something about not helping people if you didn't know whether or not they had been infected. He probably should have added that helping someone who isn't infected might be dangerous, too."

Denise felt like she could see the man's eyes well enough as they went by, and she saw something in them that made her understand what Tori meant. Even as he was begging for their help, his eyes were cold. She wondered if she would ever be able to help someone again without seeing something behind their eyes. She didn't think so.

******

Sometimes, it seemed like everyone in Watkins Glen had a boat. Whether it was large or small, it was a way of life to moor the family boat in one of the marinas on the barge canal, but lakefront property along the banks of Seneca Lake wasn't worth having if it didn't have a private dock. That was where

Denise hoped they could make their safe place for the night. She could picture the large home that had belonged to her grandparents. It was big, and it had a private dock where Brad had kept one of their boats, but it also had its secrets.

Denise kept telling Tori where to turn, taking them south but also bringing them closer to the lake, until finally, she saw the barely visible turn between low-hanging trees. It was like driving into a tunnel.

"How did you even know there was a road here?" asked Tori.

"It belonged to my family...actually, my grandparents. My parents gave it to me, and I never sold it after I married Brad. He liked to keep one of his boats here."

Thinking of her husband gave Denise a shiver. She realized that she still hadn't taken the time to grieve losing him, and the thought of Brad on the deck of his boat made her feel like she had abandoned him. She glanced at her sons in the back seat. They had been too quiet since leaving the hotel, and at the moment, they were both asleep. She noticed they were holding hands, and she was glad they had each other.

Tori saw the brief signs that Denise was feeling emotional. There were the furtive glances, first at the boys and then out the side window at trees that were too close to the car to be interesting. One hand went to the corner of her eye, and there was a quick sniffle. It made Tori think about her very short marriage to Randy, and she wondered what it would have been like for her. She felt a lump in her throat as she thought about Randy. They had talked about having a boy and a girl, and maybe ten or twelve years in the future, she would have them riding behind her in the car. That had all changed, though. The only future they had was one minute away because something could happen in the next minute to end their existence.

As if she had summoned disaster, a deer burst from the trees on the right and just as quickly disappeared into the brush on the left. Tori slammed on the brakes as hard as she could, even though the deer was already gone.

"My nerves are shot," she said. She saw that Jacob and Jalen were awake and added, "I'm sorry."

"You don't need to apologize for anything. If not for you, we would be...". She almost said they would be dead, but Tori knew what would have happened if she hadn't seen them outside the hotel. They would have died a horrible death. "I hope I've thanked you already, but if I haven't thanked you enough, this is how I'm going to do it."

Tori pressed on the gas and drove forward again, but only seconds later, the BMW emerged from the tree tunnel into a small clearing. A big house blocked their view of Seneca Lake. The driveway wrapped around the house, so she followed it until it ended on the other side.

The view was spectacular. The house sat on a rise about fifty yards from the lake, and Tori could only guess at the number of rooms. Her own family had always had money, but something told her the Warren family had been well off. A path led from the house to a private dock with a boathouse on one side at the end.

Seneca Lake was the deepest of the Finger Lakes. At over six hundred feet deep, it had been at the center of the shipping industry in New York. Barges still traveled from the canal lock near Geneva on the northern tip to Watkins Glen, thirty-eight miles to the south. Sometimes, it amazed Denise how little people knew about the lake and its neighbor, Cayuga Lake, over by Ithaca. The history and the magnitude of industrial technology seemed almost to be taken for granted. It was what was hidden under the lakes that made them fascinating to Denise.

"Is there a boat in the boathouse?" asked Tori. "Is this the safe place? We could board up the windows and doors, right?

Are there lots of supplies?"

"No, this is just a place to stay for one night. There are some things here that we need, but we at least have a backup plan if the boat's gone."

Tori looked toward the boathouse again and asked, "You think the boat's gone?"

"I don't know," said Denise. "We can go check on it after we get the boys inside where it's safer."

It felt like they had been in the car forever, and they both stretched as they used muscles that had been glued to car seats the day before. Once they were out of the car, both of them discovered they had bruises they had ignored. Tori groaned and felt for her lower back. She winced so much when she touched it that Denise got worried. After all the talk from the man on the radio, she realized Tori could be one of the *walking wounded* he had been warning about.

"Let me get a look at that," said Denise as she walked up behind Tori.

Tori didn't think anything of it and didn't try to pull away when Denise lifted the back of her shirt. Denise was shocked by the size of the bruise across Tori's back and all the way to one shoulder, but there were no teeth marks.

"What did you do to yourself?" she exclaimed. "That's nasty."

"That's what happens when you fall backward onto the top of an elevator and then from a car to a concrete garage floor," said Tori. "How about you? Are you hurt?"

Denise thought about Brad and the way his arm had gotten those long streaks that began at his knuckles and spread like spider veins all the way to his elbow. When she considered the fact that it had taken only a day for the infection to become lethal, she realized Tori couldn't be hiding any similar injuries.

"What's wrong?" asked Tori. "You looked tense for a moment, and then you relaxed."

"It's nothing," said Denise. "I was just thinking how remarkable it was that the four of us got out of the hotel without anything more serious than a few bruises."

"You call this a bruise? Darlin', I call this internal injury, and if that isn't bad enough, I wind up driving down bumpy dirt roads with my back all banged up."

Despite her own aches and pains and the traumatic state of their lives, Denise appreciated Tori's humorous whining and smiled. She hadn't found any reason to smile since sometime before the strange man walked up to her kids on the beach.

They helped Jalen and Jacob out of the back of the car and gathered together their few belongings before going up the wooden steps to the house. Denise was leading the way, carrying Jalen on her left hip, and didn't see the curtains move in a window by the door. Tori hung back, keeping Jacob out of the way while Denise went on ahead. She set her backpack on the steps and pulled the Luger from one of the pockets. She put a finger across her lips to signal Jacob to stay quiet.

"We keep a key over here," said Denise.

Denise walked straight past the door and stooped down to lift the edge of a large potted plant that had probably died over a year ago, and she was so intent on retrieving the key that she didn't see the door open as she went by. Tori aimed the Luger at the darkness in the gap as it widened, hoping that she hadn't been seen by whoever was inside the house. She watched a man step through the gap, and as he came into full view, his right arm extended toward Denise's back. Light reflected back at her from a long, steel blade.

Tori could also see Jalen's face, and he was paralyzed with fear. In that split second, Tori realized what it would have been like for her and Randy if they could have lived a normal life...

what kind of mother she would have been. She would have done anything to protect their children from the kind of fear that she saw on Jalen's face.

Jacob didn't know if Tori would pull the trigger. All he knew was that a man with a knife in his hand was extending his arm toward his mother.

"Mom," he yelled despite Tori's signal.

Denise turned in time to see the man's face. He had a linen pillowcase tied across his jaw, and it was soaked with blood. She could tell from his eyes that he wasn't one of the dead people, but he would be soon. She could guess what was under the pillowcase. Some of the spiderweb veins had already reached his left eye. It was bloodshot and weeping something yellow.

There wasn't time to wonder what happened. The crack of the 9mm Luger was especially loud in the silence of the front porch, and the silence was replaced by a high-pitched ringing sound. Tori found the Luger had a surprisingly small recoil, and the bullet hit exactly where she aimed. In her mind, she pictured a butter knife hitting the same spot.

Tori didn't question where her survival instincts were coming from. She just let things happen. She grabbed her backpack and hurried Jacob up the steps to where Denise stood frozen with Jalen on her hip. Jalen was crying and had his head buried in her neck.

The man had fallen half in and half out of the door with his feet still on the porch. Tori took one look into the gloom of the house to see if there was anyone else waiting inside. Seeing no one, she shoved the Luger into her belt, grabbed the man's ankles, and dragged him the rest of the way outside. He was too heavy for her to drag him far, so she just got him far enough out of the way for them to get inside. She grabbed a throw rug from the foyer and put it over the man's head, then pushed Denise and her children ahead of her into the house.

Once the door was shut, Tori put her face close to Denise's and said, "Snap out of it. I've never been here before, so you have to help me make sure we're alone. Can you do that?"

Denise knew that she would have pulled the trigger if she had been the one holding the gun, but everything had happened so fast. She had assumed they were safe from the moment they had gotten to the house, and she didn't even know Tori had a gun. She just felt like she had failed her children for a second time, and just like before, Tori had come to her rescue. Denise felt like they were supposed to be dead.

She blinked, and her eyes focused on Tori, only inches from her face.

"I'm okay," she said. She sniffled, sucked in a deep breath, and added, "Let me show you how I'm going to repay you. That's twice that you've saved my life."

"Twice? You don't count so well, do you?"

CHANGE

Amherst County - 2025

I always believed the way the world changed was also going to determine how we changed, but Jean and I had resisted the need to do things that had to be justified later. From the first day of the apocalypse to the moment Jean crawled onto the bridge, we had faced one brutal assault on our morals after the next, but even a blind man would have been able to see that Jean came back from the guard shack deeply unsettled. I didn't know what had happened up there, but I could see in her eyes that she was trying to deal with it. It was the way someone would try to hide pain after being shot or stabbed. They would smile and say they were fine even though the wound was obvious, but they avoided eye contact to keep you from seeing the truth.

Once we were past the debris on the bridge, we didn't waste time. We ran as fast as we could to get to the other end, and when we reached the opposite bank of the river, Jean turned onto a dirt road that disappeared into a thick forest of pine trees but ran parallel to the river.

"Where are we going?" whispered Ruth from somewhere behind me.

"It's not a good idea to stay on the road," I answered. "If

the people who blocked the bridge have any brains at all, they would have a patrol on this side of the barricade. They would most likely be on the road. Also, we need to stay close to the river and find a spot where we can see the bridge."

Wally overheard me and filled in the rest.

"We can't outrun these guys on foot, so we have to see if they're still chasing us."

"Up here," said Jean.

It was dark between the tall pine trees, but Jean had found a path to a spot that had been a picnic area before the apocalypse. There were wooden tables in a small clearing that faced the river, and from the overlook, we could see the bridge downstream. Heavy smoke was pouring from the cargo container suspended above the bridge, but we were more interested in the headlights on the road. A caravan of pickup trucks came to a stop on the other side of the bridge, and gunshots rang out as the infected dead were eliminated. We couldn't understand everything they were saying, but the shouts sounded like someone was barely able to control their anger.

We took cover behind an outcrop of rocks and watched as a large man gave instructions to the others. Apparently, he ordered them to remove the barricade on the bridge, and we understood enough of the words to know he said we couldn't have gotten too far on foot.

"We can't stay here," said Jean. "If they see the dirt road into the trees, they'll at least send someone to check it out."

I knew Jean was right, so we didn't waste time talking about it. She led the way a second time, and we followed the river bank upstream for over an hour before turning back into the thick forest. We made slow progress, but we had to avoid the paved road and any trails that seemed like they had been heavily used. We finally found one road that was overgrown with small trees and grass and walked in silence for several hours.

We kept moving until the light from the morning sun filtered through the trees. We didn't hear any vehicles in the distance, so we decided to get some rest and figure out what we were going to do next. Breakfast would have to be something simple because we couldn't risk making a campfire.

Jean didn't roll out her blanket, so I knew she didn't plan to sleep. She leaned back against a tree and crossed her legs over each other at the ankles. It might be my only chance to find out what happened at the bridge. I sat down near her feet to make sure she couldn't avoid my eyes. She knew what I was doing and tried anyway.

"Don't start," she said.

"Start what?"

"You know what I mean. You want to talk about the bridge."

"No, I want to talk about you," I answered.

"Same thing," she said, but this time, she locked onto my eyes with hers. It was a warning not to pursue it any further.

"So, if you were worried about me, I would be able to tell you to drop it?"

Jean and I didn't really get into fights with each other. Once, we got into an argument over something stupid, and the Chief had suggested that we take it outside. He meant it literally. He said he couldn't understand why people who loved each other would get into a fight when there were dead people outside the walls. He said he was sure those same dead people had families, and those families were reliving every stupid thing they had ever fought about. His observation helped us keep things in perspective when we disagreed. Jean was always needling me about something just for fun, so I knew I had at least a little bit of a safety net if I pressed the issue of getting her to talk.

Jean said, "I'm not telling you to drop anything. I'm just telling you I'm fine."

I knew I was walking on thin ice when I said it, but I had to take the chance.

"The Chief told me one time that a woman is never really okay if she says the word *fine*."

The glare I got from Jean threw out enough heat to melt the thin ice I was already walking on, but I was smart enough to follow another piece of advice the Chief's own wife had given me. She told me that sometimes you can stop talking with your mouth but keep saying volumes with your eyes.

I waited until Jean blinked, and I saw a tear roll down her cheek.

"If you can't talk about it yet, I'll be here when you're ready," I said.

I started to get up, but she stopped me, and tears rolled out of both eyes.

"I killed two men inside that cargo container."

Jean wiped her cheeks and sniffled. I couldn't remember the last time I saw her appear to be so small and helpless. I moved over next to her and put my back against the tree. I was a bit surprised when she leaned into me and sobbed, but it had always been such a natural thing for us to seek out each other when we needed support. We had met when the world fell apart, and our chance meeting had felt like the first step toward survival. I waited until she was done crying before I answered her.

"If I know you, you're wondering how we got to a point in time when we started thinking we could justify killing someone. I almost asked you if you had a choice, but I already know the answer to that question. You wouldn't have killed them if you had another choice. The real question is whether or not *they* had a choice. They were standing watch for people who would kill us if they caught us. That took the choice out of your hands. You did what you had to do."

"But I don't have to be happy about it," she said.

"No one said you do, and no one thinks you should ever get used to it. You got us across the bridge and bought us some time. Don't try to justify how you did it, and don't try to rationalize it. We're not out of the woods yet…literally and figuratively."

Jean sat up a little straighter and said, "You don't think it's safe here?"

"I don't know about here, but those people have vehicles, and we don't. They're ahead of us now, and that means we're going to run into them again, but now they're really mad. Somehow, we have to get past them."

Apparently, Ruth and Wally were thinking the same thing because they chose that moment to join us.

"Excuse us," said Ruth. "I hope we're not interrupting, but Wally and I have been talking about those people who're after us. There's only one way that we can get away from them."

"You have an idea?" I asked.

Wally said, "We have to steal one of their trucks. I also don't think we can walk to New York, so we might as well try to take one of theirs."

******

The heavily armed caravan rolled over the bridge and spread out onto every side road. It wasn't the first time they had pursued survivors who had stumbled into their territory, but no one had ever killed their people in the process. Branch had no way of knowing how many trespassers were in the area, but they had not only killed one of his best people, they had managed to set fire to the guard post on the bridge. He wondered how they had done it, and he imagined his militia was up against a well-armed adversary if they were capable of such an act. He told his men that he wanted the perpetrators brought in alive if possible, but it would be fine if they brought back their bodies.

Branch drove five miles past the bridge with enough men to establish a blockade across the road, but as the hours went by, he became increasingly agitated that they hadn't been caught. Patrols arrived at the blockade with nothing new to report, and he couldn't accept the fact that they had already gotten out of the area. The last patrol checked in just as the sun was setting, so they posted guards and set up camp.

******

We kept our plan simple. We would wait until the early hours of the morning and then make a move on any vehicle that was on the far side of their camp. The reason it was so simple was because no one had any better ideas.

It wasn't hard to avoid being caught by their patrols. The searchers made enough noise to attract every infected dead in the area, and we watched from our hiding places as they were continually distracted from their original mission. It was as if they forgot what they were supposed to be doing. After four men had passed within a few yards of us, Jean told us she had heard one say that someone named Branch wasn't going to be happy if they didn't find us, but then he disposed of a trio of infected dead and told the rest of the group it was time to move on. They didn't appear to be dedicated to their jobs. Unfortunately for them, all four of us had become proficient at stalking through the woods at night.

It was around two o'clock in the morning when we finally reached the place where our pursuers had made their camp. We found the first guard asleep at the base of a tree, and after the guilt Jean had experienced earlier, I didn't think it would be a good idea to kill him. It was a simple matter to gag him before he alerted the others.

Jean leaned close to the man's ear and whispered, "What's your name?"

She pulled the gag away far enough for him to answer.

"Wayne."

"Well, Wayne, we saw at least a dozen of the infected dead coming this way. If you make any noise, they'll find you. Do you understand what I'm saying?"

Judging by the way Wayne's eyes got wider, we didn't think he was going to yell for help. We tucked him into the gap between the ground and a fallen log as if we were doing him a favor and moved on toward the next guard.

He was easy to find because he was smoking a cigarette. It reminded me of the beginning of the apocalypse when we had slipped past guards on a bridge. Some things would never change, and as long as there were still cigarettes to be traded like currency, there would be someone who needed a jolt of nicotine to stay awake.

Wally took him to the ground from behind while Ruth stuffed a gag in his mouth. Jean gave him her little speech about infected dead finding him if he made noise, and I rifled through his pockets. I found a set of car keys and held them up where the others could see them. That was when I realized how to get our simple plan to make sense. We needed a distraction.

It took over an hour to set everything in motion, but there was still plenty of darkness we could use to our advantage, and we knew that waking our pursuers from a deep sleep would add to the chaos we needed. We retrieved Wayne from where we had left him and took both of the guards to a small clearing we had crossed earlier in the day. There was a tall tree in the middle of the clearing that was perfect for our needs. Our prisoners were blindfolded and gagged before we hung them by their feet from a sturdy limb. Their hands were tied behind their backs, and as they pulled at the rope around their wrists, they rotated in a circle. We raised them upside down until their faces were even with ours, and when we removed the strips of cloth from their faces, we told them we would tell their friends where to find them. We raised them a couple of feet higher so they would be out of reach from the ground. We didn't need for them to be eaten. We just needed to make them yell.

Ruth, Wally, and Jean got a head start while I stayed behind and lit a pile of kindling we had stacked together below the men. It wasn't big enough to burn them, but it was large enough to draw the attention of any infected dead that were in the area.

"Hey, buddy," said one of the men in a hoarse voice. "You don't have to do this. If you let us go, we won't tell anyone. I don't wanna die like this, man."

Wayne repeated what the first man said but added, "You can't burn us, man. Please don't burn us."

The small flames flickered as more of the kindling ignited, and I could tell it was big enough to do what we needed.

I said, "What kind of people do you think we are? Do you think we're that cruel?"

I didn't wait around for an answer, and I was at the edge of the clearing before I heard either of them make another sound.

One of them had rotated in a circle and saw that I was gone. His first impulse was to put all of his efforts into getting his hands untied, and I had to give him some credit for ingenuity, even if he did get a bit too loud. I stopped and listened. I didn't understand all of it, but I understood enough to know he was telling the other guy they could swing together backward and maybe untie each other.

I almost laughed as I thought, "Jiggle the bait, guys."

The campfire was probably what drew the first of the infected dead into the clearing. They were attracted to flames like moths, and even when the fire ignited their ragged clothing, they tried to get closer to the middle of it. The two men who were wriggling and swaying just out of reach only excited the infected dead more, but the icing on the cake was the distraction we had hoped for. When the men saw the bony hands reaching up toward them, they screamed.

Sound carries well at night. Everyone knows that, but even I was surprised by how well it carried when both men screamed. I caught up with Ruth, Wally, and Jean before they reached the place where we had abducted the guards and hid in the deep shadows of the fallen tree where we had tied up Wayne. We figured it was the best place to go because the rest of their group wouldn't know it was a hole in their perimeter. To our left and right, we saw the dark shadows of men running toward the screaming. They went past us without a glance in our direction, and we waited until we couldn't hear more of them coming from the camp.

"Let's go," I whispered.

We went straight through the camp, counting on the chaos to hide us in plain sight. A man came out of a tent and asked us in a breathless voice what was happening.

Jean pointed in the direction of the screaming and said, "Branch wants everyone to go help Wayne. Those people got him and someone else."

The man reached inside his tent and grabbed a rifle before running off to rescue Wayne.

"How do we know which truck to take?" asked Jean.

Wally said, "I've got that covered. We need to find an old model...something with less electronics and running on biodiesel."

We followed him as he went straight for one of the oldest pickup trucks. It was unlocked, and he pulled a handful of wires down from below the steering column. In only a few seconds, he had stripped some wires and was touching them together. There were blue-white sparks, and the engine rumbled to life. While he was hot-wiring the truck, the rest of us were busy stabbing our knives through the tires on as many pickup trucks as we could.

The timing was perfect. Just as the engine started, we heard gunshots from the general direction of the clearing where we had left Wayne and his friend. We only had seconds to spare, but Wally worked so fast that we were driving away from the camp long before anyone noticed the truck was gone.

*****

We felt like we had already been lucky despite losing our supplies and a perfectly good truck. The bonus was the fuel gauge. If it was working right, we had enough fuel to go at least three hundred miles. We even hoped the people hunting for us would be satisfied that they had relieved us of our possessions, but that was a bit optimistic. We had a good head start because of the flat tires that had to be changed, but we doubted that

Branch and his followers considered one truck to be a good trade for a bunch of tires and several dead men.

Wally used the headlights to be able to drive faster. We couldn't take the risk of running blindly into a horde at high speed, and all of the noise from the fire on the bridge and the gunshots where we had left the two guards was drawing the infected dead from the woods. Several times, Wally had to navigate around them. Twice, he had no choice but to warn everyone to brace for impact before he ran over them.

After an hour of driving, the morning sun gave us enough light for us to see further ahead, but just as importantly, we could see the road behind us. We were at a higher elevation, and we took a few minutes to stop and use binoculars. In a valley where we had crossed earlier, we could see the light reflecting from windshields. The good news was that the column of trucks was smaller than the original number, but we weren't far enough ahead to celebrate. We piled back inside the truck, and Wally increased his speed enough to make us feel like we were on a roller coaster ride.

"I only saw six trucks," said Jean.

Wally couldn't take his eyes off the road, but he added, "They probably cannibalized the other trucks for tires, but if I had been in charge of that bunch, I would have also topped off the gas tanks while they were changing tires. This is stock car racing country, and even kids know that pit stops for tires are a good time to take on gas."

"So, our luck's gonna run out?" asked Ruth. "At least that's what all the signs say on the side of the road."

She pointed at a sign that used to say there were restaurants and gas stations at the next exit. Someone had used a can of red spray paint to make a big X across the sign.

I rummaged through a backpack that had been inside the cab of the old pickup truck and found only a few useful items, but the map was of some help. I unfolded it and traced a line from our location to Ithaca, New York. I didn't pay any attention to the scribbles written with a pen in different places, but sometimes they obscured the names of towns and highway numbers.

I told the others, "If this was a perfect world, we would be able to make the rest of the trip in just under six hours, but we would still have to stop for gas one more time."

"It always comes down to that," said Jean. "Before the infected dead, when you made a trip in a car, you still had to stop for gas using your best judgment, but that was when we knew we would find gas without a problem."

"We also weren't being chased by a gang of killers who had more gas than us," said Ruth. "It doesn't make me feel better knowing that they won't have enough gas to drive back home."

"Wait...what did you say?" I asked.

Ruth repeated her comment, but before she finished, I already knew what it was she had said that caught my attention. It was something the Chief talked about constantly.

I asked Jean, "What did the Chief call it when he talked about how much fuel you would need to fly from one place to the next? You know, if you didn't land or couldn't refuel in the air?"

"He called it bingo fuel," she answered. "What are you thinking?"

"I'm thinking that those guys chasing us either don't care if they run out of gas or they know where to find more gas somewhere ahead."

Wally abruptly pulled the truck to the side of the road but left the motor running.

"Someone take over driving for me so I can look at that map."

Since I was sitting in the passenger seat behind him, it was easy for us to trade places.

I started driving as soon as his door was shut, and Wally started talking to himself as he studied the map.

"We should be about here," he said with one finger on a highway, "and if I had a fuel supply on this road that was too big to move, it would be somewhere like here."

Wally held the map so Jean was able to see it, and Ruth leaned through the gap between the seats from the front. They both smiled, and I was dying to know what Wally had found.

Jean said, "I wouldn't have expected someone to have written it on the map, but an arrow will do."

"I agree," said Wally. To me, he added, "Follow the signs to the Capital Beltway. There's a railroad terminal under the bridge before it crosses the Susquehanna River, and someone drew an arrow on the map that points at the railroad tracks."

"How far will we have to go after that?" I asked.

Wally had a huge smile when he answered.

"Maybe two hundred miles or so."

******

The needle on the gas gauge was hovering close to the red line when we reached the exit to the railroad terminal. The arrow pointed at a spot on the map not far from the bridge, and our guess was that we should be looking for a train that was hauling processed fuel from a plant somewhere along the river. Wally had focused on the map and found the processing plant a few miles south of the bridge, and we used the time we had left to talk about what we expected to find.

One major concern was that the train would be guarded, and we debated the possibility as if we were the ones who owned the fuel. We came to the conclusion that guarding the fuel would be difficult for anyone to do unless they had unlimited resources. Our shelters were equipped with the manpower and logistics to guard a fuel-carrying train, but only if they were located near the shelters.

That led us to the question of why the people from the high school didn't relocate to the railroad terminal, and the most obvious answer was that there were too many infected dead in the area. That answer became more believable as we got closer to the city of Harrisburg, and as the railroad terminal came into view, we were able to see that there were plenty of infected dead that were trapped between the long trains. We didn't have the luxury of time. Fighting the infected dead while we located the fuel wasn't an option.

We agreed that the people who were chasing us probably had the same problem when they used the terminal to resupply with fuel. That meant they had at least one tanker to transport it back to their sanctuary, and they might have an established route that was clear of the infected dead. Our suspicions were confirmed when we saw an arrow spray-painted on an access road that entered the terminal, and we should have expected the lack of originality. Both sides of the road were lined bumper to bumper with derelict vehicles, the same way as the overpass and the bridge where we had first encountered our pursuers.

Wally brought up one other problem that we couldn't answer until we reached the train.

"Fuel trains don't usually come equipped with gas pumps that fit cars. I don't know how we're going to get it from the train into our gas tank."

Jean said, "These guys aren't lazy, but they strike me as the type of people who would try to pound sand into a hole with a hammer."

"You think they attached a pump to one of the cars?" I asked. "If they did, what would stop someone else from using it?"

"Yes, but instead of hauling the pump back with the fuel, I'll bet they just hid it somewhere nearby."

I drove along the road between the derelict vehicles until I was almost to the train. A large buffer zone where a fuel tanker could turn around had been created by hundreds of cars and other debris. It formed a safe zone next to three fuel cars, so I circled and then backed up to the one in the middle. It was as good a choice as any, and I didn't have time to play guessing games.

"What now?" asked Ruth.

Jean said, "Spread out and check any of the vehicles in the barricade for their pump. Skip anything small. We're looking for at least fifty feet of hose and a manual pump, so it won't be in the trunk of an economy car."

We found it in the bed of a Ford F-150. It took all four of us to lift the heavy pump and carry it to the train, and we were relieved that we didn't have to haul it to the top of the fuel car. As every minute went by, we worked feverishly to get the gas flowing from the train to the pump and into the truck, but we watched constantly for any sign of the caravan that had followed us from Virginia. If they arrived before we were done, we would be trapped in the cul-de-sac by the train.

When Wally announced that the gas tank was full, I pulled on the hose that we had fed into the opening on top of the train, but Jean yelled at me to leave it. I assumed she meant there wasn't enough time and we needed to leave, but she had something else in mind. When I got to the truck, I saw that she had wedged the handle of the pump in the open position, and gas was spewing into the gravel of the safe zone near the train. It didn't take a rocket scientist to know what she planned to do next.

Wally had taken over at the steering wheel, and the truck was already rolling away from the train as Jean threw a burning piece of cloth toward the area where the fuel had saturated the ground. She had stuffed one end into a bottle to give it enough weight to reach her target, but the air was so full of fumes that it didn't have to go far. The explosion lifted the rear end of our truck into the air, and it bounced heavily as the tires fought for traction. Wally kept the front end under control, but we swerved from side to side until we finally straightened out and raced for the exit ramp.

We were on the Capital Beltway Bridge when we saw the caravan of pickup trucks near the railroad terminal. The explosion hadn't stopped with the fuel car that we had used. Two more tanker cars had been lifted from the tracks and dumped over on their sides. When their cargo of fuel was added to the first load, the fire sent a plume of smoke even higher into the air.

We knew better than to celebrate such a close call, but I asked Jean, "Who are you, and what did you do with my innocent wife?"

I thought Jean would be amused by my question, but her reaction told me that she was still worried.

"It's a shame to waste all of that fuel, but it was the only way to slow them down."

"You don't think they're going to give up?" asked Ruth.

"No. I think that guy in charge just has one more reason to catch us."

Wally said, "They must be low on gas, too. How will they

catch us?"

Jean said, "Branch has probably already figured it out, and he's topping off the tanks on three trucks using gas from the other three. I'll bet he has six or eight people in each truck, so we'll have about two dozen of them after us when they're done."

Wally said, "That won't take long. We bought ourselves about fifteen minutes of extra time, but I guess it's better than running out of gas."

We had two hundred miles to go with a thirty-minute lead.

VINEYARD

Seneca Lake - 2016

The old house was large, and it took over an hour to be sure there was no one else hiding inside. The basement was the worst part because it had so many dark rooms. Every corner was filled with shadows that appeared to move, and the tension exhausted the two women. It was almost relaxing to check the buildings outside the main house. They chose an upstairs room where Denise figured the boys would be safe while they checked the property and told them not to make any noise or open the door for anyone. They were more tired than afraid, so they sleepily agreed.

One of the buildings was a barn where they found an old car sitting on cinder blocks. Tori had no idea what kind of car it was. She raised an eyebrow toward Denise.

"It was my grandfather's. My husband used to talk about restoring it, but he never got around to it. I imagine it would've been worth something to someone just for parts, but I couldn't bring myself to sell it. I think it's a 1932 Ford Coupe."

Tori studied the classic car and asked, "What did you say your grandparents used to do? Were they involved with the shipping industry or something?"

"No, you probably didn't realize you were driving through

a vineyard because it was so overgrown. Thirty years of trees can really hide what was there before. They owned hundreds of acres around the house."

"That explains why we haven't been running into those dead people," said Tori. "No one else lived nearby. That man up there probably knew the house was here."

They finished checking the barn and then a second building that was smaller. It was stacked full of old and rusted equipment, so they turned in the direction of the boathouse.

The dock was in reasonably good condition because Brad Warren had at least completed that project. He wanted to keep using it as a place to take his boat out of the water, and that meant keeping the dock repaired. It stuck out like a long wooden finger into the lake. Denise led the way, but Tori kept a watchful eye on their surroundings. As they walked farther out onto the dock, she could see more of the shoreline on both sides. There were clumps of trees and bushes, but there were small, sandy picnic areas where boaters likely stopped to enjoy the peace and quiet. It technically belonged to Denise's family, but before the infection, it wasn't uncommon to see families stop for a few hours.

In the middle of one of the sandy stretches, Tori saw the bloated body of a man lying face down in the sand. He was wearing denim pants and a blue plaid shirt, and the material of both was stretched to the point of ripping apart everywhere except at the belt. Since it was probably leather, it didn't stretch as the body expanded. It looked like the body was being slowly cut in half.

"Denise, hold up just a minute."

Denise came back to Tori and followed her gaze.

She said, "That man must've gone into the water at the start of this thing, whatever it is."

"That's what I thought," said Denise. "I think I saw it in a movie or something. It takes about three days to become bloated like that."

They thought they were imagining what they saw. The man lifted his head from the sand, and his impossibly fat neck turned until his grotesque face was pointed toward them. They saw the material of his shirt split open down the middle of his back as he reached a waterlogged arm toward them.

Denise tugged on Tori's arm.

"Let's go. I don't want to see what happens next."

They were relieved when they reached the boathouse and found the boat inside. It was suspended from the rafters by a cradle lift. Denise told Tori that Brad didn't always go to the house, but he regularly came to the dock to keep the boat running smoothly. It was a bow rider that was about seventeen feet long, and it had a big engine mounted on the back.

"It's easy to use," said Denise, "and it should get us to the other side without any problems. It's only about three miles to the other side from here."

"Where are we going from there?" asked Tori. "You said there's someplace safe where we can go, and I thought this house was it. Do you have something better in mind?"

"You could say that. Maybe now would be a good time to tell you about our shelter."

"Shelter?" said Tori. "That sounds like a word you would use for something like the end of the world."

Denise tilted her head to one side as if she was letting it sink in.

"You might consider this the end of the world if you think about it. I mean, it's the end of the world as we know it. We can't survive in a world where people are coming back from the dead and eating living people, can we?"

Tori thought about the people going over Niagara Falls, wondered about where Randy had gone, and remembered stabbing someone in the head with a butter knife. It certainly wasn't the world she had been used to, and if they had faced that much in a few days, she couldn't begin to imagine what the world would be like over the next year.

"So, you have a shelter that's able to survive this?" asked Tori.

"It can survive more than this. If we can get there, we can grow old inside it without ever having to come outside again."

Tori had heard about people who prepared for nuclear war, but she had never met anyone who had actually done it. The idea of investing in supplies that would last a year or more was the reason most people didn't do it, but Denise was talking about a place where they would be safe forever.

"Is this some kind of super-shelter or something?" asked Tori.

"It's my way of repaying you for saving our lives," said Denise, "so I guess you could call it that. I know that once you're inside, you won't have to worry about whatever it is that's happening out here."

"What're we waiting for?" asked Tori.

"Tomorrow morning...so we won't get caught out on the water overnight. Even worse, if we make it to the other side, we still have to make it to Cayuga Lake. That means we have to go about sixteen more miles before we reach the back entrance of the shelter. We don't want to be forced to find another place to spend the night after we cross the lake."

******

The boys both slept through the night, but Tori and Denise wished they could sleep for just a few minutes. They eventually gave up and spent the rest of the night on the front porch, standing watch. They talked in low voices and made long pauses so they could listen for sounds that weren't supposed to be there. They heard a few branches snap and were relieved when a deer silently passed the house. It didn't seem to be in a hurry, so they didn't think it was running from something.

"Tell me more about your shelter," said Tori.

Denise thought about where to begin. The long pause was natural to Tori by then, so she waited patiently.

"It's big," said Denise. "A lot of people could survive in it for years, so I know the four of us will never be hungry. It was built by my father-in-law, but after he died, my husband continued to improve on it."

Tori said, "You mentioned something about the back entrance."

"Oh, yeah. One of the features is an emergency exit. The entrance is on the western side of Cayuga Lake. It's actually a tunnel that goes under the lake to the other side."

"Under the lake?"

Denise heard the skepticism in Tori's voice and laughed softly.

"I know what you're thinking, but it's safe. It's probably better reinforced than most underwater tunnels."

As if on cue, there was a rumbling sound of thunder in the distance, but neither of them saw any lightning.

Tori said, "I heard there were tunnels under the lakes, and

sometimes when there's thunder but no lightning, it's really the sound of tunnels collapsing."

Denise laughed for a second time but said, "There were old Indian legends about the Seneca Drums, but they stopped years ago. Brad said something about the salt mines acting as vents for gases in the tunnels."

"Wait a minute," said Tori. "Are you part of the Warren family that owns the salt mines?"

"That would be us," said Denise. "Brad's father got together with a guy a long time ago, and they decided to build a shelter that would withstand any worst-case scenario. All you have to do is be inside when disaster strikes. That's why I know we'll be safe there."

"What about the tunnel? What if those dead people are already in there?"

"First, they have to find it. It's not obvious, and there isn't a sign outside with an arrow pointing toward it, but even if they found it and got inside, the security system would take care of them."

They talked about the shelter for another hour before they realized it was getting lighter outside. Then, they decided it was time to get moving.

******

Crossing Seneca Lake was easier than driving the country roads and avoiding the dead people, but there were surprises they hadn't considered. The lake was about three miles wide, but it took almost an hour to reach the opposite side.

The bow rider lowered from the boathouse easily enough,

and the engine wasn't half as loud as Tori thought it would be, but it was loud enough to attract dozens of smaller boats. Survivors outnumbered the bodies that floated on the surface of the lake. Pontoon boats that were meant for parties or short excursions along the shorelines were anchored in the middle of the lake, and smaller fishing boats with trolling motors swarmed around them. The powerful bow rider must have made the desperate people feel like rescuers were arriving. Denise was forced to change directions repeatedly to avoid colliding with them.

"Why didn't we see them from shore yesterday?" yelled Denise over the sound of the motor on the stern.

"I don't know. Maybe they arrived during the night," answered Tori.

They couldn't have known how right Tori was. People who survived on shore had been steadily pushed toward the lake by the hordes of infected dead. The lake was surrounded by docks and boats, and everyone who had survived the first three days had been forced from their homes to their boats. Too many of them brought their injured family members with them, and the pontoon boats resembled floating hospitals. Denise felt like she should warn them, but she knew it wouldn't help. She couldn't tell them they had to throw their injured people overboard.

Closer to shore, they began to encounter logjams of bodies that floated on the surface. When she idled the boat toward them, they waved their arms in their direction and snapped their teeth at the air. Denise had Jalen and Jacob move to the middle of the boat and sit on the deck below the windshield. She didn't want them to see more than they had to as she circled around the logjams and searched for one dock in particular.

When they finally reached the opposite shore, Denise aimed the boat toward one high dock and accelerated toward the ladder at the end. Tori helped her tie a line to the ladder, and they gathered their small supply packs.

"Why'd you pick this dock?" asked Tori.

Denise pointed at a building not far from the other end of the dock. There was a sign on it that they couldn't read from the boat.

"Vehicles," said Denise. "Have you ever driven an ATV?"

Tori thought about what the initials meant and shook her head.

"I doubt it, but you've seen the way I drive a BMW, so I can probably handle it."

"I've also seen you shoot, so get your gun out as soon as we get up this ladder."

Tori climbed ahead of the boys, and Denise waited on the boat until they were all safely on the dock. She couldn't see the full length of the dock from the water, but as she put her foot on the first rung of the ladder, she was jolted for the second time in two days by the sound of the Luger. Jacob's feet appeared above her, and he was moving so fast that she was afraid he would fall.

"Mommy!"

Jalen's high shout for his mother came from somewhere out of sight, but it was followed by two more gunshots. Denise grabbed Jacob when he was within reach and plucked him from the ladder. Her impulse was to climb up after Jalen, but like his brother, he appeared above and climbed down on his own. Tori backed onto the ladder, fired two more rounds from the gun, and climbed down to join Denise and the boys.

There was a moment of panic when Denise backed the boat away from the dock before Tori could untie the rope that held them in place. The rope stretched tight and pulled out one of the rusted bolts that held the ladder to the dock, but the rest of the bolts held them in place. Above them, there was the sound of cracking boards as the railing along the dock collapsed under the weight of bodies. The infected dead rained over the side.

Most of the bodies missed the boat, hitting the water without grace and sending waves sloshing over the front seats, but one landed squarely on the rope that stretched between the ladder and the boat. Two hundred pounds of dead weight was more than the old bolts could resist, and the ladder broke free with a series of cracking sounds almost as loud as the Luger.

In that horrifying split-second, as the bottom of the ladder came toward the boat, the cleat that held the line to the boat refused to surrender. The starboard side of the boat dipped downward, and the port side went upward as if it had been hit by a rogue wave. It threatened to capsize the boat, but even worse, Jalen was catapulted into the air. He flew over his mother toward the dock and landed against Tori's chest. She was already fighting for balance but was unable to stay on her feet when Jalen's weight was added to her own. She fell backward over the side of the boat. Denise saw the fear in her eyes as Tori fell.

Jacob had spent more time on the boat with his dad than Jalen or his mom. At Jalen's age, his father had shown him how to tie off the lines, and he knew that there was only one way to free the line from the cleat. While Denise screamed and threw her own body at the place where Tori had fallen overboard with her younger son, Jacob let himself slide across the boat under the steering wheel. As he went by, he grabbed the hatchet his father had mounted next to a fire extinguisher. His feet stopped against the gunwale on the starboard side, and he held the hatchet above the cleat. One hard swing was all he needed.

When the boat fell toward the port side and rocked in the water, Denise was thrown backward onto the deck. She was surprised when she was hit in the face by the Luger that had flown from Tori's hand when she had caught Jalen. Denise grabbed the gun and frantically rushed back to the side of the boat. She aimed at the water as if she could protect Jalen from above.

Jacob pulled himself upright while the boat bounced under him. He was still holding the hatchet, but he was already thinking about the next safety rule his father had taught him. They had even practiced the man-overboard drill. He undid the snaps that held several seat cushions in place and threw them into the water around the area where Tori and Jalen had fallen. Hands grasped at the cushions, but not the hands he had expected. To make matters worse, the boat drifted toward the dock as more of the infected dead fell from above.

Denise was only intent on solving one problem, and that was finding Jalen and Tori in the water. Jacob was forced to solve the other problems, and despite Denise screaming for him to help her, he knew he had to push the boat away from the dock. He retreated to the port side to where his father had shown him the line-handling pole. It was six feet long with a hook on the end. He pulled it loose and aimed it toward the bow just as an infected dead fell from above and landed on the seats in the front of the boat. The sudden shock of the arrival of the body made Jacob charge forward with the pole as if he were in a jousting match. The dead man only had enough time to stand up before the hooked end of the pole hit him in the chest and shoved him over the bow.

Jacob didn't have time to celebrate his small victory. Like any ten-year-old boy, he felt a moment of jubilation and wished someone had seen what he had done, but he stepped onto the seats in the bow and reached out with the pole. When the hooked end stopped against the protruding ladder, he pushed as hard as he could while he braced his feet. The boat resisted at first, but he felt it give in, and the boat slid away from the dock before the next body fell from above. It almost knocked the pole out of his hands, but Jacob instinctively knew he still needed it. That was when he heard the tone of his mother's screams change.

"I found them...they're over here," she yelled.

Jacob saw that his mother was climbing over the stern. There was a platform on both sides of the engine used for water skiing, and Denise was already reaching into the water while holding onto the stern with her left hand. Jacob jumped over the seats and the stern onto the platform with her. He reached the pole toward Tori's extended hand, but just as quickly, he changed his aim and poked an ugly face in the water behind her. Denise caught Jalen's jacket in her hand and pulled. Since Tori was holding him and kicking at the water, they both flopped heavily onto the platform while Jacob wrestled with the owner of the ugly face. The infected dead had managed to grab the hook and was threatening to pull him into the water.

"Let it go," yelled Denise.

The infected dead disappeared below the surface as soon as Jacob surrendered the tugging contest. The next important part of boating safety that Jacob had learned from his father was to remove them from whatever the dangers were, and he went to the engine ignition as if his father was guiding every step. He started the engines, checked behind him to see if the others were safe, and opened the throttle as he cut the steering wheel hard to the left. The boat peeled away from the dock, and he didn't stop until they were a hundred yards from shore.

Denise, Jalen, and Tori were huddled together in a wet pile on the deck below the stern. Jacob left the engine idling as he retrieved blankets from a storage compartment under a seat. He covered all three of them and said encouraging things while they cried. He didn't know what else to do, so he just joined their group hug and waited for them to get over the experience.

It seemed like an eternity, but Tori was the one who finally realized that their ordeal wasn't over. They had only survived one more close call.

"It's okay, Denise…it's okay. We made it back."

She also took a moment to give credit where credit was due.

"You saved us, Jacob. That was quick thinking with the boat hook."

She held Denise away from her so she could make eye contact and joined Jacob with reassuring words.

"We weren't bitten. You can check us over for yourself. We got wet, but that was all."

What Tori didn't tell her was how many times she felt cold fingers on her body while they were under the surface of the water. She had held one hand over Jalen's nose and mouth until they managed to pop up high enough to gasp for air, but it felt like lead weights were attached to her ankles as she was dragged down with the dead. She also didn't tell her that one of them had managed to lock its teeth around the back of her left arm for a moment. It felt like her arm was in a vise, but it suddenly let go when Jacob poked it in the face with the pole. She would inspect it later when she could, and she expected to find a bruise, but she was sure the teeth hadn't penetrated her leather jacket.

Denise brushed back the hair from Jalen's forehead, and he made her smile when he said, "Tori caught me, Mommy. I got water in my nose, but I'm okay."

Denise lifted her eyes from his face and said to Tori, "I don't know how many times we're going to save each other, but we've got to keep doing it until we reach the shelter."

"Too bad we can't team up with someone to make it the last few miles," said Tori.

"Why can't we?"

Tori shook her head and said, "We don't have time to conduct interviews, and how do you think people will answer when we ask them if they've been infected? You said it yourself. You didn't even know your husband was infected."

As soon as she said it, she realized she had exposed the truth in front of the boys. Their lowered eyes told her that they had been holding back their feelings, perhaps out of grief or denial, but her slip of the tongue had brought some of those feelings to the surface.

"I'm so sorry," she said.

Denise pulled her into a hug and said, "Forget it. We'll all talk about it later when we can say a proper goodbye to Brad and Randy together."

When they pulled themselves up from the deck and climbed into their seats, they saw that their arrival at the dock had sparked a lot of activity on shore. The ATV shop must have been the goal of every survivor in the area, and the infection had arrived with someone.

Denise said, "I don't know why I thought I was smarter than everyone else. I thought we could just cruise across the lake, get a couple of ATVs, and ride a few miles to Cayuga Lake."

"We obviously need a backup plan," said Tori.

"We have one, but I don't think you're going to like it," said Denise.

******

Denise was right...Tori didn't like the backup plan. As a

matter of fact, she didn't know how much she would hate the plan until they were forced to use it.

When Denise told her she didn't think they could safely dock anywhere along the eastern shore of Seneca Lake, Tori was in complete agreement. The noise caused by the activity on the dock at the ATV building was drawing more and more infected dead into the open near the other docks. Bodies were spilling into the water from so many docks that the places in between them resembled overcrowded swimming pools. There were no arguments from Tori about going back to the house when Denise told her about the tunnels, but the tunnels weren't as inviting as Tori had hoped.

Denise could have suggested that they use the tunnel under Seneca Lake while they were at her grandparents' house, but she had never trusted the tunnel the way her husband had. He mined salt for a living and drove around through the tunnels for fun. He always laughed when she said she was worried that they would make a mistake and dig a tunnel too close to the lake.

She told him, "One day, you're going to open a hole in the lake, and you won't even have time to say uh oh."

He answered, "We know what we're doing. We've got tunnels all over the place under Seneca and Cayuga Lake. As a matter of fact, someday, we'll be able to drive through the mines to get from one side of the lake to the other."

Denise told Tori she and Brad had talked about it for years until one day, Brad came home and told her they had done it. He said his crew had completed two tunnels. One was under Seneca Lake, and it ran from her grandparents' house almost to Cayuga Lake. The second tunnel began in a secure location west of Trumansburg, and it went under Cayuga Lake to their shelter. She thought he was joking until he offered to take her along on a drive under the lakes. She had passed on the offer to use the tunnel under Seneca Lake, but she let him talk her into making the trip to the shelter. He said she needed to see how to get past the security features.

Denise, Tori, and the boys were in the basement of the old house in front of an open shaft that descended into darkness. A ladder with a steel cage around it was the only way down.

"Did your husband ever consider putting in an elevator?"

"It's not as bad as it looks," said Denise.

She flipped a switch near the opening. Lights lit up the entire shaft, and she could see a big piece of construction equipment sitting at the bottom. It was bright yellow and much bigger than she had expected, even though it was squat in appearance. She thought it looked a lot like a low-rider convertible with armor added to it.

"That's our transportation," said Denise. "It's used to mine salt and drive it in the front bucket to the conveyor belts. If my husband were here, he would zoom through the tunnels like you wouldn't believe, but I've never driven it. I rode with him, so I know it's just like driving a truck, but I don't want to run into the walls. I'll be going much slower."

Tori said, "Normally, I'd volunteer to drive, but I never liked driving through tunnels."

"Let's get this over with," said Denise, as she attached a safety line to Jacob. Even though there was a cage around the ladder, she didn't want to take chances that the boys would slip. She sensed they were already exhausted by the events of the day, and they had a long way to go before they were safe.

Once they were all at the bottom, Tori surveyed the dark tunnels that branched away from the area where the vehicle was parked. The ceiling was lower than she had expected, and it felt claustrophobic. She was surprised by the breezes she felt coming from all directions.

"It's colder down here than I expected," she said. "For some reason, I thought it would be hot."

"My husband told me there are more vent shafts than tunnels. Fresh air is pumped into the tunnels from several locations to prevent gas build-up, stagnant air, and even pressure equalization," said Denise.

"Don't take this the wrong way," answered Tori, "but none of that is making me feel better. How long will we be driving down here?" She tried her best to keep her voice from shaking. The idea of being under Seneca Lake for even a minute made her question their sanity.

"I don't think I'll be able to drive more than ten miles per hour, so my best guess is about twenty minutes under the lake and then another ten minutes underground until we reach the exit. Then, we have to drive to the entrance of the second tunnel. That won't take more than ten minutes. After we're inside the back entrance to the shelter, it's another twenty minutes to the end."

It seemed like the longest hour of Tori's life. They had all climbed into the mining car, which was surprisingly comfortable. She revised her appraisal of the vehicle because it felt more like a convertible Humvee. The seats were reclined slightly, and the explanation for reclining inside a low tunnel wasn't reassuring. She could guess that it was a safety precaution to keep people from getting their heads cracked open by the protrusions from the ceiling. While they were under the lake, the protrusions were overhead lights and pipes that funneled air from land vents.

Jacob and Jalen had gone on an excursion through the tunnels with their father, and both of them were enjoying themselves. The boat ride hadn't bothered them until they ran into trouble, but they felt safer inside the tunnels. At least there was no one trying to get into the mining car with them. Tori chose to treat it like a commercial plane ride. She put her head back, shut her eyes, and told herself it would be just like flying from Atlanta to Columbus, Ohio, but her seat was more comfortable.

Denise hid it well, but she was a nervous wreck. The mining vehicle had a state-of-the-art navigation system built into the dashboard. It told her which tunnel to take as she snaked from left to right and back again. As an added safety precaution, the vehicle communicated with the tunnel's mapping system, and the overhead lights changed from white to green to show her the correct path. She was grateful that it was still functioning, and she understood that they would be lost forever in the maze of tunnels if her husband hadn't installed the system. Thinking about the technology made her think about Brad, and it worried her that her boys were being forced to accept losing their father so quickly. They were dealing with it better than they should have, and she wondered if it would be bad for them later.

Without realizing it, thinking about Brad kept Denise from thinking about the drive, and time went by quickly. The floor of the tunnel sloped upward, and a green arrow indicated there was an exit ahead. She slowed her speed and remembered that the vehicle would trigger automatic doors that opened on steel tracks. It was split in the middle to open like barn doors, and it didn't occur to her what might be on the other side of the doors until they spread apart.

SHELTER

Cayuga Lake - 2016

Stories were passed through the years by family members who worked in the salt mines. Most of the stories were embellished to some extent, but the common thread was that there was a Warren family shelter somewhere in the mines. No one knew exactly where it was, but a few people claimed to have actually helped build it. In the early years of its construction, the government had hired local contractors, but when Mansfield Warren teamed up with Titus Rush, he insisted on secrecy. Construction was done by workers from distant states and never on a long-term basis. Upgrades to the technology inside the shelter were largely completed by foreign companies.

By the time the infected dead arrived near Trumansburg, New York, the shelter had taken on the same status as the monsters that had never been proven to exist in the Finger Lakes. Fishermen over two centuries had reported sightings of *Loch Ness-type* creatures in the lakes, but modern technology had never been able to locate them. It was the same for the shelter. People in the villages around the lakes believed it existed, but no one could prove it.

The lake monsters and the shelter were unproven myths, but everyone knew where the steel doors were that opened to the tunnels. They had been amused when the doors appeared in full view between the Finger Lakes. When a local newspaper explained they were the entrances to tunnels that went under the lakes, everyone swore there was nothing that could get them to go through them. Only crazy people would go into a tunnel under all that water. There were even stories circulating about people who had been brave enough to use the tunnels, but those who did were never seen again. Those stories kept people from becoming too curious, but that was before the infected dead.

The population of the quaint village of Trumansburg was barely over two thousand people, and they were scattered along the shore of Cayuga Lake, but they all knew each other well. When the infection arrived, the citizens did what came naturally to them. They bandaged wounds and cooled fevers. They joined their neighbors to fight the infected dead and ultimately found themselves fighting their friends who had died. People they had gone to church with, worked with, and grown up with were dying and coming back to life. Pastors, Sunday school teachers, and postal workers were all turned against each other in a matter of days, and in their desperation, they tried to retreat underground.

Survivors of the first few days of the infection, numbering around fifty people, established their line of last defense around those doors. They parked vehicles of all types around them and filled in the gaps with anything they could find. By the time they were surrounded by old friends who wanted to bite them, they had closed the gaps and felt secure, but they knew they couldn't last long. They spent hours trying to pry open the tunnel doors, but they couldn't make them budge an inch.

The rumbling sounded like distant thunder that was getting closer, but there were no storm clouds in sight. As the thunder became louder, the small band of survivors realized it was coming from the other side of the doors. They backed away and watched as the big steel doors opened wide. They thought the thunder was coming from the doors themselves, but the front-loading mining car burst from the opening without slowing down. The people were too stunned to do anything but get out of the way, but those who were closest to the tunnel entrance took their chance to get away. They ran into the opening and disappeared into the maze of tunnels.

******

Denise didn't expect anything to be near the doors when they opened, and she didn't even see the people at first. Even though she wasn't going fast, the mining car felt like it was speeding through the surprised crowd. Someone screamed at her to stop, and she almost did, but Tori quickly recognized what was happening inside the barricade of cars, buses, and recreational vehicles.

"Go, go, go!" yelled Tori.

Denise pushed down on the accelerator, and the machine that was used for scraping ore from the walls of the mines lunged into the barricade. It was like pushing a hot knife through butter. The barricade was shoved aside, and Denise found herself driving through hundreds of the infected dead. This time, she wasn't in a BMW. She was still in a convertible of sorts, but the heavy piece of machinery rolled easily over the dead. She flattened a path through the crowd and forced the mining car to its highest speed. By the time she reached the nearest highway, there were no more infected dead to run over.

Tori's voice was several octaves higher than normal when she asked, "How far to the next tunnel?"

"About a hundred yards," answered Denise.

"Your husband didn't think of connecting the tunnels to each other?"

"Never got around to it, but the second tunnel entrance is hidden. Everyone thinks the other entrance is to a tunnel that goes both ways. It's a good thing no one knows about the second one, or we would find a barricade around it too."

Only a few minutes later, Denise came to a stop at a cliff face near a waterfall. Tori couldn't see anything resembling a tunnel door. Denise jumped out of the yellow mining car and ran straight to the wall. She pushed aside a heavy rock and some vines to reveal a keypad and a lever. She punched in some numbers and then pulled the lever down. The cliff face rumbled and moved. Behind it was the next tunnel. After she returned to the driver's seat and rolled the mining car inside, she jumped out for a second time and pulled another lever that closed the door.

Lights brightened inside the tunnel, and Tori saw it wasn't like the one under Seneca Lake. This one was more like one of the tunnels on the West Virginia Turnpike. She didn't care for them either, but she preferred the higher ceiling and the shining walls. It gave the appearance of strength, and she didn't feel like Cayuga Lake would come crashing down on them at any moment.

"What are you doing?" she called out to Denise.

Denise answered, "How much do you weigh?"

"What?"

"I said, how much do you weigh?"

Denise was standing in front of something that looked like a computer terminal. She had her hands poised over a keyboard and was waiting for Tori to answer.

"About one hundred and twenty pounds," said Tori.

Denise gave her a skeptical look.

"The truth, please...remember the security system I mentioned?"

Tori said, "Maybe one thirty."

Denise typed on the keyboard and then got back into the driver's seat. She sat still for a minute and appeared to be waiting for something. Tori was just about to ask her what it was she was waiting for when a buzzer sounded, and a light recessed in the wall turned green. Denise pressed down on the accelerator, and they rolled forward.

"Remember when I said my husband's father had security measures installed? That was one of them. I parked on top of a scale. Then, I had to input our combined weight plus the weight of the vehicle. My input would have to match the weight being read by the scale. If I had been off by more than a few pounds, steel rods would have come out of the floor and totally blocked our path. The doors would have opened again, but the bars wouldn't reset for twenty-four hours. The thing is, there aren't any instructions at the input terminal. If someone managed to break into the tunnel, they wouldn't know what to input, and the bars would activate as soon as they got past the scale."

"I'm glad I didn't lie about my weight...again," said Tori. "How did you know the weight of the mining car?"

Denise pointed at a small tag on the dashboard.

"It's printed on all of the vehicles used in the tunnel, so you only need the passengers' weights."

Unlike the tunnels under Seneca Lake, the Cayuga Lake tunnel was a smooth ride with no twists and turns. It was brightly lit, and Denise was able to increase their speed. In only a few minutes, Tori saw the end of the tunnel, and she was surprised when they entered a cavern with parking spaces painted on the floor. The parking area was directly in front of a large door that was exactly like the one Tori had seen at her bank.

"I don't believe it," said Denise, "but we made it."

"I hope you have the combination to that thing," said Tori. "Are you going to tell me what it is?"

Denise laughed, "Why? Do you think I'm going to lock you out?"

The boys piled out of the back seats excitedly and joined their mother by the door.

As Denise spun the dial to enter the combination, Tori surveyed their surroundings. The cavern was just like the caves she had toured as a child. Stalactites hung from the ceiling way above her, and stalagmites grew up from the floor on the left and right sides of the vault door.

"Where are we?" she asked

Denise was concentrating on the numbers, but she said, "We're not under the lake anymore if that's what you're wondering, but you can't get here from most of the tunnels in the salt mines. The mines were purposely dug out around the shelter."

"So, this is the back door?" asked Denise.

"Yep, but the front door isn't as easy to find and has more security because you can reach it through the salt mine tunnels if you know which of them to use."

Denise spun a locking ring and then pulled on the huge door. It was amazing to see something so big move without making a sound.

"Welcome to your new home," said Denise as Jacob and Jalen dashed inside ahead of them. They disappeared before Denise could even pull the door shut behind Tori.

"Aren't you worried about where they went?" asked Tori.

Denise laughed. "No, they love coming here. Brad brought them here more than I did, and if I had to guess where they went, I would say they're somewhere in the vicinity of the kitchen and game room by now. There's a soft-serve ice cream machine in the kitchen, and they deserve a treat after what they've been through. Ready for a tour?"

******

Tori had imagined a bunker with curved walls and space-saving features like cots, bunk beds, and smaller appliances. When she pictured in her mind what the pantry would look like, she saw rooms stacked high with sacks of sugar, flour, and rice. The overhead lights would have wires running across the ceilings alongside heating and air ducts and snaking down the walls to switches and vents. Entertainment systems would consist of a TV set with a game console and a DVD player plugged into it. The DVDs would be stashed away inside the storage benches that doubled as furniture.

As for the bathrooms, she thought there would be a toilet inside a space as small as a closet, and the shower would be behind a curtain. Hot water would be available once a month. There would be a generator humming somewhere in the background, and it would need to be refueled twice a day until they decided to cut back and give up hot showers completely.

She thought the tour Denise offered would take about five minutes, and she assumed the soft-serve machine in the kitchen and the game room would be in one corner of the bunker. Tori didn't come close to expecting the bright, modern decor in every room.

The area beyond the vault door was spacious, but it was sparsely furnished. Tori got the impression that it had a purpose because there was a reception desk and a computer terminal that faced a few rows of chairs. She thought it was quite similar to the Department of Motor Vehicles.

Tori asked, "Is there someone else here?"

"No, what made you think that?"

"I feel like we're supposed to take a number and get checked in first," she answered while gesturing toward the seats.

"That might be the one idea my husband had that was wrong," said Denise. "He had this fantasy about saving people during a disaster, and this is the processing area for the back door. The one at the front door is bigger."

"How was the processing staff supposed to get here? I mean, this may sound like a stupid question, but I think we're having a zombie apocalypse, and do you think FEMA is going to show up?"

Denise felt a bit stung by the question because it didn't appear that Brad had a grasp on the reality of how the shelter would be used. It was like an office without an office manager. No one was in charge to make everything run smoothly.

"Brad was such a humanitarian that he disagreed with his father's reason for making the shelter in the first place. He always thought there would be time to figure out how all of this was going to work, and he thought the shelter would be populated in an orderly fashion. You know, there would be an advance notice, and people would pitch in. We would give them shelter in return."

Tori could hear the sadness in Denise's voice and regretted the sarcastic comment she had made. She was alive because she had saved Denise and her children, and if not for the shelter, she didn't know where she would be.

"I'm sorry, Denise. I must sound so ungrateful, and I even made it sound like you and your husband should have planned for a zombie apocalypse. There are probably a few things you haven't shown me yet that would've been needed in other disasters."

"There's a decontamination room over there for radioactive fallout if that's what you mean."

Denise grinned slightly when she said it, so Tori knew she was forgiven. She held out her arms and gave her new friend a hug.

"Let's see the rest of this place," said Tori.

Denise led her through a door into a spacious hallway. Framed maps and signs gave them directions to living quarters, dining rooms, the kitchen, game rooms, a theater, an infirmary, and an armory. Some of the signs had placards next to their names that read, *Special Clearance Required*. The armory, food storage, and power plant had those placards.

Their first stop was where they found the boys. Denise had been right about how they would cope with everything at first. Denise explained that they would attend school just as they always did, but of course, the plan had originally included more kids and someone being drafted to fill the role of a teacher. For the time being, ice cream cones and video games were the best therapy for them. Tori was quick to point out that her educational background would make her a good teacher, and Denise was happy to accept her offer.

"See what I mean?" said Denise. "People will pitch in."

The room where Jacob and his little brother were buried in their own world was surrounded by video screens with seating that could accommodate dozens of children. They reclined in their own gaming chairs and paid no attention to the adults. Denise and Tori didn't disturb them and quietly moved on to the kitchen.

Tori was awestruck by the layout. Part of it was designed to make them feel as if they were at home in their own kitchens. It was smaller than the main mess hall and could have been part of any kitchen in a nice home. The marble counters and the breakfast island were surrounded by well-stocked cabinets and appliances. If Tori had designed her own kitchen, this is what it would have been like.

Beyond the single-family kitchen was something she would have expected to find in any cafeteria. Stainless steel was everywhere, and it was all behind a serving line that was designed to feed over a hundred people at a time. She could see the dining room beyond. The neatly arranged tables were surrounded by chairs that had overstuffed cushions. The impression was that people would dine in comfort, even if it was just a cafeteria.

"Now, I'm going to show you something really impressive," said Denise. "We're going to go to the living quarters last because you're going to spend enough time in your room until this craziness ends. I want you to see what we have at our disposal for now."

"Until this ends?" asked Tori. "You think it will end?"

Up until that moment, both of them realized they hadn't given much thought to how long the crisis would last. When it started, they expected to see the police rescue them. Then they thought they would see the National Guard show up. When they saw a military vehicle abandoned on the side of the road, they put aside any hope of rescue and knew they had to take care of themselves. Even then, they didn't think it would be forever.

Denise thought about her sons when Tori asked the question, and she had to wonder what it would be like for them to grow up in isolation.

"It has to end," said Denise. "This can't go on forever, can it?"

Tori felt like she had a way of slipping backward. For all she knew, most of the population of the world was either dead or struggling to stay alive, and here they were safe and sound inside a shelter. She wanted to feel grateful, but it was hard to be happy for herself when she thought about the deaths she had already witnessed. Her new husband was out there somewhere, but she had no illusions that he was alive.

"I have a feeling I'm going to be apologizing to you a lot," said Tori. "We both lost someone, and I'm having a hard time being optimistic. For all we know, the military will get this under control in a week or so, and I'm perfectly willing to hang out here until they do. Now, what were you going to show me before I became all doom and gloom again?"

"Everything we need to survive," said Denise.

Three hours later, Tori wondered if the surprises would ever end. When Denise said there was an infirmary, she had expected a good supply of first aid kits. Judging by the equipment in the sterile medical suite, they could treat almost any common injury. The updated medical library had all of the information they needed for procedures that would be well beyond their medical skills, but Denise explained they always hoped there would be medically trained professionals who would find their way to the shelter during a disaster.

The armory was more than just a gun closet. The Luger that Tori had on her hip felt small compared to the array of weapons at their disposal. If Denise was right about the shelter, they would never need the weapons, but for the time being, Tori chose to keep the Luger where it was.

The next stop was the food storage facility. The dry goods section was the largest part, and Denise told Tori there was enough food to feed two hundred people for ten years. According to her math, they wouldn't run out of food for five hundred years, and that was just the dry goods. There were several walk-in freezers with packages of meat and fish, and smoked meats hung from hooks.

"How does all of this get power?" asked Tori. "Better yet, how long will we have power?"

"Brad was an engineer," said Denise. "He told me we would have power as long as there was water in Cayuga Lake."

"It's hydroelectric?" asked Tori.

Denise smiled as she explained to Tori that the hydroelectric plant was more modern than the Hoover Dam, and that engineering feat could provide power to as many as eight million homes.

"We need a fraction of that amount of power, so all we needed was a small, efficient hydroelectric plant. Brad built one."

Getting around in the shelter was a concern for Tori at first. There were stairs that went from level to level, but she couldn't imagine how they would move supplies from the storage areas to the living quarters. Denise showed her a dumb waiter that had a huge pulley on it.

"There's one of these on every floor. Since they don't need electricity to operate, there's no drain on the power supply."

Denise said it was at least a good thing they would always have more than they needed, and Tori wondered if it would always be just the four of them inside the shelter. Only time would tell, but Denise told her she thought there might be a way to help people if they arrived, and they could work it out together.

"Wait, are you saying there's outside access somewhere? Isn't that a security problem?" asked Tori.

"I should show you. If you think they're a bad idea, we can always permanently seal them, but I thought we could talk about it first."

Tori wasn't sure she heard Denise right.

"Did you just say there's more than one outside access?" asked Tori in a surprised voice that was louder than she intended. "I thought the idea behind this place was that it was impenetrable...that no one could get inside, and it would withstand any disaster."

Denise held up her hands in self-defense.

"It's not what you think. Brad and I both agreed that if we ever had to use the shelter, it would most likely be some kind of short-term disaster. You know, not an apocalypse, but if it is something that lasts months or years, it wouldn't be good for the boys to never see sunlight again."

"Why am I getting a feeling that this is going to be something I don't like?" asked Tori. "The idea behind an impenetrable shelter is that there aren't any weak spots. This sounds like it's going to be a weak spot."

"It doesn't have to be," said Denise. "We don't have to use it if it's too dangerous."

"You might as well tell me about it, though."

Denise said, "Brad had a large compound built above ground, but it's in the middle of a heavily forested area. The underbrush surrounding it is so dense that no one would ever try to go through it. They would just go around. Inside the compound, after the protective barrier of the underbrush is a barbed wire-topped chain-link fence. It's more like a prison yard, I guess."

"Nothing could go wrong here," said Tori. "If it's that dense, how would we get to it?"

"The same way we got here. There's a tunnel that goes up to the middle of it."

Tori shook her head and said, "I've seen the vault door at the back entrance, and I have all the faith in the world that no one will ever get in, but I think we would be safer if we keep that little campground closed for good."

Denise reluctantly agreed, but she hesitated long enough for Tori to notice.

"What else aren't you telling me? Is there something you haven't shown me yet?"

"One other thing…it wasn't part of the original plans. It was just something that happened."

Denise was avoiding eye contact, and Tori had to take a more defiant position in front of her. Her arms had been crossed as she listened to the description of the above-ground enclosure, but her hands moved to her hips as if she was getting ready to fight. It was the first time since they had met that their partnership had become tense.

Denise continued, "Remember when I said the tunnels of the salt mines surrounded the shelter? There was an accident. Well, it really wasn't bad enough to call it an accident."

Tori let out an exasperated sigh. "Get to the point."

"One of the tunnels was dug too close to the lake. Water seeped into the tunnel, and it had to be sealed."

Tori tried to picture what that meant to them and why it made Denise appear to be reluctant to tell her about it.

"Are you telling me that the shelter is surrounded by tunnels on all sides except one? I thought you said it was totally isolated so no one will know there's a shelter here."

"It is," said Denise, "but Brad decided we could take advantage of the mistake. Maybe I should just show you."

Tori followed Denise across the shelter. They passed some of the sections Denise had already shown her, but she noticed a gradual change in some of the construction. They went through a door that Tori had only seen in movies or television shows. It was a water-tight door like the ugly, metal doors on a ship. After they stepped through it, Denise closed it and turned a locking wheel, and she didn't have to explain why she had taken the precaution when Denise saw the wall only twenty or so feet away. It was clear plexiglass.

"What is that?" she asked, even though it was obvious.

Denise had been prepared for Tori to be unhappy about the room, but she was also ready to explain it the same way Brad had told her about it.

"It's perfectly safe. That plexiglass wall can withstand tons of pressure...even better than the materials we would've had to use to make a solid wall."

"Is there something wrong with steel?" asked Tori sarcastically.

"Wait, let me finish explaining. It serves more than one purpose. Let me show you."

Denise rushed across the room to some equipment that Tori hadn't noticed at first. She had been so amazed by the size of the clear wall that she could only think about the way they would die if it collapsed. The weight of the water would crush them in seconds. A school of fish swam by, and then accelerated away from them when they saw Denise move.

Denise was excited about the seaquarium, and she wanted to sell Tori on the reasons Brad had given her.

"Look at this, Tori. This is more than a place where we can come to enjoy watching the fish swim around in the lake."

Tori was quick to answer, "That's not gonna happen. You won't see me sitting down here getting excited every time I see a big fish go by."

Denise ignored her answer and continued, "It's got a

pressure chamber. We can actually put on SCUBA gear, get in the chamber, and pressurize to the same depth as the outside. Then we can dive in the lake."

"Why in heaven's name would we want to do that?"

Denise had asked Brad the same question, and he had told her it might be a good skill to have if they ever needed to escape from the shelter. Somehow, Denise knew that she shouldn't give Tori that same answer. Her reaction would undoubtedly be the same one she had when Brad gave her the reason.

She remembered that day clearly and had said to him, "Why would we need to escape through the water?" Brad had told her it just seemed like a good idea to have another escape route, but to distract her from the idea of SCUBA diving, something neither of them had ever done, he pointed out that the chamber had another feature that made more sense. It had a large intake shaft that propelled water through it at a high rate, and that it could capture fish. He had pointed out the value of adding fresh fish to their survival diet, and Denise had simply accepted the explanation. She wasn't worried about the glass wall, but she doubted she would ever have to even think about SCUBA diving from the pressure chamber.

Denise's long pause as she remembered her conversation with Brad made Tori ask again, "I said, why in heaven's name would we want to do that? How deep is the water, anyway?"

"Oh, I'm sorry...I was thinking about what Brad had told me when he showed me this. I think he said it's about one hundred and fifty feet deep here."

Denise started to explain that there was an intake shaft that could catch fish for them, but Tori held up both of her palms toward Denise.

"Whoa...did you say one hundred and fifty feet? Do you have a clue what the water pressure is like at that depth? As a matter of fact, that plexiglass wall makes me nervous now.

If I remember right, that's around seventy or eighty pounds per square inch. I don't know exactly because I've never even considered the possibility of SCUBA diving. If Randy and I had made it to the rest of our honeymoon, I might have tried snorkeling, but SCUBA diving isn't on my bucket list."

Tori decided she didn't want to be near that plexiglass wall for one more minute and headed for the steel door.

"Wait a minute, Tori. You need to hear the rest. Brad told me the engineers said that the wall would be able to withstand two or three times the pressure at this depth. It's perfectly safe, and there's the system that catches fresh fish for us."

"I don't want to hear about," said Tori over her shoulder as she stomped away.

She was mad as hell, and despite all of the good things about the shelter, she couldn't understand how someone could think like a survivalist one minute and then act like they needed to live in a theme park the next.

"I won't be coming down here for the view, the fresh fish, or to go SCUBA diving," said Tori, "and you shouldn't either."

Tori spun the locking ring on the water-tight door, and she felt like she wouldn't be safe again until she was on the other side of it.

"And one other thing," she said when she turned around to face Denise, who had stayed where she was by the pressure chamber, "you remember when I said I was worried about why the mines were dug so close to the lake? You said the engineers knew what they were doing. You said they knew where the lake was, and that's why they could mine under it. Apparently, they don't know, or they wouldn't have had that water problem to fix."

Tori was ranting, but she couldn't stop herself. They had been through some hair-raising days and lost their husbands, and she had felt like the shelter was too good to be true. Now that she had a good reason to feel that way, she was finally letting down the emotional barrier that had held her together since the infection started. She knew that saving Denise and her boys had been the right thing to do from the start, and she would do it all over again, but she was disillusioned by the flaws in the shelter. She would have kept ranting if not for the movement behind Denise that made her blood rush from her head to her feet.

Denise saw the way Tori stopped talking as if she had something stuck in her throat. Tori still had one hand raised in the air and her mouth open, but her eyes were aimed at a spot behind her. Denise turned toward the plexiglass wall that went from the floor to the ceiling and found herself face to face with an infected dead. It was standing on the sandy bottom of the lake, but it was leaning forward with its mouth pressed against the glass in a wide grin. It leered at her hungrily, even as a large school of small fish darted around its head, snapping up the flecks of skin that floated away from it. Every time it pressed harder to reach Denise, more skin broke free from a large wound on its jaw, and the fish darted in for more.

Denise screamed and ran toward Tori. They piled through the door almost on top of each other, but they pulled the heavy door shut and spun the locking ring. They let themselves fall to the floor in a tangle when the ring stopped.

"You don't have to say it," sobbed Denise through a hoarse throat. "That door stays shut."

ITHACA

Suburbs of Ithaca, New York - 2025

We reached the outskirts of Ithaca well after sunset. It was never a good idea to be on the move at night, but our friends from Virginia wanted to catch us badly enough to be breaking that rule, and that meant we had to do the same. They had closed the gap between us twice when we were forced to avoid small hordes of the infected dead, but we had made up the time by making sure the hordes got between us and our pursuers. While they slowed down to dispose of the infected, we increased our pace. Our last big push toward the city gave us enough time to find a place to hole up for the night.

Over the years since the beginning of the apocalypse, we had learned that any place with a good fence could be safe if you had the time to be sure of two things. First, you had to be sure there was a way to get out once you closed the gate. The second thing was to be sure there wasn't something more dangerous inside the fence than outside. In our case, outside the fence were the infected dead and a gang of angry killers who had their minds set on revenge. We didn't know how many there were of each, and if we were lucky, they were spending their time clashing with each other.

Like any other city, Ithaca had no shortage of rental storage units. In the first few years after the infected dead arrived, they went from one extreme to the other as safe or unsafe places to hide. On the first day, while hospitals were overrun and police officers fought for their own lives, storage facilities were safe for a few hours, depending on who was inside the fence with you. If you were lucky and found yourself on the inside of the fence with uninfected people who had a strong will to live, maybe you could last more than a day. Most of them were just death traps where families hid inside individual units waiting to be rescued. Sooner or later, they ventured outside for food and water, but they never made it back to their tiny hiding places.

The storage facility where we reluctantly hid for the night was probably one of the places where someone inside had taken charge. Locks had been forced open on all of the units, and everything that could be used to fortify the fence around the property had been dragged out and added to the pile. Everything from furniture, to appliances, to car parts were stacked against a wrought iron fence with spikes at the top. We had circled it twice before reaching the conclusion that it might work. There were gates on the front and back. Both were closed but not locked. That took care of the requirement to have an escape route, so all we had to do was find out if we were going to have any unwanted roommates inside with us.

Jean and I had cleared a storage facility together in Guntersville, Alabama, a few years earlier, but we had done it in broad daylight, and we had a dozen people helping us. It had been easy. We had opened one gate and driven straight through the place in a fortified van. We drove out the back gate being followed by a horde of infected dead. They were eliminated as they gathered at the gate. Once their bodies were removed, it was wash, rinse, and repeat. Four trips through the facility was all we needed to clear it of the dead, and we were free to inspect the units for useful junk and supplies.

After eight years, the storage units in every city in the

country had probably changed ownership several times. Bands of survivors would kill all of the dead inside, live within the relative safety of the fences, then either move on or find themselves on the losing side of the battle from any number of causes. Some would run out of supplies, just like the early occupants who hid in their units on the first day, and some would make a mistake that let the infection inside. Going back to the very beginning, I could remember hearing about people hiding infected relatives in the hope that they would recover. Jean had seen it on the cruise ship where she had been a nurse, and it always worked out the same way.

The Ithaca storage facility only included about two hundred units, and they were all outside in neat rows with paved streets down the middle. None were housed in a central building where it was easier to get cornered if we ran into the infected dead. There was also the added advantage of being able to climb onto the rooftops if we were outnumbered. We decided to stay together and search as a group even though it would have been faster for us to split up. I took the lead, and we stayed in single file, moving silently from unit to unit. Jean was behind me, then Ruth, and Wally brought up the rear. We didn't bother to check the units that had closed doors. If there were infected dead inside them, there was no need to disturb them. Besides, almost every door was open. Ruth had suggested that there could be survivors inside the closed units, but Jean pointed out they could be worse than the infected. She reminded Ruth that survivors hiding inside with guns might be more inclined to shoot as soon as the door opened.

We walked in single file, close enough to one row of units to be able to see further inside, but keeping a watchful eye on the row across from us. I had my machete in front of me in one hand and my flashlight in the other. I shined my flashlight into the darkness before moving on, and Jean followed my beam with the barrel of her 9mm Smith & Wesson. If she had to take a shot, it would be at virtually point-blank range, but we hoped I would be able to handle anything hiding in the dark. If Jean pulled the trigger, it would give away our position, and we would be forced to make a hasty exit through the back gate.

One by one, we went down the row until we had checked them all, then we crossed to the opposite side to get a closer look at the next row. We were in the middle of the road approaching the first unit on the end when I saw that we were being followed.

Wally was too focused on the dark interiors of the storage units. He stared into each unit as if he expected to see something we had missed. He wasn't accustomed to being last in line and didn't realize his job was to keep anyone or anything from getting close to us in our blind spot. That was why we were caught off guard. Six of the infected dead were spread out across the paved access road between the two rows of storage units. They were moving slowly, but the groaning that always began when they spotted living people was escalating into a chorus. They were between us and the back gate, and that meant we didn't have a clear path toward one of our escape routes.

Jean said in a low voice, "Maybe we can skip this row and get around behind them. We can come back and finish this row from the other side."

"That's a good idea," I said. "You take over for me up front. I'll cover us from the back. Wally, put your gun in its holster."

I was about to remind Wally that we had to stay as quiet as possible, but the sight of the infected dead behind him caused him to snap. Instead of holstering his gun, he raised it and pulled the trigger. The bullet hit the infected dead in the shoulder and caused it to spin to the ground where it landed on its face. The other five stepped more quickly toward Wally.

Jean and I didn't hesitate. Instead of going around to the next row of units, we ran straight at the infected with our machetes in front of us. Ruth practically tackled Wally to keep him from firing a second shot, but he was so panicked that he managed to pull the trigger again. The shot went so wild that it didn't hit anything except a storage unit, but we knew our only option was to fight our way through the infected dead and leave by the back exit. We had to forget about spending the night in the storage facility. If the gang chasing us was anywhere nearby, they must have heard the shots.

The infected dead were no match for us, but we felt like the clock was ticking. We didn't bother with the one infected that had fallen on its face. We cut a path through the remaining five and ran toward the back gate. Jean didn't have to check to see if I was following her, but I glanced back to see if Ruth and Wally were with us. Ruth was pulling Wally to his feet, and she wasn't being shy about the insults she yelled at him. She was a lot smaller than him, but she gave him a hard shove in our direction.

I caught up with Jean as she untied the rope we had left on the back gate. She pulled it open just far enough to slip through, and she disappeared into the dark alley outside. I pulled the gate open a bit farther and held it open for Ruth and Wally. Once they went through, I joined them and looped the rope through the bars to keep any of the dead from following us.

The lights blinded all of us. I could see Jean, Ruth, and Wally as black silhouettes frozen against the brilliance, but I couldn't see the source. The low rumble of engines idling was enough for me to guess what was behind the lights, and I found myself hoping that it was someone new. If it was the gang that had followed us all the way from Virginia, I had no illusions that they would just let us go. I took a chance and walked closer to the lights until I was partially blocking Jean.

"Well isn't that something? You guys see that? That's what I call chivalry. The man stepped right up and put himself in front of the little lady."

The voice was deep and husky. It wasn't a voice that came from a small man, and I had no doubt that it was Branch, the leader of the people who had followed us hundreds of miles. All I could do was play dumb and try to talk our way out of dying. I didn't have to fake sounding helpless because that was exactly how I felt.

I couldn't think of anything better to say, so I said, "Can you give us some help, please?"

It might not have been the smartest thing to say, but they apparently thought it was the funniest thing they had heard in a long time. I couldn't see well enough to count how many people were behind the bright lights, but it sounded like a least two dozen men. They laughed hysterically until their leader shouted loud enough for them to stop.

Branch started to say something about my sense of humor, but he stopped and said, "Wait a minute. Where'd the little lady go?"

I was just as surprised as him, so I turned around expecting to see Jean right where she had been when I stepped in front of her. Ruth and Wally were still by the gate, but Jean was gone. I didn't know how she did it, but there was no sign of her.

"Enough of this," said Branch. "Get those three and find out where the woman went."

Over a dozen men rushed forward. I was thrown to the ground, and my hands were tied behind my back. Between the legs of my captors, I saw Ruth and Wally getting the same treatment, and several men went through the gate to the storage facilities. I twisted my head from side to side to see if I would find Jean hiding somewhere in the alley. I could only guess, but she must have gotten into my shadow when I stepped in front of her, and they were so intent on me that she had made it back to the gate.

I was lifted from the ground and carried toward the lights where I was roughly dumped into the bed of a pickup truck. I made a show of making it sound like it hurt worse than it did. I knew these guys weren't going to be impressed by our toughness, and there was still a chance that I might sell them on the idea that we weren't the people they were looking for.

The big man with the deep voice leaned into the back of the truck. He grabbed me by the front of my jacket and pulled me closer to his face.

"I'm only going to ask you this once. Which one of you torched the guys at the top of the bridge?"

If Jean had escaped through the gate of the storage facility, I knew every second I bought for her would mean the difference between her life and death. I didn't think I could hold out too long, but I had to take a beating for my wife.

"Mister, I don't know what you're talking about."

He hit me hard enough to make me see white dots floating in front of my eyes, but I didn't lose consciousness. Part of me wished I had because I wasn't faking the pain anymore. I didn't know if I could take another hit, but I pressed my luck anyway.

"I don't know what you want me to say. We've been hiding here for a week. What bridge?"

Branch raised his fist again, and this time I was sure he would knock me out, but he stopped with his arm cocked. He studied me as if he were reading information written on my forehead, then pushed me flat onto the bed of the truck. He reached past me and grabbed Wally by the ankle. Wally couldn't resist as Branch dragged him over me and out of the back of the pickup truck. I saw the fear on Wally's face as he disappeared over the side of the truck, and I heard him land hard on the ground.

Branch pounced on Wally as soon as he landed, and I could

hear the sickening sound of the big man's punches. Wally made protests at first, then the protests became pleas. The pleading stopped long before the punches did. I could hear Ruth crying behind me in the truck, but I had no doubt about Wally. When Branch stood up straight, he stared down at the ground and then lifted his foot and stomped several times. I saw when he faced me again that his eyes were glazed and unfocused. I didn't know if he was trying to decide whether or not to drag me out of the truck and do the same thing to me, or if he was trying to remember who I was.

It was almost like someone flipped a light switch on. Branch went from borderline insane to incredibly sad, and it was convincing enough that it would have fooled me if I hadn't seen his rage for myself.

"Aw, man. Look what you made me do to that guy. He probably never hurt anyone in his life, and you had to go and lie to me."

All I could do was stare at the big, bald man with blood on his fists. If I didn't know better, I could have sworn that a tear rolled down his cheek. Light reflected from it and made it shine until it disappeared into an oddly well-trimmed mustache. My guess was that he was at least six and a half feet tall, and the zombie apocalypse hadn't interrupted his workout routine. His dirty t-shirt sleeves were cut off at the shoulders, probably because they were too tight.

The man leaned toward me again, and this time I didn't think he would let me live, no matter how his expression had changed. He bunched the front of my shirt in his grip and pulled me onto the tailgate of the truck until I was in a sitting position.

Face to face and a few inches apart, he said, "I think that little lady who ducked out on us means something to you. After we catch her, I'm going to use her to make you talk. You can watch, and I'm willing to bet you start talking real fast."

"It was Wally," said Ruth through a choked voice.

"What?"

Branch let go of my shirt and grabbed Ruth by her ankle the way he had grabbed Wally. He pulled her closer and propped her up against me. She had been frail before, but she suddenly seemed like there was nothing left inside her to hold her upright.

"Who's Wally?" demanded Branch.

Ruth sobbed, "My brother…the man you just killed."

"I didn't kill anyone," he said with a straight face. "Oh, wait a minute. You mean this guy on the ground? That's your brother?"

Ruth didn't acknowledge his questions. She just sobbed harder. When he said he hadn't killed anyone, Ruth had fallen for it and was hopeful. Then she saw he was toying with her, and she went from hope to grief in a split second. Despite her anguish, I knew she had said it was Wally who had killed the men in the guard shack on the bridge to save me from the same fate as her brother.

"If I had known that sooner, I wouldn't have killed him so quick. I would've taken my time. One of the men in the shack was my kid brother, so I guess we're even, but I was gonna set fire to his killer and let him burn real slow. He was only five when the infection started, and I promised our folks I'd look after him."

I felt sick to my stomach when I heard what Branch said. Jean had been going through a lot of guilt about what had happened at the bridge. She must have realized at some point that one of the guards was young, but she couldn't stop what she did. I knew Ruth wasn't going to change her story, but if Branch even suspected it was Jean, I was afraid of what he would do to them both.

Branch was about to say something else, but he was interrupted by a group of his men returning. My heart sank when I saw that two of them were dragging a limp figure between them. I couldn't be sure it was Jean, but it was someone close to her size.

"We got her, Boss. We had to hurt her a bit because she's mean, but she's alive."

I tried to turn far enough to get a look at her, but Branch grabbed me roughly by the chin and yanked my head around toward him. I thought he was going to break my neck, and my spine actually popped from the sudden twist.

"What's this woman to you, big shot? Is she your sister?"

"My wife," I said weakly.

"You lied to me, big shot. You told me you didn't know about the bridge. You still wanna claim you've been hiding here for a week?"

Ruth had already taken the blame off Jean's shoulders by giving up her brother, so she kept doing what she could to keep her alive.

"It was just me and Wally at the bridge. We ran into these people and tried to hide with them here."

Branch slapped her hard enough to knock her over, and without even a pause, he pulled a long knife from his belt. I thought he was going to use it on Ruth when he lifted his hand across his body and brought the knife down in a slashing motion, but he rotated his body to the right and violently sliced the neck of the woman who was still being held by the two men.

I don't think there had ever been a time in my entire life when I had felt so weak, so helpless, or so cold. It was like every drop of blood in my body had gone to my feet, and I would never feel warm again. At that moment, I wished Branch had held my face so I couldn't have seen her die. I should never have given in when Jean said we could go on this mission without the Chief.

I must have screamed before I cried, but whatever it was I had done, it did nothing but amuse the men. Everyone widened the circle around the woman to avoid being hit by the spray of blood, but they laughed uncontrollably at my distress. They dropped her in a heap, and all I wanted to do was go to her and stop all of that blood from coming out. Branch didn't stop me because he was enjoying it too much. With my hands tied behind my back and my ankles tied together, I landed hard on the pavement. As dizzy as I felt, I probably wouldn't have done any better with my hands and feet free. I wriggled my body against the rough asphalt until I reached her, and I let myself roll onto her body.

"Jean! No...don't."

I didn't know what I was asking her not to do. All I really knew was that she was bleeding to death, and I didn't want her to die. I was almost cheek to cheek with her, and the laughing that seemed to be coming from everywhere around me increased to hysteria when the head above the severed neck lifted backward. Bared teeth came toward my face, and I knew at any moment they would sink into me. They snapped shut just as Branch grabbed my hair and yanked me off of her.

"I'm not ready for you to die, big shot. I need to keep you alive a little longer and find out more about you. How'd a bunch of runts like you survive for so long?"

As he pulled me away, I watched the face snap at empty air, and I wondered where they had found this woman hiding and where Jean had gone. This poor woman had survived the apocalypse for the same number of years that we had, but now she was dead just because this maniac thought she was someone else. I felt grief for her and for whoever it was that loved her and wouldn't see her alive again. The grief I felt for this one poor soul was hardly enough to stop me from feeling relieved that it wasn't Jean, but it was enough to help me hide it.

For good measure, I asked Branch if he would let me bury my wife. I hoped I wasn't over-acting, but his reaction told me he bought it.

"That really was your wife? I'm sorry, man."

His laugh told me he was anything but sorry. He lifted me easily by the back of my collar with one hand and tossed me over the side rail of the truck again. I landed hard next to Ruth. She was still crying softly because her brother was so brutally murdered, but she had heard everything that happened when they slit that poor woman's throat.

"I'm so sorry, Eddie," she whispered. "I could tell from the moment I met you two that you loved each other very much."

I didn't know where Branch had gone, and I couldn't turn my head far enough to see anything but the walls of the pickup truck bed. For all I knew, he was standing right behind me listening to every word. I couldn't risk telling Ruth that Jean was alive until I knew no one else would hear me.

"I'm sorry about Wally. I don't know why Branch killed him, but I'll make him pay."

My bravado didn't earn me a slap in the back of the head or generate any amusement, so I assumed Branch was gone, but I didn't just say it for the reaction. I really felt that somehow, someway, there would come a time when I would see Branch on the ground with his throat cut. I think the thought began when he lifted me so easily by the back of my collar. There was only one man I knew who was that strong, and he was someone who hated bullies more than he hated the infected dead. A small part of me believed the Chief would be the one who put Branch face down in the dirt, even though our big friend probably didn't even know we were in Ithaca, New York.

******

Doc Bus was waiting for the Chief to land the flagship of their survival group. The runway had been secured an hour in advance by a squad of soldiers who were ready to call off the landing if too many infected dead wandered into the area. A horde had been spotted on I-20 heading south, and another squad was following them at a distance. There was no telling what had caused the horde to become organized, but the sound of an AC-130 landing near the shelter might be enough to turn them around.

When the drone of the plane's engines reached his ears, Bus lit a green smoke bomb and tossed it into clear view. They could have made radio contact for him to let the Chief know that the landing area was secure, but they always went on the assumption that someone else might be listening. Plus, the last thing Bus wanted was for the Chief to engage in a casual conversation before they were face-to-face. It was bad enough that he wasn't telling the Chief about Ed and Jean, but he was afraid he might be put in a position where he had to lie.

The AC-130 made a smooth landing, circled the field they had flattened into a runway, and coasted to a stop a few yards from where Bus waited. He saw the Chief wave from the cockpit, but he wasn't sure who was in the plane with him at first. Then he saw more familiar faces, and judging by the smiles, everyone had made it home. The door opened before the Chief shut down the engines, and the steps were lowered.

Kathy came out first, and she ran at him for the big hug she expected. Over her shoulder, he saw new faces mixed in with the familiar friends. Somehow, he managed to greet everyone and shake hands or exchange hugs without losing the smile on his face. He was glad to see each of them, but if he had tried to pull it off with the Chief first, he doubted he could have hidden the news from him. By the time the Chief's big hand grabbed his and pulled him into a hug, he had gotten the chance to fake it for a bit. It was the Chief's first comment that hit him hard enough to make him pause, and the Chief saw it.

"Not that you aren't a sight for sore eyes, but I expected a bigger party. Where's the rest of the gang? Eddie and Jean too busy to come out and welcome us home?"

Bus opened his mouth to speak, but nothing came out. The Chief was what some people called a force of nature. It wasn't just his size. It was the way he stood as if he were comfortable anywhere. It tended to make people standing near him feel comfortable. The reverse was also true. If something was bothering him, you could almost feel it in the air. With Doc Bus standing in front of him with his mouth open, the Chief's body visibly shifted, and everyone stopped talking.

"What's happened? Where are Eddie and Jean?"

It wasn't just the way the Chief stood. His tone of voice was more potent than truth serum, and Bus told him everything.

It was an understatement to say the Chief was furious. Everything had gone so well in Alaska that the unexpected news about Ed and Jean sent his good mood straight through the floor. No one in the shelter wanted to tell him that two of the most important people in the world to him had done something so stupid. The Chief made traveling seem as safe as it had been before the infection, but everyone knew he just made it seem that way. He had to be focused on getting back from Alaska safely, so telling him that Ed and Jean had gone on a mission without an armed squad of soldiers might have made him reckless. No one wanted him to rush and make a mistake that would get him killed. Not to mention everyone who was traveling with him. When Doc Bus told him, he hoped it would at least make the Chief feel better to hear the details of their mission. He told the Chief he had tried everything to stop them, including a guilt trip about leaving their son, Josh, without his parents if they didn't make it back. He also hoped the rest of the Mud Island family could calm him down.

The Chief had been over the moon since before leaving Alaska because he had gotten a surprise visit from Cassandra and Sim. They had delivered a message to the rest of the group that they had changed their minds about staying in Alaska. It had been a nice change of pace for both of them, but they knew in their hearts they belonged together with the rest of the Mud Island family. Even their old friends from Executive One had decided they were tired of hiding on the fringes of the world, and they felt like it would be the right time to start fighting back against the infected dead. The base in Alaska was in capable hands. Besides, they wanted to see if they were better suited to a warmer climate. Survival in the harsh cold of Canada had worn them down.

Now, as they all stood in a circle around Doc Bus and the Chief, there was a sense of urgency hanging over them like a cloud. They were missing two members of their family.

JALEN AND JACOB

Warren Family Shelter - 2016

The first order of business after giving Tori a tour of the shelter was a family meeting. Denise felt like she should have a long discussion with the boys about what had happened to their father and about what they had to do to stay safe. The details would be easier for Jacob to understand, but Jalen was at a far more vulnerable age. While Denise could ask Jacob to be the new man in the family, Jalen was still the baby. In a way, it would be easier for Jalen over time, but in the present, he was the one feeling the most emotion.

She found the brothers where she had left them earlier and told them to spend one more hour playing video games before meeting with her in the family living area. In her experience, giving them the extra time would make them more willing to stop playing, and one thing they were going to have more of was time. She used the hour to make the first meal in the shelter and to think about what she was going to say to the boys. Tori gave her a hand, and Denise was able to share a few thoughts with her about their new life underground.

Tori was still a little wide-eyed by her surroundings. If she didn't know she was in a shelter deep inside a salt mine, she would swear she was in a model home for a suburban neighborhood. The single-family kitchen was just like any she had ever seen, with the exception of the lack of windows. It was completely furnished with all of the same appliances, and everything was decorated to give the impression that it really was a new home. It was separated from the larger kitchen that could feed an army of people, but it wasn't so small that she would get claustrophobic.

"I was wondering," said Denise, "would you mind sitting in with me when I talk with the boys?"

"No problem. Do you know what you're going to say to them?"

"The truth…or what I think is the truth."

Tori said, "I've been trying to figure that out myself. What's the truth? Did we really just have a zombie apocalypse? Did we really just lose our husbands and everyone else we know? How do you explain that to children?"

"I guess that's why we're talking about it now before we sit down with Jalen and Jacob. I'm not as worried about Jacob. Did I tell you about what happened when I sent him to the ice machine in the hotel?"

Tori shook her head.

"I knew when he came back to the room that he would never be the same again. He was an innocent ten-year-old boy when he left the room. When he came back, he was so afraid, but something made him get over it. I think he knew how much harder it was going to be for Jalen. He knew he had to protect his little brother."

"You're lucky," said Tori. "From what I saw in the hotel, you're lucky he made it back from the ice machine, but you're also lucky he stepped up. Do you think he's figured out this could be permanent?"

"We're about to find out, but I think he's got his hopes set on being rescued. He's always believed in following the rules, and adults get their rules from teachers, police, and bosses. At least that's what Jacob thinks. The new reality is that you and I will be making all of the rules now," said Denise.

Tori was caught off guard. She hadn't thought that far ahead, but she knew Denise was right. They were likely to be the only authority figures for the boys for a long time, and she realized that she had been thrust into the role of a parent.

"Maybe we should ask them to call me Aunt Tori?"

Denise thought for a moment and said, "I like that. It will go a long way for us to think of each other as family."

"Hi, Mom. Is the food ready?"

Jacob led Jalen into the room in front of him. It was the very picture of the phrase *herding cats* because of the way Jalen weaved from side to side. Denise thought it was a good sign that Jacob was asking about food.

"Wash your hands, guys. We're going to eat and then have a nice chat," said Denise.

The familiar sounds of the boys talking over each other while Denise and Tori set the table gave them the right atmosphere for a meal, followed by the talk that Denise wished she could avoid, but Tori turned out to be the right person to help her. Jalen went after his plate of macaroni and cheese as if it were any normal day. He and Jacob didn't skip a beat in a long-running discussion about who had won the first game. Denise let them keep going while they ate because it gave them all a sense of normalcy. When they were done eating, Denise had them help clear the dishes before asking them to have a seat in the living room.

Just as the kitchen had been designed to make the shelter occupants feel more at home, the living room was for comfort. A television set dominated one wall, but Denise and Tori had agreed they would turn it on after talking with the boys.

Once they had assessed their state of mind, they would face the reality of the news together, but first, they had to make some decisions together. Everyone found a place to sit on the overstuffed sofa and recliners, and it was time to get the truth out in the open.

"We have a lot to talk about," said Denise.

She had expected a reaction, but she was surprised to see one immediately. Jalen's head lowered, and his sniffle gave away that he was holding back the tears. Denise's first impulse was to hold him, but Jacob surprised her. She had seen him protect his little brother plenty of times, but this time, he did it without having any protection for himself. Denise realized that she had been right about Jacob. He understood that literally everything had changed.

"Hey, bro...we talked about this, right?"

Jalen sniffled again, but he acknowledged his brother with a nod.

To Denise, he said, "It's okay, Mom. It's not your fault. That man at the beach made Dad too sick. We talked about it, and we want to have a...something for dad, but I don't know what to call it."

Denise and Tori were stunned, but most of all, they were grateful. Denise still didn't know how far to go with the truth, but Jacob had already been a big help with his brother.

"A memorial service?" asked Tori.

"Yeah," said Jacob. "We need to do something to remember Dad, and maybe we could do something for your husband, too."

An instant lump took shape in Tori's throat, and she found it difficult to swallow. She had been pushing back her own feelings for the sake of these two boys she had only known for a few days, but Jacob had innocently reminded her that it was okay for them to mourn now. Her own sniffle got Jalen's attention, and he lifted his wet eyes toward her. She instinctively got up from her chair and went to them. All four of them embraced each other and cried softly.

They all felt better after their group hug, and Tori took the opportunity to reintroduce herself to the boys. They were happy with her suggestion for them to call her Aunt Tori, and their agreement made it official. They were too young to call her by her first name alone, and giving her a title made them all part of the family.

"I have an idea," said Denise. "I think we just had our first memorial service. Let's mark today on a calendar, and we'll have another one on the same day every year, so we never forget your dad and Tori's husband. Agreed?"

When everyone agreed, Denise told them to get some ice cream and go back to their video games. It was an instant celebration as Jalen and Jacob rushed off to the kitchen.

"That was brilliant," said Tori.

Denise nodded, "They were at their limit, so I ended it on a high note. Besides, it's time that you and I spend some time trying to find out what's happening above ground. Brad made sure we got good reception in the shelter, and if there aren't any TV stations on the air, we should be able to find something on the internet."

The boys passed through with their ice cream on the way back to the game room, and as soon as they were out of sight, Denise suggested something a little stronger for themselves.

"Please," said Tori. "I feel like I could sleep for a week, but I don't know if I can make my mind shut down. Maybe something from your private stock will do the trick."

"It's not private anymore. Everything that's in this place is yours too, okay?"

"Okay," said Tori as she clinked her glass against Denise's.

They were surprised by how many stations were still broadcasting. Some were even running syndicated shows as if it was any normal day. There was something unreal about the contrast between the news and sitcoms. It was almost as if the sitcoms were the *real* shows, and the news broadcasts were something they could watch any time they wanted, but Denise found herself refilling their glasses only a couple of minutes later.

A tired man with a beard was reading from a list on a sheet of paper. When he lifted his eyes toward the camera, they could see the red rims even behind his glasses. He uncharacteristically ran his fingers through his hair as if he didn't know what he should be doing with his hands while he read the list.

"Shelters are closed at the following locations," he said. "We're advising that you disregard the earlier broadcasts that said to go to these locations if you need help."

The man read the names of local schools, churches, and businesses where the police had attempted to give assistance. Denise and Tori recognized the name of the ATV dealership over by Seneca Lake. Someone handed the man another sheet of paper, and the man announced that his station was still taking calls from people who were trying to locate family members or friends.

"At the top of every hour," he said in a hoarse voice, "we'll give out personal messages so you can let your families know you are safe somewhere. Just give us a call at the number on the screen."

The list of messages was longer than the previous list of shelters that were closed, and the tired man knew he had a problem when he read a message from a woman named Marlene Johnson telling her husband that she and the kids were safe at Lake City High School. It had been on the list of shelters. He scanned the list and found more messages like that one. Not knowing what else to do, he got up from his news desk and simply walked away.

Tori and Denise could have switched channels, but they were fascinated by the disappearance of the reporter, and they wondered if he would come back. It was also the television station closest to their location, and something made them feel like the local news was more important than the national news. That might change in a bit, but Tori posed a question to Denise that she couldn't answer.

"Did your husband tell a lot of people about the shelter? I mean, didn't you have neighbors or friends who you were close with?"

Denise searched her memory for any indication that Brad had given away their secret. They had talked about it plenty of times, but they always came back to the same problems. She remembered how bad it made her feel on one particular occasion. They wanted to tell their best friends, Mary and Lewis Harkness, about the shelter. Their kids went to school with Jalen and Jacob, and it seemed like protecting them was the right thing to do.

"We wanted to tell our best friends," said Denise, "so we decided we would pose it to them as a hypothetical situation. We got together for supper a lot, so one weekend we asked them what they would do if they had a big shelter and there was an apocalypse of some kind."

"What did they say?" asked Tori.

"They took the bait and talked about it like it wasn't possible to have a shelter that could be shared. Brad and I were shocked by their reaction, but it turned out to be the best way to have the discussion. Since they didn't know about the shelter, they were able to give objective opinions. They came up with a laundry list of problems. For instance, what if you invited one neighbor, but they couldn't keep a secret and told their extended family about it? It would only be a matter of time before hundreds of people who heard it from a friend of a friend would want to know if they could come to the shelter."

"I can see that happening," said Tori. "What else did they say?"

"Well, we asked them what if it could be kept secret from everyone except a few close friends, and they said it depended on the nature of the disaster. If it was a nuclear war, and if none of them were exposed to radiation, they would have to shut the door to keep the radiation out, but they couldn't accept the hypothetical belief that no one else would find out about the shelter. They said relatives and friends they never knew they had would be banging on the door wanting to get in."

"I saw that plot in an old TV show," said Tori. "Neighbors turned on each other pretty fast. What about an infection like this one?"

Denise nodded as she remembered the discussion.

"That hypothetical didn't go very far. As soon as Brad pitched it, Lewis said everyone inside the shelter would be dead within a week."

"A week? Why so soon?"

"Lewis said that you can only keep an infection out one way, and that was to keep the doors shut to start with. The more people you let inside at the start, the more likely it is that someone will be infected when you close the doors. He said people either wouldn't know they're infected, or they wouldn't tell anyone that they are."

"So, that settled it?" asked Tori. "You know, you never got around to showing me the main entrance. If it's anything like the back door, my guess would be that you and your husband decided you wouldn't tell anyone about the shelter until the last minute, and then it would be based on what's happening outside."

"We couldn't know for sure, so there's a lot of wasted space up there. You're right. We would've decided at the last minute," said Denise.

"Are we deciding now? I mean, your husband isn't here to decide, and I'm assuming I have a say in it," said Tori. "I would have to say we can't take the chance by opening the door."

Denise nodded again. "We already know what's out there. Brad and I figured the tunnels inside the salt mines would be full of people, no matter what kind of disaster happened, unless it was a flood. The reason I didn't take you to the front entrance is because I would know what's on the other side of the door."

The television caught their attention as the man returned to the anchor desk. He appeared to be more composed, and he had combed his hair. He cleared his throat and apologized for his abrupt exit, then went back to reading his list as if he had never stopped.

Denise couldn't take more of the man's defeated presentation of the information, and she switched the channel. She stopped on a major news network that was showing aerial footage of a city, and after a minute, the banner at the bottom of the screen confirmed it was downtown Atlanta. The two women had expected to see the police or military responding to the events of the last few days, but even though there was evidence of the response, the only moving people they saw were obviously dead. The failure of the response was apparent, judging by the number of dead who were wearing uniforms.

It was more of the same on every channel, but they both felt like there was more to be gained by watching for anything new than by turning it off. Plus, they had a long way to go before they even put a dent in the liquor supply. They were getting drowsy, but they woke up again when a channel showed a live broadcast from Niagara Falls.

A helicopter hovered over the Falls on the Canadian side, and the view made Tori and Denise sit up straight for the first time in hours. The camera view was in the direction of their hotel, and both of them saw it as the place where their husbands were last seen alive. Denise had a mental image of the room with her husband trapped inside, but Tori could only picture Randy in the last place she saw him. She wanted to believe that he had somehow found a way out of that nightmare, but if he had, it also meant he had left her behind. She felt a pang of guilt at the thought of him escaping without her because that was exactly what she had done. Then again, if he had escaped, he would have no way of knowing that she had survived too. Her emotions went from one extreme to the other as she fixed her eyes on the smoldering hotel. She couldn't be sure, but it appeared the fire had only burned through the upper half of the building.

A wider camera angle revealed that almost every tall building was burning, and people were going over the Falls from all directions. The area at the bottom of the Falls, where tourists had worn raincoats and gotten closer in small boats, was clogged with a mass of bodies.

"Are we the only people who got out of there?" asked Tori.

"If not for you, you wouldn't have anyone to ask that question. We would've died there," said Denise.

"If I hadn't helped you, where would I be now? I didn't have anywhere to go that compares to this."

Tori gestured in a sweeping motion with her glass, then laughed.

"I think I need a refill."

******

Television broadcasts lasted much longer than they expected. On that first night, the two women drank until they went to sleep on the sofas. They woke up with terrible hangovers, and both swore they would never drink again, but until they settled into something even close to a normal routine, drinking was probably what helped them to cope with the new reality.

On that first morning after their long night of commiserating with each other for their losses, they woke up to find the boys sitting in front of the television. They each had lap trays and were focused on bowls of cereal. Denise watched Jalen chase around a spoonful of Fruit Loops, and as soon as he caught the last one, his big brother poured him another helping from a plastic container. Her first thought was that the supply of milk wouldn't last, so she was glad they were using it first. She felt a little guilty that they had gotten their own breakfast, but she imagined Jacob had been the one who supervised it. She was glad he had taken over for her, but she wished he had made her a cup of coffee.

Tori stirred and lifted her head from a sofa cushion.

"Don't get up," said Denise. "First round of coffee is on me."

Both of her sons took a moment to say good morning, but they immediately went back to what they were watching. Denise was so groggy that she hadn't noticed they were watching cartoons until she was almost past them. She glanced at the console below the TV and saw that the DVD player wasn't turned on. She knew that she and Tori had left the TV on the news.

"Jacob, what channel is that?"

"I don't know, Mom. Cartoons were on, so we didn't change it."

Tori followed her into the kitchen and helped her with coffee and some toast. After drinking themselves to sleep, neither one cared for much more than that.

"What happened to the news?" asked Tori.

"I don't know. My guess is that the local networks went down. If we get anything, it's going to come from the big networks. I'm going to check the internet."

The internet connection was spotty at best. Besides the slow speed, it was obvious that websites weren't being updated. Major news networks had the same articles posted from the previous day, and Denise couldn't find any good news. There was one page that opened even when she selected different pages. It was a single screen with a message in bold letters. It didn't say anything they didn't already know, but what it said told them enough. The message was dated two days ago, and it said it would be updated every hour. Denise turned off the monitor.

"I imagine that same message will be there the next time I turn it on."

When they returned to the living room, they sat with the boys and watched cartoons while they let the caffeine revive them. The atmosphere of normalcy was good for all of them. Tori and Denise were content to enjoy it while they could.

ISOLATION

Ithaca Shelter - 2016

Tori, Denise, and the boys celebrated the end of their first week in the shelter with a huge chocolate cake. In the middle of it was one candle for Brad and one for Randy, and their names were spelled out with white frosting. They wished they could have included candles for everyone they had lost, but Tori and Denise agreed they wanted it to be a celebration of their survival more than a memorial, and they would have a cake every year to remind themselves they were the lucky ones. They blew the candles out together.

Denise felt like she had missed something that Brad had told her about the TV and internet reception. She couldn't believe they had been cut off so quickly, so she and Tori explored the areas of the shelter where Denise had spent less time. They learned that her husband had anticipated the loss of connection with the outside world and had installed sophisticated technology in a small theater where they could monitor the progress of disaster recovery. The shelter had a direct link with a satellite network that allowed them to surf internet channels as well as television stations. She could keep the boys busy with the DVD player in the living room while she and Tori used the theater system.

After Jalen and Jacob were tucked safely in their beds

at night, Tori and Denise retreated to the theater to catch any broadcasts they could. They didn't know how long the technology would keep working, but they suspected it would outlast the living population of the planet. Their nightly visits to the theater were meant to keep them informed, but they were also a reminder of the danger they would face if they ever forgot the rules that would keep them alive.

As they settled into the same chairs each night and poured drinks over ice, it didn't escape their attention that they were seeking the comfort of new habits. They had the same chairs, the same drinks, and the same way of searching through the channels or searching the web. Those were all things that made them feel reassured that they would be alive to do the same things tomorrow. Most conversations even began the same way, but they knew from what they saw on TV that they wouldn't always say the same things. Eventually, there would be nothing to talk about except what happened inside the shelter. That was why they began their discussions with the rules they should follow.

Three weeks into their self-imposed isolation, Denise was locating the television station in the menu when Tori asked if it would be a good idea to put the rules into writing. Denise turned on the seventy-five-inch TV and found the station, but before turning up the volume, she turned her attention to Tori and her question.

"I don't understand why we would need to."

Tori didn't want to step on any toes, but if they were going to live together, she felt like she should have some say-so when it came to the boys.

She hesitated but said, "I think the rules should be in writing and reviewed with your sons every day. You know, sort of like a pledge at breakfast."

Denise felt like someone had raised the temperature in the

room. There hadn't been any conflicts when it came to her sons listening to Tori, so she immediately felt like there had been a problem she didn't know about.

"Why?"

Tori cleared her throat, obviously uncomfortable, and said, "I heard Jacob talking about the place outside. You know, the enclosed area where it's supposed to be safe for them to go out for fresh air. We agreed that the place and the big aquarium room are off limits. Those are two of our rules."

Denise went from feeling too warm to having chills. The thought of the boys going outside frightened her more than the aquarium.

"Okay, do you want to do it, or should I?"

"I think it would mean more to them if it came from their mother. After you write down what we've talked about, maybe you could bring it up at breakfast, and then I can ask if we can go over them again the next day. It would be more natural to them."

Denise felt better, but she was still worried. She hadn't even taken Tori to the enclosure above the shelter. That's how afraid she was of its very existence.

"Maybe I should also show you the place," said Denise, "in case you ever need to get out of here in an emergency or something."

Tori was about to object when something on the TV caught her eye. She motioned for Denise to turn up the volume. Denise hit the button, and the speakers erupted with the sound of explosions.

The view was from a tall building in New York City. In all directions, smoke poured from fires that burned freely. There were no fire engines surrounding the building with ladders extended or fire hoses pouring water on the fires.

"Is this a replay of yesterday's broadcast?" asked Tori. "It looks the same."

The timing of her question fit perfectly with the arrival of a pair of fighter aircraft in the distance. They were approaching at high speed, first appearing as two fast-moving dots but growing rapidly. Light reflected from missiles as they dropped from the wings of the fighters and exploded into tall buildings. The explosions collapsed the buildings in a spectacular display.

Denise said, "That didn't happen yesterday while we were tuned into the news. I was watching the live broadcast on 911 when the second plane hit the twin towers. I remember I had a moment when my mind said I must be watching a replay of the crash. Then I realized it was live, and I felt ashamed that I had just witnessed lives being lost. I'm feeling that way now."

"Are you feeling guilty about surviving?"

Denise lowered her head, and Tori could easily guess that she was reliving that day at the beach and thinking about Brad.

"Why didn't I get up and get between my boys and that man on the beach? I just sat there and watched Brad do it."

Her voice cracked, and tears ran from the corners of her eyes.

"Here it comes," thought Tori. "We're finally going to let the grief out."

"You didn't do anything wrong, Denise. Brad did what fathers do. If you had gotten up to follow him, he would've told you to stay where you were. The last thing he or the boys needed was for you to get infected, too. Neither of you knew it was going to come to that, or he wouldn't have punched the guy in the mouth, but trust me on this one. You would've been in the way because he would've been trying to protect you too, and then maybe he would've been bitten, and you'd really have something to feel guilty about."

Tori's rapid-fire speech was like a splash of cold water in her face. Denise went from self-pity straight to the realization that she was sitting a few feet from a woman who saved their lives on the same day that her new husband disappeared. She felt guilty because she at least knew what had happened to Brad. Tori only knew Randy was gone, but instead of staying at the hotel and searching for him, she had rescued her and her sons.

Tori could see the revelation written on Denise's face and stopped her.

"You don't have to say anything. You have a right to feel grief. You don't have the right to blame yourself. You didn't do this, and neither did I. The whole world got dealt a bad hand, but at least we're still in the game."

They hugged each other and cried the way two close sisters would, and they were both surprised at how much they needed it. They had been putting on a good show by keeping it inside, and maybe part of their release was for the people on TV.

A reporter's voice got their attention as she described what they were seeing in New York. Tori and Denise wiped at their eyes and turned their attention to the view from above the streets.

"Once again," said the reporter, "these images are coming to us live from a drone camera. We just saw US military aircraft destroy a large section of downtown. We have information that there are no suspected survivors in that area, and they hope to eliminate the infected dead before they get out of the city. Targets of the bombs are primarily bridges and tunnels."

"What's she talking about?" asked Tori. "I have news for her. It's already out of the city."

The last part of Tori's comment was shouted at the TV as if the reporter could hear her. Denise let her vent at the reporter, but she put a reassuring hand on her shoulder.

"We might actually know more about what's going on than the reporter," said Denise.

Her comment seemed to spark a sudden realization, and she added, "I wonder where the reporter goes when she's not broadcasting."

Tori said, "Now I feel bad about yelling at her. It obviously couldn't be anywhere as safe as our shelter."

"I'm getting hungry," said Denise. "Why don't you try to find us something we don't already know while I make us a snack?"

"That makes my point," said Tori. "I wonder if the reporter is even getting anything to eat. Maybe we could communicate with them since we know more about what's happening than they do."

Denise saw what was happening to Tori because she had just gone through it herself, and she had to wonder how long they would have to endure survivor's guilt. She was amazed at how quickly it had left her and how quickly it had manifested itself in Tori. It was almost as if guilt was a demon that moved from host to host.

Tori realized that Denise hadn't answered her when she suggested they could contact the reporter. She turned to find Denise just watching her from the door of the theater. They locked eyes, and neither blinked for several seconds until it occurred to Tori that Denise was waiting for something.

When Tori blinked, she asked, "We wouldn't happen to have any anti-anxiety medication in the infirmary, would we?"

Denise didn't give her a big smile, but she grinned and pointed at the glass Tori had on the table before she walked out the door.

When Denise came back, Tori had switched to another channel. There wasn't much difference between what was being shown on the two broadcasts, but it was a different city. Judging by the smaller buildings and the coastline in the background, Denise guessed it was somewhere along the southern coast. Just like in New York, smoke billowed from several locations in the city, and there was no sign of living people in the streets. The only infected dead they could see were walking toward burning buildings.

"What city is that?" she asked.

"Charleston...it's bad," answered Tori. "Do you suppose if there are enough fires, they'll all be wiped out?"

Denise handed her a plate with a sandwich and chips on it and sat down to watch.

"I should've recognized it. We took the boys there last year. I don't think there's enough stuff to burn that would get them all. Besides, some of those fires will drive survivors out into the open, and if the fires don't do it, the lack of food and clean water is probably already a problem. Have you seen any living people? What's the TV station saying?"

"There's no audio. I think the station went off the air but left the equipment on."

Tori held up the remote and showed Denise that the volume was turned up all the way, but there was no sound. It was eerie to watch the camera pan across the city until they could see the entrance to the harbor. Then, it would pan back in the other direction until White Point Gardens was in view. It was a small park at the tip of the peninsular city. It was normally packed with tourists and joggers, but the people they saw crossing the park in the direction of the nearest fires weren't there for the scenery or to exercise. The silence was worse than listening to a reporter talking about what they already knew. The whole world was dying.

******

Tori thought the sealed level that housed the glass wall was her biggest nightmare. She found herself to be preoccupied with the worry that the wall would collapse under the pressure of all that water. She even woke up a few times from dreams about the shelter being flooded. She wondered if there was anything more they could do to make themselves safer from something she considered inevitable, and the only thing she could think of was that they should only live in the part of the shelter above the aquarium. She suggested it to Denise and was relieved that Denise thought it was reasonable.

Tori had explained that it was like pushing an upside-down glass into a sink full of water. The water wouldn't come up into the glass because the air would hold it down. As long as there wasn't a hole in the top of the glass that allowed the air to escape, the water would stay out. She applied the same logic to the shelter, and since they could seal off the lower floors, they should be able to keep the shelter from flooding if the wall of the aquarium collapsed. Of course, they didn't want to test the theory, so they made it a rule that all doors between levels would be kept shut, and no one could ever open a door to the outside of the shelter. Of course, there were more reasons for that rule than just to avoid the possibility of a flood. Opening doors was the only way the infection could get into the shelter.

Tori's second biggest nightmare turned out to be what she considered to be the second stupidest feature of the shelter. Tori called it nothing more than a playground for Jacob and Jalen because that was why Denise's husband had it built. When Denise took her to see it, Tori had bluntly told her it had less to do with survival than anything except the aquarium.

She added that she was convinced it would be what killed them.

Denise took Tori to the *playground* above the shelter the next day after they had agreed they needed rules. She didn't think Tori would react as much as when she saw the aquarium, but she couldn't deny it was close. They walked up through the levels of the shelter until they came to an unmarked door with two locks. One of the locks was a standard key lock, and the other was a code pad. Denise used the key first and then punched in a six-digit number on the keypad. She explained that the key lock activated the keypad, besides removing the deadbolt.

They stepped through the door into a small, circular area with a metal ladder mounted against the wall opposite the door. Denise pulled the door shut behind them and used her key again to lock it.

"When the lock inside is engaged, I can enter a new combination to the inside keypad and transfer functions to the lock above us."

Denise pointed upward at a platform about twenty feet above. Tori could see another door that was flush with the ceiling. She had never been inside a real submarine, but she imagined the hatch above her head was similar.

"And if you don't lock the door down here, the locks up there won't work?" she asked.

"That's correct, and the reverse is true. Both sets of locks can never be active at the same time. That way, both doors shouldn't theoretically be open at the same time."

Tori thought it was a good security feature, theoretically, but she imagined there would never have been any bank robberies if everything worked the way it was supposed to.

Denise climbed the ladder, and Tori followed. It was an

easy climb, but Tori could picture one of the boys falling from the ladder, and even though they had a great infirmary, she doubted they could treat a brain injury.

"Is it safe for Jalen and Jacob to climb this ladder?" she asked as she joined Denise on the platform.

"No, it isn't," she said emphatically. "Brad was a good father, but I told him he didn't think this through. He said he would install safety harnesses for them. He never got around to it, but I told him not to let them come in here until he did."

Denise unlocked the key lock and then typed on the keypad.

"As I said, if I hadn't locked the door down there, I couldn't unlock this one."

She reached upward and pushed the door with both hands. It resisted a bit, and debris fell through the opening. It was just leaves and dirt that had accumulated on top of the hatch, and they brushed it out of their hair as soon as the door was open all the way. The sky above them was blue and clear, but the odor was unmistakable.

"It smells like roadkill," said Tori.

"Did you bring your gun?"

Tori reached around behind her back and pulled the Luger from its holster. She had found a holster in the armory that was specially designed to be worn in the middle of her lower back. It was more comfortable because the side holster made her tend to bow her arm out from her side.

Denise climbed outside first, but she waited close to the door for Tori to join her. They felt exposed because they stood in the middle of a large clearing surrounded by trees and thick underbrush. Tori had expected to see a fence, a brick wall, or barbed wire, but there was nothing that resembled security. There was a sandy area a few yards away with a variety of playground equipment, but it was totally in the open.

"This isn't what I expected," said Tori. Her voice carried a note of sarcasm.

"It's not what you think," said Denise. "You don't see a break in the trees anywhere, do you?"

"No, but from what I've seen, the infected don't really care about that."

"The trees are on both sides of the fence," said Denise. "They wouldn't see the fence until they walked into it, and if they walked into it from the other side, they wouldn't be able to see through the next layer of trees."

"Is there a gate or an entrance of some kind?"

"No. That was Brad's idea. There's no need for a gate because it's not an entrance to the shelter."

Tori turned in a circle and surveyed the edge of the clearing in all directions. She didn't see an opening anywhere, so she turned again until she felt the breeze on her face and caught the odor they had smelled when they opened the hatch.

She pointed and said, "There's something dead over there."

"Should we take a look?"

Tori nodded. "Quietly...no talking even if we find something. If we see anything, just get back here as fast as possible."

The breeze shifted a little, but the closer they got to the source of the smell, the less they needed the breeze. They were able to hear the source before they reached the underbrush. Tori gently parted the bushes, and they both were able to see the remains of a man hanging from the fence. He had his arms through the straps of a backpack, and the backpack was tangled in the strands of barbed wire that ran along the top of the fence. His legs, or what was left of them, dangled below him. He thrashed the mangled stumps against the fence and growled loudly. They could guess how he died, and they knew it was a couple of days ago, judging by the smell.

Tori let the bushes close again and took Denise by the arm to guide her away from the spot. When they were far enough away, she leaned close to her ear and whispered.

"Okay, we know that one is there, but look around you. If they can't see us, then we can't see them. We have to assume there are more. There could be hundreds. Most of them are dead, but some might be alive. If they're alive, we can't help them because there's no gate, and we won't know if they're already infected."

"What if they get over the fence?" asked Denise. "We have to help the ones who make it inside. If you hadn't helped us, none of us would be here."

"I don't know," said Tori. "There's no way for us to be sure."

Denise said, "I have an idea. If someone climbs the fence and they aren't infected, we have to give them a chance to survive. Can we at least put some supplies up here for them?"

"I have a bad feeling about this. If someone finds supplies out here, then you know they'll find the hatch. They won't be able to get inside, but if I were with them, I would camp on that hatch and wait for someone to open it."

"Then we'll make it one of the rules," said Denise. "Once we put some supplies on the playground, we'll never open the hatch again for any reason."

"I can live with that," said Tori.

It took a few hours, but they raised an Army surplus tent and filled it with supplies. If someone found it, they would have a safe haven until the supplies ran out. Hopefully, it would be enough to help someone figure out a way to survive permanently. When they were done, they had a sense of satisfaction, but they also felt sad. If Brad had known there would be an apocalypse like this one, he would have given them a way to filter out the survivors who weren't infected. When they thought about it, they wondered if anyone could do that.

******

Brad Warren had prepared the shelter for scenarios that most people expected. He thought it would be a fallout shelter more than anything, and he never finished the playground near the hatch because he didn't really expect it to be safe from radiation. That was also why he chose to make a hatch instead of a real entrance. He wanted it to be flush to the ground to make it a hard target, and it had to be impenetrable. He also didn't install a security camera outside because he didn't think it mattered. If there never was a nuclear war and they were just visiting the shelter for some solitude, then they could take the boys up to the playground if they got bored inside.

Tori and Denise didn't talk about what they had found in front of Jalen or Jacob. They also didn't know that the enclosure was only one day away from being discovered by a band of survivors. The ragged group was tired and hungry from constantly running. It seemed to them like they were never more than a mile ahead of the last horde, and just when they thought they were safe somewhere, they were chased out of hiding by another group. Sometimes, it was just one or two of the infected dead, but because the main highways ran north and south between the Finger Lakes, they made natural conduits for the infected dead to find each other and form hordes.

There were eighteen people in their band, and there were times when that made it harder for them. It was hard to provide for so many people. When they did find food, there wasn't enough to go around. Some of them sacrificed their shares for others, but the infection didn't know good people from bad people, so they weren't all so generous. They were only faithful to themselves and their own survival.

At first, they panicked when they crashed through the bushes into the tall fence. A man named Jerry Lancaster was at the front of the pack. He wasn't the official leader of the group, but some of them felt like he knew what he was doing and turned to him for decisions. With the wire barrier in front of them, he didn't know if he should go left or right. The fence had old-fashioned barbed wire at the top, so he felt like he had a better chance of climbing over it than he would the concertina wire with its razor blades every few inches. His indecision was caused by the fact that he didn't know what was on the other side of the fence. For all he knew, the infected were on the other side waiting for them.

"What's the holdup?" someone behind him called out in a low voice.

"There's a fence up here," said Jerry.

A few more people joined him, and for lack of a better idea, they decided someone should go around the fence in both directions to find the gate. Jerry told them to count the sections of the fence as they went, and if they reached fifty, they should come back to the starting point.

"Why go only fifty sections?" asked one of the men who was already going to the right.

Jerry answered, "They're about ten feet apart. If you both go that far without finding a gate, we should regroup. We would be better off to all go together in one direction."

It didn't make sense to everyone, and there was some grumbling, but everyone did their best to conceal themselves in the bushes along the fence while the two scouts looked for a gate. They waited anxiously for the runners to return and almost panicked again when the two men arrived together from the same direction.

"You won't believe it," said one of the breathless men, "but the fence makes a circle a little over three hundred yards around, but there isn't a gate."

"No gate?" said Jerry. "Why? Could you see anything on the other side of the fence?"

Both of them shook their heads.

Jerry thought it over and decided it had to be safer inside the fence. He reasoned that they knew what was on their side of the fence, and if there were infected dead on the other side, they would have to deal with them. He climbed the fence and pulled a multi-tool from his belt. He cut away just enough barbed wire to allow him to get through, then he dropped over the top to the inside and motioned for the next person to follow.

The survivors climbed the fence one at a time until they were all inside. Jerry motioned for the scouts to go ahead of the group to be sure there were no infected dead inside the fence with them. They came back just as the last of their group dropped to the ground, and they had incredible news.

In a perfect world, eighteen people would have followed their leader to the large tent and the supplies, and they would have treated the discovery as a miracle. Before the infected dead, lottery winners blew through their windfalls, spending the money on things they didn't really need, but some winners were smart enough to spread the wealth over the rest of their lives. The hungry band of survivors only thought about the present, and despite the objections of a few people, there was a stampede. They filled the inside of the tent, tore open the food, and gorged themselves without regard for the future.

Turk and Darrow were two losers who had stayed with the group for one reason. They believed they didn't have to be able to run faster than the infected dead. All they had to do was run faster than the other survivors. If push came to shove, they would put the others between themselves and the infected dead. Before the infection, they lived the same way while in prison. They always made sure someone else got the blame for any trouble they started.

The discovery of the tent was an opportunity to survive longer, and sharing the food wasn't what they had in mind. As the others tore into the boxes and argued over clean clothing, the two misfits inspected a wooden box of handguns and rifles that were carefully wrapped in plastic to keep them safe from moisture. Everyone was too busy to see them loading magazines until it was too late.

Turk didn't even bother with a warning. He shot Jerry in the back as he was attempting to bring some order to the rest of the survivors. There were screams, and everyone stopped ravaging the supplies. They froze where they were. Parents pulled their children closer while a few people tightened their grip on the prizes they had seized. All of them had their eyes on Turk as he pointed the barrel of a rifle at them. He motioned with the gun for everyone to get out of the tent. Darrow held the flap aside. The unnatural smile on his face and the way he pointed at them with a semiautomatic handgun sent a clear message that he was enjoying himself.

The people closest to him stepped sideways toward the open flap, but they kept their arms wrapped around boxes and bundles they had liberated from the cache of supplies. Darrow pointed his gun at them and shook his head. He didn't have to say anything for them to get his point. One by one, they reluctantly surrendered everything they had and went outside.

The survivors were herded back to the fence amid protests and pleas, but they could tell the two criminals weren't listening. Turk told them to start climbing, and if they didn't climb fast enough, he would have to shoot more of them. He also pointed out that the noise they were making was likely to draw the infected to the fence before they could all climb to the other side and get out of the area.

It didn't take long for them to all make the climb back to the other side. Turk stepped closer to the fence and told them to listen carefully. He said he knew they were already thinking they could climb inside, but anyone who tried would be dead before they made it anywhere near the tent. To show that he meant what he said, he put the barrel of his rifle through the fence and shot randomly into the crowd. The survivors scattered through the underbrush away from the fence.

Turk and Darrow lingered by the fence for a few minutes before they returned to the tent. Turk said he had almost forgotten, but someone said there was a case of bourbon in the pile of boxes, and they laughed about the suckers who thought they were going to share it with them.

Darrow pushed aside the flap of the tent and walked straight to the supplies, but he heard the sound of the safety click on Turk's rifle behind him. He knew that sound because he had done it himself so many times behind someone else.

"You didn't think I was going to share it with you, did you?"

Darrow raised his palms as he turned around. He knew Turk would shoot him if he couldn't see his hands.

"Man, we've been through a lot together," he began, but he knew he didn't need to say more.

He had expected to see Turk standing behind him with his gun raised, but he didn't expect to see Jerry Lancaster looming over Turk's shoulder.

Turk saw Darrow's eyes shift away from him, and he turned his head to see what Darrow was looking at. He wasn't fast enough to avoid the teeth that sent fire burning through the top of his right shoulder. The sharp bite tore through his thin shirt and didn't stop until teeth hit the bone.

Darrow laughed, thinking Turk had been stupid, but Turk had the finger of his right hand inside the trigger guard of the rifle, and when the muscles spasmed from his shoulder to his hand, he shot Darrow in the stomach.

Jerry fed on Turk until Turk twitched and jerked away from him. They both found Darrow, still alive, curled into a fetal position where he had crawled behind the boxes of supplies.

DEAD END

Ithaca, New York - 2025

Despite my best efforts to stay awake, I must have fallen asleep because the pickup truck had moved during the night. After I told Ruth I would make Branch pay, I had listened to distant voices as Branch's men searched for more people. I heard Branch giving orders, and the voices moved away from the trucks. I didn't understand why he was still searching the area for more of us, but I imagined he couldn't believe he had suffered so many losses at the hands of our motley little group. I also couldn't understand why Ruth and I were still alive. He had been so brutal when he killed Wally and the stranger he thought was Jean. Even though I hoped the Chief would show up with the rest of our friends, I realistically expected that Branch had something special in mind for me.

During a quiet stretch when there were no voices, someone pulled a burlap sack over my head and tied it at the neck. I heard them doing the same to Ruth, and I heard her muffled voice as she spat out a creative burst of insults about Branch's heritage. It wasn't easy to breathe inside the sacks, so Ruth settled down after a minute or two. The stale air and the silence combined to overcome my efforts to stay awake, and I drifted off.

It was broad daylight when I woke up. Light filtered

through the fabric of the bag, and I stayed still as I hoped to hear something useful. Someone grabbed me by my ankles and yanked me from the bed of the pickup truck. With my hands tied behind my back and no way to break my fall, I landed hard on a paved surface. It knocked the wind out of me, but the pain that went through my right shoulder was the worst part. If I had been able to see it, I would have expected the bones to be sticking out through the fabric of my shirt. I did my best to bite back the sounds that I involuntarily made when the air was jolted from my lungs, but when I breathed in, the pain from my shoulder was more than I could take, and I cried out enough to satisfy someone. There was a chorus of laughter around me, and I was sure they were just getting started.

I didn't think it was Branch who lifted me from the ground because there were two of them this time. He would have done it with one hand. There was someone with an arm under each of my armpits, and the one on the right side made a special effort to rotate my shoulder joint until I couldn't bite back the pain. As soon as the groan escaped my lips, they laughed.

Through the burlap sack, the man said, "I'll bet that hurt, princess."

It's funny what people think about when they don't have any control over their lives. The Chief had told me once that he had been faced with his own death a few times, and he thought about things that disconnected him from the situation. He said it was important to remember that it was the mind's way of coping with something that seemed inevitable.

When the man called me *princess*, it reminded me of high school. I was average in so many ways that I might as well have put a sign on my own back that said, *Bully Bait*. I had average looks, average height, average build, and average talent for things like sports or band. The one thing I had going for me was a slightly higher IQ, which was another bully magnet, but I used my IQ to get out of the crosshairs of bullies by doing homework for bigger bullies. Through the pain that was shrieking from my shoulder, my mind wondered if the guy needed someone to do his homework.

My rational mind was almost pushed aside by the defense mechanism the Chief was talking about, but then I remembered the rest of what he said.

"If you let your mind protect you with useless, random thoughts when you're facing death, then your body can't do anything to help you. You have to use the rest of your brain to come up with a plan. Death isn't inevitable until you let it have the last word."

The only plan I could think of was to make myself less average to Branch. I had to have added value so he would keep me alive. My mind went from high school bullies to the present, and I pictured myself standing somewhere with a sack over my head and my hands tied behind my back. If I had any added value to offer Branch, it couldn't be something he could see, but it had to be something he wanted.

It came to me just as the sack was yanked from my head. The bright sunshine made me wince, and my first impulse was to shield my eyes. My arms couldn't move, but I tried to move them anyway, and the price was pain. My shoulder screamed at me again, but this time, the pain gave me clarity.

I didn't recognize my surroundings because I had never been to the place before, but it still had a familiar feel. The directions we had been given to the location of the shelter inside the salt mines began with, "Find the escalator used to carry the ore up to the top of the tower."

In a flash, my mind rushed back to the day when Jean got the cryptic message asking for help. She had been doing routine broadcasts on different frequencies, telling anyone who might be listening how to find our shelters. Actually, anyone who heard the messages would be directed to a location where our people could observe them. If they were survivors who needed help, they were approached by scouts wearing US Army uniforms. If they appeared to be predators, they would never know why we didn't contact them again.

The transmission came in clearly at first, but it broke down before she could get all of the details. It was a teenage boy, and he was broadcasting from a shelter where something had gone wrong. Jean got enough information for us to wonder if the shelter was part of the network of shelters designed by Titus Rush. From what she could tell, the boy on the other end of the transmission was only hearing fragments of what she asked, so the answers didn't always make sense. He seemed to hear some of her questions, but then his voice would become scrambled when he answered.

What she learned was that there were women and children in the shelter, and if they didn't get help, they were all going to die. The boy said he thought they could hold out for a few more weeks. Jean asked how she could find the shelter and what kind of danger they were facing. The boy told her the shelter was hidden in a salt mine on the banks of Cayuga Lake, a few miles north of Ithaca, New York. He said the main entrance was at the base of the escalator that carries ore on a conveyer belt to the top of the tower. The directions from that point on weren't clear, but the boy said the main entrance wasn't safe. Jean tried to find out more, but the transmission ended.

I wasn't sure how I was going to use the shelter to my advantage with Branch, but it had to be better than reliving high school memories. After all, I had skipped my high school reunion for a reason.

"How did you know to bring me here?" I asked Branch in a raspy voice. It came out so scratchy that he didn't understand what I was trying to say. Still, he heard enough to be curious.

There was a semicircle of men around me, and Branch was inside the perimeter. I think I was only about one second from getting the worst and last beating of my life when I spoke up. He was a lot taller than me, so he had to lean closer to ask me to repeat what I said.

"Water," I managed to croak.

Branch didn't appear to be happy with my request. It was either because he was annoyed that I wanted water or because he couldn't understand what I said if I didn't get water.

"Will someone please get this guy some water?"

Even though he said it nicely, it was in a voice dripping with sarcasm. When one of the men handed him a bottle of water, Branch stared at the man as if he had taken too long. He was almost gentle when he lifted my chin and poured a sip of water into my mouth. That scared me more than if he had been rough.

He handed the water back to the man and said to me, "Word for word, repeat what you said before."

He was so close to my face that I couldn't see his hands, but I imagined his fists were balled up, and if I said anything else, I would feel a fist in my ear.

"How did you know to bring me here?"

Branch must have felt like I didn't deviate from the first time I said it because he didn't hit me. Instead, he studied my face and then stood to his full height. I was pretty sure he was taller than the Chief but not as broad-chested. He turned toward the escalator with his hands on his hips and rocked back on his heels. I wasn't sure what he was doing, but my guess was that he wanted to say something that made it look like he had brought me to the salt mine on purpose. That was exactly what I wanted him to think he should do.

When he faced me again, he leaned toward me, put his huge arm across my shoulders, and held me like we were old friends. The weight of it was excruciating on my injured shoulder, but

I was thinking the whole time that the Chief would be proud of me. I had used the one talent I could claim as my own. I could use my brain against a superior power. I was reminded that my brain had a long way to go to get me out of trouble when Branch squeezed my shoulder. He apparently meant it as a friendly gesture, but it hurt like hell.

"Call me Ted. What's your name?"

My voice sounded weak when I answered, and he got that confused expression on his face again.

"Ed? Your name is Ed? Well, how about that," he exclaimed. "Ted and Ed."

Branch turned to the semicircle of men and repeated our names as if it were some reason to celebrate that our names were similar. The men apparently took it that way because they cheered as if we had just won a prize. The whole time, he kept his beefy arm across my shoulders.

"Now, Ed. What do you know about this place?"

I knew I had to give him an answer that fit with my original question, or the beating would start. Worse, I was aware that Ruth had stirred in the back of the pickup truck. If he wasn't happy with my answer, he might turn his anger on her.

"Somehow, you knew where we were going. How did you find out we were coming to this place? We didn't tell anyone."

Branch kept up the facade of friendship, but I could sense his anticipation building. I felt like I was being hugged by a coiled spring that was about to release its tension.

"That's right, Ed. I knew where you were going, so I would've caught up with you anyway, but what I really want to know is why you were coming here."

I wanted to stretch out the pause in hostilities for as long as I could, but my superpower was getting drained by the imminent danger of saying the wrong thing, so I decided that

I really had no choice but to tell Branch the truth...or maybe some version of it. It occurred to me that Jean was out there somewhere and that Branch thought she was dead. The best thing to do was to get him and his men into territory that he didn't know any better than us, and Jean would figure out that she should look for me there.

"We were coming to the shelter," I said.

******

Sitting in the bed of the pickup truck was better than getting beaten to death, so I stayed exactly where Branch had put me. After I answered his question, he alternated between walking toward the mine entrance and walking back to me. I could tell he was trying to decide how far he could take his game, pretending he knew more than he did, but he was also trying to decide if I was still useful to him. When he made up his mind, he walked over to me and picked me up like someone would have done before the apocalypse when they put their child in the top of a shopping cart.

Branch sat me down on the tailgate of the truck and said, "Can I trust you not to run off while I go take a look at the shelter?"

I thought, "Do I look stupid to you?" but I said, "You can trust me, Ted."

I had a moment when I thought I had pushed my luck by using his first name, but he laughed and said, "I'll be right back."

Branch trotted off with all of the men who had been in the semicircle, and I wondered if we were really alone. I couldn't see behind me, but I was willing to bet there were more men, maybe a dozen, where I couldn't see them. They probably had orders to shoot me if I did anything dumb.

I kept my head pointed toward Branch, but I had to find out if Ruth was still okay under the burlap sack.

"Ruth? Are you still with me?"

I saw her chest rise and fall, so I knew she was breathing, but after what Branch had done to Wally, I imagined Ruth preferred to stay inside the dark hood.

"Where are we?" Her voice was muffled, but I could understand her well enough.

"You aren't going to believe this, but we're exactly where we were going."

"The shelter? You told them about the shelter?"

"Not before they brought us here," I said. "It's still a small world, Ruth. We weren't far from the salt mines, and Branch brought us here without knowing this was where we were going. I don't know if he's been here before or if he just figured this would be a good place to torture some information out of us. I told him there's a shelter in there to buy us some time. When we get the chance to escape, we have to be ready."

"Wait a minute," said Ruth. "Are you trying to tell me these guys chased us all the way from Virginia to Ithaca and then gave us a ride the rest of the way? Then you told them about the shelter?"

Even with a burlap sack over her head, I could tell she was looking at me like I was crazy. I wanted to be able to give her a better explanation about why they brought us here, but I didn't have one to give her until I saw Branch come back out of the main entrance to the salt mines. It all made more sense because there were more men with him.

"I just figured it out, Ruth. These guys have their base in

Virginia, and they had their fuel depot at that railroad yard that we blew up, but they've already been here at the salt mines."

"I wish I didn't have this sack over my head," said Ruth. "I need to see your face to understand why you told them about the shelter, or did they already know about it?"

I chanced a quick look over my shoulder. Besides wincing in pain, I saw I had been right about Branch having more than a few men with him. There were several trucks parked about twenty yards away, and at least a dozen men were scattered around them. None of them were paying attention to me, but that hardly mattered since I wouldn't get far if I ran. Branch was talking to a man as they walked toward me. He wasn't one of the original men from the semicircle, so I could only assume he had been inside the salt mine.

"They're coming back, so I have to talk fast, Ruth. I only told them about the shelter to make us valuable to them. I think they've been using the salt mine as a base, but they didn't know there's a shelter underneath it somewhere. That's not unusual. We saw the same thing happen at every shelter in our network. People live above them and never know about the shelters. I don't know how many times people lived above Fort Sumter without ever finding the entrance."

"What happens now that they know about it?" she asked.

"That's easy," I said. "They're going to order me to show them where the shelter is, and if by some miracle I can find it, they'll expect me to open the door."

"Can you do that?"

"Not a chance," I answered. "Listen, I have to tell you something else. They think they caught Jean and killed her. I don't know who that woman was, but it wasn't Jean. I think they found her hiding in the storage facility."

"Where's Jean?"

"I don't know, but I'm glad she got away."

It was an insensitive thing for me to say to Ruth. I had forgotten about Wally because I was so busy trying to keep us alive.

"Ruth...I'm so sorry."

She could apparently hear the approaching voices as well as I could because she told me to hush and that we could talk about it later.

Branch put a big smile on his face and came off as if I wasn't sitting on the tailgate with my hands tied behind my back.

"Ed, let me introduce you to a good friend of mine. This is Jeremiah Smith. Oh, I'm sorry, but I never got your last name."

"Jackson," I said toward the new arrival.

The man actually held out his hand like we were going to shake, but then he and Branch broke out laughing like the joke was on me. I had to admit to myself that Branch made my skin crawl. The way he had killed Wally and then flipped a switch to become Mister Nice Guy was psychotic.

"Ed, I was telling Jeremiah what you said about a shelter inside the salt mine, and he says you must be mistaken because he's been here a long time and hasn't ever seen it. Of course, I told him that everyone knows about the shelter, and all we needed was someone to point us in the right direction. I figure you're the right man for the job. What do you say?"

I didn't know what I could say that would add value to Ruth, but I figured if Branch wanted to play Mister Nice Guy, I should take advantage of it.

"Sure, I'd be glad to help. Uh, is there any chance I could get you to untie my arms, and what about my mom? Can she go with us?"

It was a last-second judgment call. I watched a lot of TV before the apocalypse, and hostages were always trying to make a personal connection with their kidnappers. They usually managed to work into a conversation that a hostage had a better chance of surviving if their kidnapper saw them as a person. I was surprised that it actually worked.

"Mom? That's your mother?" said Branch.

He made a big deal out of getting her out of the truck. This man, who had only hours before beaten the life out of Ruth's brother, lifted her out of the truck with tender, loving care. He untied her and pulled the hood from her head. Ruth winced against the bright sunshine the same way I had, but she managed to overcome the hatred she felt for the man. She knew our lives depended on it. She somehow managed to thank Branch so sincerely that she could have fooled me.

The first chance she got to face me, I saw her silently mouth the word, "Mom?"

When Branch untied me, my left hand easily swung around in front of me, but my right arm stayed where it was.

Branch said in a matter-of-fact tone, "Here, let me get that for you."

He grabbed my wrist with one gigantic hand and my shoulder with the other. He pulled my arm downward and gave it a slight twist. Everyone heard the audible pop as the bone went back into the socket. I thought I was going to pass out, but relief washed over me a split second after the pain.

"I'll bet that feels better," he said with satisfaction. "Come on, everyone. Let's go see that shelter of yours. Mom, you stay here at the truck. My men can get you something to eat."

******

Jean and I had grown accustomed to living inside the shelter in Guntersville, Alabama. Most of the interior felt just like being inside a building, but when our close friend, Doctor Bus, had built the shelter, he decided to leave some of the tunnels as they were. The rough, stone-carved walls gave it a more *homey* feel, according to him. The difference between the walls in the Guntersville shelter and the walls of the salt mine was that the salt mine would only feel homey if you were the size of a Humvee. The walls in Guntersville were like theme park walls. They were a constant reminder that you were living inside a mountain, but they weren't oppressive. The salt mine just felt wrong. In some places, the support walls seemed like they were too far apart, and nothing was holding up the ceiling, but in other places, they were too close together. Dark corners were everywhere.

Ted Branch marched me down into the mine entrance with a big arm over my shoulders like we were old friends. The gloom of the mine surrounded us, and the men who were escorting us illuminated the way with weak flashlights and old kerosene lanterns. I noticed they also carried machetes that they took out of their belts as we went inside. Walking into so much darkness in a world where the infected dead weren't afraid of the dark made me remember a lesson the Chief had taught us years ago on Mud Island.

If you ever found yourself in the middle of a group of people who were all swinging blades at the infected dead, the best place to be was low to the ground. When the swinging starts, they'll take you out from all different directions. I didn't know if I could get out of the grip Branch had on my shoulders, but I had nothing to lose if I tried.

The walls inside the front of the mine were so far apart that I had to wonder what was holding up the roof over my head. Even worse, light didn't reflect off the walls and make me feel like I could see everything in the tunnel. I couldn't tell if there was a turn up ahead until I reached the next solid wall, and when the turn was to the left and the right, there was an immediate feeling of disorientation because I couldn't see the tunnel behind me.

"Which way?" said Branch.

For some reason, I didn't hesitate. I pointed to the right as if there was never a doubt in my mind. If I took a second to think about why I chose the tunnel to the right, it was only because there were half a dozen men behind me with machetes. For all I knew, Branch had told them to chop me up as soon as I made a wrong turn. Of course, I had no idea how long I could keep up the pretense, but on the off chance that I was going to make it out of the salt mine alive, I did my best to make a mental map of the turns.

Five turns into the mines, Branch asked me how far before we came to the entrance. It was the first time he had spoken since the first turn, and his voice sounded unnatural inside the cavernous tunnel. It also sounded impatient. I was bracing for the question just like a parent would be with three little kids in the backseat of a car.

The inevitable, "Are we there yet?" was overdue.

Unlike the parent who would tell the kids they would be there when they got there, I wasn't driving as much as I was navigating. I had to keep Branch and his men believing I knew exactly where I was going.

"If I remember correctly, it's not much further," I said.

Even though I was prepared, I regretted it as soon as I said it because I had intended to say it would be a lot further, and I was mentally slapping myself. I didn't have time to be too hard on myself, though. The groan came from behind us, but it was too far away for us to see where the source was. Branch's men didn't help the situation because they immediately swung their lanterns and flashlights higher in an attempt to expose the infected dead to the light. The result was a crazy melee of shadows and blind spots. We were behind the lanterns and blinded by all of the movement, and to make matters worse, the first groan was just the beginning of the chorus.

The circle around me expanded as the men stepped toward the dark tunnels to swing their machetes at the sounds rather than what they could see. One of them screamed in pain, and I didn't know if it was from the bite of an infected dead or the cut of a badly aimed machete, but it was time to follow the Chief's advice. I let my weight drop downward, and as soon as I hit the dark floor, I crawled.

YEAR ONE

Ithaca Shelter - 2017

The routines made the days go by faster at first, but routines can become boring, and signs of irritability were obvious at the beginning of the fourth week. By the end of the first year, there were almost constant conflicts between the brothers. The rules were meant to remind them of the dangers outside the shelter, but the existence of rules also bred the desire to question them.

As they gathered for breakfast, Denise placed notepads on the table next to the plates. She and Tori felt like they should try to be as natural about the process as possible so it wouldn't seem like a big deal, even though it was. There were only a few rules, mostly for Jalen and Jacob, and the big ones were mixed in with the small ones. For instance, meals were at a scheduled time, and everyone was required to be on time. After meals, there was a rotating schedule of chores, and freedom from chores could be earned by getting good grades on homework assignments. Rewards could also be earned just for following the rules consistently.

The biggest rules involved the areas of the shelter that were off-limits, and the biggest rule of all was to never give the infection the chance to get inside the shelter. Neither of the boys was physically capable of opening the big vault doors, and the access to the area above the shelter was blocked by the need for the access codes and the keys. Denise wasn't about to let them borrow the keys or tell them the access codes, but she and Tori agreed that avoiding the discussion wasn't the way to impress upon them the need for security.

Both boys ignored the notepads next to their plates. The rules had been written as needs arose, and both of them had been responsible for their fair share of the rules. One of the rules was that they were required to complete one hour of strenuous exercise every day. The shelter had state-of-the-art treadmills and stationary bikes, and because the shelter had so many corridors and levels that were uninterrupted by doors, they could jog if they preferred. The written rule said the hour of exercise could be a single method, or it could be a combination of the choices.

At first, they had accepted the exercise requirement without the need to make it a rule. Jalen and Jacob competed with each other as if it were a game, but just like any game, Jalen got tired of losing every time and refused to do his exercise at the same time as his brother. Of course, Jacob made sure to show up for his hour when Jalen was doing his workout and taunted him for being a sore loser. The result was a split lip when Jacob turned up the speed of Jalen's treadmill. The sight of blood cooled the tension for a bit, but Jalen was mad and retaliated by resetting the workout data on the stationary bike after Jacob had finished exercising, and he couldn't prove to Denise that he was done for the day. Denise felt like she had painted herself into a corner by not preventing a situation where she had to take the word of one brother or the other.

Tori told her that the problem wasn't new. It was just new to her. She suggested that it was important to get Jalen to admit he retaliated so she wouldn't have to accuse either boy of lying. In the end, she got the confession she needed from them, but one of the rules that was caused by the episode said that the truth would keep the infection out of the shelter. Neither Denise nor Tori knew for sure if the boys understood that rule, but they were trying to impress upon them that everything they did could be a matter of life or death.

When they were finished with breakfast, the boys asked to be excused and got up from the table before getting permission. Denise was bracing herself for another day of conflict, and she wasn't about to let them leave the table without acknowledging the rules on the notepad.

"Sit back down. Jalen, you can read the first rule today. Jacob, you know what to do when he finishes."

Neither of them made direct eye contact with her, but they did as they were told. When they finished, she dismissed them, and they left without another word.

"It's only going to get worse," said Tori. "I think they've forgotten how we got here and why we can't leave. Maybe we should have included them in the last news broadcasts."

"Why? So we could traumatize them a bit more?" snapped Denise.

The two women had never fought about how Denise was raising her sons. Tori was smart enough to know that would drive a big wedge between them, so she didn't even react to Denise's outburst. Besides, Denise always apologized.

"I'm sorry," said Denise. "They did better than I could have hoped when they lost their father, but maybe that's what's starting to show up now. Brad always managed to level the playing field for Jalen, so they got along well with each other. I think Jacob accepted Brad's interventions as a way of protecting Jalen from being taken advantage of by other people, but not by him."

"The only parenting experience I have is the last year with your sons, so I've been getting on-the-job training. I don't really know what to do, but do you think they've forgotten what happened, or have they blocked out enough of it that they need a reminder?"

Denise shook her head. "We can't risk taking them outside to remind them."

"I wasn't suggesting that, but can you think of another way? I think they remember it, but they resent being stuck inside the shelter. As nice as it is, it's still a prison when you get right down to it. If they felt like we had a choice, they wouldn't resent it as much."

"You think giving them a wake-up call by taking them outside would make them feel like they have a choice?" asked Denise. Her voice rose to a shout by the time she got to the last word of her question.

"Of course not," answered Tori. "It would remind them that we don't have a choice, and it's not a decision being made by you and me. Their resentment is misplaced, and we have to find a way to remind them of that."

Denise picked up one of the notepads. Rule number six restricted access to the room where she and Tori had watched the last news broadcasts. She had put passwords on the computers to keep them from surfing the internet. It was amazing that the world had died, but the internet had lived on. Websites weren't updated, but as long as servers kept their power sources, there was still plenty of surfing to be done, and it was like social media had a life of its own. Trolls still made their comments, and readers kept feeding them. That traffic was getting slower as survivors died and power failed, but there wasn't much new material that Denise wanted the boys to see.

Brad had installed an extensive local area network inside the shelter for teaching purposes, and there were fewer disputes during the mandatory classes taught by Denise and

Tori. They were both educated, and they had a lot to offer, but there was one subject that they were avoiding, and that was current events. They could teach history, but their discussion after breakfast brought them to the unavoidable question of how the history of civilization ended.

"I remember when I was in high school," said Tori. "In American History, we didn't make it through World War II before the end of the school year. I don't know what we could teach them about this stuff that's happening because we don't even know what it is."

"When was the last time you tried to find something new on the internet?" asked Denise.

"Long enough ago that I can't remember. You think we should try again?"

"Maybe we should have Jacob try. Now that he's eleven, he might be old enough."

Denise sounded hesitant when she said it, but it was obvious that she meant it. Jacob's birthday had been a few weeks ago, and it had been much different from the last few birthdays. There were no friends from school with presents, and there was no trip to the local fun pizza place. There was no doubt that Jacob remembered what had happened at the hotel, but maybe he needed to be reminded so he would be easier on his little brother and less resentful toward the adults. There was also the chance he would find something new.

There was an intercom system between some of the rooms in the living quarters, and Denise used it to ask Jacob to come back to the kitchen. He gave his usual answer that he would be there as soon as he reached a spot where he could save his game, and Denise gave her usual response that he could just pause the game. They both knew that the real reason he didn't want to pause the game was that Jalen would restart it and lose Jacob's progress on purpose.

"I have something else for you to do that you're going to like better than your game," said Denise.

Jacob moaned and complained a bit more, but he knew from experience that Denise would respond with a threat to suspend his game time if he didn't comply. They had been down that road a few times, and he knew she would do it.

When Jacob arrived, he was surprised that there really was something being offered that he would rather do. He had always wondered what he would be able to find if he were given unlimited access to one of the computers that could still access the fragmented internet. Denise gave him a stern warning to stay away from anything that resembled an adult website, but he was free to find out as much as he could about the infection.

"What about Jalen?" he asked.

"Don't worry about him," said Tori. "I'll find him and keep him busy. Do me a favor, though. If you find anything on the internet worth knowing about, talk with your mom before you talk to Jalen."

Jacob had felt *weird* when he turned eleven. It was strange, but in a good way. This new access to the outside world felt big. It was a responsibility that made him feel older, like the day he went to the ice machine in the hotel.

The sudden memory of that day sent a chill up the back of his neck, and he was surprised that he hadn't thought about it in a long time. It seemed so long ago that it was not like a memory of something that had happened to him. It was something he had seen in a movie or a TV show.

"Jacob, are you okay with this? You don't have to do it if you don't want to."

Denise had seen the distant look on Jacob's face. It was like he was seeing something far away and was watching it intently as it got closer. She thought she saw a little fear.

"No, I'm fine, Mom. I want to do it."

He didn't know how to put it into words, but he knew that he was safe if he saw it on the internet. It wouldn't be like it was when people pressed against him in the hallway outside their room.

Denise took Jacob to a computer desk in the room that had been off-limits to the boys and got him situated while Tori went to find Jalen. She reminded him again to stay away from adult websites, and that she would check his browser history if she had to. Jacob was curious, but he didn't need to be told that he would be punished by never being trusted on the internet again.

"Start with all of the news networks," said Denise. "If any of them found a way to get their websites updated, they would have the most credible information. If you don't find anything new, don't give up. Check social media sites, and then do searches using posts that seem to be recent."

"I know how to do this, Mom."

Jacob was anxious to get started, and before the infection, he had plenty of experience on computers, including how to erase his browser's search history, but he wanted to earn his mother's trust so he could make this a regular thing.

Denise gave him an affectionate pat on the head and left the room. Jacob felt absolutely liberated when she pulled the door shut behind her. He turned his attention to the computer screen and typed his first search into the browser. Five minutes into the search, he felt like he was going to throw up on the keyboard.

Most of the major news networks had gone down within days of each other, so Jacob was able to zero in on who had gotten the last word. Most of them had simply searched each other's websites and repeated what the others had said, which was common practice before the infection, but he eventually found news that was probably the last information posted by a major network. It was the last thing, but it was still more of the same bad news. The infection was everywhere. People were dying, coming back to life, and then biting people.

"Wash, rinse, and repeat," said Jacob to himself, and he wondered for a moment about that phrase. It was something he had heard said when he was playing games with people on the internet, and it gave him an idea.

There were role-playing games that allowed the players to interact with each other. They used avatars in the games and login names that were usually the same as their avatar names, but they were also allowed to actually speak with players in other cities or even other countries. Jacob usually went by the name J-War because it combined his first initial with his last name. He also thought it made him sound tough.

Jacob switched to a new window on the computer and checked the menu of applications for the one he wanted. When he opened it, he was surprised to see there were discussions only a few minutes old. He checked to see if there was any audio, and he almost fell out of his chair when a girl's voice came through the speaker in mid-sentence.

"...fix the fence better at the back of the property."

"Hello?" said Jacob.

He felt like he couldn't have sounded more stupid, but after a year of talking to no one but his brother, mother, and aunt, it seemed so strange to be talking with a real person. In this case, the real person sounded like she was around his age, and he didn't have a lot of experience with girls except online. Still, it had been a long time. The girl didn't answer at first, and he checked to see if the chat thread showed she was active. He saw that she was logged in as *Marsupial* and that she was still there. He was just about to speak again when she broke the silence.

"Where did you come from? Are you real?" she asked.

Jacob didn't know why he was so tongue-tied, but he felt like the thing to do was to get her to talk. It was making him feel so good that he couldn't believe it.

"I like your name. How'd you come up with *Marsupial*... because they're fast?"

Jacob had heard somewhere that it was funny to say marsupials were fast, but he didn't know why. It was the only thing he could think of at the moment.

He was rewarded by her giving him a short laugh before she answered, "Do you know how many times I've heard that joke?"

Jacob told himself he would have to ask his mom or Aunt Tori if they knew why it was so funny.

She went on, "No, I did like most people and combined my first and last names. My name is Marsha Sue Peele, so yeah... *Marsupial*. I go by Marsha, and I don't like my middle name."

"I like it," said Jacob. "That's actually pretty good."

"Thanks, but back to my questions. You're obviously real, but you caught me by surprise. I've been logging on for a year and talking with random people, but they always just ghost me after a while."

"Are they ghosting you, or is something happening to them?" asked Jacob.

"I think you know the answer to that question. I was just saying they ghosted me because I'd rather not think of what really happened to them. Some of them were online with me a long time before they disappeared. We used to be able to say goodbye to friends."

"I didn't get to say goodbye to anyone," said Jacob.

Since he hadn't been online with anyone in the last year, his last connection that was severed was with his father. He remembered watching his mother guide his father into the bedroom at the hotel. He knew his dad was sick, but he didn't know that would be the last time he would ever see him again. If he had known, he would've said goodbye.

"Where were you when it happened?" asked Marsha. "You know…when it all ended."

"I was in a hotel room by Niagara Falls. We were trying to go home to Ithaca, but my dad got sick."

"He was bitten?"

"No, but he cut his hand on a guy's teeth when he punched him in the face. Same thing as getting bitten, I guess. What about you?"

Marsha acted like she didn't even hear his question.

"Are you still in the hotel?" she asked.

"No, we had to get out of there. It was full of those dead people. It was pretty crazy, but we made it to a shelter my dad built. A place where we could all go if something like this happened."

"I wish we had something like that. You know, something like a real shelter, not just a place with a fence around it, but I guess we've been lucky, though. Marion and Carrie are pretty good at finding supplies and making it back to our place."

"Wait," said Jacob, "there are more of you? How many? Where are you? You aren't telling me much about you."

"I didn't get to say goodbye to anyone when it started. My parents, my brothers and sisters…I wasn't with any of them. I tried to call them when I saw the news, but my stepdad answered the phone. He was his usual charming self and wouldn't even tell my mom I was on the phone. There was a long line to use the phone, and by the time it was my turn again, the phones quit working. The people in charge at this place tried to keep a lot from us. They turned off the news, and most of the staff went home."

"I'm sorry," said Jacob. "I guess I've been taking our place for granted, but tell me more. How'd you survive? How is this server running? Are we going to lose this connection?"

Marsha lowered her voice a little. "I don't know how the others will feel about me telling you where we are. We've got it pretty good here compared to most places, and we've had our fair share of people trying to get in. Adults think that if they can get in, they can also take over."

"You don't have any adults where you are? Where are you?"

Marsha let out a heavy sigh. "I just told you. The others might not like it if I told you that."

"Who am I going to tell?" said Jacob. "It's just the four of us here, and we're not going anywhere. The shelter we're in has everything except a bowling alley, and the only reason it doesn't have one is because it wasn't finished in time."

"Okay," said Marsha, "you tell me about your shelter first, then I'll tell you about ours."

"We're somewhere inside the salt mines. I don't even know how to get here because we came in through a tunnel, but there's a main entrance that my dad brought us through when I was a kid. It was a long time ago, so I don't think I could find it again. There's another way in, but it doesn't open from the outside."

"Why not?" asked Marsha.

"Well, it's not the safest part of the shelter. My mom calls it the weak link because it goes straight to the surface. My dad thought if we ever had to use the shelter, it would at least give us a way to go outside once in a while to get some fresh air."

Marsha gave a cynical laugh and said, "I guess your dad didn't plan on people eating each other." There was something about the laugh that made her sound like she didn't think too highly of adults, and Jacob noticed it.

"Why are you making fun of my dad? At least he was with me when it started, and he got his hand cut on a guy's teeth because he was protecting us."

"Oh, hey man, I'm sorry. It's just that I haven't had good dads. My real dad left when I was a baby, and my stepdad's a jerk. My mom thinks he's a saint, but that's because he's always nice in front of her. The minute she turns her back, he's always making it look like I did something wrong. It got so bad that I finally couldn't take it anymore, so I ran away. I got caught stealing, and the jerk convinced my mom to let them put me in juvie."

"Is that where you were when it started?"

"Yeah, imagine that. Ten years old and stuck in juvie when the world ended."

"You were only ten? I didn't know they would put a ten-year-old in juvie," said Jacob.

"They will if you borrow your stepdad's car when you run away," she laughed.

"What's it like there? I mean, it can't be so bad if it kept you alive and you've got an internet connection."

"It's got a bomb shelter," said Marsha. "I think the building was made back when people were practicing for a war or something. It has those old signs on the walls going down to the basement with warnings about radiation. I guess you're right, though. At least it had a big food supply when the infection started, and the fence that used to keep us in is now what keeps them out."

"How many people are there with you?"

"When it started, there were over two hundred kids in here. Most of them were older kids, and they didn't hang around. As soon as the next shift of counselors and security guards didn't show up for work, there was kind of like a riot without all the fighting and stuff. I mean, they couldn't shoot kids, right? The guards didn't carry guns anyway. Most of the kids went to the front gate and demanded to leave, and the guards finally gave up, especially when some of the parents arrived outside the gate. As soon as the kids left, the guards did, too. There were a few resident counselors who lived in the staff wing, and some of them stayed, but they got infected. There are only five of us left now."

"Only five out of two hundred? Is it still safe there?" asked Jacob.

"You tell me," said Marsha. She sounded like she didn't really know.

Before Jacob could answer, she said, "When people left, they took all the supplies they could carry. We still had a lot, but we've been going out on supply runs to make it last. There were twenty of us here a month ago. We didn't know that one of the kids was infected until it was too late, and we lost a lot of people in one night. We had to seal off most of the building because there were infected people in the other wings. We're kind of backed into a corner now. I'm just glad it's the corner that still has internet service. Survivors still try to break into this place. It used to happen more than now, but they would always think it was safer because of the fence until they got inside with the dead."

"So, besides you, Marion, and Carrie, who else is there?"

"Amber and Shay are the other two. We were all in the same wing of juvie when it started, and we didn't know what else to do, so we just hid out in the basement. Everyone else was older than us, so all they wanted us to do was stay quiet and stay out of the way. Now they're all dead except us."

Jacob was just about to ask her if she knew more about what was happening to the rest of the world when she cut him off.

"Someone's coming. I think it's Carrie. She looks mad even when she's laughing. I'll tell her about you, but when you get to talk to her, act like you don't know anything. I'll talk with you tomorrow at the same time."

Under Marsupial on the chat log, it said she was inactive. Jacob sat in front of the computer for several minutes before it occurred to him to do a search for juvenile detention centers near Ithaca, New York. There were plenty of sites listed, but there was a large facility only about twenty miles from the shelter. It was named the Seth Duffy Center for Juvenile Rehabilitation. Images taken from satellite views showed it was a big building that seemed about right for the population Marsha had mentioned. Now, he had to decide what to do with the information.

******

"Well, that backfired," said Denise. "He was supposed to learn about what's happening outside, not find strays."

Tori almost snorted coffee out through her nose.

"Excuse me," she said as she wiped her face and fought back the tears that came with hot coffee going in the wrong direction, "but you're the mother here. You don't feel a little bad to know there are kids out there who could use a safe place like this?"

Denise had the decency to be embarrassed about her lack of empathy. Of course, she felt bad for the kids, but it was another problem to solve. For the last year, they had felt safe from the infection, and now they were suddenly in a position where they would have to open the shelter doors to help, and it wasn't like they had never talked about the fear that the infection would get inside. For all they knew, it could be transmitted in the air by now.

"It's not that I don't want to help them," she said, "but how can we do it safely?"

"I think you know the answer to that," said Tori. "We have to tell them where we are so they can come to us."

Denise was fidgeting, and after spending a year together inside the shelter, Tori felt like she knew her better than she had known Randy.

"What aren't you telling me?" asked Tori. "Something else is bothering you."

"Okay," said Denise, "you want the truth? Have you checked the main entrances lately?"

"You mean the backdoor where we came in through the tunnel?" asked Tori.

"And the main door up front."

"Why, is there something out there?" Tori hadn't forgotten the way the infected dead moved and the way they relentlessly followed their prey. She immediately assumed they had found the shelter.

Denise said, "There's no way they made it through the tunnel to the back door, but that goes to the other side of the lake. This juvenile detention facility is east of here, and there's no way we could get someone from there to the other side of Cayuga Lake. The front entrance has a problem."

"I thought you said the infected would never be able to find their way to the front entrance of the shelter," said Tori.

"I don't think I said that in so many words."

Tori gave her a raised eyebrow that indicated otherwise.

"I said it wasn't likely, or it was unlikely that they could reach the front door…something like that."

Tori kept her eyebrow raised, but the way she recalled it was something along the lines that Denise would be surprised if the infected dead made it that far into the mines, and it was more likely that they would fall down a shaft somewhere than find the front entrance.

"Okay, I'll give you that much," said Tori. "How bad is it up there?"

Denise didn't make eye contact when she said that she had checked the front security cameras after Jacob told them about the kids at the juvenile detention center.

"Ah, ha," said Tori. "You thought about bringing them here as soon as he told you."

It wasn't a question, and Denise still avoided eye contact when she answered.

"I was still worried about how we could do it because we would have to be sure no one is infected, but even if the infected dead hadn't found the front door, I don't exactly know how to navigate out of the salt mine myself."

"You mean you don't have a map? I always figured we could walk right out of here any time we wanted," said Tori.

"Brad wanted me to learn it so I wouldn't get lost down here, but I never took the time."

Tori said, "This sounds like the first line of a joke, but the punchline is too sad to get a laugh. A prepper and a procrastinator walk into a bar."

Tori let the rest of the joke hang in the air while they both waited for the other one to say the obvious. The only way was to go out through the fenced enclosure above the shelter.

"It's not such a bad idea when you think about it," said Denise. "How hard could it be?"

JUVIE

Ithaca, New York - 2017

The first step in getting the kids from the juvenile detention center was to make contact again. As long as the internet connection didn't decide it was time to fail, Jacob should be able to talk with them and give them directions to the enclosure up top. Jacob said Marsha told him to make contact the next day at the same time, and he was glad his mother and Tori wanted him to. The next step would be harder. Even though Marsha had convinced Jacob that they were a tough bunch of kids who had survived a year on their own, it was hard to believe a bunch of kids could cover the distance between the juvenile hall and their shelter. On the map, it only appeared to be about twenty miles away, but that was twenty miles where anything could go wrong. They most certainly would run into the infected dead. The one thing they had in their favor was that there weren't any populated towns in between them.

"Should we go get them?" asked Denise.

The expression on Tori's face was all the answer she needed, but Tori couldn't resist asking the obvious question.

"Besides point and shoot school, what training have you had that would make you qualified to cover twenty miles on foot and rescue a bunch of kids?"

Denise could have been offended by the question, but she knew Tori was right. She couldn't call her escape from Niagara Falls the result of advanced tactical training. She had been lucky every step of the way, and she would have died several times without Tori's help. They weren't going to be able to rely on luck.

"I don't have any better ideas," said Denise. "Do you?"

"Just one."

Tori let the words hang in the air long enough for Denise to understand whatever the idea was, it couldn't be great. She waited for Tori to tell her what it was.

"I was watching the security feed from the front door. There are a couple of front-loading mine cars out there. If we could make it from the front door to one of those things, we could drive right out of here. They probably have enough fuel in them to make it to the juvenile center and back."

Denise shook her head. "I already told you I don't have a clue how to navigate out of here."

"It seems like a shame," said Tori. "Those mindless dead things were able to find their way from the surface to the shelter."

"You're forgetting something. They might have been alive when the infection started, and some of them might have known about the shelter. Some of the shafts out there go nine hundred feet down. If the people had just blindly rushed around in the dark, they would've fallen into those shafts. That's what we would do if we just drove around blindly trying to reach the surface. Either that, or we'd run out of gas somewhere in between. I wouldn't want to be stuck out there and would probably rather jump down a shaft at that point."

Tori seemed a little shaken by the realization that the

infected dead outside the door had been alive when they arrived.

"You mean we could've saved those people out there?"

"Tell me how," said Denise. "We weren't equipped to triage them. If we had our husbands here, we could have found a way, but if we had opened that door, those people would've just rushed in and taken the shelter from us. As dumb as it sounds, we have to go get those kids."

It was time for another family meeting, but this one was remarkably different from the start. Jalen was excited by the news that his brother had found more kids, even if they were all older than him. He still felt like he would find some friends among them, and he liked the idea of bringing them in. His excitement came down a few notches when Denise explained that they didn't have any ideas about how they would get them from the detention center to the shelter without going outside.

Of course, Jacob was all for rescuing them, and just like any kid his age, he already had an emotional attachment to the girl just from having heard her voice. He was ready to go and get them himself if he had to, and he was quick to say so.

"Slow down, Rambo," said Tori. "You may be good at video games, but we're talking about real stuff now. As a matter of fact, I was watching you play a zombie game, and even though I knew it wasn't real, I got pretty nervous the way you let them get close to you before you killed them."

"That's how you get more points, Aunt Tori. You let them get bunched up first."

"Thanks for helping me make my point. Outside, the last thing you want to do is let them get close to you. Do you even know that the cannon you carry in that video game would kick like a mule every time you pull the trigger?"

Denise said, "Why haven't we been using the gun range in the armory? We should've all been learning to shoot by now. Maybe we should at least do it today to show you two dudes that shooting a gun in real life is different than a video game."

"I'll second that idea," said Tori, "but I want you boys to understand that shooting inside the gun range is still a lot different than shooting at an infected dead outside. So, don't expect us to say you can go along for this rescue."

"You're going to leave us alone?" said Jalen.

Denise stroked his hair and said, "I don't see any other way. Your Aunt and I will have to help each other. You guys can help us by working together instead of fighting."

In a very scary way, Denise thought this could be a good thing if it brought the brothers closer together again. Jalen would be eight years old in a couple of weeks, and it would be nice to have a birthday party that they all wanted to attend. When Jacob turned twelve next year, it would be obvious that Jalen would want to be somewhere else.

At the prescribed time for Jacob to sign on to contact Marsha, they gathered around the computer and logged in. The chat window said Marsha was online. Jacob put her on the speaker so everyone could hear her. She saw his name in her chat window and started talking before he had a chance to.

"Carrie was super mad at me, Jacob. She said, "Now you're going to want us to help you." I tried to tell her it's the other way around, but she gets like that. She won't listen."

"Marsha, wait a minute. I've got my mom here, and she wants to help you."

If the connection had been an old-style telephone, they would have heard the slam as the connection ended. Since it was an internet connection, the only evidence that no one was on the other end was the silence and the word *Inactive* under the name Marsupial.

"She signed off," Jacob said in disbelief.

Tori said, "She must be scared. Imagine a year up there."

"Is there a way to let her know you're still connected?" asked Denise.

Jacob pointed at the chat window and said, "She knows I am. On her window, it says *Active*. I can still type messages and hope she answers me."

Jacob typed that she should talk with them and that she could trust them. They waited a few minutes, and he added that they wanted them to come to their shelter. He told her it was really safe, and they had lots of food. They watch movies, and they make popcorn every night. When he said they have a soft-serve ice cream machine, her login changed to *Active*.

Her voice came over the speaker, and she said, "You have ice cream? You should have led with that."

"Hi, Marsha. This is Denise Warren. I'm Jacob's mother. Here with us are Jacob's brother, Jalen, and their aunt. Her name is Tori Cassidy. Are you alone, or are any of your friends there?"

"Everyone is here, Mrs. Warren. It's me, Marion, Carrie, Amber, and Shay."

Before Marsha could cover her microphone, there was a sound that caused Tori and Denise to sit up straighter and look at each other to confirm that they had each heard the same thing.

Denise said, "Marsha, was that a baby?"

Another girl spoke up and said, "Listen, lady. If babies are too much problem for you, then we don't need your help. We're doing just fine on our own."

In the shelter, they all heard Marsha say to the other girl, "Give me that back. We aren't doing fine on our own, and Allie and Bonnie need a safe place."

There were several voices for a minute before Marsha spoke again.

"How soon can you get here? We've got a big problem. The infected got past one of the barricades we put up between the wings, so we had to move into the cell block where the really bad kids were. We can't get to the kitchen or infirmary anymore. We're only able to use the computer because the security office still has power and internet, but we won't last another winter in here."

"Marsha, did I hear you right...you have two babies there? Are there any adults left?"

"No."

The single word hung in the air. It was a given that they would help the kids. They were just stunned to learn that there were babies at the juvenile detention center but no adults.

"What happened to their parents?" asked Tori.

"They were counselors here," said Marsha. "They were our friends. When the dead started coming to the gates, they stayed with us. They weren't like the ones who left. Tanya and Claire took care of us, but both of them were pregnant. After their babies were born, they told us we were their big sisters, and we would look out for them if something happened."

Denise said, "Something happened?"

They heard Marsha sniffle, and her voice broke a little when she answered.

"We didn't want Tanya and Claire to both go for supplies after the babies were born, but they did. When they came back, they had both been bitten. They only came back to tell us, then they left again. They said it was best that we didn't see what happened to them."

Tori signaled Denise that she wanted to talk, and Denise nodded.

Tori said, "Marsha, I just need to know as much as you can tell me so we can come get you. There are five of you with two babies, right?"

"Yes, Ma'am."

"How old are the babies?"

"Ummm, about six and seven months," answered Marsha.

"And how should we approach the facility where you're living? Is there a way in besides the front gate?"

There was a long stretch of silence on the other end. Tori was just about to ask again when Carrie answered. She was a bit more congenial this time.

"We made a gate in the fence by the basketball courts. It's on the north side of the building, and we're in that wing. I tied a pink rag on the fence by the gate so we could find it faster. Most of the dead are by the front of the building because that's where the road is, and the infected people inside the entrance wing make a lot of noise that keeps them interested."

"Good," said Tori. "That's what I needed to know. Okay, listen closely. It's going to take us half of the daylight hours to reach you if we don't run into any problems."

Jalen and Jacob both said, "Jinx," at the same time.

Tori didn't know what that meant, but she continued, "Be ready to leave as soon as we get there. If we want to get back before dark, we'll need a bit of luck. We might have to spend a night with you before we head back."

"When are you coming?" asked Marsha.

"Tomorrow," said Denise. "We'll get ready tonight."

******

For lack of a better name, Tori and Denise had chosen to refer to the place above the shelter as *the camp*. That was what it had become when they erected the tent and filled it with supplies, and it was too primitive for any other name. Calling it a playground felt wrong. It was just a large clearing with a fence around it, and the fence was well hidden by trees and thick undergrowth, so they thought the name suggested by Jacob was a bit pretentious. He suggested *fortress*.

They hadn't returned to the camp since the day they stocked it, and there was no way to know what would be waiting for them, so they waited until they were sure it was daylight before Tori pushed the hatch upward. She only lifted it a couple of inches before lowering it again. Tori had her 9mm Luger ready if she needed it, and in all of their planning, they had anticipated the worst. They didn't consider the weather.

"It's raining," she said as she wiped water from her face.

It took thirty minutes of precious daylight to gather together ponchos and waterproof bags.

As Tori climbed to the hatch again, Denise said, "We need to think things through better. Is there anything else we've forgotten?"

Tori was already nervous about what might be near the hatch when she opened it, and she was tired of thinking about it. The possibilities were endless, and she didn't want to think about it anymore. If there was something waiting for her outside, she just wanted to get it over with.

She stared down at Denise from the ladder and said, "Are

we doing this or not? I'm sick of talking about it. So what if we forgot about rain?"

"Sorry. Yeah, let's go."

Tori opened the hatch again, and she did her best to see through a two-inch gap if it was safe to lift it further. The grass around the hatch had grown much taller, and she knew she was being forced to just lift it open. The only consolation was that the tall grass meant nothing had been trampling the area around the hatch. That didn't mean it hadn't been walked on before, but it had been a long time ago.

As soon as Tori's feet disappeared past the rim of the hatch, Denise followed her. The rain was coming down hard, and the overcast sky made everything around them seem almost colorless. They could see the tent still standing a few yards away, but they could barely make out the trees at the perimeter of the camp. They could also hardly hear each other over the sound of the downpour.

"This is bad," Denise shouted.

Tori whirled around and put a finger across her lips. She put her face close to Denise's ear before she spoke.

"We can't try to talk. If there are people in the camp, they'll be inside the tent because of the rain. If there are infected dead, they'll be wandering around. We need to check the tent first, then we'll go."

When they had made their plans for the rescue of the kids at the juvenile center, they decided they should check the inside of the camp to be sure there hadn't been any people who had died inside the fence since their last visit. On a clear day, it wouldn't take more than thirty minutes to do a sweep along the entire fence, but in the heavy rain, it could take a couple of hours. Plus, if they split up to do the sweep, one of them could be outnumbered, and the other might be too far away to even know.

Denise knew what Tori meant. They could only hope that when they returned with the kids, there wouldn't be anything on either side of the fence that would keep them from reaching the hatch again. She nodded so Tori would know she understood.

Tori held her gun out in front of her, and Denise went to the flap of the tent first. She stood well off to the left side and gently put her fingers into the small gap to grip the material. Tori aimed the gun at the front of the tent and nodded at Denise to do it.

Denise yanked the material away to reveal the blackness inside the tent. Both of them felt the warm rush of adrenaline that was only slightly cooled by the rain, and their skin crawled at the backs of their necks as they waited to be attacked.

Both of them pulled out flashlights and aimed the beams at the black interior of the tent. The rain cut down what they could see, so they had to move closer. Tori kept her gun raised as they eased inside, and she pointed it along the beam of light. Instead of survivors huddled together for warmth, there was debris and trash scattered around the floor, but the supplies were gone. The cots that they had stacked along one side of the tent were broken down into parts, and the long wooden poles that made the frames were gone. They watched as a snake moved out of their light into the far corner of the tent.

Denise let the flap close behind them as she moved to inspect something on the other side of the tent. Tori saw it was a pile of rags that were still wrapped around bones that were only kept in place by clothing.

"Someone was here," said Denise.

Tori added, "And someone didn't make it out alive. The supplies are gone, so someone else was here. We can speculate all we want, but hopefully, the supplies helped someone. I wonder why they didn't stay, though?"

"This place is giving me the creeps," said Denise as she watched another snake slide out from under the pile of broken cots. "Why do you suppose someone took the cots apart?"

"To make weapons," said Tori. "The poles could be made into clubs or spears. Right now, a weapon seems to be more valuable than a bed."

Tori peered through the tent door and tried her best to see the inside of the camp, but she guessed visibility was only about twenty yards at the moment.

"Northeast is that way," she said. "Let's go. I won't stop again unless I see something."

She holstered her Luger, and they both pulled machetes from their belts. Neither of them had ever used the weapons, and they were much heavier than they expected, but both women had played tennis for years, and they discovered the weapons were more manageable if they carried them with one hand on the grip and the other hand cradling the blade like it was a tennis racket. Keeping the blade in front of them also made Tori and Denise feel like they would be ready if they had to use them.

Their feelings about the machetes were put to the test before they were halfway to the fence. Two infected dead emerged from the gloom of the morning rain and stumbled toward them. They were slightly to the right of Tori, but Denise happened to be looking that way and saw them first. When Denise poked her from behind, Tori's natural reaction was to turn toward her. Denise surprised herself as much as she did Tori.

In Denise's mind, it really was just like the last time she had played a doubles tennis match. Her partner was out of position for the shot, so she stepped across in front of her and put her racket up defensively. There wasn't time to wind up her arm for a return shot, so she just tried to meet the ball. This time, she hit the extended arm of the infected dead with the hilt of her machete and drove it into the second monster behind it. That put her blade into a position for her to deliver a vicious backhand, and she put everything she had into the swing.

The shock of the blade connecting with the head of the infected dead made her shoulder feel like it had been electrocuted, and she couldn't hold onto it. The infected fell into the path of the second one, so they both went down in a heap, but Denise lost her blade. It was firmly lodged in the forehead of the creature.

Tori stepped forward and used the tip of her machete instead of the long edge. She pushed it through the head of the other infected, then she used her foot braced against its ear to pull it free. Denise tried to do the same thing to retrieve her machete, but she couldn't get it to budge.

"Here, let me show you," said Tori.

The infected dead was lying on its side with the machete sticking straight upward. Tori walked around behind it and kicked the hilt with her heel to dislodge the blade, but the head of the infected dead snapped free from the body.

"I don't believe this," said Tori.

They finally got the blade free after wasting ten more minutes with Tori standing on the head while Denise pulled on the blade. The whole time, Denise apologized for getting the blade stuck. Afterward, Tori had to get her to stop blaming herself.

"Listen to me, Denise. You're looking at someone who thought she could stab one of them in the head with a butter knife. Next time, aim for the neck or use the flat side of the blade to just knock them down."

The rain didn't let up as they worked their way through the

thick underbrush to the fence, but the trees at least stopped it from hitting them with as much force. They had talked about climbing the fence, but Marsha's idea at the juvenile detention facility was better. Tori pulled a set of wire cutters from her backpack and snipped the wire while Denise kept her eyes on their surroundings. When she had a section cut in the shape of a small door, Tori pulled it open wide enough for them to go through. Once they were on the other side, they used a piece of string to tie it in place. For good measure, they dragged a tree limb over to the spot to hide the improvised gate. The limb would also make it easier for them to find it when they got back.

"We're behind schedule," said Denise.

"Now I know why your boys said jinx when I said it's going to take us half of the daylight hours to reach the detention center if we don't run into any problems. We haven't even gone a hundred yards yet."

Tori almost added that maybe they wouldn't run into any more problems, but she stopped herself in time. She kept her blade in front of her and took the lead again as they worked their way through the trees on the northeast side of the camp.

When they emerged from the trees, they could tell they were going slightly downhill, so their pace was good even if the rain made it impossible to see too far ahead. Tori walked slower to let Denise come up beside her so she could talk to her without raising her voice. With the hoods up on their ponchos, they needed to be practically face to face to tell what the other was saying.

"I was just thinking. This rain might be a good thing. Visibility is so bad that nothing can see us."

"If you say so," said Denise, "but if it's okay with you, let's not bother to stop for breaks unless we get too tired. I haven't used my muscles enough in the last year, but I don't have the urge to be sitting on a tree stump, taking a lunch break when company shows up."

"I agree about both things. When we get back, we're putting physical training on our daily schedules," said Tori.

They trudged through mud and overgrown grass until they came to a slight rise, then they found a paved road. Their legs felt heavier from the steady pace they had kept for over two hours, and any hesitation they had felt about using a road was gone with their energy. They had worried that they would be more visible on a road, and they had also reasoned that walking on a paved road would be easier for the infected dead if it were easier for them. They gave in to the temptation of walking on the road because it was easier, but it was also a valuable learning experience.

The horde materialized ahead of them. At first, they appeared to be a dark wall across the road. Tori grabbed Denise by the arm and dragged her off the right side of the road into the trees.

"Did they see us?" whispered Denise.

"I don't know, but we aren't staying to find out. We also better plan on spending the night at the detention center. If that horde is as big as I think it is, we need to let them go far enough south to be past the camp."

"Shouldn't we climb a tree?" asked Denise.

Tori kept dragging her forward as she said, "If they saw us, they'll stay under that tree until we do one of two things...fall or die of old age."

******

The rest of the trip was uneventful, and thankfully, the horde didn't see them. The rain slackened a little, and if anything good could come out of running into the horde, Tori and Denise had moved much faster than before they saw them. Judging by the position of the sun, they had made up some of their lost time. They could see a tall fence in the distance, and a few minutes later, they saw the large two-story building that had to be the detention center.

They decided not to use the road that went to the main entrance for obvious reasons. The biggest problem with roads was that the infected dead could walk on them without tripping over as many obstacles. There were abandoned vehicles that they had to walk around, and they fell down when they tripped over their own feet or some small piece of debris, but it was far easier than walking through woods or overgrown fields. There was also the fact that roads provided a longer field of vision. If Tori and Denise could see the infected dead, then the dead could see them.

The fence surrounded the entire facility, and Marsha had told them to look for the rag tied through the links about head high. They circled to the west along the back of the building until it curved around the north wing, and they spotted the rag right where they expected it to be. From their vantage point, they could see that there were at least six infected dead roaming around on the road near the front gates. They stayed low to the ground as they reached up to untangle the pieces of string that held the piece of fence in place, and they pulled it shut behind them after they slipped through the opening.

The broad patch of ground between the fence and the building had been one of the recreation areas that wasn't paved into basketball courts, and the grass had gone untended. There were already small saplings sprouting where manicured lawns had been, and in a few years, there would be plenty of trees. It was easy to stay hidden from view as they crossed the field to the building, and now that they were closer, they could also see that the inside of the perimeter fence was separated into smaller sections that prevented different ages of children from mixing with each other. It had afforded better protection for Marsha and her friends as the other wings had been breached.

Light flashed from a window as someone held a mirror out to catch the meager sunlight, and a door opened a few inches. The women crouched lower and went up a short row of steps to the door. The girl in front of them held a finger over her lips and then pointed at her ears. They could hear the infected dead at the front gate groaning, but it didn't sound like they were increasing in urgency. That was always a telltale sign that they had spotted a living person.

The young girl visibly appeared to relax.

"Marsha?" said Denise.

"No, I'm Shay. It's my turn on watch. I'll take you to the others."

Shay was barely five feet tall and slender. She wore jeans and a T-shirt, and her legs looked too long for her body. They guessed that she was nine years old, but she was also starting to show signs of malnutrition. She wasn't in trouble yet, but she needed to get on a regular diet soon. She also needed a hot bath, and her hair was in serious need of washing. It made Denise feel good about their decision to bring them to the shelter.

The hallway they used was dark, but the girls had kept it clear of debris to make it easier to walk without stumbling on anything. Shay stopped at the bottom of some stairs and moved a string of cans out of the way.

Shay said in a low voice, "The dead are on the other side of that door."

She gestured down the hall, where they could see a mattress pressed up against a wall. It totally covered the door and was held in place by a bureau.

"The mattress keeps them from hearing us, but if they ever get through there, the cans will warn us. Just so you know, there are more cans at the top of the stairs."

"Smart," said Tori. She hoped the young girl had told them about their precautions as a sign that she wanted their approval, and the smile she got from Shay told her she had been right.

Shay was quick to smile, but Carrie seemed content to keep her face in a constant frown. She met them at the top of the stairs and stood in their path as if it wasn't a foregone conclusion that they could come any further. She sized them up and finally waved them through, but the expression never changed.

"I could hear you coming a mile away," said Carrie. "Might as well ring a dinner bell."

"Don't mind her," said Shay. "She's always like that."

"I heard you," said Carrie.

The reception they got from Carrie was quickly forgotten as they stepped inside the room where the other girls were waiting. The last thing Tori or Denise expected was to have three small girls rush into their arms. They may have become tougher by surviving on their own, but they were still kids.

ESCAPE

Storage Facility, Ithaca, New York - 2025

Dark corners and blinding lights…chaos. Jean considered all of those things to be to her advantage, but being short didn't hurt. It made her invisible when the circumstances were right, and in the junkyard that surrounded the storage facility, she could blend in where a man couldn't. She had stayed behind while the Chief had taken most of the Mud Island family on wild escapades, but she hadn't just hidden inside the shelters. She and Ed had roamed and foraged around the mountains near the shelter, and they had practiced for moments like this one.

They were spread out perfectly as the ambush had been sprung, and Jean knew instinctively that standing still for one second would be one second too long. Anyone who moved after everyone's eyes adjusted to the light would be like a moving target, so Jean moved to her left and went under a derelict vehicle while everyone else tried to focus on the people who were standing still.

Jean had a random thought as she went flat to the ground and practically slid like a snake under the car. She was the one who had always needed something from the top shelf in the grocery store, and she always had to ask total strangers to get it for her. Now, she was the one who could use her height to her advantage, and not only was she smaller, but she was quieter.

She didn't stay under the car because she knew she would be retrieved quickly if she stayed in the area. Her instincts told her that she couldn't help her husband, even though her irrational side screamed at her not to leave him. Only a small part of her mind gave in to the idea that she would be totally alone and a long way from home.

The rest of her mind said, "I've changed, and I can save Eddie, Ruth, and Wally, but first I have to save myself."

Jean slipped out from under the other side of the car and saw that someone, probably one of the groups that had lived in the storage facility for a long time, had piled mountains of furniture, car parts, shopping carts, and other debris against the fence that surrounded the storage facility. It was actually a pretty good idea. If the infected dead couldn't reach the fence, then they couldn't collapse it under their combined weight.

"Too bad they needed to keep the back alley open as an escape route," she thought.

Jean only paused for a couple of seconds to listen for the sounds that would indicate they saw where she went. From what she could hear, they noticed she was gone, but they didn't see where she went. People had moved back inside the storage facility where they were loudly searching the individual units. Their confidence in their own safety was obvious by virtue of the fact that they were yelling to each other as they cleared each unit.

There was something else Jean discovered about the pile of debris. It was as if someone had carefully distributed the junk in order to keep another escape path clear. Even with very little light, she was about to crawl at a respectable speed away from the back alley. Her suspicions were confirmed when her escape path led her directly to the storage facility, and someone had made a makeshift gate in the fence. It was tied shut by a piece of wire, and since the infected dead didn't know how to untie knots, she assumed she was right about it being a backup escape route.

The inside of the storage facility was the last place she wanted to be, but no one would expect to find her hiding along the outside of the fence, especially since they thought she had made her escape to the inside. Jean lay down under the cover of the debris and made herself as small as she could. From her vantage point, she was able to watch as the cordon of searchers moved from unit to unit, and she saw when they discovered the unfortunate woman who was hiding under a pile of blankets. It was on the row that she and her friends hadn't searched yet. They would have found the woman if Wally hadn't drawn the attention of the infected dead that were behind us, and it was a small consolation to know that the woman would have been better off being found by us.

Jean felt a pang of guilt when she heard the men yell, "We found her. We found her."

The woman was kicking and putting up a good fight as Jean watched her being dragged to the back entrance of the storage facility, but more men joined in to grab her legs. One of them hit her hard, and they dragged her limp body between them.

Sound carried well at night, especially since there were no longer the sounds of a city in the background. It used to be that on any given night, there were the sounds of cars, sirens, and the whine as someone shifted gears and increased their speed on a motorcycle. In the quiet cities of the infected dead, the only sounds you would hear might be the random sounds of things that finally gave in to gravity and fell over, then the groaning that gave away the locations of the new predators that owned the cities.

Jean didn't doubt that the dead were becoming disturbed by the noisy gang of men, their vehicles, and then the screaming woman who they eventually silenced. They were probably moving toward the new noises in the city, and their groaning would begin soon. For now, Jean could hear the faint noises behind her, and she thought she could pick Eddie's voice out above them all. She knew something had happened already, judging by the pitch of his voice. She wasn't sure if it had been Ruth or Wally who had been the focus of their attention, but she mourned for them both. Then she could tell when everything changed. She could tell when the men returned with the unfortunate woman who they thought was her.

Eddie sounded like he was in complete despair, and Jean knew they had killed the woman in front of him. She also knew it was to punish him for what happened at the bridge, and even though she felt sorry for the woman, Jean hoped they would feel like they had gotten their revenge and wouldn't kill Eddie, too.

Jean was so intent on the sounds that came from the back entrance that she almost jumped when legs appeared only inches from her hiding place. Two men wearing boots stopped walking as one held out a cigarette lighter to the other.

She heard one say, "You think Branch will make us keep looking?"

"Naw, he's ready to head home just like the rest of us. We'll probably hole up in here for the night and then drive up to the salt mines in the morning. We can top off our fuel and grab some food, then head back to the high school. The salt mines aren't that far from here."

The two men walked away from where Jean was hiding, and she said to herself, "Good. I can be there before morning."

******

If I screamed loud when I thought I was watching Jean's throat get cut, it was nothing compared to Ted Branch's scream above me. In the close quarters of the salt mine tunnels, every sound was amplified, and his scream rose to a pitch I had never heard before from a man his size.

Because I had dropped to the ground, I had a front-row seat as a shiny blade flashed between me and Branch. It sliced through the tendon just above the heel of his left foot, and he grabbed for it as he fell to his knees. I would never have believed a man his size could reach such a high note, but he didn't stop there. He fell from his knees and didn't stop until he hit the hard floor with his face. There was so much mayhem around us that none of his men realized why he was screaming, but I felt myself being pulled out from under their feet before I even knew who was pulling me. I assumed it was one of Branch's men, and I didn't resist because I was still playing possum.

"Will you please quit being nothing but dead weight and get up?" said Jean.

I couldn't even see her that well in all of the dancing light from the lanterns, but I heaved myself from the floor and followed her away from the battle. Branch was in no condition to stop me, and his men were too busy to care. Jean reached back with one hand toward me, and I hung onto it for dear life.

I didn't know if Jean knew where she was going, and there wasn't time to ask her, but I should have guessed that Jean had already thought of that. Without lights, I just blindly held onto her hand as she navigated the dark tunnels. If I could have seen what she was doing with her other hand, I would have known she was keeping it pressed against the walls to follow her own mental map back to the surface. I was lost until I saw the gray light up ahead.

"Wait," I said.

When Jean turned around, I scooped her up and gave her a hug that might have killed some people. She hugged me for only a few seconds before she broke free.

"There'll be time for that and more later, Eddie. We need to get out of here before they find their way to the entrance, and there's still too much we don't know about this place. We'll never find the shelter now, not with these morons using it for a base. I mean, how stupid can they be to have a base with the infected dead inside it?"

It was fun to hear her rant about Branch and his people, but she was right. We still had to find a way to get by the men outside while rescuing Ruth in the process.

"I have a plan," I said.

There were plenty of places to hide inside the entrance of the salt mine, and Jean trusted me to take care of the men outside because I had said the magic words that the Chief always used. She hid behind some equipment while I ran out of the mine. There wasn't a backup plan, but that was only because there wasn't time to think of one.

I was already winded from running through the dark mine shafts, and my right shoulder was practically making me cry from the pain. For good measure, Branch had bled enough to get a big red stain across my forearm and chest. When I burst from the entrance of the salt mine, I certainly looked the part of a victim, so I screamed for help.

"Branch is hurt! He needs everyone inside now!"

I ran toward the men Branch had left outside, and they gravitated toward me slowly like metal shavings toward a magnet, but they weren't sure what to do at first. I saw Jeremiah Smith in the middle of them and shouted directly to him.

"Branch found the shelter…he needs help to take it, and he's hurt bad! He sent me to get everyone!"

The men moved faster once Jeremiah Smith took the bait. All twelve of them charged for the entrance of the mine like the cavalry, except one who lingered near Ruth. It worked back at their camp when we stole their truck, so I tried it again.

"He told me to watch her because I'm hurt. He needs you inside."

I hid my amazement when the man actually did what I told him to do. I waited until he disappeared behind the other men, and then I breathed a sigh of relief when Jean emerged into the light. We ran for the pickup truck, and after we untied Ruth, who was astonished to see both of us, we discovered that sometimes you could be lucky and good. The keys were in the ignition.

"Which way?" I asked Jean.

"Follow that road that goes northeast. If they get their act together back there, they'll guess we went south."

"What makes you think that?" I asked.

All three of us broke out laughing when Jean said, "I don't have a clue. You want to go the other way?"

We drove away from the salt mine, believing we were on a main highway, even though it was overgrown. It turned out to be a service road of some kind, but we had no idea where it went. We got our answer thirty minutes later when it simply ended at a wall of trees.

******

The engines would cool down on the AC-130 long before the Chief would cool down. He wanted the plane refueled and ready to go immediately, and it took everything Kathy could do to keep him from lashing out at Doc Bus for letting Ed and Jean leave. It finally fell on Iris to get her husband to at least approach the problem the way he normally solved everything else. She knew he always wanted to plan any mission, and she got him to remember it would be a mission just like the others. The only difference was who they were going to rescue.

The Chief agreed that everyone should go back to Green Cavern to prepare, but he wanted to hold a meeting with the rest of them in two hours. That was enough time to allow everyone to get a shower and a hot meal, but when he walked into their meeting room early, he found that everyone had gotten there ahead of him. It was a full house, and no one had wasted time on a shower. Some of them had brought their food with them from the cafeteria.

"I want to start this meeting by apologizing to Doc Bus."

The Chief nodded in his direction as he spoke.

"I should have assumed he would have done everything short of putting Ed and Jean in leg irons to stop them from leaving. From what I've learned in the short time since we got back, that was one of the threats he tried."

There was a slight chuckle in the room, and someone said they had heard Jean say the same thing to Bus.

"That sounds like Jean," continued the Chief, "At the same time, as dumb as it was, I'll refrain from commenting further on how stupid they were for not waiting for us to get back."

Everyone in the room could see the restraint the Chief was showing when he made his last remark. They knew he was mad, but his anger had given way to worry. There were a lot of miles between the shelter and Ithaca, New York, and they would have to search every one of them.

"We know that they've been on the road for three weeks. If they had run into no problems at all, they would have made the drive in about four days. That would allow for the time they spent getting around obstacles such as highway traffic jams and natural erosion from a lack of maintenance. In other words, they couldn't be driving fast. They also would need to find fuel, and that's been becoming more scarce as it degrades. I don't even need to mention the infected dead. They might still outnumber the living. We also need to know about the enclaves of survivors. Ed and Jean might get around roadblocks, fuel problems, and the infected dead, but there are still too many little kingdoms out there that don't operate the way we do. What do we know about groups like that on the route they're likely to have taken?"

Captain Miller raised his hand and held up a map.

"I'm ahead of you, Chief. I checked in with the other shelters to see if any of them knew of activity on the way to New York. You already know we don't have anything north of Charlotte unless someone has really kept their heads down, but we still have some satellite imagery from Huntsville. They've been tracking heat signatures."

"What are they looking for?" asked Kathy. "Man-made signatures?"

Captain Miller nodded. "That's affirmative. They're looking for anything out of the ordinary, so they have this program that's keeping an eye on every nuclear reactor on the East Coast. Our good friend Gentry Campbell said there are almost one hundred of them spread across twenty-eight states, so they cover a big area. Plus, there were a lot of nuclear-powered naval vessels in port from Georgia to Connecticut at the time the infection started. Some made it to sea, but some didn't. It might be a coincidence, but their satellite picked up a big heat bloom about a week ago somewhere that didn't have a reactor nearby."

"An explosion?" asked the Chief. "Not a reactor in port, I hope."

"A big one," said Captain Miller, "but not in a port. Previous imagery shows it was a rail yard along the river, not far from DC. It just happens to be one of the possible routes our misguided friends would be using. It could be a coincidence, but in a world where we've had to suspend our beliefs about what happens after we die, I'm willing to accept the possibility that they had something to do with it. For all we know, it was their way of signaling for help."

There was another chuckle that spread across the room, but it sounded different. If the Chief could put his finger on what was different about it, he would say it was a sign of their unity. Everyone in the room was focused on finding Ed and Jean and bringing them home.

"Thank you, Jim. Maybe that's something to consider. If we assume they made it that far, then the search area is only about a third as large as we thought."

Kathy said, "I think we should assume they at least made it halfway to Ithaca."

"There's one more thing," said Captain Miller. "Here's a satellite photograph taken at night."

He handed the Chief a picture that was grainy but clear enough for the Chief to recognize the shape for what it was.

"Someone has enough power to light up a football stadium?" he said. "When was this taken?"

"A couple of days before the big bloom in the rail yard," said Captain Miller. "One might not have anything to do with the other, but I would suggest that we put that landmark on our search map. We can at least fly over it on our way to New York."

The Chief saw that Chris Hampton had his hand raised. Hampton had been one of the most solid members of their group, and the Chief valued his input. He was glad to see he had something to add, and he called on him.

Hampton stood before he spoke, and his comments had a sobering impact on everyone in the room.

"I know our goal is to find our friends alive, and I hate to be the one to say this, but there's a big difference between a search and rescue operation and a recovery operation. Ed and Jean aren't floating in a life raft somewhere waiting for the chance to shoot a flare as a plane flies over. The odds are really against them. That's why I propose we send a ground operation to follow the route they would have followed, and at the same time, we can fly up to Ithaca and search from there backward."

There was a general clamor in the room of people who agreed and disagreed, and the Chief had to raise his voice to get everyone to calm down.

"We aren't going to get anything done if we argue about it," he said. "I want to thank Hampton for reminding us that every minute…every second could count, and even though I trust all of you to give your honest opinion, I've already decided on Plan A and B. The ground forces will leave within the hour to retrace their route. They'll be escorted by the MRAP, and if they encounter difficulty, the AC-130 can be at their location quickly. In the meantime, we'll fly the same route instead of a direct route to Ithaca. I want to do a pass over the high school football stadium in Virginia and then the rail yard that blew up."

"If they left clues along the way," said Kathy, "We aren't going to spot them from the air."

The Chief nodded and said, "I know that, but this is the part Hampton got right. There are more ways to die out there than there used to be, and one of them is probably a paramilitary group that's so crazy that they light up their base at night. I want to find out what Ed and Jean had to deal with when they went through Virginia. Besides, it's not exactly out of our way. Let's go, people."

Within the hour, the entire Mud Island family was loaded into the AC-130 and ready to go. Captain Miller and a squad of soldiers were already on the road in the MRAP. They hoped their mission would be cut short by a message from the Chief saying Ed and Jean had been located, but until they were told to turn around, they would try to retrace their route to Ithaca.

FAMILY TIES

Juvenile Hall - 2017

Tori and Denise both knew it would be better to wait until the next morning to make the trip back to the shelter. There was no way to move a group of children quietly over twenty miles of terrain that was crawling with the infected dead. It was going to be hard enough to do it during the daytime, but in the dark would be impossible. Both of them were well aware of the probability that one or both of the infants would begin to cry on the trip, and when that happened, they would be forced to run.

The first order of business was to be secure for the night and to get food into them all. The girls had been resourceful with supplies, but they had been rationing for a long time, and the infants needed the formula Denise had carried with them. Denise also broke out a couple of jars of baby food in case the two little girls didn't drink the formula. It turned out that her worries over the food were unnecessary. The babies ate it hungrily and fell asleep fast with their bellies full.

Tori took care of the older girls while Denise fed the babies, and she took the opportunity to get to know them better. She found that Marsha was as outgoing in person as she had been over the computer. Like the others, she was in need of a bath, but Tori could tell she would be a pretty little girl when she was cleaned up. She figured Jacob and Jalen were going to be head over heels in love when they met them. Marsha acted as the spokesman for the group, but they all turned to each other as if no one was the clear leader. Tori had expected the permanent frown on Carrie's face would ease up a bit once she ate some food, but she hadn't come close to a grin. Whatever the girl had seen in the last year, it had left a mark on her soul that couldn't be erased. Still, Tori hoped she would feel better once they were safely inside the shelter.

Amber was by far the quietest one in the group. She watched as Marsha and Shay told Tori everything about the first days when the infected dead arrived, and Tori noticed she sat up straight like she was still in school. The rest of the girls laid back against the walls of the room like teenagers. She was just about to ask Amber a question when Marion spoke up. Tori had hardly been aware of her because she had just been watching everything that went on around her.

"She wasn't supposed to be here," said Marion.

Tori was surprised because she had simply been about to ask Amber to tell her something about herself. Marion had just shown Tori she was the perceptive one in the group.

"What do you mean by that?" asked Tori.

Marion nodded toward Amber and said, "She wasn't sent to juvie like the rest of us. She was just here when it started. Her mom worked in the kitchen, and she brought her with her when it started."

"Oh, I'm sorry."

Tori didn't know what else to say because she could have said the same thing to any of the children. She just studied Amber and the way she sat up so straight with a half-smile on her face.

Marion crooked an index finger toward Tori to indicate she

wanted her to come closer. Tori leaned toward her so Marion could whisper in her ear.

"Her mom is one of those dead people in the hall. Amber thinks if she's really good, her mom will be okay."

Tori realized Marion wasn't trying to be mean. If she were, she wouldn't have whispered privately to Tori. She would have blurted it out for everyone to hear. Tori suddenly felt the enormity of the trauma in the room. It wasn't just a group of kids feeling pain over their losses and the confusion that had happened in their lives. It was a collection of damaged children. Marsha, Marion, and Shay were all taking it in stride because they had stronger defense mechanisms, but Amber hadn't come to terms with the reality of the situation yet, and something had happened to Carrie that made her feel like she would never be happy again.

"Marsha, could you do me a favor?" said Tori. "Split up this food while I have a little chat with Marion."

Marsha and Shay dug into the prepackaged MREs that Tori and Denise had brought along, and they helped Amber get hers open. Tori noticed as she and Marion left the room that they were all acting like big sisters toward her even though they were the same age.

"You guys have all been looking after Amber and the babies?" asked Tori.

Marion nodded, "Amber is kind of…innocent?" she said as if she wasn't sure if she had chosen the right word. "I mean, she's a good kid. She didn't get in any trouble like the rest of us, but it feels like she got punished more than we did. It's not fair that her mom had to die in front of her. Me and the others, we know our parents are probably dead, but at least we didn't have to see it happen."

Tori felt like the empathy from the girls toward Amber spoke volumes about the way they really were before the infection, despite the fact that they were inmates of a juvenile detention center. All of them deserved to be safe inside the shelter.

"Tell me about Allie and Bonnie. They're both so young."

Marion shrugged, but Tori saw her lower lip quiver a little.

"What do you want to know? Their moms were good to us. They didn't have to stay, but they were both pregnant when the infection started. We told them to leave us, but they said they couldn't. Besides, where were they going to get free babysitters with all of this going on?"

Marion sniffled and wiped at the corner of her eye with the back of her hand.

"Allie's mom really said that to me. The other counselors were leaving, and they weren't even offering to take us with them, but Ms. Duncan and Ms. Sandler said they would take care of us. They said we were all sisters, and they would be our moms."

"So, they both had their babies here with you guys a few months ago, then they got infected?"

"Yes, Ma'am. Do you have kids?"

"Me? No, but Denise has two boys about your age back at the shelter. With a little luck, we'll all be back there together around this time tomorrow night. Now, you must be starving. Let's get back to the others."

******

Denise had forgotten a lot about caring for babies, and she realized that most of it she had just set aside in her memories once the boys had learned to talk. Then it was like a whole new ball game raising kids. From the moment she picked up Allie to feed her the first time to the moment the babies woke up for their next feeding, she had worried about how they were going to travel twenty miles without one of them crying. She had a hard time sleeping and was running on pure adrenaline by the time they were ready for the trip.

Tori had gone around and helped each girl pack their meager belongings and made sure everyone was ready to go at sunrise. Every minute would count, or they would be stuck in the open when the sun went down. When the first light from the sun spread across the trees in the distance, they opened the door and ran bent over at the waist through the tall grass. Tori and Denise carried Allie and Bonnie, wrapped securely in slings across their stomachs. Both babies had been awakened and fed an hour before sunrise, so they had gone back to sleep. Without a sign of rain and with both babies sleeping peacefully, Tori and Denise felt like they just might have a chance to make it.

As the morning wore on, they stayed in a single column without talking. Denise led the way with Tori following behind the girls. From the back of the group, she was gratified to see the way they constantly watched for the infected dead, but she was especially moved by the way they helped Amber get over fallen trees or across ditches. The terrain was mostly flat, but none of them were prepared for a cross-country run. They stopped before noon and huddled up in a deep ditch. Allie and Bonnie woke up hungry, and the timing was good because the infected dead decided to show up while everyone was in hiding.

Tori was perched on the edge of the ditch while the rest of the group was eating. Marsha was feeding Bonnie across from Denise, and she saw Tori extend her hand toward them. Tori kept her hand palm down to let everyone know to stay down and stay quiet. Then she flashed her fingers to warn them it was a horde. Marsha got everyone's attention, so they were watching when Tori flashed five fingers repeatedly. There were at least thirty of them. When she was done, she let her body slide down the bank of the ditch until she was with the whole group.

"We need to move," she whispered. "Stay in the ditch as low as you can. Most of them are on the road, but some are walking along the shoulder and could fall into the ditch close enough to see us."

Everyone moved quietly, but it was closer than they would have liked. Tori had just gotten around a slight turn in the ditch when she heard the first of the infected dead tumble over the edge. She looked down at the baby inside her sling, and she saw that the little girl was awake and watching her. Tori didn't know when babies begin to recognize smiling faces as friendly, but she did her best to put on a smile. Bonnie returned the smile, and Tori felt the determination she needed to get everyone back to the shelter. Behind her, she heard the infected dead landing on top of each other, but she caught up with the girls and urged them on.

They made good time without rain pelting them, and they could see the camp as the sun was getting low in the west. Denise got her bearings and led them to a spot where the trees appeared to be thick, but she had carefully broken a couple of branches to point toward the fence. The underbrush was too thick for the infected dead to walk around freely, but it would still be dangerous if one ran into the fence and was stuck walking along it. She knew that had happened before she even saw it.

It appeared to be alone, but it had already heard them as they hurried toward the tall fence. There was no way they could hide the sound of seven people running through the bushes. Denise pointed toward it, but Tori saw she was also pointing at something else. The infected dead was practically wrestling with the big tree branch that they had used to mark the spot where they had cut the fence. They would have to kill it to get inside.

Carrie said, "What're we waiting for?"

Denise and Tori had survived the hotel and the trip to the shelter. Along the way, they had eliminated a handful of infected dead with a desk, a butter knife, a car, and a gun. Carrie, on the other hand, had survived above ground for over a year, and one infected dead wasn't a problem. They watched as the girl jumped onto the fence and climbed it like a squirrel up a tree. Carrie tossed her jacket over the barbed wire and spread it apart. She went over the top, dropped to the ground, and ran along the inside of the fence until she was face to face with the infected dead.

"Here, stupid. I have something for you."

Carrie shook the fence until the infected dead leaned close enough for her to shove a long knife through its head. As if it were no big deal, she went over and untied the string on the fence and pulled it open for the others.

******

Tori was right about the girls. They all cleaned up really well. As for the boys, Jalen and Jacob acted like they had never seen girls before. Jalen was totally blinded by the sight of Amber because she was so vulnerable compared to the others. Jacob and Marsha acted like they had known each other for years because they had met online. All of the girls wanted soft-serve ice cream and to see the game room.

It was the beginning of a new way of life for all of them. Outside the shelter in the real world, there had always been foster families raising children, and maybe somewhere else, there were families that had been formed when survivors found each other, but the shelter population grew from four to eleven because of a brief internet connection. Along with the population growth came the biggest challenge of all...raising teenagers in a closed environment.

In the days before the infection, parents had support systems they could rely on. The schools, churches, and peer groups all filled roles in the lives of the kids, but the group that came together in the shelter hadn't done so well in society. For one reason or another, four of them had been taken out of the general population and incarcerated. Marsha, Marion, Carrie, and Shay had never really known normal lives, and they needed to learn how to get along in a community that had rules. That meant conflicts would arise, and conflict resolution was almost a daily chore after the honeymoon wore off.

Jalen and Amber were constant companions and gave the other kids as much space as they could. It didn't go unnoticed by Denise or Tori, and as any good parents would do, they arranged supervision as best they could to keep the adolescent attractions from becoming bigger problems.

It was an understatement to say Jacob had his hands full. Marsha was pretty, and they already had a connection, but that left Marion, Carrie, and Shay without someone to share their affection, and as Denise and Tori knew all too well, girls would compete for boys. They constantly sought Jacob's attention and approval, and they grew frustrated by his attraction to Marsha.

Despite the hormonal adolescent Olympics, the newness of the shelter and the unending safety that surrounded them made them grow as a family. Denise took on most of the childcare duties with Allie and Bonnie, while Tori became the teacher and crisis counselor for the older kids. When she established formal school hours, they called Denise the principal because Tori would send them to see her if they didn't listen.

Routines fell into place that gave the eleven survivors in the Ithaca shelter new ways to pass the time. Family breakfasts were riotous releases of energy that were generally like food parties because the *juvie* kids had done without variety for so long. Pancakes and waffles were the most requested meals because, as Marion explained, maple syrup was the first thing to go after the infection started. It was worth more than money on the very first day.

Everyone helped to clean up the kitchen and the dishes after breakfast, and there was one hour allowed for video games before school started. Meals, school, and video games were always at the same hours, but there was still plenty of time for mischief. The kids didn't have a chance to get bored because there were still chores, such as laundry and making beds, but sometimes they needed to discover something new. It was a big shelter, and exploring was a way to fill their time and satisfy their curiosity.

The armory was off-limits, and the locked door that opened into the *seaquarium* had a warning sign on it that made it clear that trespassers would face Tori's wrath. She never displayed real anger in front of the kids, but they all sensed it was a sore spot. The only time Carrie asked her why they weren't allowed to go past the door, Tori hadn't answered. The cold stare on her face had been all the answer she needed, and Denise had quickly changed the subject.

The written rules of the shelter also clearly stated that no one could open the main doors or the hatch to the camp. Otherwise, they were all free to explore during their free time. They were quick to discover that the shelter was like a big hotel with plenty of unoccupied rooms. That made it harder for the adults to keep up with Jacob and Marsha, but when Denise and Tori talked about it, they agreed it would only get worse if they tried too hard to prevent it. All in all, life inside the shelter became what they hoped it would be.

Time worked its magic because there was still enough to do besides daily routines. Video gaming was unrestricted, but the freedom to play whenever they wanted caused the kids to develop other interests. Jacob and Marsha used the extensive library of computers to design a botany lab, and they tapped the power from the hydroelectric plant to create a farm under artificial lighting. By the end of their first year, they were harvesting fresh vegetables. The fruit trees took another year, but as they became teenagers, they picked their first crop of oranges and lemons.

Denise and Tori were worried that Marion, Carrie, and Shay would become too independent because they didn't have boyfriends, but the girls were surprisingly drawn to other projects in the shelter. No one would have suspected that the three of them would form a science and math club after Jacob and Marsha complained that they needed more output from the hydroelectric plant. Maybe it started as a project to attract the attention of Jacob, but the unintentional side effect was that it was actually interesting to the girls.

Their success led them to work on other projects in the machine and wood-crafting shops. Carrie, who still frowned like it was a hobby, took an interest in medicine and spent hours reading journals. She might not have ever developed a good bedside manner, but patients would always believe she was serious about the profession. By the time she had her seventeenth birthday, all of the inhabitants of the shelter called her Doctor Carrie.

Birthdays and holidays made them all feel like time flew by because they were constantly celebrating them. They also had memorial days for the mothers of Allie and Bonnie because they had stayed behind at the detention center, even though they could have left. Their babies had most likely survived because they had made that selfless decision. Of course, they also had a day set aside for Randy and Brad. Year after year, the survivors grew and remembered.

Jacob would be the first of them to turn nineteen, and Marsha was close behind, as were the other girls. Denise was worried about seeing grandchildren being born into such a damaged world, but she was bracing herself for the inevitable. They considered themselves to be adults long before their birthdays, but for some lucky reason, there were no big announcements until the day when they told Denise they wanted to get married. It wasn't a surprise, and in some ways, it was a relief. Her son had grown six inches taller than her, and she would have expected him to fall in love and get married if there hadn't been an apocalypse. The couple wanted the marriage to take place after Jacob's birthday.

Amber was a little older than Jalen, but she had been good for him. After he had endured the first year under the thumb of his big brother, he had matured with an even temperament, probably because Amber had been more of an outsider than the rest of them, and she needed his innocent nature. Overall, Denise felt lucky that her sons had grown up as well as they had, considering the circumstances.

******

The 2025 day of remembrance for Randy and Brad would have been just as the others had been, but every year, the day had become more of a celebration than a memorial. Time had faded the pain of their loss, but it had also dulled their memories about the infection. They had been safe for too long. Allie and Bonnie didn't know anything about the infected dead, and no one really knew how much they should be told or when to tell them. The girls from the detention center remembered better than Jalen and Jacob because the boys had been safe for nine years, but they had also been lulled into a belief that the infection couldn't get inside the shelter. They had no way of knowing that their complacency could cost them so much.

Denise felt like she should have seen trouble coming and somehow gotten in front of it. From the beginning, she had put responsibility on Jacob's shoulders. She had no way of knowing he had been traumatized by his short trip to the ice machine. Then, he had lost his father without having a chance to say goodbye, and that day was followed by the frantic escape from the hotel. She had missed the signs when Jacob made his little brother the target of his emotional wounds. It just seemed like a phase all brothers go through, but that changed when the girls arrived.

Jacob wasn't jealous of the affection given to the new arrivals because Marsha compensated for his losses. It had spared Jalen from Jacob's vindictiveness and had even helped Jacob hide the part of himself that was still damaged. For almost seven more years, he was able to give the outward appearance that everything was fine. Marsha didn't even disagree with him when he told her his plan.

It was after supper, and everyone had settled into whatever it was they wanted to do before going to bed. It was fairly customary to see the young couple stroll away hand in hand for some time alone. No one even paid any attention to which direction they chose. On this particular evening, they reached the large waiting area by the big front door of the shelter and sat in two of the seats that had been intended for people being processed into the shelter, but Jacob had turned them around to face the great vault door. They put their feet on the seats that had been behind theirs, and he draped an arm around her shoulder.

Sometimes, they spent their time watching the infected dead on the security cameras. The dead gathered at the large vault door and milled around as if waiting for something, but then they would wander off into the dark tunnels when a noise caught their attention. This time, the couple simply sat quietly for several minutes and enjoyed each other's company.

"I've decided what I want for a wedding present," said Jacob.

Marsha laughed a little and said, "You're supposed to be thinking about what to give me."

"I've got an idea for that, too, but I want something special."

"Well, so do I," she answered.

She saw that he had something on his mind when he didn't take the bait and talk about what she wanted.

"What's up, Jay?"

Marsha had shortened his name the way some girls had done before the infection. She could remember them talking about their crushes, and they would call their favorite actors by pet names as if they were their boyfriends.

"Through that door, and at the end of the main shaft near the entrance of the mine, there's an office that belonged to my dad. I've been thinking about some of the things he had on his desk, and he told me they would be mine when I grew up."

"Like what?" she asked.

"Well, the main thing is a baseball. My dad caught a home run ball at a World Series game and got it signed by the guy who hit it. It was a big deal to him. I think it was in 2009, around the time my brother was born, and my dad was a big Yankees fan. He said it was worth a lot of money, but he said it would make him happier to give it to me on my eighteenth birthday. We went to a game together before the infection, and it was all he talked about."

"That's sweet," said Marsha. "I wish I could've met your dad."

Of all the things she could have said, that was the one thing that solidified in his mind that he had to go after the ball. It was like the ball was a piece of his father, and it was just sitting on the desk, waiting for him to come and get it.

"What else did he have up there?"

Jacob thought about the last time he had seen the desk, and he remembered the little things that fathers have with them at work. There was a coffee cup with World's Best Dad written on it. They had given it to him for Father's Day a few years before the infection began. There were also framed pictures of the whole family. They were all smiling at the camera and happy. Jacob wanted to just see the desk as it had been, almost as much as he wanted to bring back the things on it.

"When should we go?" asked Marsha.

"I can't take you with me. It's way too dangerous."

"You can't go by yourself."

Jacob pulled his long legs off the seat in front of him and turned to face her.

"I need you to stay here to open the door when I get back. I don't know the combination, and I can't ask my mom for it. She would freak out on me. You can watch for me on the security camera."

"Why don't you let me go for you?" asked Marsha. "That way, it would be like a real present from me. Besides, I can take care of myself out there. I did it before."

"You mean when you were in juvie? That was a long time ago, and it was different. You guys were outside. It wasn't like being inside a mineshaft. You're crazy for even suggesting it."

Jacob smiled when he said it, so it didn't come across as mean, but she knew he meant it. She also knew she wouldn't be as brave inside the mine as she had been in juvie. Besides, they didn't have any choice back then, and playing hide and seek with the infected dead was different when you could see them better.

"You're right, but like you said, that was a long time ago. What makes you think you can make it to the office? You were a little kid when you did it with your dad."

Jacob pictured himself riding with his father in a mine car. To him, it felt like it was just yesterday, and he could see every turn. In reality, there were about a hundred turns, and he hadn't paid attention to most of them. He had been a kid who simply loved to ride through the mine with his dad.

"How long will it take? You won't be gone long, will you?"

Jacob got that far-away look again as he thought about riding in the mine car. He had only been ten years old, so he had paid even less attention to the amount of time it took than to the exact number of turns. It hadn't taken long to make the drive, and in his mind, it couldn't take much longer to walk to the top and back.

"If I take my time? My guess is about an hour to go up to the top. I probably won't need that much time coming back down. I'll have to sneak past the infected people going up, but they're so slow that I can just run by them. Since it's all downhill coming back, they'll just fall when they try to catch up."

Jacob laughed at the thought of dodging the infected dead. They would reach for him, but it wasn't like they would ever have a chance to catch him. He imagined himself taunting them into following him, and then he would run away. It was thrilling to think about.

"I have an idea," said Jacob. "Let's do it like this...we'll use the lights. After supper tomorrow, when everyone goes off to do their own thing, we can go to the power plant and turn on the main lights in the tunnels. They still work, and I'll be able to see where I'm going the whole time. You can wait at the vault door, and when you see me coming, you can open it for me."

BREACH

Ithaca Shelter - 2025

"I'm a little nervous about this," said Marsha. "Are you sure this is a good idea?"

Jacob laughed, "No, I'm actually sure this is a bad idea, but what's the worst thing that could happen? I think when I'm back, we'll both be glad I did it. Look at it this way. If I don't at least try, I'll never be satisfied with myself."

"Promise me one thing. If you run into trouble, turn around and come back. No matter how close you get to the top, give up if it gets bad."

"It won't get that bad."

He wanted to be reassuring, but he knew that he wasn't even sounding reassuring to himself.

"Promise me," she insisted.

"Okay, I promise. If it gets bad, I'll come back."

"Even if you're almost there," she added.

"Even if I'm almost there."

The couple drifted away from the rest of the group after the dishes from the evening meal were done, and no one noticed when they turned to the stairs that went down to the power plant. They both knew their way around the hundreds of switches and breakers that went to the various parts of the shelter, and they knew the power to the mine shafts was mostly in one panel. They were all turned off except two. One was to the security cameras on the other side of the vault door, and the other was the string of lights in the immediate area outside the door.

Jacob put his hand on the first switch at the top of a long row and pushed it to the right. A small tag on the switch changed from red to white, indicating that power had been turned on somewhere in the mine. The label on the switch said it was Section E, but Jacob didn't know if it was where he was going or not. All he knew was that all of the switches had to be turned on.

The lights on the ceiling of the power plant flickered, and Jacob hesitated before pressing the next switch.

"Did I do that?" he asked Marsha.

"How should I know?"

"If it does that every time I press a switch, someone's going to notice and come check to see if there's a problem."

Jacob braced himself for another flickering light as he pressed the second switch, and he knew if it did it again, he would have to abandon his attempt to reach his father's office. When the switch clicked into place, and the white label appeared, the light may have dimmed slightly, but it didn't flicker.

"Keep going, Jay. I think it's okay."

Jacob was buoyed by her confidence, so he pressed the third and fourth switches more quickly. They didn't see a change in the lights, so he rapidly went down the row clicking them into place. When they were all on, they breathed a sigh of relief.

"Okay, let's hope that was the hard part," said Jacob.

It only took ten minutes for them to get to the big waiting room at the main entrance, and they went to the monitor for the security camera first. The lights were brighter outside, and they could see further into the tunnel. There was only one infected dead, and its back was to them as it walked slowly up the sloping tunnel.

"I wish we could've gotten into the armory so I could at least have a machete," said Jacob.

Now that the moment had arrived, he was feeling more of the nervousness that adrenaline causes, and he was shifting his weight from one foot to the other. His nervous behavior was making Marsha nervous too, and she heard it in her own voice.

"Here, put these on."

She handed him a pair of thick leather gloves. He pulled them on and felt a little better.

"At least I can punch them in the mouth and not get cut the way my dad did."

It felt as stupid as it sounded, and Jacob was getting cold feet about the whole idea.

"Don't test that theory," said Marsha. "A tooth can go through leather."

For one long minute while Jacob stood with his hand wrapped around the handle of the door, he considered changing his mind. He even said to himself not to open the door. Marsha spun the big wheel that allowed the handle to move to the unlocked position and took a step back to give him room.

Jacob heard the mechanism inside the door as it slid large rods out of their slots, and he gave himself time to say one more thing before pulling the door open.

"You don't have to lock it. Just push it shut after I go

through. If more of them come down the tunnel, they won't know they could push it open."

When Marsha nodded that she understood, Jacob pulled the door open and went through the gap. It occurred to him that he forgot to kiss Marsha first, but when he turned to make up for the oversight, he saw the gap in the door disappear. He felt like it was a bad omen.

Alone in the tunnel, the ceiling above him was higher than he remembered, but he could see further up the tunnel and the way the ceiling seemed to dive toward the floor. It was high enough to walk upright, but he could easily touch it with his hand. The one infected dead they had seen was nowhere in sight, so Jacob set off at a fast pace up the slope.

It didn't take long for Jacob to realize he had no idea which tunnel was the right way to go, and an early decision turned out to have a major flaw. The first time he came to a fork, one sloped downward, and one sloped upward. Jacob figured it was an easy choice to always go upward. When he eventually came to a fork that had three choices, he wasn't so sure about which one to pick because two of the tunnels went upward. Jacob decided he would always pick the tunnel that went upward and to the right. He thought it was a good idea to be consistent, and it meant he would only need to make left turns on the way back.

That reasoning would have made sense if every right turn continually brought him closer to the entrance of the mine. He went about fifty yards before coming to another fork. This time there were three choices, and they all went downward. Jacob decided to stick to his first rule of always going upward, so he backtracked to the last fork in the tunnels and took the fork in the middle because it also went upward. It was also *almost* in compliance with his rule to go to the right.

Panic was still far from his mind when Jacob navigated several easy decisions, but there was something new that he hadn't expected. The muscles in his legs were cramping. First, his calves burned, and the sensation worked its way up to his hamstrings. He didn't have a clue that he had walked the equivalent length of ten football fields, and he had gone up eleven stories inside the mine. He stopped for a minute to rest and to rub his calves, and his next mistake caught up with him...he was thirsty.

"How did I forget to bring water?" he said out loud.

Jacob spoke in a low voice, but the answer seemed much louder and closer than he could believe. He spun around in a circle and tried to tell where the groan had come from. Logic told him it was somewhere ahead of him since he hadn't encountered any of the infected dead where he had already been. Despite his aching muscles and the sudden thirst that quickly became a dry mouth, he ran back the way he had come. He stopped at the last fork he had come to and made another mistake when he made a right turn. In his mind, he was being consistent. In reality, he had made a wrong turn.

The next fork in the tunnels was something new. There were three forks in front of him, and two were dark. He didn't know if they were supposed to be lit up the way the others were, but he knew he didn't want to go into one with just a flashlight. That was the one thing he had remembered to bring with him, but there were too many shadows, and the beam from the flashlight seemed to be swallowed by the pitch black in front of him. He leaned toward one of the dark tunnels and listened. It was quiet, but there was a breeze that blew out of the darkness as if the tunnel mouth was breathing on him. The air was warm and stale, and he could imagine why the salt mine had bad breath.

Jacob chose the tunnel with the lights on and hoped he wouldn't come to any forks where all of the choices were bad. Things got better as he came to three new levels in a row where all of the tunnels had lights, and all of the choices included one on the right going upward. His situation felt better, but he had a nagging feeling that he should turn around and go back. The thought sat in a corner of his mind like that odd feeling you get when you mean to do something, but you can't remember what it was. When it finally dawned on him why he was feeling that way, he realized it was because he knew for certain that he was lost, and reaching the entrance of the salt mine wouldn't help him find his way back to the shelter.

He turned around at the next fork and looked down the tunnel he had just used. It looked just like any of the other tunnels going downward, and a flash of hope washed over him when he saw footprints. All he had to do was follow his footprints back down. He made the decision to give up trying to reach the entrance, and that was when the real panic hit him. It wasn't just a feeling that he was going back. It was a feeling that he wasn't sure he could find his way back.

Jacob picked up speed as he made one turn after the next, always choosing the forks that went downward, and he thought he recognized the places where he had been. Footprints went toward all of them. He only slowed down to see if he could recognize his own, but more often than not, there were too many. He had never had the opportunity to do any long-distance running, and he had never learned how to control his breathing, so he ran with his mouth open and sucked in the dust from the salt mine. His dry throat became even more parched, and his breathing was accented by a rasping wheeze from his irritated lungs.

The tunnel abruptly ended with no exits. Jacob found himself standing at a dead end with footprints all around him. Even in a panic, he understood that he had not only chosen the wrong tunnel, but the infected dead had been where he presently stood. How long ago was the question he had to answer. Despite the cramps in his legs, a jolt of fear-induced adrenaline made Jacob run. He blindly took turns down tunnels regardless of where he saw footprints, and he fell awkwardly through one tunnel that dropped straight down to the next level.

The vertical drop through the shaft was only about ten feet, but he didn't have time to brace for the impact. It knocked the wind out of him, and he made a loud whooshing grunt that was promptly answered by three infected dead. They had fallen through the same shaft and had obviously crawled away, unable to stand on bent and broken legs. Jacob was stunned by the fall but was fortunate that he could still stand. He had to go past the other victims of the shaft, and they grabbed at his pants as he went by. He shook their brittle hands from his legs and ran for the next tunnel.

Jacob didn't realize when he started to cry, but tears made his eyes sting, and he dragged a dusty sleeve across them. He was almost blinded by the tears and dust as he made another turn and ran straight into an infected dead. The emaciated creature was knocked to the ground, and Jacob was amazed to see he was in the tunnel with the high ceiling. The big vault door was moving, opening inward, but at least a dozen of the infected dead were gathered near it and would get there before him.

******

Marsha became more emotional with each passing minute. Jacob was way overdue, and she debated leaving the monitor to go for help. He had guessed that he would be gone less than two hours, but he was already gone for three, and the second hand on a clock near the entrance was sweeping relentlessly past another minute. Denise and Tori would be furious, but at least they could bring guns and go after Jacob. Then she worried about what would happen if Jacob came back while she was gone. If she wasn't there to let him in when he came back, he might be cornered outside the vault by the infected dead. She didn't know what was drawing them to the door, but a steady stream of them had arrived while Jacob was gone, and they were gathering close to the place where the door would open. It was out of her view, but a red strobe light blinked above the camera outside the door. It turned on when she activated the camera, and a corroded wire to the red light was responsible for the electrical hum that was being broadcast into the tunnels.

When Marsha turned the camera on to watch for Jacob's return, the humming began, and without turning up her own volume, she couldn't hear the groaning that grew louder as the infected dead gathered in the chamber outside the door. There were so many below the security camera that she wondered if Jacob wasn't already back and had somehow reached a perch above the door. She came to the conclusion that there was no way he could tell her he needed help, and she had to open the door. If he were out there, he could die if she didn't open it soon. She decided to take the chance.

When Jacob guessed there were at least a dozen infected dead between him and the door, he wasn't aware that the door had already been opened far enough for more to flow inside. Marsha had been quickly overwhelmed by the size of the crowd and had retreated as the dead pushed the door inward. It was way too much pressure for her to force it shut, and she had backed away with only a folding chair to use as a shield. She held it up and forced the infected dead that was in the lead to fall backward into the one behind it, but all she did was buy herself a couple of minutes to retreat further from the door. Behind the pileup, the lobby was filled with infected dead. They spread out like a noisy crowd at a sporting event.

Jacob was grateful for the heavy gloves Marsha had given

him because he felt the vise-like pinch of teeth on his fingers through the leather more than once as he used his hands to throw emaciated bodies aside. Somehow, he found his way to the front of the crowd and burst through the logjam inside. He saw Marsha backing away from at least six of the infected dead. She swung a folding chair back and forth at them, but her arms were clearly getting tired, and the chair swung lower and lower. He grabbed the last of the infected dead in front of him and gave them a hard push into the others.

Marsha couldn't see Jacob behind the infected that were reaching for her. She just kept swinging the chair and brushing their grasping hands away from her body. When Jacob broke through, he had to wrestle the chair away from her to keep her from hitting him by accident. He scooped an arm around her waist and pulled her away from the waiting room. The vault door opened further as dozens of infected dead forced their way inside. The bright lights and the chaos inside the waiting room were broadcast into the salt mines as a summons to hundreds of infected dead that had been standing still in the darkness, waiting for something to draw their interest.

Jacob pulled Marsha into a corridor away from the waiting room, but he was surprised by how quickly the area surrounding them was filled with the dead. It never occurred to him that the dead would move faster if they were pushed from behind. He got himself and Marsha through another pair of doors into a cafeteria that had been intended to cater to a large number of refugees. It was supposed to be a safe place, so the doors swung freely without locks. As soon as they swung shut behind Jacob and Marsha, the doors bulged inward again, and the infected dead swarmed into the room.

The tables and chairs in the cafeteria offered some resistance to the forward movement of the horde. Jacob pushed Marsha ahead of him toward the kitchen doors, but as they ran, he upended tables and chairs in their path. It allowed them to gain some advantage, and they reached the kitchen doors well ahead of their pursuers. They kept going until they were able to reach the doors they could lock behind them, but they knew they couldn't go back and lock all of the doors to the rest of the shelter. Over the years, there had never been a reason to lock doors, and it was too late to start now.

"We have to warn the others," said Marsha.

"My mom and aunt are going to kill me."

"You mean us," she added. "They're going to ask me why I didn't stop you, and I can't think of a good reason right now."

"That's because now we know what a dumb idea it was."

Jacob was out of breath when they burst into the living area. Tori had her feet curled under her in an overstuffed chair and had a book open on her lap. Denise had just returned from tucking in the children and was ready to settle into the sofa cushions with her own book. The two women knew without asking that something bad was happening, but Denise knew her son well enough to read the expression on his face.

"What did you do?" she asked in an accusing tone.

"It was my idea, Mom. Marsha didn't want to do it."

"Stop with the whole responsibility act and tell me what's happening."

Tori was already on her feet and ready to get between them, but she also sensed it was going to be bad news, and there were only two things she could think of that would be really bad. One was that they had gone into the off-limits area where the seaquarium was, and the other was that the infected dead were inside the shelter.

"They're inside, Mom. I'm sorry. It was my fault."

Denise cut him off sharply, "How many?"

"I don't know…a lot," he said in a weak voice.

Tori grabbed his arm and turned him toward her, but her gaze was on Marsha. Whatever Jacob had done, she knew it had to involve Marsha.

"Where? Were you able to lock them up in another section?" she demanded.

Marsha answered, "Only in the sections we came back through. There wasn't time to go around to the other doors and lock them."

Denise pinned her eyes on her son's face and said with controlled anger, "We can deal with how it happened later. Right now, I want you to get the rest of the kids and relocate as many of the things we need as you can to an upper level."

She pushed him toward the door to get him moving, and he knew she was really angry because she had never done that before. Even when he paused for a moment to try to say he was sorry again, she cut him off.

"Focus on food for Allie and Bonnie."

Her voice was so sharp and on the verge of a shout that he bit his tongue and left to do what she said. He had Marsha on his heels, and as glad as they were that they didn't have to stay in the room to face more anger, both Jacob and Marsha felt the sting of her words behind them.

"Don't do anything else that's stupid," yelled Denise.

******

Tori didn't waste time finding her shoes, and her bare feet slapped on the tile floor as she and Denise ran toward the front entrance. There also wasn't time to go to the armory for weapons, and Tori wasn't wearing her Luger as much as she used to. She regretted not having the weight of the holster on her hip.

"We have to find out how far they've gotten so we can go around them and lock the doors," said Denise.

Tori caught her arm and said, "I have a better idea. Let's concede territory and lock the nearest doors across the whole level. If any of them get locked in with us, we can deal with them, but we have to cut off every place they can enter this level."

They locked the first door they came to and then began the long process of running through cross corridors to the next vulnerable hallway. Twice, they locked the doors just as the infected dead were about to enter their level, and they could only hope that none had already gone through those intersections.

When they were sure they had locked all of the access points, they went down the stairs to the armory level to get some weapons. It was going to be a long night, but they had to be sure there were no infected dead in their living area. Normally, they would have enlisted Jacob to help them, but neither of them trusted his judgment at the moment. They pulled on vests with ammo pockets and loaded up on 9mm magazines. They each took two Smith & Wesson semiautomatics and clipped their holsters to their belts.

Tori said, "Let's not get caught in a close-quarters fight. We need to be quick about it if we see any."

"I still want to bring this just in case," said Denise.

She held up a machete before she slid it into her belt, then she handed one to Tori. She took the weapon, but she planned on shooting from a distance as often as possible.

"Stay together or split up?" asked Tori.

"I don't know yet," said Denise. "We may need to stay

together just to be sure neither of us gets cornered. How many do you think got inside?"

Denise was almost breathless as she asked the question, and they both realized they hadn't been forced to face the dead for too long. They also hadn't been in a battle with this many. It was almost like they weren't in shape anymore.

"We should've trained for this," said Tori. "I think Jacob was trying to tell us this one is really bad. A lot of them got in. Even if we live through it, the cleanup is going to be hell."

"One step at a time," answered Denise. "My son and Marsha can do the cleaning as punishment."

Heavily armed with weapons and adrenaline, the two women went back up to the main level to begin their search for intruders. They locked the lower level door behind them and advanced into the first hallway. The first two sets of doors they came to were locked. Denise produced a big piece of chalk and wrote CLEAR in big letters on them. They didn't make it to the second set of doors before they knew the real work had begun. The doors were open, and the sounds from inside were unmistakable. Small knick-knacks on shelves clattered to the floor in both rooms, and each crash was accompanied by groans as if there was excitement to be found in breaking decorations.

The shelter had been designed to make its occupants feel at home wherever they were, and this particular section had been one of the many apartment levels. When they first arrived at the shelter, they kept all of the doors closed and locked, but as time went by, the closed doors became symbolic of the emptiness of the shelter. Denise told Tori she felt like they were back in the hotel and that the closed doors reminded her of the evil that had been trapped inside the rooms. For that reason, they had opened many of the rooms as a reminder that there was nothing inside to be afraid of. They left the rooms nearest to the stairwells locked because they were strategically located by the nearest escape routes.

Tori tapped Denise on her arm and gestured with her hand to indicate they should close the doors. She couldn't say it out loud, but it occurred to her that it would be better to trap the infected dead inside the rooms instead of going in with their guns blazing. They could always come back and clear the rooms one at a time after the infected dead were contained.

Denise understood the hand gesture, and she silently pulled the first door shut while Tori did the same across the hall. There was no real need to lock the doors because the knobs were round, and the infected dead had never mastered the art of gripping door knobs and turning them. The closed doors masked the sounds inside, and the pair of women moved to the next rooms, but not before Denise wrote *NOT CLEAR* on the doors. It would have been great if their luck had continued, but just as they reached the doors, they were discovered by a pair of infected dead that came out of the door at the end of the hall. Just as the dead always did, they announced their discovery with loud groans. Between the women and the new arrivals, there were eight pairs of doors to be closed, but the infected dead answered the calls from so many of the rooms that there was no sense in paying attention to where they came from.

"Back up to the stairwell door in case we have to retreat," said Tori. "We have time to make each shot count."

It was a good thing she suggested it because they had been standing at the next pair of open doors, and the dead emerged from the dark rooms as they backed away. Tori and Denise shot them at point-blank range as they stepped carefully toward the stairwell door. Denise didn't need to be told to unlock it again.

Tori fired three shots in rapid succession, and three of the infected fell to the floor. She might not have felt the need to carry the Luger with her all of the time, but she had spent plenty of time on the gun range practicing. As she adjusted her aim toward another group, Denise shot two more. The bodies fell in the path of the others that mindlessly advanced toward them, and her next two shots missed as the infected tripped over their comrades.

"Wait," said Tori.

They both stood with their guns ready, but they had the advantage of knowing what was going to happen. The dog pile in the hallway grew as the infected dead in the back pushed forward. Tori stepped toward them until she reached the first open door on the right, and she calmly pulled it shut. Denise did the same on the left side, then they stepped closer to the crowd of reaching hands, took aim, and shot two more. They moved from target to target until none of the infected were moving. They closed another pair of doors that were within reach, but the pile of bodies had created a barricade they couldn't cross.

Denise was considering whether or not she could climb over the bodies when she noticed Tori's feet.

"Where are your shoes?"

"There wasn't time to put them on."

"Well, you have to make time now because you aren't stepping on that mess barefooted."

Tori wasn't going to debate that with Denise, but the number of infected dead in the hallway gave her an idea of what they were up against, and there were always going to be bodies to step over.

Tori said, "We can backtrack to the living quarters and get some boots, but we need to take a different approach to clearing each floor. Instead of coming to their level and clearing them all the way back to the main entrance, we should go to the floor above the main door and come down behind them. Let's get that door shut first."

"Good idea," said Denise. "As long as they're still coming

inside, we're going to have targets to shoot at."

It only took about fifteen minutes to backtrack to the living quarters and then go up to the level above the main entrance. The lobby that had been intended to be used as a processing area for crowds of survivors had a vaulted ceiling, and the level above it had a balcony that allowed them to see the waiting room below. Denise knew her husband had dreamed of standing on that balcony to watch as his shelter welcomed people who had nowhere else to go. She doubted he ever imagined the chaos they saw below them. There were at least a hundred infected dead crowded inside the lobby, and more of them were at the open door to the salt mines.

"How much ammo did you bring with you?" asked Denise.

"Not enough," said Tori as she took aim.

When they ran out of ammunition, the lobby was still packed with the infected dead, and more were forcing their way inside. All they could do was retreat.

RETREAT

Ithaca Shelter - 2025

"Leave that," shouted Jacob. "We need to take food, water, and first aid supplies."

"We won't need blankets?" answered his brother.

Marsha answered for Jacob, "We're only moving to the upper level. We're not going outside."

"Not yet," snapped Jalen. "When Mom gets back, she's gonna put you outside. You'll be lucky if she even gives you a blanket."

They didn't need to see Carrie's face to know her usual frown was replaced by outright anger. They could hear it in the way she gritted her teeth together when she spoke.

"You two are such whiners. When we get through this, I'm going to make sure you both get punished. You too, Marsha. I can't wait to hear you try to explain why you and your boyfriend thought it would be a good idea to open the door."

Marsha opened her mouth to defend herself and Jacob, but even Amber had heard enough. She was still just as shy as she had been when she was stranded at the juvenile detention center, but she knew when it was time to speak her mind.

"Enough fighting! Don't you all realize how bad this is? Do

you want to go back to how we were living outside? You're scaring Allie and Bonnie to death."

Everyone stopped what they were doing. They saw that Amber was right. Barely eight years old, the two girls sat next to each other, holding small bundles of their belongings. The tears on their cheeks were enough to get everyone else in line. They were too young to remember what life was like outside the shelter. All they knew was it was bad, and neither of them wanted to go outside. There were monsters outside.

"I'll be back in a few minutes," said Jacob.

"Where are you going?"

Jacob could hear the pleading in Marsha's voice, but Amber's scolding words and the scared faces of the youngest girls had hit him hard, and he knew he had to do something to make up for his stupid mistakes.

"Just wait for me, or go ahead without me if I'm gone too long. Help them get to an upper level, and I'll be right behind you. I have to do something."

The living area was too close to the breach, and Jacob heard gunshots echo through the shelter as he made his way to the computer room. He shut the door behind him and hoped he had enough time to send a message. Time was short, so he collected his thoughts as the computer powered up. He clicked on the recording app as soon as the cursor appeared on the screen. Saving even more time, he broadcast the message as he recorded it, then put it on a loop so it would continue after he was gone.

"If anyone is listening, my name is Jacob Warren."

Jacob went on to give a brief history of the shelter, its location, and its occupants. He described the situation they were in and asked anyone who heard the message to please come help them. Jacob realized that he was taking a chance that someone bad would hear the message, but he also knew the upper levels of the shelter weren't a permanent solution. The middle levels, the parts that sustained them in the shelter, were being swarmed by the infected dead.

As Jacob made the recording, the memory of the crowded hallway in the hotel came back to him. In his mind, he was still a young boy clutching the ice bucket against his stomach as if it were a shield. He could still see the angry faces, and for a moment, he remembered them as being infected dead. They weren't living people who were trying to escape from the hotel. They weren't just angry hotel guests who didn't like that he was trying to push to the front of the line at the elevators.

A voice from the computer speakers pulled him back to the present.

"Hello? Say again?"

It was a woman's voice, and Jacob wasn't even sure it was real. He had already put the message on a broadcast loop, and the cursor was poised over the STOP button in the app. There were gunshots in the room next door, and he didn't know which was worse, getting caught by the infected dead or getting caught by his mom. He was supposed to be getting the other kids to an upper level, and even though he was doing something important, they might not give him the benefit of the doubt after what he had already done.

Jacob took a chance and stopped the broadcast loop for just a few seconds.

"Hello, I don't have time to explain. Our shelter is being overrun by the infected, and I have to get the rest of the kids to an upper level. Listen to the rest of the recording, and come help us if you can."

Jacob clicked on the button again before the woman could answer. His recording played again, but as he ran for the door, he heard her yelling for him to wait. Whoever she was, she didn't know how close the horde was to the computer room, but there was something in the way she called out to him that made him believe he had done the right thing. She sounded like she would help them if it were at all possible.

Jacob pulled the door shut behind him and went into the nearest stairwell to the upper levels. He only made it up the first set of stairs to the landing and was on the first step of the stairs that would reach the next level, when the door he had just gone through burst open. His mother and Aunt Tori practically fell through the door. They immediately put their hands against the door to close it, but the weight of the bodies on the other side was too much for them. They leaned their shoulders against it and pushed as their feet slipped and slid on the floor.

Jacob went down the steps in two long strides and slammed against the door. The sudden surge from their side was just enough for the gap to close and the lock to click into place. They could hear the groans from the other side, but the door would stay shut until the infected dead learned how to use a key and turn a doorknob.

"Thank goodness your husband went with knobs and key locks instead of panic bars when he built this place," said Tori.

Denise was about to say something back to Tori's comment, but it sank in that her son was why they had been able to close the door. That meant he wasn't where he was supposed to be.

"Jacob, why are you on this level? Aren't you supposed to be upstairs helping the rest of the kids?"

The last thing Jacob wanted to do was admit he had been on the other side of that door only moments ago. If he hadn't left the computer room when he did, he would have been trapped in there as his mother and Aunt Tori retreated from the horde. They would never have known he was there, and from the looks of it, they wouldn't have been able to close the door in time. The retreat would have spilled over into the stairwell.

Jacob didn't want to lie to them, but telling the truth might not score enough points to keep them from getting mad.

"I made one last trip to the armory," he said.

Luckily for him, he was still wearing the heavy vest he had put on when he needed the pockets for extra ammunition. He put one hand on a pocket that bulged with 9mm magazines for the handguns.

"I was on my way back up when I heard the shooting, so I waited on the landing in case you needed help."

"Good thing you did," said Tori. "There's no way we would've gotten that door closed."

"Don't expect that to get you out of hot water," said Denise, "but at least you made one good decision today. Were Jalen and the girls on an upper level already?"

"They were just leaving for there when I came down here."

"Let's go," said Denise.

It only took a few minutes for them to catch up with the rest of the kids, and Jacob was quick to pull Marsha aside to tell her what happened. When he got to the part about the woman on the radio, he had to stop her from blurting out the good news.

"We can't tell anyone," he whispered urgently.

"Why not?"

"I told them I went to the armory one last time. They'll kill me if they find out I was in the living quarters. It was really close. The horde broke through just after I got out. Ten more seconds, and I would've been trapped."

"Did the woman say she would send help?"

"There wasn't time to talk. To be honest, I don't even know how we got connected. The internet's been down for a long time. I think it might have been just a lucky connection with the shortwave radio. I don't know. That's been Jalen's pet project."

"Maybe we should tell him."

"Are you kidding? He's madder at me than everyone else. He would go straight to my mom. Just remember, if anyone says anything to you, I went to the armory."

The couple joined the rest of the group and gathered together their backpacks and boxes of supplies. Denise was busy with the two youngest children while Tori checked off items on a list. When they were ready, they moved out like a caravan toward the next level access.

One of the safety features on every floor was a wall-mounted ladder that led to the next level. They preferred to use the stairs, but Tori hadn't spent the last few years just reading and watching old movies. She had kept herself busy by finding ways to improve security measures. The stairwell doors could be locked with a key, and they were locked before the survivors migrated to the upper levels, but the simple truth was that the infected dead couldn't climb. Tori had ensured that every hatch was opened easily and that there were small stores of supplies near each hatch.

"How many levels are we going to go up?" asked Tori.

Denise furrowed her brow and said, "I think we need to have at least one level between us and the infected. We can go up one more for now and stand watch over this hatch to see what's happening on the main level. Jalen, can you make sure Allie and Bonnie get situated upstairs? I'm taking the first watch?"

The question had been posed to Jalen, but Amber answered for him. Even though Amber was a couple of years older than Jalen, they were as much a couple as Jacob and Marsha, and it was clear for the time being that the older couple had fallen from Denise's good graces. So far, no one had died as a result of their misguided adventures, but their standard of living was upended.

Once again, backpacks were carried to another access ladder and lifted upward as they climbed to the next level. When the last pair of feet disappeared through the hatch, Denise breathed a sigh of relief, knowing that everyone was safe. She leaned over the open hatch and listened for any sounds from the level they had evacuated. She could hear distant echoes from the infected dead that were still bouncing against the stairwell doors. Another sound had her worried, though. She focused all of her attention on that one sound and tried to decipher what it was. Something crashed to the floor and shattered just out of her field of vision. Somehow, the infected dead had already made it into the living quarters, and Denise wondered if she and Tori had missed some of the doors.

A shadow appeared, followed by a severely decayed monster. It stood almost directly below her, so she looked down at the top of its head and shoulders. The bones across its right shoulder appeared to be barely held in place by strands of tissue, and when the monster turned from side to side, the arm below the dislocated shoulder swung like a pendulum. Denise could swear she saw the tissue stretch even further, and she almost gasped out loud when the weight of the arm became too much for the last ligament. It fell heavily to the floor, and the monster walked away from it, oblivious to the fact that it had shed part of its body.

Denise held her breath and was lost in thought as she stared at the motionless limb.

"What keeps them going?" she asked herself. "Why don't they die?"

She couldn't put her finger on it at first, but there was something different about the arm. It was partially covered with the tattered remnants of a shirt sleeve, but the exposed portion of it was an odd color. She could have passed it off as the bruising from trauma, but there was something else. It was more like the dark bruise was on the surface of the skin instead of under it. Denise pushed herself up from the floor and went to the access hatch across the room. She only had to climb far enough up the ladder to stick her head through the opening and call out to Carrie. Since Carrie had become their resident physician, she wanted her opinion.

"I need you to see something," said Denise.

Denise backed down the ladder and went back to her perch over the living quarters. When Carrie joined her, she pointed at the arm near the bottom of the ladder.

"Is there something wrong with that arm besides the fact that it fell off a dead man?"

Carrie studied it from a distance. Her constant frown deepened when she came to a conclusion.

She asked Denise, "Have you ever seen a mummy?"

"Only pictures," said Denise.

"That arm has been mummified," said Carrie. "My guess is it was exposed to the salt in the mines for several years, and now it's like a walking cured ham."

"Gross," said Denise. "I wonder what that means for us. Do you think it's making them break down or fall apart faster?"

Carrie shook her head, "No, the opposite. It's making them tougher, you know, sinewy. It's like stringy or chewy meat."

She snapped her fingers and said, "Beef jerky. It's turning them into beef jerky, but since people are more like pork, I guess you would call it pork jerky."

Denise held up a palm at Carrie.

"You can stop there. Thanks for the colorful insights. Do me a favor and go back upstairs. Tell the others I'm skipping lunch today. Have someone relieve me in four hours."

Denise settled in next to the hatch and watched as the infected dead stumbled over the arm that was deposited by the first one. The room below gradually filled until the dead couldn't move around, and she was fascinated by the way they came to a complete stop when they couldn't go anywhere else. She guessed there were at least thirty squeezed into the room, and it seemed almost like they were going to sleep until one of them looked up. She didn't move a muscle. She didn't even blink her eyes, but somehow it knew she was a living person. It let out a groan that caused every infected dead in the room to respond.

With no encouragement from Denise, the dead pushed and shoved against each other to get closer to the open hatch. She felt like she was looking down into a blender because of the way new faces replaced the old. She imagined that the one-armed man didn't stand a chance of regaining his spot below the hatch. They might not be able to climb, but they had no problem shoving each other out of the way.

By the end of her shift guarding the hatch, Denise felt like there were no new faces to see. She became strangely detached from them as the infected dead and began seeing them as the people they used to be. Even as they reached for her and snapped hungry jaws, she imagined which of them had been doctors, lawyers, housewives, firemen, or farmers. She also wondered if they would ever know a world without the infected dead.

Tori climbed down the ladder across the room and made her way over to where Denise sat. After living in the shelter with her for years, she knew her friend well enough to know Denise had been watching the dead faces below her for the entire time, and that she had gone down a mental rabbit hole.

"I would guess that you've been planning something we could do to take back the shelter, but that thousand-yard stare in your eyes tells me otherwise," said Tori.

Denise didn't take her eyes off the faces below, but she said, "I wish I could say there's something we can do. I think I spent the first hour playing out different scenarios."

"Think of anything that wasn't totally useless?"

"Naw, it mostly came back around to shooting fish in a barrel. I thought maybe we could just make every bullet count, but we would still be living above a pile of bodies we couldn't remove. I tried to at least estimate how many there are, but the way they keep trading places with each other makes it impossible to be sure. I finally got to a point when I realized it doesn't matter how many there are. Even if we kill them all and then shut the doors to that room, we would still be stuck with the bodies."

Tori leaned over the hatch and watched the faces as they turned toward her and then were pushed away by the swirling force of the crowd.

She said, "Something has to draw them out of the room."

"That's the conclusion I came to," answered Denise, "but I always came back to the same questions. How many are there, where are they, how can we redirect their attention, and where can we get them to go? Of course, there's also that one last question...what happens to the person who gets the infected to follow them? It's a suicide mission."

"You've been sitting here thinking for too long. You need some sleep. Why don't you let me take over for you? Go upstairs and spend some time with the kids, then catch a few hours of shuteye. I'll take over for you here."

Denise didn't feel like moving from her spot. She felt paralyzed and hopeless. What made her eventually able to push herself from the floor was the realization that getting up and doing as Tori suggested was the only thing she could do. She couldn't sit there forever, and she couldn't force the infected dead to leave the shelter.

******

It was hard to believe that a week had gone by while the eleven shelter occupants adjusted to living on the upper level. Tori led scouting parties to the other rooms on their level to make sure they were secure, then they inspected the few remaining levels above them. She did an inventory of everything useful, and if they ever regained total control of the shelter, they planned to redistribute essential supplies. They had learned the hard way that they should not have kept all of their food on levels below the main living quarters. They also learned that the infected dead smelled worse as time went by. The room below theirs smelled like a sewage treatment plant, and they had been forced to close the hatch rather than keep watch over the crowd in the living quarters.

As for plans to retake the shelter, they were still stuck on some of the big problems. They could use the upper levels to outflank the horde that occupied the main level, but they didn't know how to do it without sacrificing someone.

Although they had been able to carry enough supplies to last a few weeks, the level hadn't been intended for the long-term comfort afforded by the living quarters. The room above the place where they stood watch over the infected had been a recreation room, so they had passed the time playing ping pong, pool, and board games. Unfinished jigsaw puzzles were spread out on folding tables, but mostly they played cards. It didn't take long before boredom led to frayed nerves, and frayed nerves led to disputes. It was during one of the disputes that Marsha let it slip that maybe help was coming, and they would be able to clear out the shelter again.

"What would give you that idea?" asked Shay.

They were sitting across from each other while playing poker for pretend money. Shay had always had the most even disposition of them all, but along with her even disposition, she had become very observant. If someone had asked her who was the most likely to bring about a disaster inside the shelter, she would have nailed the answer on her first try. It had become harder for her to keep her even disposition because she felt like Marsha hadn't taken responsibility for her part in it.

Marsha tried to pretend she hadn't heard Shay's question. Jacob's warning was clear on his face, and Marsha tossed three cards on the table face down.

"I'll take three," she said.

"I said, what would give you that idea?" repeated Shay.

Marsha's resistance continued until Shay raised her voice, and since that was an uncommon occurrence, it drew the immediate attention of Tori and everyone else in the room. Denise was vaguely aware that Marsha had said something about being rescued, but she had quickly dismissed the comment as speculation. It seemed to her that Marsha was just engaging in wishful thinking, but Shay raising her voice was way out of character.

Denise asked Tori, "Did I miss something?"

Denise pushed aside the diagram of the shelter she had been studying and focused her attention on the card game.

"That's what I was wondering," said Tori.

Shay was like a bloodhound on the scent of something it was tracking, and she wasn't about to let it go. She laid her cards on the table and leaned forward.

"I asked you a question, Marsha. What would give you the

idea that someone might be coming to help us? Don't try to act like you didn't mean it."

Jacob pushed his chair back from the table and stood up.

"Well, I think I'm done playing cards for the day. Who wants to play ping pong?"

"Sit down," said Denise.

Everyone was silent as Jacob returned to his chair. He didn't take his eyes off the pile of cards in front of him, and he knew he was the one who was going to be forced to help Marsha get out of trouble.

Before Denise or Tori could order either of them to explain what Marsha had meant, Jacob blurted out, "It's not Marsha's fault. She kept it secret because I told her to."

Denise directed her attention to Marsha instead of Jacob.

"Young lady, if we live long enough for you to get to marry my son, you need to remember what he talked you into before. If he tells you to do or not do something, it might not be the best thing for your health."

Denise's comment stung Jacob, and for a few seconds, he was that scared boy clutching an ice bucket again, but this time, the angry expressions weren't on the faces of strangers. His brother was smiling, but he knew it was because he was enjoying seeing his big brother squirm. None of them felt like Denise had been hard enough on Jacob for opening the shelter door. Marsha had been his accomplice, but he had been the mastermind, and their existence had been in doubt ever since.

When Denise returned her attention to her son, Jacob was ready to confess, but he still felt like he had done the right thing. He understood that he had taken a risk and had come within seconds of being trapped two levels below, but if the loop was still broadcasting, there was a slim chance that he had done something that would save them.

"Remember when I helped you and Aunt Tori close the door in the stairwell? I wasn't on my way back from the armory. I went to the computer room and sent out a message through the shortwave link. I put it on a loop so the message would keep repeating. A woman answered before I had to get out of the room."

"A woman?" said Denise. "Did she tell you who she was? Is she near the shelter?"

Tori cut in, "We don't know if this is good or bad. We could use a little help, but I don't know what someone else could do for us. On the other hand, we might not want strangers finding us. They might just take the shelter away from us."

Jacob knew he was on thin ice, and anything he said could make it worse, but Tori's observation was at least a stay of execution. Denise needed to weigh whether or not it had been the right thing to do, and he saw his opening.

"Mom, I know it was a risk, and you wouldn't have let me do it if I had asked you first, but I had to make up for what I had already done. I had to do something."

Denise felt the emotional warmth she had always felt as a mother, and just like he had flashed back to the hotel and the ice bucket, she had a sudden memory of that day and how they had been forced to leave the father of her children locked in a hotel bedroom. She had to ask herself if they would ever know again when they were making a good or bad decision, or would they only know after they saw the results.

"That was a week ago," said Denise. To Tori, she said, "What do you think?"

"We don't have enough information, but if we assume the woman was part of a larger group, I think we can also assume they would see some value in the shelter even if it was breached. It depends on how much Jacob told her."

They both turned their attention to Jacob, and there was no way he was going to withhold the truth. His eyes moved to a spot on the ceiling to his left as he pulled up the memory of what he said in his message.

"I said, there are eleven survivors living in a shelter located somewhere near the bottom of the salt mines, a few miles north of Ithaca, New York. Two of the survivors are only eight years old, and we need help. The shelter has been breached, and we're sealing ourselves off in the only part that's still safe."

"That's all?" asked Tori. "That's not enough for anyone to go on. They would have to bring an army into the salt mines just to find the shelter."

"What did the woman say?" asked Marion.

It was almost like there had been a spotlight on Jacob the whole time, and everyone had forgotten that Marion, Carrie, Amber, Jalen, and Shay were in the room. Bonnie and Allie were too young for the discussion and were busy with a puzzle in the far corner of the room. Now the spotlight was on an expectant audience that was eagerly waiting to find out if they were going to be forced to survive in a recreation room for the rest of their lives.

"She asked me to repeat what I had already said and to tell her more about how to find us, but there wasn't enough time. I told her I had to go, or the infected would get me."

Jacob sounded defensive and was pleading for them to understand, but he suddenly remembered something.

"I think she said something else after I put the message on a loop and ran for the door. I think she said she could be here in about two weeks."

They could have heard a pin drop in the room as everyone let the last part sink in. Denise and Tori were staring at each other as if either of them knew what they should do. It came to them both at the same time, and they both started to speak. Denise stopped and let Tori say it.

"We have to be outside for them to find us."

******

The best outcome they hoped for was that the infected dead would eventually wander out of the shelter through the same door they had used to come inside, but they were fairly sure that wasn't going to happen. They spent hours discussing ways to make them want to leave, and the only thing they could come up with was to set off an alarm somewhere in the mines. The problem they couldn't solve was always the same... how to do it. As crazy as it sounded, the best suggestion came from Carrie.

The constant frown on her face hid the fact that she was serious when she said, "If we can't go out past them, maybe we can go outside and come around behind them."

Everyone thought she was joking, and a few of them laughed, but they all became silent when she continued.

"One or two of us could go out through the hatch and go to the entrance of the mine. We could go in just far enough to set up something that makes noise, and it would draw the infected out of the mine and maybe even out of the shelter."

Tori said, "Our options must be pretty slim when we start talking about a bad idea as if it's our best chance. We should have been planning for something like this years ago instead of just waiting for something to go wrong."

"At least my idea is better than opening the front door," said Carrie. The comment was made to Tori, but everyone knew it was intended for Jacob. The only thing that kept Jacob from answering was the unspoken warning on Denise's face.

Boredom wasn't the only thing causing tempers to flare. They had enough food to last until they figured out their next step, and the water supply was still functioning, but the upper level lacked a fully functional bathroom. There was a toilet and a sink, but there had never been a need for a shower to be installed on that level. Also missing was the ability to wash their clothes, and there hadn't been time to gather clothing when they evacuated. To add insult to injury, the toilet paper shortage was critical. There was enough to last several years, but it was two floors below the living quarters.

Two weeks into their self-imposed exile to the upper level, they gave in to the inevitable and made plans to go out through the hatch. What they would do when they got there would be decided by what they found. They also wondered if the woman who spoke with Jacob would really come to their rescue.

OUTSIDE

Ithaca Shelter - 2025

The last time any of them had gone to the enclosure above the shelter was when they had brought the girls back from the juvenile detention facility. Over the years, they had talked about going outside to inspect the fence to see if it was still intact, but they had always found a reason to put it off a bit longer. They finally came to an unspoken agreement that there was no real reason to ever go there again. If the fence was still standing, maybe survivors had been lucky enough to use it for protection, but they had become used to the isolation of their fortress of solitude, and going outside might lead to unintended consequences.

They never openly admitted their decision to stay below ground was because they didn't want to know if there were people out there who needed their help, but Denise and Tori both knew they had the same reservations. They had no hesitation about rescuing the girls from the juvenile detention center, but that was because they were kids, and they were able to learn a few things about them in advance. Even though the enclosure above the shelter was much closer, they couldn't just pop the hatch open and take a peek to see if it was safe. They might open it and find nothing, but they could also find out it was populated with the infected dead. So, they eventually just ignored it.

Jacob wanted to be the one who opened the hatch. He argued that he was physically more capable of dealing with whatever might be outside than Tori or Denise, but they made it clear it wasn't his physical ability that was in question. His reasoning skills were what had cost them their security, and they didn't want to make another mistake while he was trying to make up for the last one. That was why they chose Jalen to go out first.

The plan was simple. Jalen would open the hatch just far enough to see if it was clear. Unfortunately, that meant he would only know about what was in front of him. If his field of vision was clear, he would open the hatch far enough to climb outside, and he would close the hatch behind him. Inside, Tori would immediately engage the lock behind him.

The extra precaution of locking the door made Denise nervous, and she felt like she was sacrificing her younger son, but the alternatives were more deadly. If there were survivors inside the fence, they might pull the hatch open by force. If there were infected dead inside the fence, they could overwhelm Jalen while the hatch was open and then block Tori from pulling it shut. If no one was there, Jalen would knock on the hatch in a predetermined pattern to let them know it was safe to come outside.

When they were ready, Jalen climbed the ladder and only turned back long enough to give his mother a half smile as he held up one hand with a small wave. She returned both gestures, and Tori moved into her position close to Jalen's legs. He unlocked the hatch and lifted it a couple of inches. Sunlight poured through the small gap and made him wince, but at least the weather was clear, and he could see a wide stretch of the compound outside. Nothing moved within his field of vision.

Denise and Tori had repeatedly stressed that he had to move fast. If someone or something was behind the hatch and saw it move at the moment he opened it, he might only have two or three seconds to make a decision. He had to either go or pull it shut again. Jalen immediately felt like he had waited too long, even though it was only seconds. He didn't know what made him able to go as quickly as he did because his legs felt like they were weighed down by concrete blocks. He pushed upward and shoved his body outside. As soon as his legs were clear, Tori pulled the hatch into place and turned the lock.

Time seemed to stop inside the small chamber where Denise and Tori waited for the knock that would signal it was all clear, and Denise held her breath. When she finally exhaled, they both knew it had been too long. They exchanged worried looks, but neither of them spoke for fear that their voices would mask the sound they were waiting for.

Outside the hatch, Jalen sensed the presence behind him before he turned around. There wasn't time to regret that he hadn't sensed it sooner, and something told him he didn't even have time to face whatever it was behind him. When he landed far enough from the hatch, he heard it slam shut and knew Tori would lock it before he got to his feet, so there was no going back. Jalen pulled his feet under his body and launched himself forward like an Olympic sprinter coming off the starting blocks. He didn't risk a glance backward until he had run over ten yards, and when he saw what was behind him, he didn't slow down.

In the wide field behind the hatch, a horde of the infected dead saw the teenage boy running away from them. They would never be able to move as fast as Jalen, but as long as they could see him, they would continue their pursuit. Tori had told him several times not to let himself be cornered. She warned him not to bother to look for the place where they had gone through the fence when they had left before, unless he had enough time. It had most likely become too overgrown by tall bushes, and he could climb the fence faster. Jalen thought he had time to look for it, but he followed her advice and used his forward momentum to jump high up the fence. He easily reached the top, dodged the barbed wire, and dropped onto the other side.

The next piece of advice he remembered was what to do if he was forced to go over the fence. Denise stressed that he couldn't stay by the fence because the infected dead inside would gather near him and become loud. If there were more outside, they would be drawn to the commotion. Jalen dropped to one knee and focused his attention on the trees and bushes that hid the enclosed compound. When his father had built the shelter, he didn't want the fence to be detected by casual observers, so he had invested in the cultivation of a dense ring of trees to hide it. The trees still hid the fence, but Tori warned Jalen to watch out for infected dead that may have been entangled by the undergrowth. She didn't have to tell him how bad it would be if he stepped on one of them.

More light came between the trees in one place, so Jalen carefully picked his way toward it. Keeping a constant watch on where he put his feet and staying as quiet as he could, he finally reached the rim of the protective forest. He couldn't be sure, but he thought he was facing north, and he stopped to think about what he was supposed to do next. They had talked about as many possibilities as they could, and this had been one of them.

Finding himself alone on the other side of the fence was not what they had hoped for, but Tori had pointed out it was better than several other possibilities. When she listed some of the less desirable outcomes, Denise almost called off the whole plan. Tori had to remind her that there could already be a rescue party waiting outside, and they couldn't survive much longer with most of their shelter inhabited by the infected dead. When they came to the conclusion that Jalen might need to get out of the compound in a hurry, they had to admit that he didn't have many options after that, but he would hopefully be uninjured and breathing.

The plan they had agreed on was that Jalen should use the daylight hours to find a safe place to spend the night if he was stranded outside the fence. If there was enough time left during the day, he could look for signs that rescuers were in the area, and he could try to find a way to get back to the hatch undetected. Judging by the size of the horde inside the compound, he doubted that would happen, but he wasn't ready to give up on the possibility. He knew that someone, most likely his mother, would wait for days to unlock the hatch.

Jalen leaned against the thickest tree that protected him from view and checked the items he had brought with him. He wore a small backpack that held a few days' worth of rations and some medical supplies. Under the straps of the backpack was a machete that was safely covered in a sheath. A canteen of water was on his left hip, and a 9mm Smith & Wesson semiautomatic was on his right hip. He pulled the gun out of its holster to be sure the safety was still on, even though he had done the same thing several times before climbing the ladder. He resisted the urge to take a sip of water to soothe his dry throat and chose a stick of gum instead.

Chewing furiously at first, his nerves settled a bit, and he decided he had to give up the safety of the trees to begin following the plans. Behind him, the horde finally reached the fence and began a chorus of groans. He doubted they felt frustration, but he didn't have time to think about whether or not they would ever stop making noise. Jalen stepped out from behind the tree, and the last time he could remember being more exposed was when he had been a little kid playing on a sandy beach as a strange man stumbled toward him.

******

Our pickup truck still had plenty of gas left in the tank, but we had run out of road. I couldn't think of a time when I had ever come to a dead end without seeing a warning sign first. The trees in front of us formed a barrier so thick that it seemed like the road was intended to go through them, but the builder of the road never got around to clearing a path.

"What now?" asked Jean. "We can't go back the way we came because we would have to go right by the salt mine. If Branch was in a bad mood before, I expect he will execute his own people if he can't find us."

"That's your fault," I said.

Despite our predicament, my teasing comment got a laugh out of Jean.

"You two never stop," said Ruth.

Jean said, "When we do, check to see if we're still breathing."

We slid out of the truck and walked around the front to face the wall of trees. There were no sounds of engines in the distance to announce the arrival of Branch and his men, but all three of us had spent enough time in the woods over the last eight years to know what we should hear. Ruth pointed it out first.

"No birds. They most likely flew out of the area in the last ten minutes or so."

We all listened closely for the telltale sounds of whatever had caused the birds to leave. Behind us, the engine of the pickup truck dinged and popped as the metal cooled, but in between pops, we all heard the distant groans.

"How far away are they?" asked Jean, even though we could all make a good guess.

"Not far," said Ruth, "but they're not getting closer or moving away. I think they're staying in one spot."

"Not a big horde," said Jean, "but enough to worry about."

The sound of the horde was coming from somewhere beyond the dense trees, slightly to the right of where we stopped the truck. Jean was the first one to see movement to our left.

"Well, I'll be..."

She left the sentence unfinished and pointed as a slender, teenage boy came out from behind a tree and ran crouched over as if he was trying to stay undetected. His medium-length hair and generally clean appearance weren't what we would expect to see on someone his age surviving the apocalypse. He was wearing a green shirt that helped him blend into the background, and the gear he carried looked like it had taken careful planning. Whoever he was, he had probably been with other people up until now.

The boy didn't seem to be aware of us until Jean raised her arms over her head and yelled.

"Hey, kid. Over here!"

******

The last thing Jalen expected was a woman's voice, and when she yelled to get his attention, his first reaction was to freeze. He stood up straight and stared at the three people facing him from less than thirty yards away. Something told him that they would only be a threat if they had tried to avoid being seen, and as he stood frozen in his tracks, the petite woman with short black hair waved. He didn't know if they were there to rescue him and the others, but he hoped so, and he mentally reminded himself that his first goal outside was to find shelter, but his second goal was to look for signs of rescuers. Jalen returned her wave and then ran to meet them.

******

There was something very familiar about the way we met Jalen. It reminded me a little of the day when I had gone out on my boat to practice shooting at targets. It was back at the beginning of the infection. My uncle, Titus Rush, had said to stay inside the shelter and never open the door for any reason, but I had gotten stir crazy and didn't follow his advice. That was when I met Jean. She floated into my life on a raft along with my good friends Kathy and the Chief. She yelled at me in the same way she yelled at the kid who stood in the clearing between us and the wall of trees.

I saw him wave back at us, take a hesitant step our way, and then run toward us. Even at a distance, I could see tears streaming down his cheeks.

"I can't believe it," he shouted as he got closer to us. "Are you the lady my brother talked to?"

"Your brother? The one who put the distress call on a loop?"

"His name is Jacob. I don't know if he told you that, but yeah. He sent the message because he was trying to clean up the mess he had made of everything. We were fine until he opened the door of the shelter and the infected got inside."

I said, "That sounds familiar. It was something of a family

motto when the infection started. I'm Ed, this is Jean, and this lady is Ruth."

The boy hooked a thumb toward his chest and said, "Jalen. Is it just you three? I thought there would be more of you."

Jalen sized us up and added, "You don't even have much in the way of guns and stuff."

"It's a long story," said Jean, "and we don't have time to give you all of the details right now."

Jean glanced toward the truck and the road we had used until it came to a dead end.

"Are you being followed or something?" asked Jalen.

"By some particularly angry people," I said. "Can you take us to your shelter?"

He nodded and pointed at the trees, "I can get you close, but we have a little problem. The infected are inside the fence."

"The fence?" I said.

"I'll show you."

Jalen led the way into the thick bushes down the path he had taken away from the groaning. As we followed him, we were grateful to leave the road behind. We felt like we were swallowed by the trees and the underbrush, but we were invisible if Branch and his men showed up. The downside was that the groaning was louder as we got closer. Jalen stopped when we reached a spot where we could see movement on the other side of a tall, chain-link fence. We did as he did and knelt on one knee.

"The fence makes a big circle, and there isn't a gate," he whispered. "The trees hide it all the way around, but once you're inside and away from the fence, it's all clear. In the middle, there's a hatch that can only be opened from the inside. It goes down into our shelter."

"How'd the infected dead get inside the fence?" I asked. "And why did you come out?"

"I thought you said we needed to hurry," said Jalen.

"We didn't say it," answered Jean, "but it would be a really good idea. Just tell me one thing. Did you know any of those infected dead on the other side of the fence?"

Jalen shook his head. "No, they must've been survivors who climbed the fence and then died inside. Maybe one of them was infected and spread it to the others."

"Good," said Jean. "Then you won't mind if we get rid of them."

I reached over and pulled the machete from Jalen's back and said, "I need to borrow this."

Jean was already at the fence, drawing the attention of the horde. As soon as the first one arrived, she shoved her machete blade through the wire into its face. The blades were almost too big to go through the links, and I could hear the blade sing in a high-pitched squeal as it rubbed against the fence. When I joined her, my blade did the same thing, and I struggled to keep my grip on the handle. It was hard work, but the sound of the horde decreased as we eliminated them.

When the last one was quiet, Ruth said, "I don't think I can climb that high. You can leave me here."

"Wait," said Jalen.

He set his backpack on the ground and dug through one of the pockets. He held up a pair of wire cutters.

"The plan was to use these if there was time."

Jean took the wire cutters and quickly snipped the wires in the outline of a gate. She held it aside until we all went through, then pushed it back into place. We had been around the infected dead long enough to know they still had shoestrings, so Ruth and I quickly collected enough to tie the fence in place.

"I wish we had time to move these bodies and to hide this gate, but we're lucky to get this far before Branch and his men show up. Where's that hatch, Jalen?"

******

Denise stayed under the hatch waiting to hear the signal to open it. Tori knew she wouldn't leave until she found out what happened to Jalen, so she didn't even try to talk her into taking a break. She brought her some food and water, but Denise just shook her head.

"It hasn't been that long," said Denise. "I won't start to worry until it's at least a few hours."

Tori almost pointed out that it had been over an hour, but she knew better than to speculate about what had happened outside. None of the possibilities were good. She just hoped that whatever had happened, Jalen was handling it. If there were a way for him to safely knock on the hatch, she hoped he would find it. She was about to try to get Denise to at least drink some water when the knock came. It was the exact pattern of raps they had practiced, so they knew it was Jalen and not someone else. There was always a chance that someone was making Jalen do it, but they had decided beforehand that there was nothing they could do if that happened, and it would most likely be a situation that got Jalen killed if they didn't open up.

Denise launched herself upward and unlocked the hatch. It swung upward, and Jalen's smiling face appeared. There was movement behind him, but Denise could only see him through her tears. Tori didn't show her hand down by her thigh because she was hiding a semiautomatic pistol there. The safety was off.

"I did it, Mom. I found the lady Jacob talked to."

Jalen was excited, and Tori relaxed as she flipped the safety on with her thumb. Jalen didn't hesitate to climb inside, and the newcomers were right behind him. Tori had to back out of the narrow chamber around the ladder to make room for them, but she saw that they didn't appear to be a threat.

******

We followed Jalen inside the hidden shelter. I wasn't sure what we would find, but I expected it to be like something my uncle had designed. As I was about to discover, the Warren family had worked closely with Titus Rush in the early days of construction. Not surprisingly, they had eventually gone their separate ways due to disagreements. Titus and I always got along with each other well, maybe because I was a kid when we were around each other. He had a harder time getting along with other adults.

After quick introductions, we followed the woman Jalen called his aunt as she led the way. She explained that we were on an upper level of the shelter, and that the main floors were overrun by the infected dead. Her details about how it happened were somewhat abbreviated, and we learned later that she was trying to be tactful since it was Jalen's brother who started the chain of events that caused them to be exiled from the living quarters.

We reached the recreation room and were greeted by kids who were mostly teenagers, but two little girls in the group couldn't have been a year old when the infection began. They had a hundred questions, and everyone was asking them at the same time. Denise held up her hands to gain control.

"Enough, everyone. We have a lot to talk about with these people. Give them a chance to catch their breath, and I'm sure they'll answer your questions for you."

After we got settled in around a card table, a couple of the teenage girls opened some boxes of food rations and passed them out. The box was labeled as emergency rations, and they explained that there was better food in the living quarters, but they didn't have time to bring much when they evacuated. Plus, the kitchen was one of the first places that was overrun. We saw the way Jacob lowered his head when the others talked about how things had been before then, and we made sure they knew we appreciated the food. It had been some time since our last meal, and we didn't have to fake being hungry.

We answered questions as we ate and asked a few of our own. The two women and the kids were amazed and excited when we told them our own stories. We didn't dwell on the part about how Jean and I had set off on the rescue mission without being officially sanctioned to do so, but we did include the fact that we were being pursued by people who were as dangerous as the infected dead. Our first priority was to assess the possibility of retaking the shelter. After that, we would work on a plan to contact our own people to let them know we needed help.

Denise took us down one level to show us what it was like in the living quarters. When she opened the hatch, the smell hit us pretty hard. She was about to close it quickly to spare us from losing our meal, but Tori stopped her.

"Wait a minute."

Tori pointed at something below.

All I could see was a dimly lit room that was populated with the infected dead. Most of them were reaching toward us and groaning incessantly. I couldn't tell what she was pointing at, but Jean saw it.

"Is there supposed to be water down there?" asked Jean.

Denise leaned closer and covered her mouth in shock. She could see that the infected were wading in water that was ankle deep.

"No, there's not, and there's only one place that much water could be coming from."

******

In the days before the infected dead, tourists flocked to Niagara Falls. Fishermen scheduled their vacations on the Finger Lakes as religiously as pilgrims visiting a holy shrine. The New York State Canal System didn't get nearly as much attention from tourists and fishermen despite the fact that it was made up of five hundred and twenty-five miles of canals and locks that allowed shipping across the state. In comparison, the Panama Canal always got more attention despite the fact that it was only one-tenth as long.

Another important function of the canals and locks, other than shipping, was that they controlled the flow of water that would flood the countryside when the annual snowfall melted. The locks in the canals remained either open or closed, depending on the position they were in when they were last used. For over seven years, excess water was diverted into Cayuga Lake instead of being evenly distributed throughout the system. As the depth of the lake increased and the water crested the banks, so did the water pressure that pushed against the huge observation window at the bottom of the

Warren family shelter.

The tremor that passed through the shelter when the window collapsed had gone unnoticed by the survivors on the upper level. If they had been outside the door where Tori had placed a sign that said the area was off limits, they would have heard a booming sound only moments before being hit by so much water and debris that they wouldn't have had the chance to even wonder what happened. The water crumpled the walls and consumed everything in the lower levels before it began to seek higher ground.

In much the same way as a cup could be pushed upside down into water and preserve the air inside, the air held captive in the shelter kept the water from rising at first. The lower levels flooded and pushed back against the air in the shelter, and on the main level, there was a gentle breeze that rushed across the lobby toward the open vault door. The breeze became wind that could be heard above the groaning of the infected dead. At greater than two hundred pounds per square inch, Cayuga Lake forced its way into the shelter.

It was ironic that the open door kept the water from flooding the entire shelter, but the main floor became deep enough to develop a steady current across the large waiting room. Tables, chairs, and the infected dead were washed from the lobby and became a dam across the doorway. The water rose deeper behind the logjam and threatened to fill the lobby, but the pressure finally pushed the obstruction forward into the salt mine. Endless tunnels and shafts became underground rivers as the lake continued to find new places to go. When the dam broke, a tidal wave of bodies and debris pushed through the opening with a crashing sound that rivaled Niagara Falls. The survivors in the upper level of the shelter heard the sound and had no idea what it was, but they knew it had something to do with the water that had become shin-deep on the infected dead one level below them.

SEARCH AND RESCUE

Ithaca, New York - 2025

The Chief increased his forward speed after circling the rail yard near Washington, D.C. Smoke was still drifting upward, and he took the AC-130 in close enough to see that it had been a really hot fire. Judging by the size of the debris field and the twisted railroad cars, he understood why the heat bloom had registered on the monitoring system operated by Gentry Campbell. He radioed Captain Miller and told him he was sure Eddie and Jean had something to do with the fire. It was just too big of a coincidence that it happened along their route.

Captain Miller reported that his ground force had just engaged a small militia at the high school stadium near Lynchburg. It was a short fight, and they weren't sure why the people opened fire on the MRAP because they didn't have any weapons capable of penetrating its armor. He said that there were only a few men at the stadium, and they were cutting them loose after confiscating their weapons. What Captain Miller learned from the men was that their leader, a man named Ted Branch, had taken most of the militia with him to hunt down some people who had killed his brother and a few other men. They described Branch as being unpredictable and violent.

The Chief asked if they knew anything about Eddie and

Jean. Captain Miller said the guys he spoke with didn't have any details about the people Branch was after, but that they would be dead if Branch caught them. The Chief told Captain Miller he would just have to find them first. Before he signed off, Captain Miller had to give him the bad news that he didn't have enough fuel to reach Ithaca, New York. The Chief had hoped his good friend would be able to liberate some fuel from the militia, but they had been forced to send what extra fuel they had with Branch when he left. Captain Miller drained their tanks and had enough to get home, but they agreed they couldn't risk losing the MRAP over a fuel shortage.

Kathy joined the Chief in the copilot's seat as he signed off, and he broke the news to her.

"We've got enough people," said Kathy, "but that's not what I'm worried about."

"I didn't know you were worried about anything."

"You know what I mean. Do I have to say it?"

She had that challenging expression on her face that she got whenever she felt like something was so obvious that she shouldn't have to put it into words. Sometimes it was safer to just play dumb and let her say it, but time was getting short, and they didn't have time to beat around the bush.

"Okay, I'll admit it. Beyond flying to New York, I don't have a plan."

Kathy clamped one hand over her chest and leaned forward as if she were in pain.

"Here comes the drama," said the Chief.

Kathy would have enjoyed dragging it out a little longer, but she also knew they would be over Ithaca soon.

In a serious voice, she said, "You've got nothing? Do you even know where we can land? I've been in back with the rest of the gang, and they have a message for you."

Kathy held out a folded map that showed the area around the salt mines, and then she pointed to the southern tip of Cayuga Lake.

"That's Ithaca down there. Sim said he doesn't think there's a flat enough place to land that doesn't have seven years of trees and brush growing on it."

"What about roads?"

"I know you've landed this thing in some tight spots, Chief, but not this time. If we have to land at the Ithaca airport, and that's assuming we can land there, we still have to either walk or find transportation to get to the mines. It's only ten miles, but we're talking about searching for two friends who are in the general area while being hunted by a militia."

"Does the gang have any suggestions?"

He used her reference to the Mud Island family in order to keep it light, but he would never admit that he was more nervous than usual. He believed in having plans and backup plans. As a matter of fact, that's what bothered him the most about Eddie and Jean going off to help someone in New York. Other than going there, they didn't have a plan at all. It bothered him even more that he was being forced to do the same thing. He wasn't given enough time to make a plan.

"As a matter of fact, they had a good one," said Kathy.

The Chief hadn't expected her answer, but he was glad to hear it, and when she told him what they had come up with, all he could say was, "Not bad...not bad at all."

******

Ted Branch tipped the scales at around two hundred and

thirty pounds, and that was a lot of weight for someone to carry around with a severed Achilles tendon. He was still fuzzy on the details of what happened in the dark tunnel. He was aware that they were possibly surrounded by the infected dead, but it wasn't anything they hadn't dealt with before. There was a sudden, searing pain above his left heel, and he fell helplessly to the ground. He didn't know why he couldn't stand up, but he felt more pain when he put his weight on his left foot than he had ever felt in his life.

Branch had spent time in prison before the infection, and the first month of his incarceration was spent in a prison hospital ward recovering from a gunshot wound. He had been shot by an undercover officer during a drug deal, and he didn't think anything could have hurt more. When his tendon was severed, he learned that he would rather be shot.

Some of the militia didn't make it back to the surface, but seven of them, including Branch, reached the entrance of the mine without being bitten. Four men weren't so lucky, and just like Stevie when he fell from the overpass and landed on the *meat pile* at the bottom, a bite from the infected dead was a death sentence. One of the bitten men had practically carried Branch out of the salt mines, but everyone knew that there was no cure for a bite. Branch said he was sorry to the guy, but he ordered the uninjured men to do what they had to do. One by one, they were executed.

"Hey, Boss. The truck is gone."

Jeremiah Smith had led the last of the men into the mines when one of the captives ran outside screaming that Branch needed help. Now, he was practically admitting that he had been responsible for the escape by falling for the stunt, but Branch didn't know that for sure. Smith realized he had to come up with something fast, but he wasn't actually known for quick thinking.

"We killed all three of the prisoners before we came to help you. They said you were hurt and needed help, and I figured we couldn't guard them and help you, so we shot them."

Branch was seeing Jeremiah Smith through a haze of pain, but sometimes pain made him see things more clearly.

"All three of the prisoners? Did you say three?"

Smith mentally counted how many people they had captive and realized he had seen the little woman with short hair when he ran into the mine, but he didn't know who she was.

"Yeah, the guy, the old lady, and the little woman."

Branch thought back to the night before and wondered how many people had been at the storage unit.

"So, if you killed them, where are they?"

Smith turned in a circle and searched the area outside the entrance of the mine. He had a hopeful moment when he saw a couple of infected dead in the distance. They were walking slowly in their direction.

"I guess we didn't put them down permanently, Boss. They must've come back and then walked away."

"Uh, huh," said Branch. "Then I guess they stole the truck, too."

Smith stared in the direction of where they had parked the truck, and when he turned back toward Branch, he only saw the barrel of the handgun for a split second before Branch pulled the trigger. Branch lowered the gun, but when he looked at the remaining men, they all thought they were next.

Branch said, "Someone find me a truck. It's not like we didn't have more of them here."

Since their militia had used the mines as a staging area, it didn't take long for the men to return with a truck. While they were gone, Branch had endured the efforts of one man to bandage his leg. Without surgery, there was no chance he would ever walk normally again, and he knew it. The only thing that helped him see through the pain was the thought of what he would do to the people when he caught them. The first thing he planned to do was cut three pairs of Achilles tendons. He said he wanted to see if those people could crawl fast enough to get away from the infected dead.

Branch couldn't believe he was down to five men, and it was all because of the same group of people. They had been a thorn in his side ever since they showed up near the stadium. He had lost his kid brother, a bunch of men, and his fuel supply, all because of them. Now, he couldn't walk without help, and he was down to five men and a truck.

"Anyone have an idea which way they went?" he asked the men.

One of them pointed to the spot where the truck had been parked when they left Smith to guard them.

"They must've hit the gas hard enough to spin the wheels when they left, Boss. The tracks start out deeper, then they settle out a bit, but the driver must've turned the wheel kind of hard at the fork because the tires bit deep again."

"Are you saying they went north?" asked Branch.

"Yessir."

"Then why don't you say that?"

Branch was getting impatient and was worried about them getting such a big head start. He had the men carry him to the truck and slide him into the passenger seat. He cursed at them the entire time. He wanted to drive, but there was no way he could use the pedals. The imbecile who brought them the truck had found an older model with a clutch. The thought of having to ride around in the passenger seat for the rest of his life made him hate the three people even more.

They drove north, and it turned out to be a short chase.

They found the abandoned pickup truck parked at the end of the road and stopped next to it. All they could see were trees. The men all jumped out of the truck and fanned out to find any tracks or clues to where the people had gone. While they searched, Branch sat in the truck and fumed about the pain in his leg, but he scanned the area and watched for movement in the trees. Against the blue sky, the familiar wingspan of a vulture circling in one spot caught his eye. The bird disappeared almost immediately, which was a clear indication to him that the bird knew something was already dead. If it had circled again, it would have meant something was injured.

Since the beginning of the infection, Branch had seen vultures land on the infected dead while they were still moving, but there were so many to feed on that they usually played it safe and fed on the dead that had been lying still for a while. This particular carrion-eater had circled once while Branch had been watching, and then it had dropped out of sight.

Branch let out a sharp whistle to get his dwindling gang to pay attention, then he pointed toward the trees and yelled.

"Vultures are feeding over there. Check it out."

All five of his men turned in the direction he indicated. Four of them went toward the trees, but the last man put one hand up to his face to shade his eyes.

Branch yelled, "What's up, Harlan? You don't believe me? Go with the others. Find out what those vultures are feeding on."

He wasn't used to repeating orders, and he would have shot Harlan if he hadn't already lost so many people, but Harlan still didn't move from where he stood. Branch opened his door to get out, and the only thing that stopped him was the pain he caused himself by moving too quickly. He reached down and clasped his hands around his ankle and weathered the worst of it, and he was genuinely surprised when he sat up straight and found Harlan standing by his window.

"I'm sorry, Boss, but I thought I saw something else, and I wasn't sure."

Never short on sarcasm, Branch said, "I'm happy for you, Harlan. Are you sure now?"

"No, Boss, but I thought you would want to know what I thought I saw."

Branch forced himself to stay calm as he asked, "Why would I want to know what you *thought* you saw if you aren't sure what it was?"

"Because we haven't seen a plane in a long time, Boss."

Branch's eyes moved from Harlan to a spot over the man's shoulder, and he saw a very brief flash as sunlight reflected from something in the sky. It was gone so fast that he would have thought it was his imagination if Harlan hadn't seen it the first time. Harlan saw Branch's reaction and spun around, hoping to see it again.

"Did you see it, Boss?"

"I don't know what I saw. Go find the rest of the guys, then get back here and let me know what the vulture is feeding on."

Branch heard the man trot away, but he kept his eyes on the patch of blue sky where he thought he saw the plane. A part of him felt like it was too much of a coincidence. First, those people showed up and made him and his militia look like fools. They were always one step ahead of him. Then, there was the revelation that the salt mine had a shelter hiding in its depths. If he had really seen an airplane, he also had to believe it was connected to the people and the shelter.

He was still watching the sky when his men emerged from the trees. They were moving fast, so he was sure they had found something. He would have been happier if they had come back pushing the escapees ahead of them.

When they were close enough, he understood that one of them was yelling, "Someone killed a horde, Boss."

******

"What can we do?" asked Tori.

The question wasn't aimed at anyone in particular, but I felt like it deserved an answer, even if I didn't have enough information to give her one. I had my own questions.

"Any idea where the water is coming from?" I asked.

I didn't expect my innocent question to make anyone mad, but Tori was clearly upset by it, and Denise appeared to become defensive.

"I told you this would happen," accused Tori.

Denise answered, "We don't know for sure."

Jean leaned into the hatch and watched the infected dead slosh around in the water.

"Is it just me, or does it seem like it's not getting deeper?" she asked. "Is there a way for the water to escape from the shelter on that level?"

I saw Denise throw a glance at her older son, Jacob. He had come down from the recreation room along with the rest of the teenagers. Only Amber had stayed upstairs with the two little girls, Bonnie and Allie. The rest were curious about us newcomers and wanted to be part of whatever was about to happen. I didn't think they realized yet that we weren't exactly the cavalry riding to their rescue.

Tori answered for Denise, "The main entrance to the shelter is on that level, and someone left the door open."

"The shelter door is open?" I asked with just enough shock in my voice for them to understand how alarmed I was. "Is that how the infected dead got in?"

Jacob cleared his throat and said, "That's why I did the distress call."

"You're who I spoke with," said Jean. "So, the infected have had two weeks to find their way from the salt mine into the shelter. Did you manage to stop any of them before you retreated?"

"Fifty or sixty," said Tori. "We trapped some inside rooms where they're probably still bumping into the walls. We closed off some hallways and kept a few more from getting into the main living area, but the biggest part of the horde that was outside the vault door came straight through the kitchen into the level where we lived. That's not the bad news, though. If water is at the level below us, then the supply levels are all flooded. Our food, armory, and medical bay are all under the living area."

"Why can't we just leave with you guys?" asked Marsha.

Ruth had stayed quiet, but I had to give her credit for being there when we needed her.

"I have an idea," she said. "There's a lot of planning to do, and the grown-ups need a few minutes to talk."

She didn't wait for them to answer, and she managed to ward off the questions from the teenagers as she herded them to the ladder and up to the recreation room. She followed them up and closed the door at the top of the ladder.

Jean said, "Remind me to thank her for that. Now, there's good news and bad news. The good news is that we have lots of friends who can come to help us. The bad news is that we weren't doing so great by the time we got here."

Jean and I told them what had happened on our way to help.

We left out a few details that were best kept to ourselves, such as the fire bombing on the bridge, but I think they understood. It was enough for them to know that we made some enemies along the way, and now we were fugitives.

"Is there any possibility we could get to the radio gear your son used to contact us?" asked Jean.

Denise pointed at the infected dead below us.

"We'd have to get through them, and if there are twenty inside that room, there are twenty more trying to get in there with them."

Tori added, "It was a computer setup that got a satellite connection. The room wasn't exactly waterproof. All of the outlets and surge protectors are submerged by now. As a matter of fact, I'm surprised the breakers haven't tripped for the upper levels."

"There you have it," I said. "You aren't worse off than you were, but we haven't improved things, either."

"I don't know about that," said Jean. "We came here to help them, so let's help them. I don't think staying here is an option, and that means we have to lead them back to the shelter in Alabama. We can stop at Ruth's cabin for a few days to rest up, and maybe we could make it to the shelter in Charlotte."

"We also have to use a different route," I added. "We can't get too close to Branch's territory. He still had people out there. That means our best bet is to go around the long way to Ohio and then south to Alabama."

Tori and Denise were in complete agreement about leaving. They said they doubted that clearing the shelter was possible, but we weren't so sure it couldn't be done with help. All of that would have to wait, though. Our first priority was simply getting home. As we assembled our backpacks and got ready for the long trip, we told them more about ourselves. They had plenty of questions, but everyone needed rest because we decided we would leave at dawn. Still, they wanted to hear more before we turned in.

Ruth had heard some of the stories, and she interrupted several times to ask us to tell them more about the Chief and Kathy. She said she couldn't wait to meet them, and she wished Wally had lived long enough to join our group. She was sad about what Branch had done to Wally, but she was remarkably understanding about how the infected dead had caused some people like Branch to become the worst versions of themselves.

"You never know," she said, "he might've been a great guy before the infected dead came along."

I doubted Branch had ever been a decent person, and I felt like the apocalypse was just an excuse he used to live without morals. Even though I couldn't see what he was doing when he killed Wally, I could still hear it as if it had just happened, and my only regret was not knowing for sure that Branch had died in the dark tunnels of the salt mine.

"Ruth, when you meet the Chief, you're going to see how the infected dead made good people better and bad people worse. I don't believe Branch was a good guy before this all happened. I still remember when I met the Chief, Jean, and Kathy. He was so big that I would have been afraid of him if he hadn't been with two attractive women."

"You're going to love all of our friends," said Jean, "and I think the Chief is going to come up with a plan to clear out your shelter. It's too valuable to let it go to waste."

"You're too optimistic," said Tori. "I don't doubt that you're going to be able to help us get to your home. I mean, you made it this far, but the shelter has an idiotic amenity that is probably responsible for the flooding."

Tori went on to describe the transparent wall that let them see the bottom of Cayuga Lake, and we saw her point about saving the shelter. That was one hole that couldn't be plugged.

I said, "It wouldn't be the first shelter that had to be abandoned. The shelter in Columbus, Ohio, might be safe to restore someday, but the damage at the main entrance would take an army of engineers years to fix. I guess the best thing we can do is just get you guys to a safe place."

We finished packing our bags before midnight and then got settled in for a few hours of sleep. Judging by the tossing and turning and occasional whispers, I don't think anyone slept well. Jean poked me just before dawn, and I told her I was already awake. It was a sleepy group that assembled at the ladder to the hatch.

Tori climbed up to be sure it was clear, and after what had happened with Jalen, she wasn't taking any chances. She had a semiautomatic pistol in her right hand as she pushed the hatch up with her shoulder. We were all bracing ourselves for trouble, but after a few seconds, she said it was all clear. She pushed the hatch open and was almost completely outside when we heard the shots. Tori screamed in pain and fell back down the ladder. There were enough of us in line to break her fall, but a big, red blossom was spreading across her right shoulder.

Jean and Carrie pulled her to one side and immediately went to work stopping the bleeding, but I knew I had to get the hatch closed. Instead of going straight for the handle on the hatch, I reached outside and opened fire, shooting without a target. I saw a group of men ducking for cover and fired a few more rounds. I saw one of them fall backward, but couldn't swear it was because he was hit. While they took cover, I pulled the heavy hatch back into place and locked it. I heard several bullets clang against the metal only inches from me.

Tori was mad more than anything. The bullet had gone straight through her shoulder beneath the clavicle. It probably broke some bones, but judging by how fast Carrie was able to slow the bleeding, the bullet had missed any major arteries. Everyone helped to get her back to the recreation room while I stood guard at the door. I didn't think the men were going to be able to get through the door, but if it was Branch and his men, I knew they would never leave. I was sure we would be waiting inside for a long time.

Jean and I pulled Denise aside to talk about our options. We knew we couldn't survive forever in the upper level of the shelter. There were too many of us, and even if we had enough supplies, no one could mentally withstand our overcrowded conditions.

Jean asked Denise, "Would we even have a chance if we tried to reach the main door? I mean, I know the shelter is full of the infected dead, but what if we retraced the route you and Tori took when you closed off some of the rooms?"

Denise shook her head.

"Even if we could make it through the main rooms below us, the big waiting room by the vault door was like one of those logjams during a flash flood. From what I've seen, those things don't drown. They might be packed together in a twisted mess across the door, but they're still biting. Not to mention what's on the other side of that logjam. We could never find our way out of the salt mine. It goes thousands of feet below Cayuga Lake, it's full of infected dead, and some of it could be flooded."

"So, that leaves going out to face Branch and his men," I said. "He had about a dozen men before, but I'm pretty sure he's only got half as many now."

"What would it matter if he had six or twelve?" asked Jean. "If he only has one or two men now, all they would have to do is sit behind the hatch and wait for it to open."

Jacob came over to our corner of the room and waited for Denise to ask him what he wanted. The kid was still desperate to find a way to make up for his stupidity, and his mother was having a hard time letting it go. The expression on his face wasn't enthusiastic, and I got the impression that he wasn't bringing us good news that would help our situation. As a matter of fact, it was like he was being forced to pour salt on his own self-inflicted wounds.

Denise seemed almost content to ignore him, but she finally asked Jacob what he wanted. As I expected, he had some bad news, and he got right to the point.

"The water is deeper in the main living area. I went down to see if I could think of something to do to help, but when I opened the hatch to take a look, an infected dead practically floated into the room. Jalen and I got some duct tape and covered all the seams around the hatch, but it won't hold too long. The best we can do is keep it from filling up the next level too fast."

Denise groaned and covered her face with her hands.

"It's worse than you think," she said. "We might slow down the water in that room, but all of the rooms connected to it will need to be sealed too, and even if we stop it, what's the point? We still can't stay."

"That's not all," said Jacob. "The water smells rank."

I added, "It should smell rank with all those rotten bodies swimming around in it."

We checked on Tori and found Carrie had convinced her to take some pain meds and get some sleep. That was the best thing for her at the moment because we were between a rock and a hard place. Branch and his men were probably camped behind the hatch outside, and the water in the level below us had already loosened the tape on the seals around the hatch and was seeping in. The only thing we could think of was to surrender to Branch. Maybe he would let everyone else go if we turned ourselves over to him. In the end, we decided it was our only option, and we drafted him a letter.

Mr. Branch,

There are eleven innocent people in here with us. Most of them are young and have done nothing to you. If we turn ourselves over to you, will you please let them go? Knock four times on the hatch if you agree.

Ed

"Do you think we can trust him if he agrees?" asked Denise.

I shook my head and said, "No, but we've seen people do stranger things. We just don't have any other choices."

Jean and I got on the ladder together. If we unlocked the hatch and lifted it just far enough to slip the letter outside, we could get the hatch closed and locked before it was pulled open by Branch's men. If they did manage to get a grip on it and pull it open, there were three of us with guns aimed upward. It could be really ugly, but there wasn't much else we could do.

Jean turned the lock so slowly that there wasn't even the slightest sound, and we pushed the heavy hatch upward less than an inch. I pushed the folded piece of paper through the gap, and we closed the door. Since the letter was short, we didn't think we would have long to wait, and since we didn't think Branch was really someone we could trust, we got our guns ready.

******

Ted Branch had been busy. After the brief exchange of

gunfire, he had taken up a permanent position directly behind the heavy metal hatch. From there, he had directed his men to gather anything they could find to create defensive positions. If anyone came out of the ground, they would be shot before they could find a target. All five of them were arranged in a semicircle around the front of the hatch, but Branch was resting comfortably with his injured leg elevated on top of it.

He felt the movement under his leg, but it was so slight that he didn't remove it. When the letter popped out and the door shut, one of his men ran forward and scooped it up. He knew better than to read it before handing it to Branch, so he passed it quickly to his boss.

"Well, how about that?" said Branch. "They want to know if we'll let everyone else go if they surrender."

The man who handed him the note asked, "Are we gonna do it?"

The glare Branch gave him was enough of an answer. He pushed himself up from the ground using a crutch he had fashioned from a broken tent pole and hovered over the hatch with his fist poised to knock, but he had a sudden revelation. He pointed at the door as he moved back to his position behind it.

To the man who had handed him the letter, he said, "Knock on that hatch four times for me."

ASSAULT

Ithaca, New York - 2025

When Kathy explained the plan to the Chief, he felt better than he had since first learning that Ed and Jean had gone out on the road by themselves. To him, going on a mission without a plan was like carrying a gun without bullets. The idea she had was also so simple that he didn't know why it hadn't occurred to him.

"Who's going to jump with me?" he asked.

"Garrett and Jon have the most flight experience, so they can take over for you and find a place to land. If they can land at the airport in Ithaca, they should have enough people with them for protection, so I figured Anne and Susan were a logical choice to stay with them. Sim wants to come with us, but he's never jumped before, and I didn't think you wanted to carry someone with a broken ankle, so I convinced him to go with them."

The Chief said, "So, that leaves you, Tom, Iris, Cassandra, Hampton, and Colleen. All of you have jumped out of airplanes before?"

"Believe it or not, yes. I think Cassandra's the only one with as many jumps as you, but the rest of us have at least a couple of recreational jumps apiece. We also only have enough parachutes for seven of us."

Garrett Carson came into the cockpit with a big smile on his face.

"Ready for me to take over for you, Chief? I can't wait to get some time flying this beast."

"Just don't fly off with it," said the Chief. "Got your copilot with you?"

Jon King appeared behind Garrett and said, "Right here, Chief. I'll make sure to keep an eye on your plane."

"Please do that. I suppose you heard what I did to the last guy who stole my plane."

"We did, and it left a lasting impression on us," said Garrett.

They exchanged a few handshakes and backslaps as the Chief and Kathy climbed into the back of the plane to join the rest of the group. Most of them already had their parachutes on and were helping the others with their straps. Cassandra was in the middle of an explanation about the difference between jumping from a small plane that could go slower and a plane like the AC-130. They would have all enjoyed the opportunity to do a high-altitude, low-opening jump referred to as a HALO jump, but they didn't think they had the time to do it right. If someone got their calculations wrong, they would end up scattered over the countryside.

"Listen up, everyone," said the Chief. "Kathy is going to brief you on the mission plan. I'm part of the team, but she's running this show since she came up with the idea."

As the Chief finished getting their attention, they all felt the plane's nose tilt downward and accelerate, and they reached for handholds. Cassandra had already told them it was going to happen fast, and if anyone had any second thoughts, the opportunity to stay in the plane was an option, but don't block the door. They were going to be doing static line jumps because they were coming in around seven hundred feet. They had to be on the ground fast because they were targets while they descended.

Kathy barely had time to tell everyone that they could expect some serious turns and acceleration when Garrett and Jon went into the first part of the plan. She and the Chief helped each other into their chutes with their feet spread wide to brace themselves. The plane dipped, leveled, turned, and then climbed at high speed.

******

"What's that sound?" asked Branch.

The question came out in a harsh tone. The man who was about to knock for Branch stood with his feet spread wide over the hatch. He was leaning forward with his fist extended, but he stopped short because Branch sounded like he was accusing him of something.

"I didn't do anything yet, Boss," the man said defensively.

The other men were all in their positions with guns aimed at the hatch, but one by one, they stood up and turned in circles. The sound was just a steady hum at first, but it was getting louder. In the days before the infected dead, the sound wasn't a novelty, but after nine years, they were no longer accustomed to hearing it, and they had lost the ability to locate the source.

Branch felt like he should recognize the sound, but he couldn't accept the possibility of what he was hearing. The hum grew in intensity so fast that he didn't accept the answer until his eyes told him he was right about what he was thinking.

The plane appeared over the treetops so low that the wash from its propellers made the trees around the enclosure sway madly. Even though it was over a hundred yards away when it appeared, it rushed at them so fast that they ducked before it passed over them. Something spread out from its sides in a wide, fan-shaped shroud that blanketed the entire clearing within the fence, and in seconds, no one could see anything through a cloud of white smoke. Branch and his men yelled at each other, but they scattered or threw themselves to the ground. Someone blindly fired a few shots, but no one could see who it was or what they had shot at. Branch yelled angrily to stop shooting as bullets whizzed by him.

The sound of the plane's engine went from a hum to a roar, but as it flew farther from them, it seemed to become a high-pitched whine. Branch and his men couldn't see it, or they would have known it was accelerating as it increased altitude and was making a steep turn.

******

Jon King's voice came over the speakers in the main cabin of the AC-130.

"First pass is complete. Smoke has been deployed, and visibility within the target zone is zero. Be advised that hostile forces are concentrated in the middle. Completing our turn and now leveling off at seven hundred feet. The red light is on for jump in five, four, three, two, one...."

As Jon made the announcement, the seven members of the Mud Island family bunched together in a tight group at the open door. They had to get out in seconds, or they risked someone landing outside the target area. When the countdown finished, they jumped almost on top of each other.

******

"What's taking so long?" I asked Jean in a whisper.

No one could hear me outside even if I shouted the question at her, but my nerves were tingling. I didn't know if someone was going to yank the door open and start shooting as soon as we unlocked it, or if, by some miracle, Branch decided he could be generous and let the others go.

"I don't have a clue," said Jean. "Maybe he's thinking it over."

From below us, Denise said, "There's a third possibility. I don't know how smart this guy is, but he could be just having fun waiting for us to pop the hatch. Maybe he figured out that we're desperate."

******

The smoke was so thick that the man straddling the hatch tripped and fell over it. When he pushed himself upright, he fell for a second time as he collided with Branch. As hard as he tried to help his boss to his feet, Branch seemed more interested in lashing out at the man. His severed Achilles tendon screamed in pain, and the stitches that had crudely held the tissue in place tore open. The two men wrestled themselves apart, but they couldn't see each other anymore.

Branch crawled forward on his knees, and his hands

recognized the slope of the ground that formed the lip around the hatch. He couldn't see anything else, but finding the hatch made him feel like he had some control. He turned his head from side to side, searching the white cloud for anything that moved, and he was convinced that the people inside the hatch had something to do with the plane. Maybe they had even come out of the hatch while he had been distracted by the plane. Instead of knocking on the metal door, he beat on it furiously with both fists.

The hum was coming back, but this time it was farther away. Now that Branch knew for sure that it was a plane, he could tell it was at a higher altitude. He instinctively leaned his head backward and strained his eyes against the whiteness. He couldn't see anything in any direction, but he saw something in his own mind clearly. All he had to do was ask himself why the plane had dropped smoke bombs on them, and if he answered correctly, he wondered how much time he had. Branch had become the leader of his militia by being smart, and from his own military experience, he knew that the smoke was a prelude to an assault. He mistakenly assumed the assault would come from the fence around the perimeter of the enclosure instead of above.

******

Jumping into the dense, white smoke was risky, but if Jon King had timed his red light well, the jumpers would all land away from the trees but inside the fence. Once on the ground, everyone would stay where they landed until they established contact with each other. The first signal from each of them was simply two clicks on the switch of their handheld radios.

Before the jump and according to the plan, Cassandra had

handed out small laser pointers. The Chief explained to those who didn't already know that the green laser pointer beams could be seen through the smoke, and once everyone signaled they were on the ground, they should press the button for two seconds. As soon as they turn off their laser pointers, they should move five feet to their right and drop to the ground. The hostile forces would see the beams, and they would most likely shoot where they had seen the beams coming from.

"If you're lucky," said the Chief, "you'll be in a position to locate and shoot the person who shot at your beam, so have your weapon ready when you hit the ground."

One of the hardest things about parachuting is the landing. On a clear day, it can still cause an injury, but in the thick smoke, it was a teeth-jarring jolt that no one could prepare for. They each did their best not to let it make them grunt out loud when the ground suddenly appeared, but in Kathy's case, it helped her find Colleen. Kathy was still getting out from under her parachute when she heard Colleen grunt only a few feet away. She crawled over to her quickly and helped her get out of her harness.

"Was I that loud?" whispered Colleen.

"No, I wouldn't have heard you if you hadn't landed on top of me. Signal on your radio even though we're together."

Both of them made the signal, and they heard five more responses.

"Move with me when I use the laser pointer," said Kathy.

Kathy pressed the button for two seconds, and then they moved together to the right. Two shots came from behind them, so neither of them was facing in that direction. They heard the bullets pass over them, but before they could sight in on the possible location, there was a second series of shots, followed by two laser pointers. Cassandra and Hampton appeared through the smoke close to where Kathy and Colleen hid on the ground.

Hampton gave his wife a hug and said in a low voice, "You two drew out a couple of them with one beam, so we must be right on top of them."

Tom and Iris found each other closer to the fence, and they ran into the wire enclosure on their first move after using the laser pointer. They heard the shots that were fired about thirty yards away and moved in that direction. As they got closer to the center of the target area, they heard someone arguing, and they knew it wasn't one of their group. They were too disciplined to give away their positions like that. The voices were obviously angry because they couldn't see, but they had heard the shots.

Tom whispered, "If they keep up the arguing long enough, we'll be able to find them without baiting them into shooting."

Iris seemed to blend into the smoke because of her long, silver hair. She whispered just loud enough for Tom to hear, "I've got them. Ten more yards. I see three of them."

When she and Tom were closer, she said just loud enough and in an even voice, "Lay your weapons on the ground, lace your fingers behind your heads, and you won't have to die today."

Two of the men hardly paused and immediately did as they were told. The third held onto his rifle for a heartbeat, but not far away, a green beam pierced the smoke. Two seconds after that came the familiar sound of someone shooting at the beam, and then came the sounds of several people shooting together and eliminating their targets. The third man guessed that someone had gotten one of his friends and quickly put his rifle on the ground.

"Three prisoners," whispered Iris into her radio.

Ted Branch didn't understand that the strange sound he

heard through the thick smoke was the sound of a parachute canopy collapsing in on itself. For some reason, it reminded him of a movie he had seen before the infection. It sounded like big wings flapping in the movie, but then the victim discovered it was Dracula swirling his cape.

He called himself stupid for even thinking it, but he still felt the crawling sensation on the skin below the hair on his neck. He put his hand on the spot, fully expecting to find a spider or something with lots of legs crawling on him. After all, he had been sitting on the ground a long time, and he had no urge to become exposed by standing up. Nothing was there, but he still felt like something was close by, and he had to get it before it got him.

Branch rolled over onto his stomach and brought up his semiautomatic pistol. He pulled the trigger three times, hoping to catch his unseen attacker by surprise. There was no indication that he shot anything, and the sound of his own gun had left him deaf.

"Deaf and blind," he said out loud over the ringing in his ears. "Who's there?"

Branch had been in near total darkness in the salt mines when something sliced through his Achilles tendon. The helplessness that he felt when it happened made him much more terrified than he would have felt if he had been able to see what was happening. The same helplessness washed over him again as he felt his body slide forward and his left leg leave the ground. It felt like his damaged ankle was caught in a vice grip, and he was lifted upside down into the air. He brought his gun up to point it at the mountainous shape that had picked him up. He didn't feel like he could miss, but the hand that gripped his ankle suddenly twisted hard to the right. His body spun like a rag doll, and when he pulled the trigger, he shot wildly into the smoke.

The Chief dropped Branch on his head and stepped forward,

putting a huge boot on top of Branch's gun. He felt like there was something appropriate he should say about the situation, but he saw that the man was unconscious.

"Well, that's disappointing," said the Chief.

He noticed the big man on the ground had a piece of paper in his left hand. The Chief took it from him and unfolded it, but before he read it, he got his opportunity to make a signature comment.

"You don't mind if I read this, do you? Nod if you mind. Okay, I'll take that as a no."

******

I think all of us stopped breathing when we heard four knocks on the steel hatch. It meant a world of possibilities when we opened the door, but none of them were likely to be good. It most likely meant Ted Branch was going to kill us, but we hoped he would spare the others. At the very least, we expected to pay a price for crossing his path. How painful he made it, and how long he delayed it, was entirely up to him, but the outcome was inevitable.

I hugged Jean one last time and reached up to unlock the door while she pushed upward. Both of us had our guns ready, and as the heavy steel moved upward, the hatch was filled with white smoke. A large hand reached toward us, and the face that loomed above the hand wore the biggest smile.

EPILOGUE

Ithaca, New York - 2025

The smoke over the enclosure was being blown away by the breeze, but Garrett Carson couldn't resist one more low pass over the group of people on the ground. The low flyby caused the smoke to swirl and dissipate further. He wagged the wings of the AC-130, then turned south toward Ithaca, where they would wait for us at the airport.

I watched as Kathy and the Chief helped carry Tori out of the shelter. She was pale, but I had no doubt they would make sure she made a full recovery. Iris already had the two youngest girls, Allie and Bonnie, sitting with her on the grass, where they talked nonstop about the fun things they were going to do together with the other kids in the Guntersville shelter. It made me think of our son, Josh, and I couldn't wait to see him. I had no doubt that my little boy was going to enjoy meeting the girls. Hampton, Colleen, Cassandra, and Tom were busy with the rest of the kids and organizing their supplies for the trip to Ithaca.

Jean and I were given warm hugs, but everyone knew there would be a good old-fashioned tongue lashing in our future. Ruth and Denise were being treated like royalty and were told to get some rest before the trip. There was still enough time left in the day for the journey south, so the Chief hurried everyone else along. I tried to approach him once, but he politely let me know there would be a right time and place to talk about the trouble we had caused.

Not far from our activities were our prisoners. There were four left alive, including Ted Branch. When he had regained consciousness, he was surprised to find that they were surrounded by a well-armed assault team. He had always suspected he was going up against more than just me, Jean, and Ruth, and the arrival of our friends somehow made him satisfied that he had been right. He was actually smiling, but I doubted he would be so smug when the Chief decided what he was going to do with him and his men.

Jean and the Chief walked away from the rest of us to talk privately. I figured he would go easier on her than he would on me, so she gave him the details of our trip. She had also witnessed the way Branch had shown no mercy when he killed Wally and that unknown woman his men found hiding in the storage facility. I couldn't hear what they were saying, but I knew the Chief well enough to understand what the occasional hard glances toward Branch meant. Ted Branch would have to pay for those lives.

When they finished talking, Jean came over to stand beside me. The rest of the Mud Island family stood together in a group, but everyone could tell the Chief needed a few minutes to process what he had been told. He walked away and kept his back to everyone. His broad shoulder muscles were bunched with anger.

Jean said, "I told him that Branch would have killed us if we had opened the door, and I wasn't sure he would have spared the children's lives. We were only seconds from finding out."

After a few minutes of private deliberation, the Chief suddenly turned and walked toward the prisoners. We could see the smile disappear from Branch's face as the Chief got closer, and he tried in vain to ward away the Chief's big hand.

The Chief lifted the man from the ground and carried him toward the open hatch. He motioned with his other hand, and Kathy understood he wanted the other three prisoners to be brought along.

We all formed a wide circle around the dark opening so we could hear what the Chief said.

"I have never wanted to be a judge and jury, but I also never thought there would be an infection that makes people turn into monsters. One thing I'm sure of is that there were monsters before the infection, and the apocalypse just gave them the opportunity to be the people they wanted to be before we lost the rules of society. The infection didn't make them this way, and if there was any decency in them at all, they would have used their powerful personalities for something good. Instead, they thrived on the opposite."

The Chief paused for a moment, but his eyes were on Ruth.

"I can't bring back your brother, but I hope you find some justice in what I'm about to do."

To Ted Branch, he said, "You wanted to get inside this shelter? Let me give you a hand."

The Chief dangled Branch's feet over the opening and let go. Needless to say, it wasn't a smooth entry because Branch was a big man, and the opening was narrow. There were plenty of metal things to bang into on the way down, and judging by the number of times Branch yelled, he hit most of them.

"As for you three," the Chief said to Branch's men, "no one made you follow him, but you don't get to stop now. You can climb down the ladder, or I can drop you on top of your boss."

The Chief stepped aside and pointed at the hatch, and he didn't have to say it twice. The men fought each other for position, but they all eventually managed to disappear through the opening. The Chief closed the hatch behind them.

"Do you think a little C-4 would warp this thing shut?" he asked Cassandra.

She studied it for a moment and said, "Too much would blow the lid off, but a small charge might do the trick. How did you know I had some with me?"

"I would've been more surprised if you didn't."

The small explosion was still more than they wanted, but it worked. When the dust settled, they saw that the hatch and the surrounding escape tunnel had collapsed inward, and it was doubtful that it could be opened again without a bulldozer.

"Is everyone ready to go?" asked the Chief. "All the activity around here has probably gotten the attention of every infected dead in the state."

The Chief was right. As soon as we all reached the other side of the fence, we had work to do. We avoided the largest groups and eventually outran the stragglers. It was close to sunset when we reached the airport in Ithaca, New York. Along the way, we encountered a few random infected dead, but luckily, there hadn't been any really big hordes. Our long column of people must have looked like a small army of survivors to our friends waiting at the airport.

I caught up with the Chief and risked his temper to let him know that Tori and Denise had a special request.

"You're not going to sneak in any excuses, are you?" asked the Chief.

I shook my head. "No, this isn't about me or Jean. It's about them. They want a favor."

"Okay. What do they want?"

******

Ted Branch sounded like he had a severe head cold when he spoke. In reality, his nasal passages were blocked by dried blood because he had broken his nose on the metal rungs of the ladder. He had several broken fingers, and his whole body ached. He swore he would find a way out of the dimly lit room where he and his men were trapped, and he would get even with the man who had dumped him down the hole.

They rummaged around the recreation room and found a few useful items, but what he wanted them to find more than anything was a way out of their new prison. They found a hatch in the corner of the room that they hoped would be the answer, but when they opened it, they found nothing but water.

Branch leaned over the opening and stared at the dark liquid. It wasn't long before he realized the water level had risen about an inch while he tried to penetrate it with his eyes.

"It's getting deeper," he said, "but wait until those people find out that I'm a good swimmer, and I can hold my breath for a long time."

Without waiting for the other three to agree, Branch put his feet through the hole and disappeared into the water.

******

From the air, the sight was even more majestic. The infected dead hadn't been able to diminish the beauty of Niagara Falls, even though they had polluted the water and still continued to do so. The Chief understood why Tori and Denise wanted to see it one more time. They needed to say goodbye, and as they told the Chief, they needed to see it one last time to prove it had all been real.

Niagara Falls was supposed to be a beginning for Randy and Tori, but it had become their ending and the beginning of something sinister. Tori knew she would never know what happened to Randy, but in her heart, she believed he died making sure she would live. Whatever happened, he died protecting her. As for Denise and her sons, they wondered if Brad was still trapped inside the hotel room, and not knowing for sure was in some ways even more painful than Tori's loss.

The Chief slowed the forward speed and did a lazy circle around both sides of the border between Canada and the United States. They were able to see the hotel from every angle, and everyone crowded around the gun ports and windows for a better view. The building was mostly burned, but they could still see the parts that would forever be in their memories. The fire had burned itself out before it reached the floor where Denise and her boys had left Brad, and there were still infected dead in the plaza that faced the waterfalls. In the river above the falls, they could see bodies still being swept along in the current until they dropped into the mists below. As they said their final goodbye, they also had to ask if it would ever stop.

ABOUT THE AUTHOR

Bob Howard

ABOUT THE AUTHOR Bob Howard (1951-) was born in New Jersey to an Army Sergeant from Ohio and a mother from Romania. He was moved from one Army base to the next, and before he began high school in Huntsville, Alabama, he had lived most of his life overseas in Germany and Okinawa with brief stays in Maryland and North Carolina. He credits his imagination to his exposure to different cultures and environments at an early age. He began reading science fiction and fell in love with post-apocalyptic novels. He still has an original copy of the first one he read in 1966, The Furies by Keith Edwards. He joined the Navy after high school and continued to move from one base to another, including a submarine base at Holy Loch, Scotland. He eventually stayed in one place when he got stationed in Charleston, South Carolina. He graduated with a BS in Psychology from the College of Charleston and married his wife of 40 years. His son still lives in Charleston, but his daughter has married and made a home in Ohio where the Howard family has its earliest recorded roots. Through the years he has had one passion that he wanted to fulfill, and through The Infected Dead series, he is getting to live that passion. Creating a book is something so many people want to do but never have the opportunity, and after writing these books he believes the sky is the limit. He plans to write for the rest of his life because it is enjoyable beyond his wildest dreams. As for the zombie genre, he saw Night of the Living Dead when it originally hit the theaters, and he believes until recently it didn't receive the attention it deserves.